# The Complete Screech Owls

## Volume 3

### Roy MacGregor

McCLELLAND & STEWART

This omnibus edition published in 2006 by McClelland & Stewart

**Library and Archives Canada Cataloguing in Publication**

MacGregor, Roy, 1948–
   The complete Screech Owls / written by Roy MacGregor.

Contents: v.1. Mystery at Lake Placid – The night they stole the Stanley Cup – The Screech Owls' northern adventure – Murder at hockey camp – v. 2. Kidnapped in Sweden – Terror in Florida – The Quebec City crisis – The Screech Owls' home loss – v. 3. Nightmare in Nagano – Danger in Dinosaur Valley – The ghost of the Stanley Cup – The West Coast murders.

ISBN 13: 978-0-7710-5484-6 (v. 1)     ISBN 10: 0-7710-5484-X (v. 1)
ISBN 13: 978-0-7710-5486-0 (v. 2)     ISBN 10: 0-7710-5486-6 (v. 2)
ISBN 13: 978-0-7710-5489-1 (v. 3)     ISBN 10: 0-7710-5489-0 (v. 3)

   I. Title.

PS8575.G84C64 2005     jC813'.54     C2005-903880-2

We acknowledge the financial support of the Government of Canada through the Book Publishing Industry Development Program and that of the Government of Ontario through the Ontario Media Development Corporation's Ontario Book Initiative. We further acknowledge the support of the Canada Council for the Arts and the Ontario Arts Council for our publishing program.

Typeset in Bembo by M&S, Toronto
Printed and bound in Canada
Cover illustration by Sue Todd

This book is printed on acid-free paper that is 100% recycled, ancient-forest friendly (100% post-consumer recycled).

McClelland & Stewart Ltd.
75 Sherbourne Street
Toronto, Ontario
M5A 2P9
www.mcclelland.com

1   2   3   4   5        10  09   08   07   06

# Contents

# Nightmare in Nagano

# 1

"TOASTED BUNS!"

Travis Lindsay could only shake his head in wonder. The Screech Owls had been in Nagano, Japan, less than an hour, and already Nish was spinning out of control.

"WE GOT TOASTED BUNS!"

The Owls had just checked in to the Olympic Village where they would be staying for the next two weeks. They'd been issued door keys, divided into groups, and assigned to different "apartments" in the large complex that would be home to all the teams competing in this special, once-in-a-lifetime "Junior Olympics." Travis was sharing with Dmitri Yakushev, Lars Johanssen, Andy Higgins, Fahd Noorizadeh – and, of course, his so-called, perhaps soon to be *former*, best friend Wayne Nishikawa.

"COME AND GET YOUR BUNS TOASTED!"

Rarely had Travis seen Nish this wound up. Travis and the other players had been carefully hanging up their clothes or putting them neatly in drawers, when Nish, as usual, had simply stepped into the bedroom he'd be sharing with Travis, unzipped his bag, turned it upside down, and let shirts and pants tumble into a heap beside his bed. Then he'd gone "exploring."

It took him less than a minute to find out that Japan was the land of the heated toilet seat.

"*Fan-tas-tic!*" Nish had shouted out in triumph. "*At least one country still believes in the electric chair!*"

The rooms were not very warm. The elevator and the stairs were all on the outside of the building, the wind-blown snow powder dancing around the walkways as the Owls had made their way to their little apartments. The apartments were heated, but still cool compared to homes in North America. Each bathroom had its own heater, and the toilet seat itself was wired for heat, with a small red dial on the side to control the temperature. Nish had instantly cranked theirs up as high as it would go.

"THIS IS BETTER THAN WEDGIES!" he had screamed before heading out to crank up all the other toilet seats before anyone else discovered this little miracle of technology.

Travis just shook his head.

He still had unpacking to do. And after eighteen hours of flying, and six hours sitting in a bus as it climbed up from Tokyo into the snow-capped mountains that surrounded Nagano, he was exhausted. His own bed back home couldn't have looked more inviting than this tiny bed with the crisp sheets folded back, waiting for him.

Travis was so tired that not even the screaming and shouting from the other apartments was going to stop him from slipping in between those covers for a quick nap.

"YOU'RE GONNA DIE FOR THIS, NISH!"

That was Sarah Cuthbertson's voice. And if anybody could get revenge on Nish, it would be Sarah.

⊚

The Screech Owls had come to Nagano through a remarkable series of coincidences. Several years earlier, their small town of Tamarack had "twinned" with Nagano, which considered itself small by Japanese standards, even though it had close to a hundred times as many people as there were in Tamarack. But "twinning" had been popular at the time, and centres throughout Japan had been approaching North American towns and cities and setting up exchanges. Nagano and Tamarack were both tourist centres. Both had long and snowy winters. Both had ski hills within easy reach. Both were surrounded by bush, but farther from the city, Nagano's bush became mountains, whereas Tamarack's bush just became more bush.

There had been exchanges in the past between the two towns. One of the Tamarack service clubs had gone to Nagano several years back, and a Nagano high-school band had come to Tamarack and put on a wonderful concert at the town hall – but in the past few years, as Nagano had prepared to host the Olympics, there had been no contact.

Now, with the Winter Games over, the town of Nagano had sent out the most surprising invitation: Would there be a hockey team in Tamarack that would like to come over and play in Big Hat? Big Hat, of course, was the main arena at the Olympic Games. It was here that Dominik Hasek of the Czech Republic team had stopped five players from Team Canada, one after the other – Theoren Fleury, Raymond Bourque, Eric Lindros, Joe Nieuwendyk, Brendan Shanahan – in that amazing shootout that had eliminated Canada. And it was here that the brilliant Hasek had then shut out the mighty Russians. In a single season, Hasek had won the Olympic gold medal and, four months later, been named, for the second year in a row, the most valuable player in the National Hockey League.

But now that the Games were over, the city of Nagano had decided to turn Big Hat into a huge gymnasium. It would never again serve as a hockey rink.

There would, however, be one last gasp. The head of Japanese hockey, Mr. Shoichi "Sho" Fujiwara, had talked the city of Nagano into putting on one final tournament at Big Hat. He had even received approval from the International Olympic Committee to use the official Olympic symbol and call this once-in-a-lifetime tournament the "Junior Olympics." It would feature Japan's future Olympic stars, or so hoped the organizers. The best peewee teams in Japan were invited. A team was invited from Lake Placid, New York, where the Winter Olympics had been held nearly twenty years earlier, and an invitation had gone out, as well, to the Canadian town of Tamarack.

Both Lake Placid and Tamarack readily agreed. Not every Owl was able to go, of course. Jeremy Weathers, their No. 1 goaltender, had a family vacation booked to Disney World and wouldn't be able to make it. But Jenny Staples, the backup, was more than up to the challenge. And for once the fundraising was not left up entirely to the Owls and their families. The service club was pitching in with a new wheelchair and enough money to cover the cost of Data going along as a special "assistant coach." The local radio station was putting up some money. The town council voted five thousand dollars toward the exchange. A Canadian airline, as a goodwill gesture and to promote its own links with Japan, offered free passage for the players and coaches.

What seemed like a financial impossibility one week, was a certainty the next: the Screech Owls were off to Nagano!

No one, of course, took the trip as seriously as Nish. He called the visit his "homecoming" – ignoring the fact that his great grandfather, Yasuo Nishikawa, had left Japan for Canada a whole century earlier. Nish, who had once proudly claimed he didn't know a single word of Japanese and didn't care, was suddenly the self-proclaimed expert on the Land of the Heated Toilet Seat.

He had been insufferable since the plane had taken off – and not just because he twice tried to "stink out" the section where the Owls were attempting to catch some sleep. Nish was so excited, he didn't fall asleep until just before the plane landed. And now, while everyone else seemed to be having trouble dealing with the jet lag – the dizzying effect of convincing your body that it hadn't missed a night of sleep – Nish was running ahead of them all, as if he had somehow picked up the energy they had lost.

He acted like he knew everything. Back home he'd called up his grandfather to get some Japanese sayings, and was shouting "*Moshi moshi!*" to everyone he bumped into.

"It means 'Hello,'" he explained to Travis, as if Travis was some infant who had never heard the spoken word before.

"'*Arigato*' means 'Thank you.'"

"Thank you," said Travis with some sarcasm.

"*Arigato*," said Nish, entirely missing Travis's point.

He told everybody to be careful with their shoes. "You can't walk into a house or restaurant with your shoes on," he said. "You have to have slippers."

Nish turned out to be right about the shoes, which rather impressed some of the other Owls. As they found their rooms in the Olympic Village, they discovered small blue slippers waiting for them at the entrances. The slippers slid on easily, and almost instantly the Owls had taken to skating about the small apartments, the new footwear sliding effortlessly on the highly polished floors.

That first evening, after Travis had taken his little nap, and Nish had practically electrocuted the entire building, the Owls gathered with the other teams in the large tent that had been erected between the buildings and which would be their gathering place for meals and relaxation for the remainder of their stay. Tonight was to be the opening banquet, with the mayor of Nagano and other area dignitaries welcoming the teams to the first-ever, and probably only-ever, Junior Olympic Hockey Tournament.

Muck Munro, the Owls' coach, had laid down the law. Dark pants, no jeans. White blouse or shirt and tie. Team jacket. "You're not here just representing your town," he told them. "You're here representing your country."

That seemed to upset Nish's plans. He had told Fahd he was headed out to find a store where he could buy a package of adult diapers. He told Fahd – and Fahd, of course, had believed him – that he was going to go to the banquet as a sumo wrestler, his big stomach hanging out over the diaper, and that he planned to spend the evening "belly bumping" the players on the other teams.

"I think he needs a straitjacket, not a diaper," said Sarah.

"You should have been sitting next to him on the plane," said Fahd. "He needs a diaper, all right."

Nish was, of course, kidding. But he did go out to explore, and came back about an hour later even more expert on the subject of Japan than he'd already been, if that were possible.

"Japan," he announced, "is the most civilized country on Earth. If you can't find what you want in a vending machine, it doesn't exist."

To prove his point, he began laying out his vending-machine loot on the bed, pulling treasures from his jacket pocket as if they were stolen jewels and the rest of the Owls were his accomplices gathered in some back alley.

"Cigarettes," he announced, dropping two packages down on the bed.

"You're not old enough to buy smokes!" Fahd protested.

Nish shrugged a world-weary shrug and yanked something from his other pocket. A can, and a small bottle.

"Beer," he announced. "And whisky."

"*Where'd you get this?*" Fahd almost screeched.

"Vending machines. Anybody can use them. You just put your yen in and push any button you want."

"You don't even smoke!" said Sarah, disgusted.

"And you *certainly* don't drink!" said Fahd, still alarmed.

"You just watch what the ol' Nisher drinks," Nish announced, reaching into an inside pocket of his jacket.

He pulled out a tall blue can. On the side was one word in large white letters: *Sweat.*

Nish held out his can of "Sweat," smacked his lips, pulled the tab, and hoisted the drink high, guzzling it down until he'd finished half the can.

He pulled the drink away, burped loudly, and held it out, his eyes having taken on their most kindly look.

"A slug of Sweat, anyone?"

"*I think I'm gonna hurl!*" yelled Fahd.

Nish tossed the drink to Travis, who caught the skinny blue can before it spilled onto the floor. He held it up to his nose and sniffed quickly. It didn't *smell* like sweat. The idea that anyone would produce a drink that would taste like the inside of a hockey bag was a bit much for Travis to believe, and he sniffed again. It smelled almost sweet. He glanced at the writing on the side. Most was in Japanese, but there was also some English: "Pocari Sweat is highly recommended as a beverage for such activities as sports."

He took a taste: sweet fizzy water. Nice. Perhaps it was just a misspelling: "Sweat" instead of "Sweet."

"It's okay!" said Travis.

"What do you say?" Nish announced grandly. "Do the Screech Owls have a new team drink?"

"Sounds good to me," Travis said, passing on the can of Sweat so others could try a sip of the sweet, cool liquid.

Nish was in his glory. The Owls were hanging on his every word. Phoney or not, he had established himself as the Owls' expert on Japan.

"Muck says we gotta look nice," Nish announced next. "But we gotta act right, too. You meet people here, you don't shake their hands, okay – you *bow*."

To demonstrate, he stood back, set his heels together, and made a deep bow to Sarah, who giggled and bowed back.

"No handshakes," Nish barked. "*Bow.* You got it? *Bow.*"

"What about high-fives?" Wilson asked. "What do we do when we score?"

"What you always do," Nish said with a wicked grin. "Shout '*Way to go, Nish!*'"

**2**

**M**uck would be pleased, Travis knew, as the Screech Owls assembled by the entrance to the tent and awaited the arrival of their coach. Travis had taken special care in combing his hair. He had moved the blond curl back off his forehead. It made him look older, he thought, more mature. More like a team captain.

They were all there. Wilson and Andy the tallest, by far. Gordie Griffith still managing to look like a little boy and a skinny teenager at the same time. Sarah with her blonde hair in a neat ponytail. Jenny with her flame-red hair shining like it had sparkles in it. Dmitri with his hair slicked down, and Lars with his hair so light and dry it seemed like it might bounce off his head just from walking. And Nish, of course, wearing his beloved Mighty Ducks of Anaheim cap.

"You hoping they'll mistake you for Paul Kariya?" Sarah kidded.

"Very funny," Nish said, but refused to remove the cap. Travis understood why. It had, after all, been given to Nish by

Paul Kariya at the end of the Quebec International Peewee Tournament, and Nish had hardly taken if off since. It was, for him, the symbol of his greatest moment on the ice – he'd scored the winning goal – and his greatest moment *off* the ice, as well. He had met his great hero, Paul Kariya. And Kariya had forgiven Nish for letting on that they were "cousins" just because they were both of Japanese heritage.

Muck came along with Mr. Dillinger, the team manager, and Mr. Dillinger was pushing Data in his fancy new wheelchair. Data looked great. His dark hair was combed perfectly and he had put on his new blazer with the Screech Owls logo over the heart. It was amazing what Data could do with a single hand: loop a tie, button his cuffs, tie his shoes, practically anything that anyone else could do with two. Data, the electronics nut, had a video camera small enough to hold in his one good hand, and was using it to sweep the scene, lingering on each player as he recorded their first day in Nagano.

Both Muck and Mr. Dillinger were in suits, but Mr. Dillinger, his happy red face grinning, his bald head shining, looked far more at ease in his fancy clothes than did Muck. Muck kept pulling at his collar, and he kept scratching the top of his legs as if the pants itched him. But if Muck didn't much care for how he was dressed, he seemed to like what he saw in his team. His only adjustment was to pluck the Mighty Ducks cap off Nish and slam it into his stomach before announcing it was time to go in to the opening banquet.

The Owls were put at the same table as the Olympians, the peewee team from Lake Placid. The Olympians were wearing beautiful red–white–and–blue tracksuits, the U.S. flag emblazoned across the back with the Olympic symbol and "1980" stitched on beneath. The Owls knew that 1980 was pretty much a sacred year in Lake Placid – the year the home team, the United States, had won the Olympic gold medal.

There were more than a dozen teams crammed into the tent. There were the two teams from North America, at least ten from Japan, and even two from China, where hockey was just beginning to be played.

The teams were shy of each other, but gradually they began to mingle as they were prodded by their coaches and the tournament organizers. Nish made a great show of bowing to various members of the Japanese teams, who giggled shyly into their hands and bowed back. The Japanese all seemed to have their own cards – kid versions of the business cards Travis's dad sometimes gave out – and Nish seemed to be the only North American player there with cards to hand back: hockey cards of NHL stars, usually, but also a few of his treasured "Wayne Nishikawa" cards from the Quebec International Peewee Tournament. Nish was a huge hit, with his Japanese looks and his treasured Mighty Ducks cap, which was now back on his head. One by one, Japanese players lined up to try on the cap that had been given to Nish "by the great Paul Kariya himself – my *cousin*."

Muck and Mr. Dillinger were invited to the head table. Sho Fujiwara, recognizing a hockey man like himself in Muck, did a quick switch of the place cards that indicated the seating arrangements so that they could sit together and talk – and Muck seemed to be having a wonderful time of it in this strange, foreign country where his game served as the common language. At one point, Travis even noticed Muck showing Sho a break-out pattern by using the water glasses and salt and pepper shakers to illustrate the Owls' game plan.

Sho opened the ceremonies with a hilarious account of his own experiences as the Japanese goaltender for the 1960 Winter Olympics in Squaw Valley, California. In Japanese, and then English, he told the kids what it was like to be on the very first hockey team that ever played for Japan, and the pressure they were under. They sailed across the Pacific rather than flew, so they'd have time to work on new skills on the way across. "Not stickhandling," he said with a wide smile, "but learning how to eat with a knife and fork."

He soon had the kids screaming with laughter. Each member of the Japanese team had been issued an official Japanese Olympic team shirt and tie for the trip, and they had worn them each day aboard the ship as it had made its way across the ocean, practising three meals a day to do without the traditional chopsticks and eat with the knives and forks they would be expected to use in North America. "We landed in Vancouver," he said. "First thing we all did was go out and buy a new shirt and tie each. Our official ones we had to throw away, we'd spilled so much food on them!"

Sho then introduced the head table. Besides Muck and Mr. Dillinger and the head of the Lake Placid and the Chinese teams, the mayor of Nagano was present, as was the head of the service club from Tamarack, the head of the local sports federation, and a few local businessmen, including Mr. Ikura, the man who owned the largest of the nearby ski resorts, who stood to extend an invitation to all the teams to come to his hill for a day of skiing and snowboarding – "free of charge" – before the end of the tournament. He was, of course, cheered wildly.

After the introductions, they served the food. Nish insisted he was going to eat his with chopsticks, and made a grand gesture of getting his sticks ready and pushing away the knife and fork that had also been laid out at his plate.

"What's *this*?" demanded the Japanese expert as the first plate was placed in front of the Owls.

"Sushi," announced Sarah.

"I thought you'd have known all about sushi, Nish," said Jenny.

"What *is* it?" snarled Nish. "It looks alive!"

"It's raw," said Sarah. "Raw fish."

"Whatdya mean? They cook it at our table, like that steak they do in restaurants?"

"You eat it raw," said Jenny.

"I'm not eating anything that hasn't been cooked!"

Travis looked at the plates as they landed in front of him. The sushi looked more like artwork than food. It was beautiful, each piece perfectly laid out on a little roll of rice with small, green sprigs of vegetable around it. On each roll of rice there was a slice of fish, some very pale, some very red, and some, it seemed, with tentacles.

"Is that what I think it is?" Travis asked Sarah.

Sarah followed his finger.

"It's octopus," she said. "Raw octopus."

Jenny, who seemed to know a great deal about sushi, took over. Like a patient teacher, she pointed to each piece of sushi laid out on the plates before them.

"This one is eel."

"*Yuuucckkkk!*" said Nish.

"Squid."

"*Yuuucckkkk!*"

"Raw eggs."

"*Yuuucckkkk!*"

"More octopus tentacle . . ."

But Nish was already up and scrambling. He had his Paul Kariya cap over his face and was bolting for the far exit as fast as he could move. Travis noticed that Data had pulled up near the table in his wheelchair and had recorded the entire scene. Good old Data – they'd want to show *that* one day!

Travis couldn't help laughing. He had seen Nish act like this once before, when the team was visiting the Cree village of Waskaganish and Nish had eaten, without realizing it, some fried "moose nostrils." But Nish had come around eventually, and had eventually eaten, and enjoyed, beaver and goose and even some moose nostril. He would come around here in Japan, too. He had to. He was, after all, Mr. Japan on this trip. And this was Japanese food.

Travis tried the sushi cautiously. Sarah and Jenny and Lars had no concern about it, and ate happily. Travis chose the raw tuna to start – he had tuna sandwiches most days at school – and it wasn't bad. He tried dipping it in the small bowl of soya sauce and green mustard that Jenny held out to him. It tasted even better. He tried the salmon and it was delicious. He tried the octopus, but it was rubbery and made his skin crawl – particularly when he bit down on one of the tentacles – and he spat the rest of it out into his napkin and stayed away from the octopus from then on.

Toward the end of the meal, Sho stood up and introduced the mayor, who would be making a few welcoming remarks to the teams.

The mayor rose slowly, seeming to bask in the applause from the assembled players.

He was an older man – but even so, Travis thought, he moved slowly.

As he got to his feet, he seemed a bit unsteady.

Concerned, Sho reached for the mayor's elbow.

Muck leapt to his feet and rushed to help, his chair tipping over and clattering onto the floor.

The mayor reached for his throat, then plunged straight forward, his face twisting horribly as he fell across his plate, the legs of the head table giving way under him and the entire table – trays of sushi, flower arrangements, glasses of water, knives, forks, and chopsticks – crashing down onto the floor with him.

Mr. Dillinger, who knew first aid, pushed his way through and reached the mayor. He turned him flat on his back, yanking his collar loose.

He bent down, his ear to the mayor's open, twisted mouth.

He looked up, blinking at Muck and Sho Fujiwara.

"*He's dead!*"

# 3

arah leaned over the chair in the sitting room, her chin in her hands, her eyes red-rimmed from the shock and strain of the hours since the banquet the night before.

"I've never seen anyone have a heart attack," she said.

"My grandfather had one," said Travis. "But he drove himself to the hospital – it wasn't like this at all."

"He looked like he was being strangled."

There had been no hope for the mayor of Nagano from the moment Mr. Dillinger bent down over him. An ambulance had arrived quickly, and the body had been removed at once, but the shock lingered.

For once, even Nish was quiet. Suddenly electric toilet seats and drinking Sweat didn't seem quite so funny. They hadn't known the mayor of Nagano, none of them had even been introduced to him, but he had been thoughtful enough to come out and welcome them to his city.

They were feeling sorry for the mayor and sorry for themselves when the door opened and Muck came in. The coach was dressed much more normally now, in an old tracksuit and his team jacket. But he didn't look normal. Muck's face was grey and serious.

"It wasn't a heart attack," he told them.

"What was it?" The question, of course, came from Fahd.

Muck took some time answering. Travis, sitting closest to him, could see his big coach swallow several times. A muscle on the side of Muck's cheek was twitching.

"The police say . . . he was . . . poisoned."

"*Poisoned?*" Travis repeated, hardly believing it.

"How?" Fahd asked again. "We all ate the same meal."

"I told you that sushi stuff was poison," Nish said.

"*Shhhhhh,*" Sarah ordered. This was no time for Nish's stupid humour.

"They found traces of blowfish in his stomach," Muck said.

"*Blowfish?*" Fahd asked. "What the heck's *blowfish?*"

By lunchtime, they all knew everything there was to know about blowfish. Called *fugu* in Japanese, the blowfish is able to inflate its body by swallowing water or air so that it swells into a ball. The Japanese treasure the ugly creature as a great delicacy, and chefs are trained for years in how to clean the fish so that none of the poison that is found in some of its internal organs spreads into the flesh. Even so, about a hundred Japanese a year die accidentally from the deadly poison.

"It wasn't an accident," Muck had told them. "There was no blowfish on the menu. Someone had to deliberately put it on the plate he was served."

"Who would want to do something like that?" Fahd had asked.

"The police have taken the two chefs in for questioning."

Travis's mind was racing. Why would anyone want to kill that nice old man? Travis had no idea. He knew nothing about the mayor, not even his name. And why would they kill him at the hockey banquet? In front of a couple of hundred peewee hockey players?

It suddenly struck Travis: *I am a witness to murder. I have seen one human being killed by another human being. And the way murders are usually solved is by questioning the witnesses.*

*What did I see?* Travis asked himself. *Nothing.*

*What do I suspect? Nothing.*

*What do I know? Nothing.*

"There's nothing we can do about it," Muck said after the Owls had discussed the matter at length. "It's unfortunate, and we are all sorry for the mayor's family. Mr. Dillinger is sending our sympathies to them. But the matter is now under investigation by the police – nothing to do with us, nothing to do with this hockey tournament. The best thing we can do is move on."

"Do we know who we're playing yet?" Lars asked.

Muck pulled out a schedule. He opened it, scanning sections he'd already underlined in red ink.

"Our first game is Thursday morning against the Sapporo Mighty Ducks."

"The *Sapporo Mighty Ducks*," Nish said with a sneer. "What a joke!"

"Maybe the rest of your 'cousins' will be on the team," said Sarah.

"Very funny."

"Are they any good?" Travis asked.

"Don't know," Muck said, stuffing his schedule back into his breast pocket. "That's why we need to practise. We're on in an hour – get your stuff. Mr. Dillinger and I have a little surprise worked up for you."

"What?" Fahd asked.

Muck smiled. "If I told you, it wouldn't be a surprise any more, now would it?"

# 4

ravis was glad to get back home – because that's how he felt on skates, on ice, in his own hockey equipment, surrounded by his own smell, his own teammates, with everything in its place, everything where it should be. His eyes knew where the net would be without even looking. His shoulder had a sense of the boards. His imagination held a thousand different ways to score a goal.

There is something universal about the way a skate blade digs into the first corner on a fresh sheet of ice, Travis thought, as he took his first spin around the Big Hat ice surface. This was the same ice surface where Dominik Hasek had put on the greatest display of goaltending the world had ever seen. But it felt no different than the arena back home. Travis and the Owls had skated on the Olympic rink in Lake Placid, and they had played in the Globen Arena in Stockholm, where the World Championships had been played – but the sound of his blade as it cut through that first corner was the same as in Lake Placid, in Sweden, the same, for that matter, as on the frozen creek where they sometimes played at the edge of town back home.

On skates, Travis had a different sense of his body. He felt bigger, because of his pads. Stronger, because of his skills. Faster, because his body was pumping with so much pent-up emotion that he felt he *needed* to play almost as much as he *wanted* to. Now that he was on the ice, everything felt right: Sarah was sizzling on her skates just ahead of him, Nish puffing back of him as they went through their wind sprints, Dmitri's skates barely touching the ice surface as he danced around the first and second turns, Lars striding low and wide, the European way.

Everything was right here. Murder did not exist here.

Even Muck's whistle felt right: music from centre ice. Travis and Sarah cut fast around the far net and headed for the coach, the two of them coming to a stop in a fine spray of ice. The other Owls came in spraying as well, Muck waiting, whistle to mouth, until the last of them – Nish, naturally – came spinning in on his gloves and shinpads, the toes of his skates looping odd circles in the ice behind him.

Travis had raced to centre so automatically that he hadn't even looked up. He hadn't noticed that Muck was not alone.

"This, here, is Mr. Imoo," Muck said, indicating the little man beside him. "He's a Buddhist priest, so show him proper respect. He also knows his Japanese hockey."

The Owls stared in wonder. If this was a priest, none of them had ever met another one like him. Mr. Imoo was grinning ear to ear; but his front teeth were missing, top and bottom! He was wearing hockey equipment, but the socks were torn and there seemed to be old dried blood on his sweater.

"Mr. Imoo runs the local hockey club, the Polar Stars – but he's also a priest at the Zenkoji Temple, which you'll be touring later this week. Mr. Dillinger met him at the temple and asked Mr. Imoo if he'd mind coming out to practise with us."

"It is great honour," Mr. Imoo said, bowing deeply towards the Owls.

Nish, who was on his skates now, immediately bowed back, even deeper, causing Mr. Imoo to laugh.

"I see you already have Japanese player," he said.

"Half Japanese," Nish corrected.

"Half *nuts*," Sarah added.

"*Moshi moshi*," said Nish, ignoring Sarah.

"*Moshi moshi*," Mr. Imoo said back.

"I thought Buddhists were non-violent," said Fahd.

"Not the hockey-playing Buddhists," said Mr. Imoo, smiling. "But there's only one of them, me. I lost my top teeth in that corner over there. Keep an eye out for them, please."

The Owls laughed, knowing the teeth would have long been swept up by the Zamboni, if, in fact, the story were even true – which they figured it was, given how fierce Mr. Imoo looked in his ragged hockey gear.

"Mr. Imoo is going to give you the secrets of playing hockey in Japan," said Muck.

"Buddhist secrets," Mr. Imoo grinned. "Very special secrets, only for Screech Owls."

"Listen to what he says," said Muck. "And remember it tomorrow."

"The secret to Japanese hockey is to shoot," Mr. Imoo said.

"That's no secret," Fahd insisted. "Even Don Cherry knows that."

"But in Japan is different," said Mr. Imoo. "Japanese hockey very, very different from North American hockey."

By the time Mr. Imoo was through explaining, the place in Travis's brain that held his hockey knowledge felt as if it had been invaded by an alien force. It made absolutely no sense – hockey sense, anyway.

Japan, Mr. Imoo explained, is a very formal place. Younger people, for instance, are always expected to step aside for their elders, and it applies as well to hockey. On his team, there are *koohai* players – the younger ones, the rookies – and the older players are called *sempai*. The *sempai* rule the dressing room. The older players sit together, talk together, and bark out orders to the younger *koohai* players.

"*Koohai* have to tape the *sempai* sticks," said Mr. Imoo, "have to get them drinks when they want them – even have to wash their dirty underwear!"

"Seems sensible to me," said Nish.

It would, thought Travis – Nish was the oldest player on the team.

"At least that way your long underwear would finally get cleaned," Sarah said.

But Nish wasn't listening. He seemed hypnotized by Mr. Imoo. He had moved up close and was standing next to him, nodding at everything the Buddhist priest told them.

"Japanese hockey is trying to change this," said Mr. Imoo, "but it is very, very difficult to change old habits. On the ice, the younger *koohai* will never take a shot – they always pass to a *sempai* to take the shot."

"Good idea," agreed Nish.

Mr. Imoo grinned. "This has major effect in hockey. Goaltenders check to see which player is older player and wait for him to get the pass for the shot. Don't have to worry about younger players."

"I like that," said Jenny, the goaltender.

"Goalies also not good in Japan," said Mr. Imoo. "Everyone is afraid of hurting goalie in practice, so no one shoots – not even *sempai*. So goalies not get good through practice. That's why I say secret against Japanese hockey is to shoot puck. Shoot puck, score goal – simple, eh?"

"Yes!" shouted Nish, banging his stick on the ice. Several of the other Owls followed suit. Mr. Imoo grinned widely, the big gap of his missing teeth making his grin all the more infectious.

"You must play like *samurai* – great Japanese warriors, afraid of nothing, attacking all the time. Okay?"

"O-kay!" Nish shouted, banging his stick again.

Muck stepped back into the centre of the gathering. "We're just going to scrimmage. But I want to see shots, okay? Lots and lots and lots of shots. I want quick shots, surprise shots, any shots you can get off, understand?"

"You bet, coach!" Nish said, slamming his stick again. Muck winced. He didn't care to be called "coach." He said that was what American football players called their coach. Canadian hockey coaches, he always said, went by their real names.

"I need a volunteer for goal," said Muck. "We've only got Jenny here. We need another for the scrimmage."

"You got one right here!" said Nish, whose enthusiasm seemed to have gotten the best of him.

As one, the entire team turned and stared at Nish, who was about to bang his stick again on the ice, but now was beginning to blush beet-red. "Why not?" he said.

"You said shoot, didn't you?" Sarah said to Mr. Imoo.

"That's right, *shoot*."

"Hard?"

Mr. Imoo smiled, realizing the play that went on between Sarah and Nish.

"Hard as you can."

Travis often wondered if other athletes loved their particular games as much as hockey players loved theirs. Did baseball players enjoy practice? Did the Blue Jays or the Yankees ever play a little "scrub" baseball or "knocking out flies" while they were waiting around to play a real game? Did the Pittsburgh Steelers ever play a little "touch football" while gearing up for the Super Bowl?

He doubted it. But hockey players were different. Hockey players *loved* to play a dozen silly little games. Scrimmage, like this, was best of all – a time when you could try any play you wanted, a time when mistakes counted for nothing and no one even bothered to keep score. But there were also contests to see who could hit the crossbar, who could score the most one-on-one, who could hang on to the puck longest, who could pick a puck up off the ice using only the blade of the stick, who could bounce a puck longest on the stick blade, who could bat a puck out of the air best . . .

Scrimmage was when Travis's line shone. Sarah at centre, Travis on left, the speedy Dmitri on right wing. Sarah the play-maker, Travis the checker, Dmitri the finisher.

Sarah made certain they lined up on Jenny's side – with Nish, wobbling in thick pads, his head covered by a borrowed mask, heading for the far net. Mr. Imoo, laughing, skated beside him. The two seemed to have struck up a special friendship – or perhaps Mr. Imoo, like everyone else, was merely amused by Nish's wild antics.

And Nish, of course, was making the most of it. Pretending he was Patrick Roy, he started talking to his goal posts, patting each one as if it were a guard dog that was there to help him out. He lay on his back and stretched like Dominik Hasek. He sprayed the water bottle directly into his face. He charged to the left corner and smashed his stick into the glass before returning to the crease, daring anyone to try to score on him.

Wayne Nishikawa, *samurai* goaltender.

Muck let them play. No instructions. No whistles. He simply let them do what they wanted, watching as they got a feel for the larger ice surface, and watching Mr. Imoo as he scrambled around on his skates and shouted at the players to "*Shoot!*" almost as soon as they got the puck.

Sarah picked up the puck behind Jenny and broke straight up through centre, Dmitri cutting away from her on the right. The moment Gordie Griffith made a move toward her, Sarah flipped the puck to Dmitri, who broke hard down the boards before firing a hard cross-ice pass to Travis.

Travis was ready to shoot, but couldn't resist his little back pass to Sarah. Muck hated the move; Travis loved it. When it worked, it looked brilliant; when it didn't work, it usually meant a breakaway for the other team. But this was scrimmage, so he tried it.

Sarah was expecting the trick pass and already had her stick raised to one-time a slapshot. The puck came perfectly at her, and she put all her strength into the shot, trying to drive it right through Nish if necessary.

The shot was high and hard.

It clipped off Nish's skate blade, smashing against the glass behind the net!

Travis heard three sounds. The puck hitting the glass. Sarah's scream of surprise. And Nish's hysterical laugh.

Travis hadn't even looked at the goal. He did now, and saw Nish lying flat on his back, head sticking up the ice, the heavy pads crossed casually and the skates resting high up one post near the crossbar.

"*Save by Hasek!*" Nish shouted.

He did it all practice long. He sat on the net, his legs dangling, and made saves. He lay on his side on the ice, head resting on his glove hand, and made saves kicking his legs high. He wandered out of the crease and dived back whenever one of the Owls fired a shot at his net, timing his slide just perfectly.

Whatever Nish was up to, it was working.

How it worked, Travis had no idea. Luck? The Japanese gods? Buddha? Or just Nish, trying, and accomplishing, the impossible. Mr. Imoo had tears in his eyes from laughing.

"No one on Earth plays hockey like you!" Mr. Imoo shouted at Nish.

"No one on Earth does anything like him," Sarah corrected.

"He is true *samurai*!" Mr. Imoo pronounced.

Muck blew his whistle long and hard at centre. The Owls skated over to Muck, Nish last, as always, and falling to his pads as he arrived.

"I saw some things I liked," Muck said. "And I saw some things I didn't like."

He turned his gaze on Nish, who had his goalie mask off and was smiling up at Muck, blinking innocently.

"Tournament rules require us to have two goaltenders," Muck says. "You just won yourself a job, Mr. Nishikawa."

Nish's eyes stopped blinking. They opened wider in shock.

His mouth opened as well.

And for once, no sound came out.

# 5

n the evening, the Screech Owls went down into the heart of downtown Nagano. It had been Mr. Dillinger's idea, and it turned out to be a good one. It stopped the Owls from thinking about the murder.

Data brought along his video camera, and Mr. Dillinger and Travis and Sarah took turns pushing Data's wheelchair along so that Data could use his good hand to record the scene for when they all got back home.

Travis had never seen anything like this unfamiliar city. What struck him was not so much the people moving everywhere, the cars and the buses and the policemen's whistles at the intersections, it was the powdery snow falling to earth through the brilliant lights, the still-busy stores, and the million different things for sale in packaging so strange that Travis often didn't know whether they were to be worn or eaten. It was like some wild combination of the Santa Claus parade, Disney World, the Eaton Centre in Toronto, Niagara Falls – and a world Travis had never even imagined.

Nish, of course, was acting as their tour guide – even though he himself had not yet been downtown. But obviously he had been quizzing his new pal, Mr. Imoo. He knew there was a McDonald's at Central Square. He knew how to work the vending machines so the team could get cans of Sweat, the new team drink. He knew that the area was renowned for its huge, delicious apples, still looking fresh at the end of the winter. He knew that the main street was called Chuo, that the main department store was halfway up it, and that the Buddhist temple, where Mr. Imoo was a priest and where they would be touring on Saturday, was at the far end. When they crossed at one of the busy intersections, they could see up to the temple in the distance, like some fantastic fairytale setting in the light falling snow and the magical glow of the downtown lights.

Nish, however, didn't know everything.

"What're they wearing?" Fahd had asked, pointing at some shoppers.

Travis had seen others like them before. Every once in a while they would come across someone on a bus or in the street wearing a curious white gauze mask across the mouth and hooked by elastic over the ears. They looked like doctors and nurses about to head into the operating room.

Mr. Dillinger knew. "Health masks," he said. "People with breathing problems wear them when the smog gets bad. A city like this traps smog between the mountains. The masks cut out the pollution."

"We should get them for Nish," Sarah said.

Nish, who had only partially been paying attention, turned around. "What's *that* supposed to mean?"

"Think about it, Stinky."

Nish let the comment pass. His mind was apparently on more important things. From the moment Muck had named him backup goaltender for the game against Sapporo, he had taken his new role to heart.

"Great goaltenders," he had announced to the boys sharing their little apartment, "are nuttier than fruitcakes. You have to be eccentric to play goal."

He had gone down the list of great goalies as if counting off points for an exam. Jacques Plante, who used to knit his own underwear. Glenn Hall, who used to throw up before every game and between periods. Patrick Roy, who talks to goal posts and insists on stepping over the lines in the ice rather than skating over them. Goalies who have secret messages painted on their masks. Goalies who talk to themselves throughout the game, as if they're not only playing but also doing the play-by-play.

"Mr. Imoo's going to help me," Nish announced as they walked along. "He's going to work with me until I'm the first goalie in history to have a force shield."

"A *what?*" Travis had asked.

"He's an expert in martial arts, too – not just a Buddhist priest. He's the greatest guy I ever met. He's got a black belt in judo and he knows tae kwon do, and he's going to teach me how to do the Indonesian 'force shield.' It's a little-known Asian secret that'll give me superhuman powers."

"You already have superhuman power," said Sarah. "Unfortunately, it's in your butt."

"Back off," Nish said. "Look at what I got here."

Nish flattened out a piece of carefully folded paper.

"This is the address of a restaurant where a friend of Mr. Imoo's can bend spoons."

"What's so hard about that?" Jenny asked.

"He doesn't touch them, that's what's so hard about that."

According to Nish, the restaurant was located in what seemed to Travis to be a back alley. It was a narrow passage leading off the main street, not even wide enough for a car to get down. They walked along, Travis growing nervous, until finally Nish stopped and pointed at what looked like little more than a run-down house.

"This is it."

"Your Mr. Imoo's pulling your leg," said Sarah.

"Ha!" snorted Nish. "Let's go."

Nish pulled the front door open and stepped inside. Fahd followed, then Andy, then the rest of them. Travis had to turn Data's chair around and back him up over a small step, but he managed it easily.

Sure enough, it was a tiny restaurant, with barely enough room to hold them all.

A woman came out from behind the cash register clapping her hands together and smiling. Obviously, she was expecting them. She began speaking – very fast and in Japanese – to Nish, who kept bowing and saying, "*Moshi moshi!*" to her, which only made her smile all the more.

She called back into the kitchen and a man wearing a white apron came out, also smiling and bowing. Nish held out his piece of paper. The man took it, nodding as he wiped his hands on the front of his apron, and laughed when he realized why the kids were really there. He had business cards for them all – but in Japanese, of course, so Travis had no idea what they said.

Travis was shocked at the reception. Back home, he thought, kids like him and Nish and Sarah were often regarded with suspicion the moment they walked into a store or a restaurant on their own. Often, they couldn't get anyone to wait on them. They got ignored in lines. It was as if somehow, at the age of twelve or thirteen, they'd just broken out of prison, where they were serving life sentences for shoplifting and armed holdups.

But not here. Not in Japan. There was such trust, such open acceptance, even if they were just kids. The woman had an Olympic pin for each of them. Sarah, luckily, had a small Screech Owls crest to give her in return. A man who had been sipping a large bowl of soup picked up and moved off happily to give the Owls and the restaurant owner more space at the one large table in the place.

Just then, the door of the restaurant opened again. It was Mr. Imoo, his ragged hockey bag over his shoulder, a stick in one hand, and a huge Band-Aid over his nose that oozed with fresh blood.

Nish seemed ecstatic to see his new hero, racing to help Mr. Imoo unload his hockey gear.

"What happened to you?" Nish asked.

"Good hockey game tonight," Mr. Imoo grinned.

"Who won?" Fahd asked.

Mr. Imoo grinned again. "Game or fight?"

Mr. Imoo seemed particularly pleased with his little joke. He explained it, in Japanese, to the restaurant, tapping his injured nose a couple of times while everyone else laughed and giggled.

Whatever Mr. Imoo was, thought Travis, he wasn't at all like the minister of the church his family attended back home.

The woman brought over a handful of spoons.

"How come he doesn't use chopsticks?" Fahd asked.

Nish turned to him with a look of astonishment combined with disgust.

"Chopsticks," he informed Fahd, "are made of wood."

"My goodness," said Sarah, "*such* an expert."

Giggling, the man placed one of the spoons in the centre of the table, and then fell very quiet. He seemed to withdraw into his body, his arms folding tightly over his chest. His eyes were closed and he began to rock slightly, as if gathering his energies.

Mr. Imoo, the snow still melting in his hair, also went quiet, not even bothering to wipe away the long drop of melted snow that rolled down one cheek.

The Screech Owls fell silent too, but most of them slyly looked around to catch the eye of a friend, their expressions all asking the same question: *What on earth is going on here?*

But not Nish. Nish was even rocking slightly himself, his eyes almost closed but open just enough that he could keep them on the restaurant owner.

The man grunted once and opened his eyes. He had somehow changed, as if almost hypnotized, and it seemed he was now totally unaware of their presence.

He reached out his index finger. Slowly, carefully, he ran it lightly along the length of the spoon, almost as if he were reaching out to tickle a cat's stomach.

Suddenly his hand moved with astonishing speed, the fingers fanning, and in the blur Travis thought he must have lost sight of the spoon, for when the hand pulled back, the spoon was still there, in the centre of the table – but twisted almost in a perfect circle.

"*Outstanding!*" Nish said, nodding his head rapidly.

"How'd he do that?" Fahd asked.

"It's a trick," Sarah said.

"No trick," Mr. Imoo said.

"Can I film it?" Data asked.

Mr. Imoo spoke quickly, in Japanese, to the man, and the man nodded back in agreement.

"Go ahead," Mr. Imoo said to Data. "This is special one for Sarah."

With Data's camera rolling, the man placed another spoon in the centre of the table, then reached out and gently took Sarah's hand in his. Sarah seemed nervous, and Travis could see that she was blushing, but she let the man guide her hand to the spoon and place her fingers over it to feel that it was made of stainless steel.

He took her hand in his again, and while her hand rested on his, for a second time he ran a finger lightly along the spoon, flicked his fingers once, and another curled spoon lay on the table.

Sarah yanked her hand back as if it had just touched fire.

"Is it hot?" Fahd asked.

"N-no," Sarah stammered. She reached out and carefully picked up the bent spoon.

"For you," the man said, gesturing that Sarah should take it.

"Th-thank you," Sarah said, blushing deeply now. She took the spoon, rolled it once in her hand, and then placed it proudly in her lapel buttonhole.

"*Arigato*," she said to the man. "Thank you."

The restaurant owner got up and bowed deeply. He seemed very pleased that Sarah had thought his spoon worthy of a fashion statement.

"Mr. Imoo's going to teach me how to use the force shield," Nish announced to no one in particular.

"You already bend your stick blades too much," said Lars. Everyone laughed.

"You laugh now," said Nish. "You won't be laughing when ol' Nish starts sending players flying with a flick of his glove."

Mr. Imoo giggled and put a hand gingerly to his battered nose.

"Force shield not protect me tonight, that's for sure."

t was the morning they were to travel to Mount Yakebitai, site of the first-ever Olympic competition in snowboarding. On the way they passed through some of the most spectacular scenery Travis had ever seen, but not all the Owls were interested in looking out into the bright, sunlit day.

"Put on a movie!" Nish had screamed from the back.

"Open a window!" Sarah, sitting directly behind him, screamed a moment later.

Mr. Dillinger went to the front of the bus and tried to arrange with the driver to put a movie on the bus's video system, but the driver, unfortunately, had no movies.

"Shoot," moaned Nish. "I wanted to see *Godzilla* in the original Japanese!"

"Hey, Data!" Sarah called ahead to where two seats had been removed to accommodate Data's chair. "Put on your tape. I want to see how that guy bent those spoons."

"Yeah!" shouted Fahd. "Me too."

Everyone was in agreement, and Mr. Dillinger set about rigging the machine so it would play what Data had recorded so far of the Screech Owls' great trip to Nagano.

"Where is it?" Mr. Dillinger called back to Data as he began pushing the "rewind" button on the machine.

"Not too far," said Data. "About now!"

Mr. Dillinger pushed the "stop" button, then "start." A picture began dancing, badly out of focus, on the screens throughout the bus.

Mr. Dillinger fiddled with the tracking buttons and the picture came into sharp focus. It was the opening-night banquet.

"Too far!" called several voices up and down the bus.

"*Hey!*" Nish shouted. "*Hold it right there for a second!*"

Mr. Dillinger looked back, startled.

"*Pause it!*" Nish shouted. "*Pause it!*"

Mr. Dillinger hit the "pause" button. Travis looked closely at the screen. There seemed to be nothing of importance on it. Just a waiter carrying a tray of sushi toward the head table.

"It's a mistake," Data said. "I didn't know how to work the camera then."

"*No!*" Nish shouted. "*Back it up a touch!*"

Mr. Dillinger pushed "reverse" and then "play."

"*That's the creep who dumped me!*" Nish shouted, anger in his voice.

Travis turned in his seat, startled. *What was Nish going on about?*

"Whatdya mean?" Fahd called out.

"The night of the banquet. Remember when I left the tent?"

"I remember when you ran out crying like a baby," said Sarah.

"I thought I was gonna hurl, remember?"

Sarah rolled her eyes at Travis. Why did they have to go over all this again?

"So?" Lars said. "*This guy* made you throw up?"

"No-no-no-no. When I was out in the entrance. This guy comes running through like something's chasing him. Bowls me right over."

"Maybe he didn't see you," suggested Fahd.

"He saw me all right. He had to step over me to get past. I see him again, he's dead meat."

"What're you gonna do?" shouted Andy. "Blow him apart with your force shield?"

"Very funny," said Nish. "Very, very funny."

Nish folded his arms over his chest and closed his eyes. Whether he was just shutting out the shots he was taking from his teammates or gathering his forces to bend Andy like a spoon, Travis couldn't tell.

But he could tell that Nish was upset at whatever had happened to him. It did seem odd to Travis. People in Japan were so polite. They seemed always to be apologizing for no reason. And he had never seen anyone move so fast unless it was on skates.

*Why would a waiter be running through that way anyhow? The kitchen was in the other direction, and through revolving doors.*

*And wasn't this just about the same time that the mayor had stood up and dropped dead from the blowfish?*

Fahd asked what everyone else was thinking: "Is the death on the tape?"

"A bit," said Data.

"There's no need for anyone to see that," said Mr. Dillinger, his thumb hard against the "forward" button. "Who wants to see the spoon bend?"

"Me!"

"We do!"

"I do!"

"Me!"

Mr. Dillinger pushed the "play" button and the fuzzy picture cleared to show the little downtown restaurant. The woman was just coming to the table carrying the spoons.

A cheer went up through the bus.

But not from Travis. There was something about what had happened to Nish that was bothering him. Something to do with a man running away from a murder that was just about to happen.

# 7

f there were no such thing as the magic of skating, Travis thought, then he would choose snowboarding as the perfect way to travel through life. If he loved nothing more than the sense of his sharp skates on a new, glistening sheet of ice, he loved almost as much the feeling that came from a sharp carve on a good snowboard.

He liked to get his hands down low, his knees bent, and the carve so deep that his hips all but brushed against the snow as it flew past him. A few quick curves, a jump, a quick tail grab, and a perfect landing, immediately into another hard, hard carve, the snow sizzling beneath the board almost exactly as ice will sometimes sizzle beneath your skates.

Travis was not the best snowboarder, but he was pretty good. Best were Sarah and Lars, who were probably the best technical skaters on the team, and fastest, as usual, was Dmitri. But Fahd wasn't far behind. Fahd, in fact, was a far better snowboarder than skater, and Travis was secretly delighted that his friend now had something to brag about.

Nish was hopeless. Well, not exactly hopeless, but he had no patience, expecting his expertise in hockey to serve him just as well in snowboarding. He also thought – or claimed to think, anyway – that snowboarding should be a contact sport. But Nish felt that way about every game he played. He was convinced that baseball would be more fun if you could tackle the runners.

The Owls had been welcomed to Mount Yakebitai by Mr. Ikura, the owner of the ski resort and, according to Nish's information from Mr. Imoo, the owner of several of the top ski and snowboarding hills in the area. He was reputed to be a very, very wealthy man, and was renowned for his generosity. Of his generosity there was no doubt: he had met the Screech Owls with free passes, free board rentals, and a voucher for each youngster for a full meal at the cafeteria.

"*It's not sushi, is it?*" Nish had whined.

"Anything you want," said Mr. Ikura.

"Dairy Queen Blizzard!" shouted Nish.

"What's that?" Mr. Ikura asked.

"Just ignore him," suggested Sarah. "We all do. And thank you from us all for your kind gift."

Sarah had then presented Mr. Ikura with a team windbreaker, and he had put it on to great cheers from the team. He had thanked them and told them to enjoy their day on the hills.

After his first couple of runs, Travis had come to a smaller hill near the bottom to work with Nish on his carving. Nish wanted to improve, but seemed willing to allow only his best friend to know how bad he really was.

They were working on Nish's crouch when Mr. Dillinger

and Data came along, Mr. Dillinger pushing Data on a special sled. Data was filming again with his camera.

"Put that thing away!" shouted Nish, embarrassed at being caught. "Or else."

"What're you gonna do?" Data laughed. "Use your force shield?"

"I don't want any pictures, okay. Not yet, anyway."

Mr. Dillinger headed back toward the lodge, and Data stayed with the two boys, content to watch without filming, at least for a while. Nish worked hard, sweat covering his face, and Travis was delighted with how quickly Nish's snowboarding was improving. He seemed to have mastered the balancing, and once you had that, you were away.

"Go ahead," Nish told Data with new confidence. "You can take some shots of the master now."

Data picked up his camera and began shooting again. Not just Nish, but the entire hill, the lodge, and a Toyota 4x4 that was crawling up the steep road toward them.

The vehicle came to a stop just the other side of some nearby trees. Two men got out and pulled a Yamaha snowmobile from the back, followed by a heavy sled, which they attached to the rear of the snowmobile.

Hill workers, Travis presumed, after a quick glance, but then he noticed Nish was staring fiercely at them.

"The guy in the red coat," Nish said.

"What about him?"

"Isn't that the guy who ran me over?"

Travis looked hard. He had heard the stupid jokes about how all Japanese look the same, and he had heard that there were

Japanese jokes about all Westerners looking the same, and he knew that neither was true, but still, he couldn't tell whether this man looked all that much different from any other hill worker he'd seen that day.

"It's the creep, okay," said Nish. "Check the eyebrows."

The eyebrows did stand out. Very dark, and slanted in a V that gave him a slightly mean look.

"Maybe," Travis said.

"No 'maybe' about it. That's him."

"I'll get a shot of him," said Data. "Then we can check it against the other shot."

"I'll take my own shot, thanks," Nish said, bending down.

Nish quickly packed a good hard snowball, reeled back, and let it fly. The snowball flew past the trees separating them and crashed into the side of the snowmobile.

The two men looked up, startled.

Nish shook his fist. "MOSHI MOSHI!" he shouted.

"'Hello, hello'?" Travis translated, puzzled.

Nish grinned sheepishly. "Well, I didn't know what else to say."

The man with the mean eyebrows gave a quick, hard look at the boys and then turned away.

"Got him!" shouted Data.

"Nah!" said Nish. "Missed him."

"No," Data corrected, patting his video camera. "*I* got him."

"That's really going to hurt him," Nish said sarcastically, shaking his head and boarding away, carving like an expert until, leaning too tight into a turn, he fell flat on his face, the snow spraying around him.

"*Got that, too!*" Data shouted triumphantly.

**8**

ravis caught up to Sarah, Dmitri, Lars, and Jenny at the top of the gondola run. It was a glorious sight – the sun sparkling on the thick snow, the clouds below them, tucked tight as thick blankets to Mount Yakebitai. It was snowing down there, but at the top, high above everything but the neighbouring bright white mountain-tops, the day was picture perfect. Travis wished Data could get up here with the video camera, but Data had gone back to the lodge and Nish had stayed out on the smaller hill to practise.

They did a long run together, Sarah taking the lead and all the others trying to follow, not only her run but her every move. If Sarah pumped a fist, all five pumped a fist. If Sarah jumped and tucked or did a special grab, everyone did. They dropped down through the clouds and along a high ridge until they noticed some signs indicating danger, and Sarah pulled to a sharp stop in the shelter of some pines. The others pulled in beside her.

"Fun, eh?" Jenny said.

Travis smiled at her. Jenny's face was flushed bright pink. Snow was falling on her cheeks, and melting from the heat as fast as it landed.

Lars was biting into a mittful of powdery snow.

Dmitri was closer to the edge of the pines, staring out over the dangerous slope where no one was to go.

*And then the mountain exploded.*

---

Just the roar alone would have terrified Travis. But a moment after the terrible sound hit them, the world began to slip away from under the Owls, and they hit the ground, screaming.

*Mount Yakebitai was falling!*

"*It's an avalanche!*" Sarah screamed, barely audible over the devastating roar.

"*Hang onto the trees!*" Lars yelled.

Travis rolled to one side, over and over, until he could wrap his arms around one of the pines. The tree was shaking – but holding. Dmitri held on to a pine beside him.

The snow below the Owls seemed to be bucking like a horse. Travis could hear Jenny screeching, but he could also see that she had managed to grab a tree.

He lifted his head higher, the sound almost deafening. He could see out through the pines to the dangerous slope, and he had a sense of being in a moving car.

It felt like he was flying with the trees *up* the hill!

He looked again and realized it was the mountainside slipping down, not him going up. The slope seemed to be sliding like a cloth off a tipped-up table, the roar building and a plume of snow rising thicker than any of the clouds that ringed the mountain.

The roar began to recede, but the ground still shook.

*Or is it just me shaking*, wondered Travis.

The five Screech Owls lay against the safety of the pine trees until the roar stopped. The sky was still filled with rolling snowflakes when they finally stood, but the avalanche was over. They were still alive.

Jenny was crying. Lars put his arms around her and held her. Travis wished he had enough nerve to do it, but knew he couldn't. He wished he could be that comfortable around other people.

Sarah was creeping to the edge of the pines. Dmitri grabbed her arm.

"Don't!" he said. "There could be a second one any minute."

"Where's it headed?" Sarah asked.

"Toward the lodge," Dmitri answered.

Never had Travis snowboarded so well and so fast – but it meant nothing to him except getting to the bottom of the mountain as quickly as possible. They had to find out if anyone was hurt.

Dmitri went first, body crouched, board singing on the snow. He led them in a high loop away from the avalanche area and into clearer skies that had not yet filled with the burst of powdered snow that had risen like a cloud of smoke from a bomb blast. Sarah followed. Then Travis, Jenny, and Lars bringing up the rear and making sure Jenny was all right.

Travis felt his heart jump when the lodge came into view. *It was safe!* There were skiers and boarders milling about, all staring up toward the practice hill where one edge of the avalanche had rolled over the top like a giant wave.

The five boarders raced down and several of the other Owls, and Muck, came stomping through the snow to greet them. Mr. Dillinger and Data were waving from the deck outside the lodge.

"*You're all right! You're all right!*" Fahd called.

"*We're fine!*" Sarah called back. "*But it was close!*"

"Everyone here okay?" Lars asked.

The others turned to Muck.

Travis looked at the big coach. Maybe it came from running through the cold air, but Muck's eyes were glassy and red around the edges.

"We can't find Nishikawa."

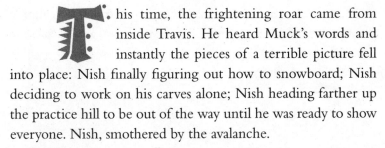

his time, the frightening roar came from inside Travis. He heard Muck's words and instantly the pieces of a terrible picture fell into place: Nish finally figuring out how to snowboard; Nish deciding to work on his carves alone; Nish heading farther up the practice hill to be out of the way until he was ready to show everyone. Nish, smothered by the avalanche.

"NNNNNOOOOOOOO!"

The Owls all turned at once toward the hill where the avalanche had lapped over onto the ski runs. Several trees were broken. Snow was piled up as if ploughs had just cleared the world's largest parking lot. Huge banks of snow had risen out of nowhere, it seemed, the flying powder still in the air and now glittering in the sun that had just broken through.

Already rescue crews were out. Vast snowmobiles like army tanks were rolling out across the hills, and rescue workers in bright-yellow ski jackets were racing toward the trees.

Travis reacted without thinking. He kicked off his board and began running toward the area where he had last seen Nish.

"*Travis!*" Muck called from behind.

Travis didn't stop. He ran farther and then looked back. The rest of the Owls, Muck included, were following, Muck hobbling over the snow on his bad leg.

The Owls were a team, and a teammate was in trouble.

Travis was sweating heavily now. His heart was pounding, his throat burning. He knew he was half crying but didn't care. Nish was his greatest friend in the world.

He blamed himself for what had happened. He should have stayed with Nish. But Travis had abandoned him to show off with his other friends.

And now Nish was gone.

Travis tried to keep what might have happened out of his head, but couldn't. He could see Nish turning, screaming, and the great wall of sliding snow burying him, crushing him.

Right now, Nish might be trying to scream for help – gagging on snow and slowly losing the fight to stay alive.

The rescue workers were out on the avalanche section now. They were crawling on their hands and knees and pulling behind them thin hollow rods that looked like gigantic long straws. Several of the rescuers were already working with the rods, inserting them into the snow and prodding deep below the surface. If somehow Nish was still alive, he would be able to breathe through one of them until they dug him out!

Travis felt his heart skip with hope. The rescuers obviously felt there was a chance. A million tonnes of snow wasn't like a million tonnes of rocks. Nish might still be alive!

Travis found himself praying. He was crying and praying and creeping along on his hands and knees as if he half expected to see Nish's Screech Owls' tuque sticking out of the snow, or hear his muffled voice complaining about sushi or something.

"What the hell is everybody looking for?" A voice behind him asked.

"*Nish!*" Travis called back impatiently.

"What?" the voice asked stupidly.

"*We're looking for Nish!*" Travis repeated, anger in his voice.

"*What?*" the voice repeated.

And then it struck Travis: *he knew that voice as well as his own!* Still down on his hands and knees, Travis turned his head.

Nish was standing there, his mouth full and his hand stuck deep in a bag of potato chips.

"What's up?" Nish asked.

"Where did *you* come from?"

"The tuck shop. Look, they got real chips there – just like at home."

Travis stood up, now, and did what only minutes before he'd thought himself incapable of – he hugged Nish.

"*Hey!*" Nish protested. "Back off. You'll crush my chips!"

Now everyone noticed him. The Owls came flying at Nish as if he'd just scored the winning goal in overtime. Even Muck came racing over, his bad leg in pain but his face laughing as he reached into the crush and rubbed a big, snow-covered glove in Nish's face.

"C'mon!" Nish shouted. "You're crushing my chips!"

But no one was listening to him. They piled on, and soon the bag of chips was as flat as if the avalanche itself had rolled over

it, Nish's protests growing increasingly muffled as more and
more Owls leapt onto the pile.

⌾

"It's a miracle," said Mr. Dillinger. "An absolute miracle."

The Owls had gathered just outside the tuck shop at the
lodge. Everyone, it seemed, had bought a new bag of chips for
Nish, who was in his glory now. Between mouthfuls he held
court, as if he had, in fact, been swept away by the avalanche,
but was such a superior snowboarder that he had simply ridden
the wave of snow like a surfer to the safety of the tuck shop.

Everyone had been accounted for. Not just every Screech
Owl, but all the hundreds of skiers and boarders who had been
on the hill that day. Mr. Ikura, the owner – his face drawn with
concern – had gone around and apologized to everyone who
had been here. As if all this, somehow, had been his fault.

"A miracle," Mr. Dillinger kept saying.

Eventually, word came up the mountain that the roads were
once again open. The Screech Owls were tired and cranky and
just wanted to get back to their rooms and rest up for the game
against Sapporo.

The bus was loaded and warming up when Muck and Mr.
Lindsay came back from the area where the rescuers were still
investigating the slide. A watch would be kept throughout the
night in case there was any more movement.

For the time being, Mount Yakebitai was closed for business.

Travis was sitting close enough to the front of the bus to
overhear Muck talking to Mr. Dillinger.

"Apparently they've never had an avalanche at this time of the year before," Muck was saying. "Mr. Ikura says it doesn't make any sense to him."

*How could it make sense?* thought Travis.

*The mayor murdered . . . Now an avalanche . . .*

*What was going on in Nagano?*

# 10

**N**ever had a hockey game felt so welcome. The Screech Owls had come to Nagano to play in the "Junior Olympics," but to Travis it seemed that hockey had become the furthest thing from anyone's mind. *Murder. An avalanche. Nish almost killed.* It was time to get back to something that made sense to the Owls.

They went by bus to Big Hat. Travis had instantly seen where the large arena got its name – it looked like one of the old hat boxes his mother kept in the attic, only thousands of times bigger. The dressing rooms were huge. The rink was a marvel.

The Sapporo Mighty Ducks, unfortunately, weren't very good. They had about a half dozen excellent skaters, but only one puck-handler, and a very, very weak goaltender.

Sarah had taken Mr. Imoo's advice to shoot a little too much to heart. She fired the puck in right off the opening face-off, which she had won easily with her little trick of plucking the puck out of the air before it landed and sending it back between her own skates. A quick pivot, a shoulder fake to lose the

Sapporo centre, and Sarah wound up for a long slapshot that cleared the blueline, bounced once, and went in through the goaltender's five hole.

Next shift, Andy Higgins, who with Nish had the hardest shot on the team, fired a slapper from outside the blueline that stayed in the air all the way and went in over the Sapporo goalie's outstretched glove.

Owls 2, Mighty Ducks 0.

Several of the Owls were laughing on the bench.

"Next player who shoots from outside the blueline will sit the rest of the game," Muck announced. He did not sound amused.

The message got through immediately. From then on, the Owls were careful not to embarrass the Japanese team. They carried the puck in to the Mighty Ducks' end and made sure they set up a play before shooting, and the Mighty Ducks' goalie gradually began to gather confidence.

Travis found when he was on the bench he was paying more attention to the way the Ducks played than to the Owls. He kept trying to figure out which players were the older ones. And sure enough, it seemed Mr. Imoo had been right: the younger players always gave the puck to the older ones if they had a chance.

Jenny, however, had very few chances. And whatever came her way, she easily blocked.

By the end of the second period, the Owls were up 5–0, with Dmitri scoring on a breakaway, Fahd on a tip-in, and Liz on a pretty deke after being set up to the side of the net by Wilson.

The third period was just about to start when Muck made his announcement.

"Nishikawa – you're in."

Nish had been sitting on the end of the bench, practically asleep in the heavy, hot goaltending equipment. He hadn't expected to play at all. As backup, he'd concluded his job in Japan was to entertain at practice and daydream during games.

"I can't go in," Nish protested. "I'm no goalie."

"Get over the boards before I throw you over them," Muck said.

Nish scrambled to get onto the ice, but his big pads caught as he vaulted the boards and he fell, heavily, to the ice, causing the first huge cheer from the Japanese crowd at Big Hat.

Jenny came off to a lot of backslapping and cheering from the Owls. Muck put a big hand on the back of her neck and squeezed, a small message of congratulations from the coach.

It took Nish about five seconds to get into it. He hopped over the lines on his way to the net. He talked to his goal posts. He sprayed his face with the water bottle. He skated over to the boards and hammered his stick against the glass, returning fast to his crease, where he slammed his stick hard into each pad and set himself, ready for anything.

The Mighty Ducks must have thought the Owls were putting in their *real* goaltender, for Travis could see concern on their faces and hear it in their voices.

*Of course*, Travis realized. There were no girls on the teams here. They assumed Jenny was the weak player and Nish was the star – especially when he acted like a star.

Whatever it was that the Mighty Ducks were thinking, it changed their style. Instead of holding on to the puck too long and trying to get it to an older player who might get a shot, the Ducks started throwing long shots into the Screech Owls' end.

The first one went wide, Nish dramatically swooping behind the net to clear the puck as if he were Martin Brodeur.

The second one skipped and went in under Nish's stick!

Owls 5, Mighty Ducks 1.

The goal brought the Ducks to life. They began skating harder. Their one good puck-carrier began to challenge the Owls' defence and twice slipped through for good shots. The first hit Nish square on the chest. The second went between his legs.

Owls 5, Mighty Ducks 2.

"Where's his force shield?" asked Sarah, giggling.

Twice more the Ducks scored, and in the final minute they pulled their own goalie to try to tie the game.

Sarah's line was out to stop them, Travis hoping he might finally get a goal, even if it was into the empty net.

But the Sapporo Mighty Ducks had other ideas. They were flying now, and the good puck-carrier beat Travis and then Dmitri before putting a perfect breakaway pass on the stick of one of the Ducks' better skaters.

He split the Owls' defence and came flying in on Nish, who went down too soon.

The Duck fired the puck high toward the open top corner.

Nish, flat on his back, kicked his legs straight up.

The puck clipped off the top of his skate toe and hammered against the glass.

A second later the horn blew. Game over.

Nish was last into the dressing room, his uniform soaked through with sweat, his big pads seemingly made of cement.

"I guess I saved your skins," he announced. "If it wasn't for me, we'd have been lucky to come out of that with a tie."

**11**

ack in the dressing room, Travis was first to notice something was wrong. His clothes were hung up in a very strange order. If he had taken off his jacket first, then his shirt, then his pants, they should not be on the peg pants first, then jacket, then shirt. Not unless they'd been taken off and replaced by someone in a hurry.

"How'd *your* clothes get on *my* peg?" Fahd was asking Andy.

This was even more curious. There was no mistaking big Andy's clothes for anything of Fahd's.

"Someone's rifled through my hockey bag," said Lars.

"Mine, too," said Jesse.

They carefully checked through everything, and nothing appeared to have been stolen. Mr. Dillinger apologized, saying it hadn't seemed like they ever locked dressing-room doors in Japan, so he hadn't insisted. But someone had obviously been in the room.

The mystery began to clear, if only slightly, once they got back to the Olympic Village apartments. Travis had the key to their apartment in his left pants pocket – or so he thought. When he dug deep for it, he found nothing.

Travis wasn't alone. Three others couldn't find their keys either.

Whoever had stolen them had known where the Owls were staying and had raced back to the Village before the team arrived. Someone had been inside the little apartments. Drawers were left open and clothes thrown about the rooms.

"Looks like I unpacked for everybody!" said a surprised Nish when he saw what had happened.

No one could figure out what the burglar was after. Money? Clothes? It was hard to figure out, because nothing had been taken.

@

In the morning, still with no idea why their apartments had been broken into – the Screech Owls set off to visit the Zenkoji Temple. They took the bus down to the train station and walked up Chuo street toward the sacred temple.

Mr. Imoo met them at the front gate. Until he smiled, the Owls might not have recognized him. He was wearing the frock of a Buddhist priest and looked much like any of the other priests hurrying about the entrance to the various temples – except, of course, for the missing teeth.

"You must see all of it," he told them. "Zenkoji is nearly three hundred years old. But even before that, for hundreds of years, this was a place of worship. Come – let me show you a bit."

Mr. Imoo's tour was incredible. He showed them the walkway

to the main hall – "There are exactly seven thousand, seven hundred and seventy-seven stones here," he told them. "Good mathematics problem, designing that" – and he showed them the darkened area in the main hall where the sacred image of Buddha is said to be, which only the highest priests are ever allowed to see.

"More important than Stanley Cup!" Mr. Imoo said, laughing.

Travis couldn't figure him out. Here he was, a priest in a church – Travis guessed this Japanese temple was much the same as a North American church – and though it was clear that the hundreds of visitors milling about were deadly serious, Mr. Imoo was forever joking about things. "Buddha likes laughing," he said at one point. "Buddha enjoys good joke same as anyone."

He showed them the huge stone pots where visitors burned incense, the air sickly-sweet with the smell. He showed them a statue of a man where older visitors lined up just to rub their hands over the smooth stone. "Binzuro," Mr. Imoo explained. "Smartest doctor who ever lived. They rub him to feel better. Try it – it works!"

Some of the Owls did rub their hands over the smiling figure, but they could feel nothing. "Because you're young," Mr. Imoo said. "Come back to Nagano when you're old – you'll see it works."

Mr. Imoo had his own chores to do and couldn't stay any longer, but he left them with a tour guide and some maps of the huge temple complex and told them all that there was one thing they really should do if they got the chance.

"You must experience *O-kaidan*," he told them. "Under the main temple is tunnel. You can see people over there lining up for it. It is very dark down there. Sometimes people get frightened.

But when you reach the end, you will find the way out. Stick to the right. And feel for the latch to the door. We call it the 'Key to Enlightenment.' I can not explain it to you, but after you have been through it, you will know."

"I'm going right now!" said Nish.

"You certainly need some enlightenment," said Sarah.

"I'm not going down in some stuffy room with him," Fahd said. "Nish'll stink it out."

"*This* is a temple!" Nish barked at him, outraged. "You don't do things like that in a place like this."

"*Hey!*" cheered Sarah. "It's working! Nish finally sees the light!"

"C'mon!" Nish said to Travis.

Travis shook his head. "Maybe later."

Travis moved off quickly. He only had to imagine the dark tunnel underneath the temple and he shuddered. Travis hated enclosed dark spaces. He didn't even like long elevator rides. He'd do whatever he could to avoid going.

Travis moved on toward the souvenir section, where visitors were lining up for incense and postcards and small silk banners with paintings of the temple on them.

Data wheeled up to him, smiling and excited.

"The others are going to push me through," Data told him. "Here, you hang on to the camera. There's no point taking it down into a dark tunnel. Take some shots of the other temples if you get a chance."

Travis nodded. It was a beautiful sunny day. The pines surrounding the temples were bright and dripping with melting snow.

There were pigeons strutting all over the walkway. Hundreds of them. Thousands of them. An old woman was dumping out bags of dried bread, and the sound of hundreds of more pigeons landing was almost deafening. They darkened the sun. They landed on her arms, her shoulders, her head, all around her. People cheered and children danced and cameras were raised to record it all as the old woman, grinning from ear to ear, stood with both arms out and pigeons by the dozen tried to find a roost on her.

*Got to get this for Data*, Travis thought.

The video camera was easy to work. He simply pointed and pressed a button with his thumb.

Everything seemed smaller through the lens. Smaller, but somehow sharper. A cloud of pigeons would fall, another would rise, and in the centre of the shot the old woman turned as if on a pedestal, her grin almost as wide as her outstretched arms as the pigeons fought for a foothold.

A small child ran out into the middle and spooked the birds, a thousand wings roaring as the pigeons rose as one and headed back toward the trees. The child spun, bewildered at their sudden disappearance. Travis giggled, knowing he had caught a delightful scene on Data's camera.

He raised the camera back toward the old woman and for the first time saw, through the lens, that someone was pointing at him.

It was Eyebrows.

*The waiter who had run over Nish.*

*The man at the ski hill.*

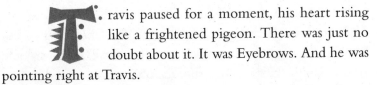

# 12

**T**ravis paused for a moment, his heart rising like a frightened pigeon. There was just no doubt about it. It was Eyebrows. And he was pointing right at Travis.

*How does he even recognize me?* Travis wondered, the camera still raised to his eye.

But there was no time to figure out how. Eyebrows was scowling and beginning to move around the square in Travis's direction. There was another man with him, and he was headed around the square in the other direction.

There was no time to ask questions. Travis knew he had to get out of there.

He stepped backwards and turned, but there was no exit behind him – only a long walk to another temple, and no visitors there.

His best bet was the crowd. But to get back amongst the people, Travis had to go straight ahead.

The pigeons were landing again by the thousands, the old woman dumping out another large bag of broken bread. The clamouring sound of the birds was enormous. The crowd of tourists was growing.

Travis checked the sides of the small square. Both men had their eyes fixed on him and were circling toward him, sticking to the outer edges of the square so they could skirt around the loose circle of tourists.

Travis had no choice.

Like the small child, he broke straight for the centre. The pigeons exploded, rising in terror, their thousands of wings blurring Travis's view as he raced past the old woman toward the other side.

Some of the people had covered their ears, the sound was so great. Others were making faces at him, as if disgusted that he would be so thoughtless. But there was no time for Travis to stop and explain.

He allowed himself only one backward glance as he headed back toward the main temple area.

*Eyebrows was running! And right behind Eyebrows – the other man!*

Travis ran flat out now, twisting and turning through the heavy crowds of pilgrims and tourists, pigeons flying, families scattering as the little foreigner in the Screech Owls jacket broke as fast as he could for the front gates, where the largest crowds seemed to be.

Travis's mind was racing too. He couldn't stop and ask for help: who here would speak English? And he couldn't seem to lose himself in the crowds. His team jacket and his face set him apart from everyone else.

*I have to hide!* Travis thought. *But where?*

And then it struck him.

*The tunnel.*

If he could reach the tunnel, he might find the rest of the team there. Or Muck or Mr. Dillinger.

But the tunnel was dark and airless, with thick, heavy walls bearing in on him.

There was nothing for it. He turned just enough to see that the men were gaining, and he knew it was now only a matter of time before one of them reached him. And then what would the people watching do? Help him? Not likely. They'd assume that the men had been chasing Travis to get him to stop running and scaring up the pigeons. He'd never be able to explain. They'd take him away. He had no idea what for, but he knew it would be bad.

Travis flew over the seven thousand, seven hundred and seventy-seven stones heading to the main temple. He slipped through the thickening crowds as if he were on skates, dipping and deking to find an opening. He was now moving faster than his pursuers.

Up to the main temple he flew. At the top of the wooden steps he saw that everywhere in front of him were mats covered with the shoes and boots of people who had gone inside. Knowing he must, he kicked off his boots and ran, in his socks, over the soft spongy matting that led to the rear of the temple.

There were pilgrims there, lining up to head down into the tunnel.

Apologizing, Travis eased his way through. No one seemed to mind very much. They must have thought he was just catching up to his teammates. Perhaps that meant Nish and Sarah and everyone else were still down there. He hoped so.

A few feet into the tunnel, the dark and silence descended on him like a blanket. There was no sound but for the breathing of others in the tight line working their way along the nearest wall.

Travis tried to breathe deep, and felt his nostrils fighting to seal out a rush of damp straw – the smell of the mats on the tunnel floor.

*He couldn't breathe!*

His heart was pounding now, slamming against his chest as if it, too, desperately wanted out. His breath was coming fast and jerky, never enough, and he choked.

He reached out and felt for the wall. He tried to remember what they'd been told: *Stick to the right wall, trust in yourself, and you will feel the key.*

Travis lunged against the wall, finding instant comfort in its solidity. He held Data's camera tight with his left hand and felt ahead with his right as he inched along. He thought he might be crying.

He almost dropped the camera, and then it struck him.

*The camera!*

*Data's video camera!*

That's what they were after! They hadn't recognized him at all. They saw the Screech Owls jacket – and the camera!

That's what they had been searching for in the dressing room. That was why they had stolen the keys and broken into the apartments. But they hadn't realized that Data had a separate apartment on the ground floor.

Data had recorded something on the camera that they wanted. *But what?* Did Eyebrows have something to do with the murder?

There was Eyebrows at the banquet. And Eyebrows and one of his friends at the ski hill. But what was the connection?

It didn't matter that Travis couldn't figure it out. It was enough to know that the men were after the camera, and he had the camera.

Should he leave it? Just drop it, and let them have it if they could find it here?

No, he couldn't do that. He had a responsibility. If the camera was that important to them, it must be important to the police as well.

Travis tightened his grip on the camera and edged along a little farther.

*There were sounds behind him – something rubbing along the wall!*

What was it he was supposed to look for in the tunnel?

A key? The Key to Enlightenment?

Travis reached out, praying. He reached out – and then felt it.

*A hand. A strong hand – tightening about his arm!*

A thousand pigeons seemed to take off in his chest.

He felt himself being yanked back, hard.

"*This way!*"

Travis was choking. *That voice! It wasn't Muck or Mr. Dillinger or any of the Owls!*

Travis couldn't even scream. With the strong hand drawing him along, he slipped and tripped and slid toward the far end of the pitch black tunnel. He was being dragged away.

But the hand didn't hurt him.

There was a sound: wood rubbing on wood, and then something giving.

The light hit him, a thousand flashbulbs in his eyes, a shot right to the head that sent him reeling back, almost falling.

The hand still held him.

"You're okay now," the voice said.

Travis looked but couldn't see. His eyes were overwhelmed with the light. He held his hands over them, and when he looked through the cracks of his fingers, he saw a familiar toothless grin.

*Mr. Imoo!*

# 13

**M**r. Imoo had saved Travis — *BUT FROM WHAT?* His fear of dark enclosed spaces? Of getting lost forever underneath the temple?

What if Eyebrows had simply wanted to get even for Nish's snowball? But if that was the case, why would he bring another guy along with him? Another mean-looking guy.

Mr. Imoo had only noticed that Travis had headed into the tunnel and was seeming to take a very long time coming out the other end. He hadn't gone down to rescue Travis from any murderers or anything, just to show him the way out. Visitors often panicked and froze in the tunnel, apparently.

"It happens," said Mr. Imoo. "Don't worry about it."

But Travis couldn't stop worrying. What was going on? Had he been right — was it the camera they wanted? And if so, what was in the camera that was so important to them that they'd break into the Owls' residence and then chase Travis into a sacred temple?

When they got back to the Olympic Village, Travis got Sarah and Nish to sit down with him and go through the video cassette. There was the waiter, and it certainly looked like Eyebrows. And there he was again at the ski hill. And there was Nish tossing his snowball.

"It's me he wants," Nish said, almost bragging.

"But why break into our rooms?" Travis asked.

"I don't know. Maybe he meant to play a trick on me but couldn't figure out which bed was mine."

"That hardly takes a rocket scientist to figure out," countered Sarah. "Just look for the unmade one with all the clothes dumped on the floor."

"Well, what then?" shot back Nish. "You tell us."

Sarah shook her head. "I don't know. There's something to this, though. Travis is right."

Several times they went over the tape. A waiter. Two men unloading a snowmobile and a sled. No poison. No explosives. Nothing.

"I still think we should show it to the police," said Travis.

"Show what?" Nish asked. "There's nothing there."

Travis sighed. He and his friends were missing something, he was certain, but he didn't know what.

"We better get going," said Sarah. "We've got a game at two."

○

This time the Screech Owls were up against the Matsumoto Sharks, a much better team than the Sapporo Mighty Ducks.

Big Hat was almost filled for the match, and the sound when the Sharks came out onto the ice was almost as loud as if an NHL team had arrived. No one booed, however, when the Owls came out after them. The Owls' parents cheered from one corner, where they were all sitting together with their Screech Owls banners and Canadian flags, and the rest of the packed rink applauded, politely, as if the Owls had come to Nagano for a spelling bee instead of a hockey tournament.

The Sharks passed well and weren't afraid of shooting. There was no sense here of older *sempai* or younger *koohai* players. And the goalie, from what the Owls could gather during warm-up, was excellent, with a lightning-fast glove hand.

"I should be playing the point," Nish said to Travis during the warm-up. "We're going to need my shot."

Travis nodded. Nish might be right. But Muck still had him playing backup goal, so Travis didn't think there was any chance Nish would get into this game. If the Owls were going to win, they'd need Jenny in net all the way.

Muck started Andy's line, just to surprise the Sharks. Andy's line checked wonderfully, but they were slow compared to Sarah's line, and when Muck called for a change on the fly, it seemed to catch the Sharks off guard.

Dmitri leapt over the boards and took off for the far side of the rink, looping fast just as Sarah picked up a loose puck and rattled it hard off the boards so it flew ahead of Dmitri and beat him over the red line. No icing – and Dmitri was almost free.

Travis joined the rush. There was one defender back, and he didn't seem sure what to do: chase Dmitri or block the potential pass.

Dmitri solved his opponent's dilemma by cutting right across the ice, straight at the backpedalling defenceman. The defender went for Dmitri, and Dmitri let him catch him, but he left the puck behind in a perfect drop pass.

Travis read the play perfectly, and picked up the sitting puck to burst in on goal. A head fake, a dipped shoulder, and the Sharks' goaltender went down.

Travis backhanded the puck high and hard – right off the crossbar!

The ring of metal was followed by a huge gasp throughout Big Hat. The goal light went on by mistake, but the players knew Travis hadn't scored.

The defenceman who'd been fooled picked up the puck and backhanded it high, nearly hitting the clock.

The puck slapped down past centre, and was scooped up by a Sharks forward in full flight. A clear breakaway!

Jenny came wiggling out to cut off the angle. The forward faked a slapshot, delayed while Jenny committed to blocking the shot, and then held on until he had swept farther around her, lofting an easy wristshot into the empty net.

Travis came off and looked down the bench toward Nish. His friend had his goalie glove over his face, afraid to look for fear Muck might be signalling him to go in.

"Defence stays back," Muck said calmly. "That doesn't happen again, understand?"

Everyone understood. There would be no more breakaways.

Little Simon Milliken got the Owls moving later in the period when he cut off a cross-blueline pass and broke up centre, a Sharks defenceman chasing frantically.

Simon waited until the last moment, and instead of shooting, dropped the puck back between the chasing defenceman's legs, perfectly on Liz's stick.

The play caught the Sharks' goaltender off guard. He'd counted on Simon going to his backhand, leaving the far side of his net open.

Liz fired the puck hard and true, the net bulging as a huge cheer went up from the little Canadian section.

Heading into the third period, the score was tied 3−3 when Sarah took matters into her own hands. First, she set Travis up for an easy tap-in on a beautiful end-to-end rush. Then she sent Dmitri in on a breakaway, and he did his usual one fake and roofed a backhand. Then Sarah herself scored into the empty Sharks net in the final minute.

Owls 6, Sharks 3. But it had been a lot closer than it looked. They had won, yes, but no one felt good about how they had played. The Screech Owls had looked sloppy on defence, and defence was an area of the game in which they all took enormous pride.

"We play like that against Lake Placid," Muck said in the dressing room, "and we won't have a chance."

Muck and Mr. Dillinger had scouted the Lake Placid Olympians when they'd played the night before. A strong team with excellent skaters and one tremendous playmaker, the Olympians, Muck figured, would be as strong an opposition as the Owls had ever faced.

"We play like that again, and we won't have a chance," Muck repeated.

No one said a word. Travis knew that Muck was looking around the room. He could sense that Muck had looked at Jenny and wondered if the Owls would be in better shape if Jeremy were with them. He knew that Muck had looked, as well, at Nish and wondered if perhaps they shouldn't have Nish and his big shot playing out instead of sitting on the bench in goaltending gear he barely knew how to put on.

But Muck could hardly change things now. If he did anything with Nish, Jenny would think that Muck didn't have enough faith in her, which would only make her more nervous. He had to stick with Jenny, and was forced, also, to leave Nish where he was.

"If Lake Placid wins tonight, it's going to be them and us in the final," Muck said, finally. "Do you think you're ready for it?"

No one spoke. Travis knew, as captain, he had to say something.

"We can do it," he said.

"We'll win," said Sarah.

"Good," said Muck. "That's what I want to hear."

*But did he believe it?* Travis wondered.

*More important, did the Owls believe it?*

# 14

**T**ravis had never known Nish to take his studies so seriously. Every morning, when the Screech Owls didn't have a game or a practice, Nish was off with Mr. Imoo, either at the Zenkoji Temple or at a special *dojo* near the Olympic Village where Mr. Imoo trained several students in the strange art of the Indonesian "force shield."

Nish seemed filled with wisdom, even if he couldn't yet curve spoons or, for that matter, even convince one of Sarah's hairpins to bend a bit when he tickled it one day at lunch. Other students, Nish claimed, could break bricks and boards with their foreheads.

"There's a master in Indonesia," he said, "who can pick a bullet out of the air."

"A *shot* bullet?" Fahd asked.

Nish looked at Fahd as if he were an idiot. Everyone else looked at Nish as if he were making it up.

But Travis had to give his old friend credit. Nish was applying himself to this newfound interest much more than Nish had ever worked on math or science or English. Mr. Imoo seemed to understand Nish perfectly. He was even starting to make jokes about Nish stinking up the *dojo*.

Nish didn't mind. He was going to master this. Before the trip was out, he was determined to find his own force shield.

The Screech Owls had one more practice at Big Hat before the championship weekend. Muck ran some drills and had the Owls practise tip-ins on Jenny at one end and on Nish at the other. He had his reasons.

"Lake Placid made the final easily," Muck told them later in the dressing room. "They are an excellent team. They know how to get traffic in front of the net, and they know how to get point shots on the net for tip-ins and rebounds. That's why we were working on the same thing ourselves today. I want to get our goalies comfortable with what they'll be facing."

Muck finished talking, but he didn't look finished. He walked around the room and cleared his throat a couple of times. No one said a word. Even Nish sat quietly, his goalie mask still on top of his head.

"Mr. Dillinger will talk to you now," he said.

Muck walked toward the dressing room and held the door open for Mr. Dillinger to come in. Mr. Dillinger looked worried. He was rubbing his hands together.

"I've just met with the Nagano police," said Mr. Dillinger.

"Any word on the break-ins?" Fahd asked.

"No," Mr. Dillinger said, shaking his head.

"More blowfish?" Fahd asked.

Mr. Dillinger shook his head again.

"The avalanche," he said. "They've found some evidence that it was set off deliberately. They found dynamite blasting caps up the hill."

Travis snapped back, striking his head lightly on the wall behind him. *Dynamite!* So that was why the avalanche had started with such a bang. It was an explosion!

"What for?" Andy asked with a slight tremor in his voice. "Were they trying to kill us?"

"The police don't know," said Mr. Dillinger. "But they want us to be very careful from here on out. They don't know if there's any connection between the break-ins and the avalanche – maybe even the murder of the mayor – but they're afraid to take anything for granted. From now on, we stay together in groups of at least three, all right? And we stick to the Village and the hockey rink."

He looked around the room, his big eyes pleading for understanding. Mr. Dillinger looked very hurt. This was hardly the way the trip to Japan had been planned to go.

Travis had never heard the phone ring in his room before. It caught him by surprise. He'd been brushing his teeth, and Nish had been sitting, cross-legged, on his bed, his eyes closed, deep in concentration.

It took a moment for Travis to locate it. There was a desk against one wall and the telephone was on the floor beside it, covered by several sweaty T-shirts belonging to Nish.

He picked it up. But what should he say? "Hello"? Or "*Moshi moshi*"?

"Hel-lo," he said, uncertain.

"Travis – that you?"

"Yeah . . . *Data?*"

"It's me. Nish there?"

Travis looked over at his roommate, still seemingly deep in a trance.

"I think so."

"Good. Get down here. *Quick!*"

Travis had no idea what had Data so worked up, but it was clear from his voice that he was very, very excited about something.

"C'mon," Travis said to Nish. "That was Data. He needs us."

Nish made no sign of moving.

"*Hey!*" Travis yelled. Nish's eyes popped open. He was back in the real world.

"What's up?"

"Data needs us – let's go!"

To get to Data's ground-floor apartment, they had to cut across the courtyard and through the tent where the teams ate their meals. They picked up Sarah and Jenny along the way.

"We're supposed to be in groups of three or more," Travis explained. "Data needs us."

The four Screech Owls found Data's door unlocked when they got there. They let themselves in.

Data was in his wheelchair. He had a small television on top of the desk and a tiny video cassette recorder beside it.

"The man at the desk sent this to me with some movies to watch," Data explained. "But I set it up to see what our tape looked like so far."

He had the tape paused at the point where Nish threw the snowball at Eyebrows.

"Did you check for explosives?" Nish asked. "I bet it was Eyebrows who started the avalanche."

"It might have been," said Data. "But there's nothing there. See for yourself."

Data ran the footage of the men pulling up in the Toyota 4x4 and unloading the snowmobile and sled. The Owls pulled up chairs or sat on the edge of Data's bed and went over it carefully several times, but there was nothing remarkable. Whatever was in the sled was out of sight. It could have been dynamite; it could just as easily have been blankets or shovels. No way would the video ever convince the police that Eyebrows had started the avalanche.

"There's nothing there, see?"

"We see," said Sarah. "But you found something, didn't you, Data?"

Data looked at her and nodded.

He seemed a little frightened.

"I want you to watch this."

Data rewound the tape, then stopped it and pressed "play" to see where he was. It was the banquet, near the end.

"Here's where Eyebrows runs me over!" announced Nish.

"It's before that," said Data, pushing the "rewind" button again.

When he had found the right spot, Data turned to the four friends. "I'll just play it straight," he said. "You tell me if you see anything."

The four leaned closer to the television and Data pushed "play."

The picture cleared. It was the beginning of the banquet. They saw the teams heading for their places. There were shots of the Screech Owls sitting down.

The camera then scanned the head table, just as Muck and the others were taking their places.

Sho Fujiwara, the man in charge of Japanese hockey, was reaching out an arm toward Muck. He was pulling him over, smiling and gesturing for Muck to sit.

Data hit "pause."

"See anything?" he asked.

"Muck and Sho," said Jenny. "They sat together, remember?"

"What about it?" asked Nish. "I saw nothing."

"I'm going to run it again," said Data.

The machine whirred back, clicked, then started again at just the right place.

Sho Fujiwara was standing at the table. He saw Muck and called him over. They seemed like old pals, happy to be together. It made sense for them to sit side by side.

As Muck stepped up onto the raised platform and headed toward his new friend, Sho deftly switched a couple of the place cards showing who should sit where.

Data stopped the machine.

"See?" he asked.

"He changed the seating plan so Muck could sit beside him," Travis said. "Big deal."

"Your point?" asked Sarah.

"Watch again," said Data. "You can read the place cards if you look closely."

He played the same sequence again. Sho called Muck over. Sho switched the seating around.

Data stopped the machine.

"The mayor was not sitting where he was supposed to."

Again he played the sequence.

Data was right! To get Muck beside him, Sho had to switch the names around on the head table. Muck had ended up beside him, but the mayor had bumped Mr. Ikura over one place.

"The blowfish wasn't meant for the mayor," said Data. "Whoever the murderer is, he wanted to kill Mr. Ikura."

They stared at the machine on "pause," nothing moving on the screen, but images racing in their minds.

Data was right. If it hadn't been for the switching of places, the mayor would have been one seat over.

Someone must have brought the blowfish out to a designated spot at the head table, the place where Mr. Ikura was supposed to be sitting.

The waiter? Is that why he ran – because he'd realized the mistake too late?

And is that why Eyebrows was up to no good at Mr. Ikura's ski hill?

"We better take this to Mr. Dillinger," said Sarah. "He'll want the police to see this."

# 15

he police arrived within five minutes of Mr. Dillinger's call. They brought translators, and they even had a precision video player that could freeze a single frame of tape so that it looked like a sharp, crystal-clear photograph. Travis couldn't believe how efficient they were.

Nish was in his glory, bowing left and right to every Japanese person who looked like he or she might be even remotely connected to the investigation. He acted as if he alone had solved the crime – even if, so far, no crime at all had been solved.

The police interviewed Muck about the switch in places at the head table. They brought in Sho Fujiwara and interviewed him separately, and then Sho and Muck together. They interviewed Data alone, Travis alone, Nish alone, Sarah alone, and then talked to them in a group. Nish was taken to a special investigative van that had pulled up outside the Olympic Village and was asked to look at possible suspects on a computer screen. He claimed he had found Eyebrows within a matter of minutes.

The police packed up and left. They made no mention of what they were going to do. No hint of what might happen now. Nothing.

Six hours later, they were back – with the full story.

The man the Owls called Eyebrows – "I identified him," bragged Nish – was a well-known *yakuza*, a Japanese gangster. "*Yakuza* means good for nothing," explained Sho Fujiwara, who was also called back for the meeting with the police. "We have bad people here in Japan, too."

Eyebrows had been hired to do the murder. But the mayor of Nagano was never intended to be the victim. The man they wanted to kill was Mr. Ikura, the owner of the ski hill. The blowfish plot had, apparently, been Eyebrows' idea, and he had botched it so badly – dressing up like a waiter and serving the poisonous dish to the wrong person at the head table – that he'd been scrambling to make up for it ever since.

The avalanche was also Eyebrows' idea. He was worried that the very thugs who had hired him might now want to kill him for botching the job, so he'd tried to frighten Mr. Ikura into selling off.

That turned out to be a huge mistake, and a key break in the case for the police. Mr. Ikura had been under enormous pressure to sell to a corporation, but had refused to do so. This company had plans to turn the site of the Olympic skiing and snowboarding competitions into a major international tourist complex for the very rich, complete with a huge chalet development, that would have closed off the hill to the likes of the Owls and the people of Nagano. Mr. Ikura could have made millions by selling, but chose not to.

He was saying no to the wrong people, apparently. When they couldn't convince him to sell, they hired Eyebrows to kill him, believing that Mr. Ikura's heirs would quickly agree to the sale.

If the death looked accidental, no one would ever connect it with the sale. Eyebrows' idea was that the blowfish poisoning would look like a heart attack. But when he accidentally killed the mayor of Nagano, he aroused the police's suspicions. The sudden death of a well-known politician could not go uninvestigated, and the police had ordered an autopsy that discovered the blowfish.

Even so, there was still nothing to throw suspicion on the big corporation and its plans for Mr. Ikura's ski lodge. It wasn't until the avalanche that the pieces of the puzzle finally started to fall into place. First, the avalanche was out of season, and while looking for the cause they had found the dynamite caps not far from where they figured the slide had started.

The final, essential, clue was Data's video. It not only placed Eyebrows at both the banquet and the ski hill – with no real proof of wrongdoing, the police pointed out – it also showed the switch of places at the head table.

Once the police knew that the intended victim had been Mr. Ikura, and that the avalanche had been deliberate, they quickly came up with a pretty good idea of what had happened.

Data's tape had also helped the police track down Eyebrows' accomplice. The man helping Eyebrows unload the snowmobile and sled from the Toyota 4x4 had cracked almost immediately.

He hadn't even known what Eyebrows had in the sled. And once he realized he was caught up in a murder, he told them everything he knew – including where to find Eyebrows.

"He's in jail right now," Sho told the Owls. "And he'll probably spend the rest of his life there.

"The City of Nagano – all Japan, for that matter – is deeply indebted to you, Mr. Data. We thank you and your friends."

Data was a hero. The newspapers came to do stories on him. Television stations came to interview him.

"I identified the guy," Nish told each and every one of the reporters as they and their film crews arrived at the Olympic Village.

But no one was interested in Nish. The hockey player in the wheelchair – the master sleuth, the Canadian Sherlock Holmes – was the biggest story in Japan. Next to Anne of Green Gables, he was, for a few days, the most-beloved young Canadian in all of Japan.

"I identified the guy," Nish kept saying.

arah was first in the Big Hat dressing room. When Travis made his way in, he could tell at once that she was pumped for the championship game against the Lake Placid Olympians. Her eyes seemed on fire.

"One for each of you," she said as she handed each arriving player a small plastic package.

"Hide them until I give the signal."

Nish, as always, was last into the room, dragging and pushing and half kicking his hockey bag. He dropped his sticks against the wall, letting them fall against the others that had been set there so carefully and sending them crashing to the floor like falling dominoes.

No one said a word. Nish looked around at them, seemingly disappointed that no one had noticed him.

He had an open can of Sweat and took a huge slug of it before he sat down, burping loudly as the gas backed up in his throat.

Even with your eyes shut, Travis thought to himself, you would know when Nish had arrived in a hockey dressing room. The crashing sticks. The dragging bag on the floor. The burping. The long, lazy zip of the hockey bag, and the terrible sweaty odour that rose up from inside. The rest of the Owls had given up asking him to wash his equipment. "Sweat is my good-luck charm," he said. "Smell bad, play good."

Nish took off his jacket and shirt, stood up, burped again, and walked to the end of the dressing room, where he slammed the washroom door: part of his hockey ritual, as certain as fresh tape on his stick, as sure as the drop of the puck.

"*Now!*" Sarah hissed.

Everyone dipped into the little packages she had handed out. Some began giggling when they saw what it was that Sarah had brought for them. They had to move quickly.

The toilet flushed, and from behind the closed door Nish groaned with the exaggerated satisfaction he always displayed at this moment.

The door banged open, Nish pumping a fist in the air – and then he saw the Owls.

Sarah had issued each team member a face mask, the kind the Japanese wore to keep out pollution. They were all wearing them, all sitting in their stalls, staring at Nish over the white gauze that covered their noses and mouths.

"What's *that* supposed to mean?" Nish said.

"Think about it," Sarah said, her voice muffled.


Muck came in pushing Data. Data started giggling when he saw the masks, but Muck said nothing. Nothing ever seemed to surprise Muck, thought Travis. Not even Nish.

Mr. Dillinger came in and did a double take at the kids in their masks, but he, too, said nothing. He went about his business, filling the water bottles, getting the tape ready, making sure there were pucks for the warm-up.

Sarah removed her mask and the others followed. Muck waited until everyone was ready, their minds back on the game.

"The rink is full," said Muck. "The whole town came out to cheer Data – that's what I think – but they deserve to see some good North American hockey, too. If hockey's going to take off in this country, they're going to have to see what a great game it can be.

"I want a clean game. I want a good game. I want these people to know how much we appreciate them coming out to watch."

The door opened again and Mr. Imoo popped his head in. He was grinning ear to ear, the gap in his teeth almost exactly the width of a puck.

"Good show today, Owls," he said.

Mr. Imoo turned to his prize pupil, Nish, who was beaming.

"Nish," he said. "I think you're ready."

Travis looked at Muck, who cocked an eyebrow. What did Muck think? Travis wondered. That Mr. Imoo thought Nish was "ready" to play goal? Not likely, not against the Lake Placid Olympians, that was for sure.

Travis glanced over at Nish, who seemed to have assumed a new, calm look. It was no longer the Nish who was always desperate to be the centre of attention. It was a Nish filled with poise and confidence.

Travis couldn't help it: he wished Nish wasn't playing goal.

They would need him on defence, and even if Muck never put him in, Nish wouldn't be much use to the Owls sitting at the end of the bench.

But he also knew there was no choice. Tournament rules were rules: they had to have a second goalie. If only Jeremy had been able to come. He hoped Jenny was going to have a good game.

"Okay?" Muck said. He was staring at Travis.

Travis understood the signal. As captain, he was to lead them out onto the ice.

"*Let's go!*" Travis shouted, standing up and yanking on his helmet.

"*Screech Owls!*" Sarah called as she stood.

"*Let's do it!*" called Lars.

"*Owls!*"

"*Owls!*"

"*Owls!*"

# 17

ravis had never been in such a game!

He had played in front of large crowds before – larger even than this one, which filled Big Hat – but never in front of a crowd that cheered every single thing that happened.

The biggest cheer, so far, had been when the crowd had first noticed Data coming out onto the ice, pushed by Mr. Dillinger. They had risen to their feet in a long standing ovation. Data had waved and smiled and probably wished it would be over with, but Travis knew how much this meant to his friend. The Japanese were all grateful for what he had done.

He had heard crowds cheer and boo before, but never one that seemed to find no fault with anything. They played no favourites. They did not boo the referee or the linesmen. They cheered the goals and the saves equally. They were cheering, he supposed, for *hockey*.

And the hockey was fantastic. The Screech Owls and the Lake Placid Olympians were evenly matched. Jenny was outstanding in the Owls' goal, but so, too, was the little guy playing net for the Olympians. He had an unbelievable glove hand, and had twice robbed Dmitri on clean break-aways, the Screech Owls forward going both times to his special backhand move that almost always meant the goal-tender's water bottle flying off the top of the net and a Screech Owls goal.

Muck was matching lines with the Lake Placid coach, and he seemed to be enjoying the game as much as anyone. Mr. Dillinger was handling the defence door and Data the forwards', so every time Travis came off or went on, he felt Data pat him as he passed.

Sarah's line was on against the top Olympians' line – Sarah the playmaker matched with Lake Placid's top playmaker, a big, lanky kid with such a long reach no one seemed capable of checking him. The big playmaker had two good wingers, too, which meant that Travis had to pay far more attention to defence than offence.

Muck wanted them to shut down the big Lake Placid line. It made sense. Sarah was the best checker on the team, by far, when she put her mind to it – and when Sarah was sent out in a checking role, she seemed to take as much pride in stopping goals as she did in making them happen.

The Owls scored first when Andy's line got a lucky bounce at the blueline. The puck hit some bad ice as it was sent back for a point shot and bounced over the defenceman's stick and out to centre. Andy, with his long stride, got the jump on both defence and broke in alone. The Lake Placid goaltender made a wonderful stop on Andy, stacking his pads as Andy tried to pull him out and dump it into the far side, but the rebound went straight to little Simon Milliken, who found he had an empty net staring at him.

Two minutes later, the game was tied up. The big Lake Placid playmaker went end to end, losing Sarah on a twisting play at his own blueline and faking Wilson brilliantly as he broke in. The big Olympian dumped the puck in a saucer pass to one side of Wilson and curled around him on the other side, picking up his own pass to come in alone on Jenny. Two big fakes, and Jenny was sprawled out of the position and the puck was in the back of the net.

Between the first and second period, Muck told Sarah to step it up. "You're taking your checking too seriously," he told her. "If you have the puck, he can't have it."

Sarah knew what Muck meant. Her line started the second period, and she snicked the puck out of the air as it fell, sending it back to Wilson.

Dmitri broke hard for the far blueline, cutting toward centre.

Wilson hit him perfectly. Dmitri took the pass and sent it back between his own legs to Travis, who stepped into it as he crossed the blueline.

Sarah was slapping the ice with her stick. Travis didn't even look. He flipped the puck into empty space, knowing she would be there in an instant – and she was.

Sarah was in free. The goaltender began backing up, preparing for a fake, but she shot almost at once, completely fooling the goalie and finding the net just over his left shoulder.

"That's more like it," Muck said when Sarah and Travis got back to the bench. He put a big hand on each player's neck as they gathered their breath. Travis liked nothing better in the world than to feel Muck do that. The coach didn't even think about it, probably, but it meant everything.

Andy then scored on a pretty play, sent in by Simon on a neat pass when Simon was falling with the puck. Andy went to his backhand and slipped the shot low through the sharp little goalie's pads.

Into the third period, the Olympians began to press.

The big playmaker came straight up centre and swept around Sarah, who dived after him, her stick accidentally sweeping away his skates.

The referee's whistle blew.

Travis cringed. The Owls could hardly afford to lose their best player just now. But Sarah was going off. The referee signalled "tripping" to the timekeeper, the penalty door box swung open, and Sarah, slamming her stick once in anger at herself, headed for it.

The crowd cheered politely. Travis giggled. He couldn't help himself.

The Olympians needed only one shot to score on the power play. It came in from the point, and Jenny had it all the way, but just at the last moment the big Lake Placid playmaker reached his stick blade out just enough to tick the puck, and it changed direction and flipped over her outstretched pad.

Screech Owls 3, Olympians 2.

The Lake Placid team started to press even harder. Travis wondered if they could hold them back. *If only they had Nish on the ice. If only Nish wasn't sitting there, on the end of the bench, in his goalie gear . . .*

The Olympians' strategy was to crash the net, hoping to set up shots from the point like the one that had gone in on the power play. When the defence shot, the forwards tried to screen Jenny in front, attempting either to tip another shot or allow one to slip through without Jenny seeing it coming.

The game was getting rough, but the referee was calling nothing.

The right defenceman had the puck, and Travis dived to block the shot, shutting his eyes instinctively as he hit the ice.

He waited for the puck to crash into him – but nothing happened. When he opened his eyes, he saw the defenceman deftly step around him, closing in even tighter for the shot.

The defenceman took a mighty slapshot. Jenny's glove hand snaked out. *She had it!*

But then the big playmaker crashed into her.

They hit, and Jenny gave, flying toward the corner, the big playmaker going with her and crashing hard on top of her into the boards.

The whistle blew.

Mr. Dillinger was already over the boards, racing and slipping on the ice, a towel in one hand.

Jenny was groaning. She was moving her legs but still flat on her back, the air knocked out of her.

"*No penalty?*" Jenny was asking the referee.

The referee was shaking his head. "Your own man hit him into her," the referee said.

The referee was pointing at Wilson. Wilson didn't argue. It was true. He had been trying to clear the big playmaker out from in front of the net, and he had put his shoulder into him just when Jenny made her spectacular save.

Travis glided in closer to Jenny. He was exhausted, his breath coming in huge gulps. He knew that this time, this game, he was covered in sweat.

Mr. Dillinger was leaning over Jenny.

He looked up, catching the referee's eye.

"Just the wind knocked out," he said. "But she's hurt her arm, too."

"You'll have to replace her," said the referee. "We have to get this game in."

Mr. Dillinger winced.

Travis winced.

If Jenny couldn't play, that meant only one thing.

*Nish was going in!*

Jenny was up and holding her arm cautiously. She had tears rolling down her cheeks, but whether that was from the pain or the fact that she couldn't go on, Travis couldn't say.

The big playmaker brushed by him, reaching out to tap Jenny's pads.

"Sorry about that," he said. "You played great."

Jenny smiled through her tears. Travis could tell how much that meant to her, the best player she'd ever faced showing her that kind of respect. Travis was impressed. It was a very classy thing for the big Olympian to do.

"I'm ready," Nish announced.

Muck didn't seem convinced. But he had no choice. He stared long and hard at his new goaltender, who was standing in front of the bench, his mask on top of his head, spraying water directly into his face.

"Do what you can," Muck said. "And don't worry about it."

But Nish was into it. He sprayed the water, spat another mouthful out, yanked down his mask as if he were a fighter pilot about to take off, jumped over the red line, jumped over the blue-line, skated to where Mr. Imoo was standing, clapping, smashed his stick into the glass, then turned and headed for his net.

A quick few words with his goal posts, and he was ready to go.

Nish, the *samurai* goaltender.

It was over, Travis figured. They could barely hold the Lake Placid team with Jenny playing her best. How could they hold them off now with Nish in net? Nish, who didn't know the first thing about playing goal.

"Let's just get it over with fast," Sarah said. "And hope we don't embarrass ourselves too badly."

The Lake Placid team seemed to take new energy from the fact that Nish was in net. Whether it was because they were impressed by his hot-dog moves or because they knew how weak he was, Travis couldn't tell. But suddenly the Olympians were even stronger.

Sarah, however, had her own ideas. If Lake Placid was going to score, the big playmaker wouldn't be the one to do it. She began playing as furiously as her opponent, sticking to him with every move, lifting his stick when he reached for passes, and stepping in his way whenever he tried for the fast break.

It didn't seem to matter. The Olympians tied the game on their very first shot, a long bouncing puck from centre ice that skipped funny and went in through Nish's skates.

"Oh, no!" Sarah said as they sat on the bench watching.

"This is going to get ugly," said Travis.

Next shift, one of the quicker Lake Placid forwards broke up-ice, and the big playmaker put a perfect breakaway pass on his stick.

But Nish took the forward by surprise, coming out to block the shot like a defenceman instead of waiting on it like a goalie, and the shot bounced away harmlessly.

"*Way to go, Nish!*" Travis found himself yelling as he turned back up-ice.

Nish seemed to find himself over the next few minutes. It wasn't pretty – it wasn't like anything anyone had ever seen before – but it worked. He kicked, he turned backwards, he threw himself, head-first, at shots.

And not one got past him.

"That idiot's playing his heart out!" Sarah said when her line came off for a rest.

"I know," said Travis.

"We owe him a goal for all this, you know."

"I know."

Next shift, Sarah raced back to pick the puck away from Nish's crease. He was flat on his back, looking like he was making snow angels instead of playing goal, and he cheered her as she took the puck out of harm's way and up-ice.

"*Do it, Sarah!*"

Sarah played a quick give-and-go with Dmitri, who fed

the puck back to her just as she hit the Lake Placid blueline. She slipped past the defenceman and curled so sharply in the corner, the other defenceman lost his footing and crashed into the backboards.

Travis had his stick down before he even imagined what he might do. It was as if his stick was thinking for itself. It was down flat and out in front of him, and Sarah's hard pass hit it perfectly, a laser beam from the corner.

Travis didn't even have to shoot – the puck cracked against his stick and snapped off it, directly into the open side of the Lake Placid net.

Travis had been mobbed before, but never like this.

He felt them piling on, one by one, and then the huge weight of the goaltender, who had skated the length of the ice to join the pile: the *samurai* goaltender.

"*We did it! We did it! We did it!*" Nish was screaming.

"We've done nothing yet," corrected Sarah. "There's still five minutes to go."

"Don't worry about it," Nish said. "I've got everything under control."

It seemed he had. The game started up again with the Owls leading 4–3, and Nish took everything the Olympians could fire at him.

With a minute and a half to go, and a face-off in the Owls' end, Lake Placid pulled their goaltender.

"Sarah's line," Muck said. "And nothing foolish. We protect the lead, okay?"

They understood. No trying for the grandstand empty-net

goal. If it came, it came, but their first job was to protect Nish and the lead.

Sarah dumped the puck out, but not far enough for icing. Travis and Dmitri went on the forecheck, twice causing the defence to turn back.

They were killing the clock. So long as the Olympians couldn't rush, the Owls didn't care how long they held on to the puck.

The big playmaker circled back, picking up a puck the Lake Placid defence dropped for him.

He was in full flight.

Travis had the first chance and foolishly went for the poke check. One quick move of the big playmaker's stick and he was past Travis and moving away from Dmitri.

Sarah stuck with him, leading him off along the boards and into the corner, where he stopped with the puck.

*Ten seconds to go!*

Sarah moved toward him and he backhanded the puck off the boards, stepping around her and picking the puck off on the rebound. A play worthy of Sarah herself.

He circled the net, Nish wrongly stabbing for the puck as he passed by the far side.

*Nish's goal stick flew away to the corner!*

The big playmaker fired the puck to the point and crashed the net.

The shot came in. Nish kicked it away.

Wilson and Sarah hit the big playmaker at exactly the same time, sending him crashing into Nish, who fell hard.

*Nish's glove shot to the other corner!*

*Three seconds to go!*

He had no stick. He had no glove.

*And the defenceman was winding up for a second shot!*

Travis had never seen Nish move so fast. In a flash he was back on his skates, crouching to face the shot.

The defenceman slammed into the puck, sending it soaring off his stick toward the net. Sarah dived, the puck clipping off her back and heading now for the top corner.

*A bare hand snaked out, and the puck seemed to stop in mid-air!*

*The horn blew!*

*The Screech Owls had won the Junior Olympics!*

After that, Travis could remember only bits of what happened.

The Screech Owls – Muck and Mr. Dillinger and Data included – had hit the ice instantly, racing to congratulate Nish, who simply sat back in his crease, holding the puck above his head as if it were some great trick he'd pulled out of his own ear.

They mobbed him.

The doors at the far end of Big Hat had opened up and an official delegation, led by Sho Fujiwara, came out. They were followed by a long line of women dressed in beautiful traditional costumes, each carrying a cushion, and each cushion holding a medal.

They had played the Canadian anthem, with the Canadian flag going up on a huge banner.

Everyone in the building had cheered.

After the anthem, the Lake Placid Olympians formed a line and shook hands with the Screech Owls.

Jenny went through the line with her right hand in a sling. When she came to the big playmaker, he dropped his sticks and gloves and hugged her.

There were cameras on the ice now, and they captured it all.

Nish was at the Zamboni entrance. He was hauling Mr. Imoo out onto the ice. Mr. Imoo, his missing teeth more noticeable than ever, was sliding and hurrying out to join in the celebration with his star pupil.

Nish took the puck he'd saved – "The Greatest Save in the History of International Hockey," he would later call it – and gave it to Mr. Imoo, who seemed honoured.

"I caught it with the force shield," he explained.

Travis, the Screech Owls captain, was now face-to-face with the big playmaker, the Lake Placid Olympians captain.

Travis looked up. The big playmaker was grinning. He looked as if he'd won himself.

"Great game," he said.

"Maybe the best ever," Travis said.

They shook hands.

"Ever see a crowd like this?" the big playmaker asked.

"Never."

"We should do something for them," the big playmaker said.

It took them only a moment to decide what.

They waited until the medals had been given out. Travis felt the gold around his neck and watched while the silver medals were awarded to the Lake Placid team.

Then, on a signal from the big Olympian, Travis motioned for all the Owls to skate to centre ice with him.

He went and got Muck, who came reluctantly. Mr. Dillinger pushed Data.

The big playmaker gathered all his team and coaches as well.

Then at centre ice they turned, first to one side of the rink, then the other, then the far ends, while the fans continued to stand and applaud.

And they bowed.

*Arigato.*

A thank-you to Japan.

**THE END**

# Danger in Dinosaur Valley

# 1

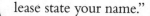

"Please state your name."

Travis Lindsay had never shaken so much in his life. Not from the cold wind of James Bay. Not from the thrill of Disney World's Tower of Terror. Not even from the emotion of seeing Data wheeled out onto the ice the night of the benefit game.

This was different: this was pure nerves.

Travis was terrified.

He was not so much frightened of a lie – which was why he was here – but petrified, to the very bottom of his twelve-year-old soul, of the *truth*.

"Your name?"

The man asking the question was staring at Travis, waiting. He was an older man – an officer of the Royal Canadian Mounted Police – with a white brush cut so thick and stiff it looked as if he could sand wood with the top of his head. His face, however, was soft and flushed. He had his uniform jacket off, and there were sweat stains under the arms of his shirt. A second Mountie, younger, square-jawed and unsmiling, sat closer to the window, where he was surrounded by computer equipment and switches. An open Pepsi can was on the desk in front of him, condensation beading on the sides. Travis was suddenly aware of how badly he himself wanted something cold to drink.

Travis cleared his throat to answer. A green line on the computer screen jumped. The Mountie monitoring the line checked off something on a pad.

"T–Travis Lindsay," he finally said, his voice catching.

Even in the heat of the small room, he could feel the shiver of cold metal on his skin. There were electrodes taped over his heart and to his arm, and sensors attached to his temples and even to the index finger of his right hand. He tried to tell his body parts not to jump – but they seemed to belong to someone else.

"Address?"

"Twenty-two Birch Street, Tamarack." He tried to be helpful: "You want my postal code?"

The Mountie asking the questions shook his head. The other Mountie looked up at him, blinking, and again checked something off on the pad. *Did he think Travis was trying to be smart?*

"This is just to set the parameters of the computer," the first Mountie said. "Just relax, son."

*Relax?* Easy for him to say. He wasn't the one on trial here, in the middle of the strangest land any of the Screech Owls had ever visited.

How could Travis possibly relax when he'd just seen his best friend, Wayne Nishikawa, leave this same room in the Drumheller RCMP headquarters with tears streaming down his red cheeks? How could he relax when so many of his teammates were waiting in another room to go through the same gruelling experience. Sarah was out there. And Lars. And Jenny. And Jesse. And Andy. Each one of them waiting to take a lie-detector test.

It seemed the whole world had been turned upside down. It was March break, and yet the younger Mountie had just pried open the window, and the welcome breeze that fluttered the paper on the desks felt like summer. Over the hum of the computer, Travis could hear the river churning behind the curling rink across the street. Between the Owls' departure from Tamarack and this dreadful moment, winter had vanished like one of those time-lapse shots the nature shows sometimes had of flowers opening in super-fast motion. One day winter snowploughs in the streets, the next day flooding along the low riverbanks.

There were television cameras in town – somehow, word had got out – though this was no nature program. This was closer to science fiction, but there was no button on a remote to push so that the two Mounted Police would simply flash into a shrink-ing dot of light on a dark screen. This was real life – *only it couldn't possibly be! Could it?*

"All right, Travis," the first Mountie said, apparently satisfied with the levels he was getting off the monitors, "I'm going to ask you a series of questions, now. You're simply to answer them honestly, understand?"

Travis cleared his throat again. The green readout line jumped sharply.

"Yes, sir."

The Mountie asking the questions smiled gently, then began.

"You are a member of a hockey team, correct?"

"Yes."

"The name of the team?"

"The Screech Owls."

"And you're out here for a tournament, isn't that right?"

"Yes."

"The name of the tournament?"

Travis's mind wasn't working right. He couldn't remember. The Prairie Invitational? The Drumheller Invitational? The Alberta Invitational? Was the word "peewee" in there anywhere? He didn't want the two Mounties to think him so stupid, so he tried to bluff his way through the question.

"Prairie Invitational . . . ?" he answered hesitantly.

The green readout light jumped, a squiggly line like a ragged mountain range forming on the screen. The two Mounties looked at each other.

The first Mountie smiled. "Care to try again, Travis?"

Travis coughed. The line jumped. "I, I don't remember exactly," Travis said. "*Something* Invitational. I'm sorry."

"Drumheller Invitational Peewee Tournament," the first Mountie said, smiling as he scribbled something in his notes.

The man didn't appear at all bothered by Travis's error. In fact, he looked oddly pleased, as if Travis's little mistake had confirmed something. Travis didn't know if that was good or bad, but it seemed the lie detector would react whenever he wasn't absolutely certain of his answer. He would do no more guessing. And he would certainly not be lying – whether he was hooked up to a lie detector or not.

"What happened yesterday to you and your teammates, Travis?"

Travis sucked his breath in deep. He felt like he was going to explode. In trying so hard to appear calm, he was only making it worse. His arms and legs were jumping on their own. His throat felt dry and tight. But there was no choice but to begin, and to let the machine do its job. It was all so incredible to Travis. He was no longer sure himself what had happened – and what he had seen.

"We, we went out on the bikes . . ."

"Where?"

"Out along the river. We wanted to look for hoodoos."

The Mountie nodded, one eye seemingly on Travis, the other tracking the readout line of the computer. The line was a little wiggly, but steady, with neither high jagged mountains nor sharp valleys.

"And?"

"And we also wanted to see where Nish had been."

"Who's Nish?"

"Wayne Nishikawa. We call him Nish."

"Your friend."

"Yes."

"Nish had already been there?"

"Yes."

"And what made this place so interesting?"

"It was where he saw . . . the . . ." Travis's throat went thin as a straw. He could barely breathe, let alone speak.

Both Mounties looked up, waiting.

"Where he saw the what, Travis?" the first Mountie asked.

"The . . . the *thing* he saw."

"The *thing* he saw?" the Mountie repeated. Travis thought he could detect a little sarcasm there. Clearly, they didn't think Nish had seen anything at all.

"Yes."

"Did you believe Nish had seen anything?"

"No," Travis said. "Not then, anyway."

The Mounties exchanged the quickest of glances. Travis noticed that the second Mountie, the one handling the computer, was smiling slightly. Travis didn't like the look of that smile.

"And did you find the right place?"

"We rode off the trail and back over some hills," Travis said. "I'm not sure exactly where we were . . ."

"Did you see anything?"

Travis looked down, swallowing hard.

"Yes." He spoke almost defiantly, certain that he would be challenged.

"And what did you see, Travis?"

Travis moved his lips but nothing came out. He tried to breathe in, but his lungs had frozen. He felt slightly dizzy and shifted in his seat. He wanted to scream. No wonder Nish had run out of the room crying. Travis felt close to tears himself.

"What was it you saw?" the first Mountie asked again.

"I, I'm not *sure* . . ." Travis said.

Both men looked at him hard.

"Do you mean you might have seen *nothing*?" the first Mountie asked.

"No."

The Mountie's red face darkened further.

"But you're not *sure* what you saw?" he asked, his lips narrowing.

"No, not that. I know what I saw. But I can't *believe* what I saw."

The first Mountie smiled, encouraging.

"Just say what you think you saw, then."

Travis sat up in his seat, blowing air hard out of his cheeks. He swallowed and looked directly into the Mountie's eyes.

"A dinosaur."

Travis looked from one Mountie to the other, waiting for a reaction. The first Mountie was staring down at his monitor, watching the thin green line. The second was also staring at a monitor.

The first Mountie expelled a burst of air just as Travis had done moments earlier. The colour had drained completely from his face. He looked ashen.

Travis knew why. He felt queasy himself.

*The line hadn't even flickered!*

**2**

*here to begin?* Travis wondered. He had already telephoned home to talk to his mother and father, and even though they'd been sympathetic and supportive, Travis couldn't shake the feeling that they didn't believe him either. And who could blame them? If his best friend Nish had come up with this story, Travis would have aimed his index finger at his right temple and spun it around and around and around. It was absolutely *insane*.

The Screech Owls hockey team had flown to Calgary, Alberta, on a sparkling-clear and bitterly cold March day. They had stuffed their thick winter coats into the overhead containers and settled down with their books, and portable CD players and iPods, and hockey magazines for what was sure to be one of the greatest Screech Owls escapades of all time.

They were headed for the town of Drumheller, where the Owls were going to combine a hockey tournament with a tour of the famous Badlands and a visit to the world-famous Royal Tyrrell Museum. At the Royal Tyrrell, they were going to learn all about prehistoric life in North America. They were headed, claimed Data, who always seemed to know about such things, to "The Dinosaur Capital of Canada."

They would be seeing prehistoric fossils and models of the giant reptiles that had lived in the Badlands nearly a hundred million years ago – a time so far in the past that Travis and the rest of the Owls couldn't even comprehend its distance. Data said to think of it this way: at twelve years of age, they had each been alive 4,380 days, or 105,120 hours, or 6,307,200 minutes. If every minute of their lives had really taken twenty years to live, that's how long ago the dinosaurs lived in Alberta.

"Every minute *does* last twenty years!" Nish had roared. "At least when you're in Mr. Schultz's math class!"

The Owls were so excited about the trip they had all but forgotten about the hockey. Muck Munro hadn't been able to get off work and so they were without a coach. One of the assistants, Ty Barrett, had managed to get time off, but Ty wasn't that much older than the Owls themselves. Control of the team had pretty much fallen to Mr. Higgins, Andy's father, and good old Mr. Dillinger, who had actually taken an extra week off work so he could drive the Screech Owls' bus to Calgary, meet them there, and then drive them around Drumheller and the surrounding area while the tournament was on. Once it was over, Mr. Dillinger was going to drive all the way back home while everyone else flew.

They could never have afforded the trip if Mr. Higgins hadn't become involved. Before Andy's family had moved to Ontario so Mr. Higgins could supervise a huge gas-pipeline project, he had been an executive with one of the biggest oil companies in Alberta. Through years of travel, he had built up enough air-travel points, Andy once said, to fly the family five times around the world. When Mr. Higgins then won a special airline draw that gave him a million bonus points on his air-travel program, he had generously donated all his points to the Owls. The entire team was able to fly out and back – at no cost at all to the players!

Once Mr. Higgins got involved, there was no holding him back. A big man with a salesman's gift for persuasion, he had easily talked Mr. Dillinger into taking the old bus across country so the Owls would have cheap transportation once they got to Calgary. He also arranged accommodation on the outskirts of Drumheller where an old friend of his, Kelly Block, had a sports camp that specialized in motivation and teamwork. They might not win the hockey tournament, Mr. Higgins had said at a meeting of all the players and their parents, but they'd come back a better team!

Most of the parents had seemed quite pleased with the arrangement, and were even excited about the idea of a moti-vational sports camp. Travis had noticed, however, that Muck, who had earlier said he might not even come to the meeting, slipped out of the hall before it was over. From his seat by the window, Travis could see Muck walking in the freezing parking lot, his breath lingering in heavy clouds as he moved slowly back and forth on his bad leg. He knew Muck well enough to know that the coach was unhappy about something.

Now that they had arrived, Travis thought he knew what had disturbed his old coach. Following supper that first night in

Drumheller, he had overheard Mr. Higgins and Kelly Block talking, and he hadn't liked the tone Kelly Block was using. The camp owner – an athletic-looking man with his blond hair strangely combed over the bald spots – seemed to be dumping on Muck, whom he didn't even know, for being old-fashioned and out of touch with modern coaching techniques. At one point Block had even said it was "time for the Screech Owls to move on, get a new coach who understands the way the game is played today." Travis had felt his cheeks burn with anger. Already he didn't like Kelly Block.

"*Mental* Block" was the nickname Nish had already given the head of the sports camp, and it seemed to be sticking – at least when the Owls talked to each other in private.

Travis had tried to imagine the trip west for weeks, but his daydreams had fallen very far short of reality. Three hours into their flight, they had flown straight into a chinook that had blown up across the Rocky Mountains from the United States. The plane had bounced into the rush of warm air from the south like a fishing bobber in a rough current. Poor Nish barely had time to scream "I'M GONNA HURL!" before he turned pure white and was reaching for a barf bag.

They landed in summer weather – an entire hockey team wearing three layers of clothing, including long underwear, and carrying their bulky Screech Owls parkas, scarves, tuques, and heavy winter mitts. It was as if they'd flown to Florida, not Calgary. The heat made them itchy and cranky. Mr. Dillinger, who was there to meet them, was having trouble with the bus overheating and twice had to stop to let the engine cool down while the Owls filed out along the shoulder of the road in their shirtsleeves and marvelled at the extraordinarily warm wind.

"It's a chinook," Andy said.

"We get sudden thaws back home in Tamarack sometimes," said Fahd.

Andy shook his head sharply. "Not the same thing. You only get chinooks out here. I've seen them last for more than a week."

They drove with the windows open, the tired travellers dozing, the road straight as a ruler, the landscape flat for the most part and sometimes rolling slightly. There were small lakes in the fields from the quickly melting snow.

They were passing through a small town – Beiseker, the sign said – when, up ahead in the bus, Sarah suddenly broke into wild laughter.

"*We're in Nish's home town! They even put up a statue to him!*"

Everyone sat up and looked outside. They were passing a baseball diamond, and then a park, and in the middle of the park was a large black-and-white statue of – *a skunk!*

The big statue even had a sign with the skunk's name: SQUIRT.

Nish stood in the aisle, turning as he bowed in acceptance. "Thank you very much, thank you very much."

Soon, however, the joking died down. Several of the Owls were asleep. Travis put his jacket against the window and leaned against it, one eye barely watching the rolling fields and the telephone poles pass by.

The next thing Travis knew, he was being jarred awake by a wildly honking horn. Travis sat up sharply, his chin on the seat in front. All the other Owls were also popping up wide awake.

At the front, Mr. Dillinger's bald head was turning rapidly back and forth as he leaned on the horn and tried to see if everyone was up and watching. He was laughing and excited.

"*Get ready to drop off the edge of the Earth!*" Mr. Dillinger shouted, giggling at the end of his warning.

"THE ROAD'S WASHED OUT!" Nish screamed from the back of the bus.

Travis stared ahead through the patch in the windshield where the wipers had cleared the muddy spray from passing vehicles. To either side he could still see the wet brown fields of the flat Alberta countryside, but up ahead the ground – and the road they were following – had vanished!

"HERE WE GO!" shouted Mr. Dillinger. "HANG ONTO YOUR HATS!"

Travis could not even get his breath. The bus rumbled on, Mr. Dillinger seemingly unconcerned that up ahead there was no road whatsoever, just open space and fog!

"WE'RE GONNA DIE!" Nish shouted. "WE'RE ALL GONNA DIE!"

The bus hurtled towards the edge, then *dropped*. Not like a stone, but like a glider, sailing down into thick fog.

Travis felt his ears pop as the bus seemed to float, down, down, down the steep slope of the highway into the fog.

It really did seem they had dropped off the edge of the Earth, just as the old explorers were warned would happen if they dared set out to sail *around* a world that everyone knew was flat as a board.

"WE'RE GONNA DIE!"

Travis didn't have to see Nish's face, or anyone else's for that matter, to know that they were as delighted as he was by the thrilling ride. This was an added bonus.

A hockey tournament.

A visit to a fabulous dinosaur museum.

And a brand-new world to explore.

This was going to be an unbelievable Screech Owls adventure.

# 3

*uestion 3: would you rather pass wind or make a speech?'"* Nish read out loud from his dressing-room locker. "WHAT IS THIS?"

"Aren't they pretty well the same thing for you?" Sarah asked from a stall on the other side.

The Owls all had their heads down, trying to fill in the blanks on a document they were balancing on the tops of their shin pads and hockey pants. They had just had their first practice at the Drumheller arena – a marvellous rink, where the Zamboni drove onto the ice through the mouth of a dinosaur and green dinosaurs were painted into each side of the faceoff circle – and then Kelly Block had handed out an eight-page questionnaire that he said would help him get to know the team. He wanted what he called "psychological profiles" of the whole team.

Travis understood some of the questions – "*Do you feel you have leadership qualities? . . . If you play well but the team still loses, are you satisfied?*" – but a good many of them made no sense whatsoever. The Owls were asked about their ambitions and interests, as might be expected, but also about daydreaming and private fears and, as Nish had just loudly pointed out, even passing wind.

"GIVE ME A BREAK!" Nish shouted from the corner. "'*Question 14: Would you rather kiss a member of the opposite sex or finish your homework?*'"

"I picked homework," Sarah said.

"I'd rather pick my nose," grumbled Nish, burying his head in the final page of the questionnaire.

Kelly Block came in and rounded up the finished questionnaires. He had that slightly knock-kneed, bounce-on-the-balls-of-the-feet way of moving. He was wearing expensive running shoes without the laces tied up, and he had on a track suit with his name stencilled over the heart and the name of his business – Camp Victory – emblazoned across the back.

Camp Victory must have been mostly a summer operation, for it had a musty smell to it that suggested the place had only recently been opened up and still needed some airing out. Fortunately, it was like summer right now. If it had been typical March weather, and the windows had remained locked up tight, the camp buildings might have been unbearable. Travis figured Kelly Block spent most of the winter months working for big companies like the one Mr. Higgins was with. Judging from Block's clothes and the expensive 4x4 sports utility vehicle he drove, Travis figured he must do pretty well as a motivational psychologist.

Certainly, he had spent a lot of money setting up this camp. There was a main building with a full gymnasium – weights, workout bikes, treadmills – and a kitchen that served meals so good that Nish forgot he'd seen the golden arches of McDonald's on the drive into town. There were individual cabins, each with four beds and the hottest, softest showers Travis had ever been under. There was a small enclosed rink for Rollerblade hockey, a basketball court, and a "garage" filled with mountain bikes, good ones with full shocks.

The Drumheller area was a mountain-biker's dream, with deep valleys and high rounded hills and natural trails everywhere you looked. The camp was out along the Red Deer River, half-way to a suspension footbridge at Rosedale that headed deep into the hills. They had already been out past Rosedale to see the hoodoos – bizarre, cartoon-like pillars of rock the shape of mushrooms and monsters that had been formed by thousands of years of erosion – and there were said to be more hoodoos farther up a trail beyond the swinging bridge. It was more like they'd come to another planet than another town.

"We did die when the bus went over that hill," Nish announced. "And this is heaven!"

"Not if *you're* here, it isn't," corrected Sarah.

In Mr. Dillinger's old team bus, they had toured the town and the surrounding countryside. Drumheller was fascinating, with dinosaur models – some of them life-size – at every corner, and dinosaur murals painted on most of the buildings. They visited the Little Church, a building so tiny they had to take turns just to get inside and see. "SEATS 10,000," a sign said. "SIX AT A TIME."

"How come they don't have a little priest?" Nish asked aloud when the others were trying to sit and kneel in their seats. "And a little Bible and a little God and a little Jesus?"

"How about a little *quiet*?" Sarah said over her shoulder.

They stopped for the better part of the afternoon at the fabulous Royal Tyrrell Museum of Paleontology, a huge complex on the other side of town, deep in the high, barren hills. Travis had seen dozens of museums in his lifetime, but never one so spectacular as this. It sat, like a spaceship on the moon, perfectly placed in what seemed its very own canyon.

Outside were bronzed, full-sized models of various dinosaurs. Travis thought if the museum weren't there, someone who happened to walk in here over the hills could easily think they had stepped back in time a hundred million years. It sent a shudder of excitement up his spine.

Mr. Higgins had arranged for a special tour of the museum. Mr. Dillinger got Data's wheelchair out of the bus, and Sarah was quick to move in behind it to push him around. The Owls set off, and were soon swarming around displays of huge jawbones and skulls of dozens of prehistoric beasts, including one magnificent model of what looked like a giant flesh-eating Tyrannosaurus rex. The monster was fighting a couple of small, vicious Domeosaurs over the bloody remains of a dead Parasaurolophus.

"Sick," said Jenny.

"Awesome," said Fahd.

"It's not a Tyrannosaurus," corrected Data. "It's an Albertosaurus."

"Good for you," smiled the guide. "A much tougher beast than T. rex. How did you know that?"

"I study dinosaurs," Data said, blushing.

"I want to see an Ontariosaurus!" called Nish.

"Sorry," said the guide. "There's no such thing."

"That's not true," Sarah whispered to the rest of the Owls. "There's Nish. He's creepy. He's got a brain the size of a peanut. He makes your skin crawl. And he's from Ontario."

Nish turned sharply as the others began giggling. "*What's so funny?*" he demanded. But no one would tell him.

Travis had never had such a marvellous day. The Owls were taken on a hike around the neighbouring hills, and were shown where fossils had been dug out of the ground. They were told that alligators had once lived here. They were told that there were still dangerous beasts about, not dinosaurs but poisonous snakes and scorpions and black widow spiders, and that they had better be careful where they stepped.

The Owls visited a lab and saw scientists cleaning newly dis-covered fossils and getting ready to assemble the skeletons. They saw fossils embedded in rocks, and whole reconstructed skeletons, and artists' depictions of life, and death, as it must have been more than a hundred million years ago. They learned that dinosaurs might have lived to be as much as 150 years old. They learned that no one really knows what the largest dinosaurs were, though the Brachiosaurus stood as tall as a five-storey building and weighed as much as eighty tonnes. They learned that the smallest dinosaur was no bigger than a chicken, and that the toughest dinosaur was not, as they had thought, Tyrannosaurus rex. The most fearsome of all was a little featherweight called Deinonychus, which was no bigger than a man but could move so fast and slash so quickly with its long, sickle-shaped claws and razor-sharp teeth that no dinosaur would dare tangle with it. They learned that they were standing on the richest dinosaur land known on Earth: some thirty-five different dinosaur species had been identified in the Alberta Badlands.

"There's so much we don't know," said the guide. "Before 1824 they didn't even know dinosaurs once existed. We don't know whether they were cold- or warm-blooded. We don't know what colour they were. We don't even know what they sounded like."

"Did they fart?" a small voice squeaked from the back.

"Excuse me?" the guide said, trying to see who had spoken.

No one spoke. Travis cringed, knowing at once who it was.

"You said something, young man?" the guide said pointedly to Nish.

"N–no," Nish mumbled.

"I didn't think so," the guide said. "If you have something to say, please tell us all, though, will you?"

"O . . . kay," Nish mumbled even lower.

"Ontariosaurus," Sarah said. Everyone, the guide included, laughed.

"Actually, young man, we do have something over here you might be interested in."

They crossed to a special display, and the guide stopped in front of what appeared to be a polished rock.

"Any idea what this might be, young man?" the guide asked Nish.

Nish looked, his eyes squinting with suspicion. "N–no."

"It's *coprolites*. Anyone have any idea what that means?"

The guide looked around. Data was raising his hand.

"Yes?" the guide asked.

"It's dung, isn't it?"

The guide's eyes lighted up. "Good for you. Yes, dung. Prehistoric poop. This one's probably twenty million years old."

"Does it still smell?" Nish asked.

"A smell wouldn't last twenty million years, young man," the guide said, shaking his head.

"You obviously haven't spent much time around Nish," Wilson said, breaking up the group.

"*Very funny*," Nish snapped, and stormed off.

It wasn't a good day for Nish at the Royal Tyrrell Museum – but that was nothing compared to the evening he had back at Camp Victory. After a good meal, the Owls had been sitting around, talking about their wonderful day at the dinosaur museum, when Kelly Block walked in and announced that their day wasn't done yet.

"We are going to build a team," Block announced.

"We already are a team," Nish protested, but he wilted under the stern gaze of Kelly Block.

"You are, are you?" Block asked, his eyebrows rising.

"We're the Screech Owls," Nish said weakly.

"Your name?"

"Wayne," Nish said.

"Nish," Fahd corrected.

Block smiled. "So, Mr. Nish, do you know what makes a team?"

Nish had turned crimson. "I guess. . . . Kids who play together. A coach."

Block laughed. It was an ugly laugh. It seemed fake to Travis, and it had an insulting tone to it. "Not even close, mister."

Block, who had been sitting cross-legged on the floor as he talked to them, suddenly sprang to his feet. He stood himself in front of Nish.

"Stand up," he instructed.

Nish reluctantly got to his feet. Travis could see that he was sweating.

Block pulled a chair out from a table and set it in the middle of the floor.

"Stand up here," Block commanded.

Slowly, Nish climbed up onto the chair and stood.

Kelly Block pulled a handkerchief from his jacket pocket. "Lean towards me," he commanded. Nish leaned forward and Block tied the handkerchief over his eyes. He then straightened Nish up, keeping one hand on Nish's arm to keep him from falling.

"You," he said, pointing towards Sarah. "Back there." He pointed behind Nish.

Travis realized at that moment that Kelly Block was no fool. He had already understood that there was a rivalry between Nish and Sarah.

Sarah rose, smiling, and stood where she was told behind Nish.

Block stared up at Nish.

"I'm going to push you over backwards," he said. "One of your teammates will catch you. Do you understand?"

"N–no," Nish said. His voice shook.

"I assure you that one of your teammates is behind you and will stop your fall," Block said. "Do you believe me?"

"I–I guess so."

"You don't sound very certain."

"I can't see anyone."

"But it's your teammate. Wouldn't they automatically be there to save you?"

"I don't know."

"You don't know," Block said with sarcasm. "You don't know. What kind of 'team' is that, where you don't know your own teammates?"

"I don't know." Nish repeated. He sounded near tears.

"I'm going to push you back," Block warned. "Are you ready?"

Nish was breathing hard. "N–no."

"Your teammate is there, waiting to catch you." He turned to Sarah. "Are you ready to catch him?"

"Yes."

Travis could see Nish jump with the realization that it was Sarah waiting behind him. Sarah, who never let Nish get away with anything. Sarah, who knew exactly how to wind Nish up or shut Nish down, whatever the situation required.

"Here goes," Kelly Block said.

He placed a large hand over Nish's chest, and pushed back. Sarah prepared to catch him.

Nish buckled! He folded and toppled forward rather than back, falling into Kelly Block's big hands instead of back onto Sarah.

Block caught Nish easily and ripped off the handkerchief.

Travis noted Block's smile. He had expected this.

Travis could see the terror in Nish's eyes. And humiliation. And anger. He had been singled out, he had been tested, and he had failed. Nish wouldn't look at Sarah, who also looked hurt. She had wanted to catch Nish. Travis knew she would never have let Nish fall and hurt himself.

But Kelly Block was ignoring both of them. He was standing in the centre of the room, bouncing on the balls of his feet, his hands out in front of him as if he were holding a phantom football. He nodded his head knowingly.

"There is no team here," he announced. "We have a lot of work to do."

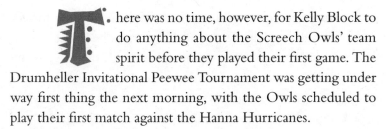

here was no time, however, for Kelly Block to do anything about the Screech Owls' team spirit before they played their first game. The Drumheller Invitational Peewee Tournament was getting under way first thing the next morning, with the Owls scheduled to play their first match against the Hanna Hurricanes.

"That's Lanny McDonald's home town!" Data had shouted as Mr. Dillinger read out the schedule to the Owls gathered in the dressing room.

"Maybe they've all got big red moustaches!" Nish shouted.

Travis giggled, thinking of a bunch of twelve-year-old boys and girls skating out looking like they were Yosemite Sam from the Saturday-afternoon cartoon shows. He was a great fan of Lanny McDonald, even if he'd never seen the Hall of Famer play in the NHL. He knew that Lanny had scored a big goal for the Calgary Flames the year they won the Stanley Cup, and he knew, of course, that Lanny McDonald not only played with heart, he approached life the same way. He'd come all the way to Tamarack, after all, for the big fundraiser after Data was hurt by the car.

It was time for the Screech Owls to hit the ice.

"LET'S GO!" Sarah called, slamming her stick hard onto the concrete floor of the dressing room. Travis, the captain, hadn't even put his helmet on yet! He scrambled to catch up, joining in the shouting.

"C'MON SARAH – A COUPLE OF GOALS!"

"MAKE YOUR FIRST SHOT COUNT, DMITRI!"

"BE TOUGH, LARS! BE STRONG!"

"MOVE YOUR BIG BUTT, NISH!"

Travis moved quickly through the door leading to the ice surface, Data slapping the rear of his pants as he passed. Travis had come to count on Data's slap as much as he needed to hit the crossbar in warmup. Data being there meant a lot to the Owls – he had, in some ways, become as important a coach as Muck himself. Not for how he planned out the games and changed the lines, but for how his own intensity and desire seemed to rub off on the others.

Travis stepped out onto the ice of the little arena knowing there was nothing he'd rather be doing. It might have been like summer outside, but in here the air was cool and the ice as hard as glass. He could hear his skates dig in on the corners. He could hear the buzz of the crowd. It seemed as if the entire town of Hanna had driven down for the game. Travis hit the crossbar on his first shot, a high snapper over Jenny's left shoulder. He slammed his stick triumphantly into the boards as he swooped past the net and turned back towards the blueline.

The crossbar was a good omen. Sarah took the opening

faceoff and turned her back on her checker, giving her time to send the puck back to Nish, who was already in motion. Nish crossed his own blueline and – just as his skates touched the tail of the green dinosaur on the Owls' side of centre – sent a high, looping pass up the right side for Dmitri, who timed it perfectly, snaring the puck just as it crossed the Hurricanes' blueline. There were cries in the crowd that Dmitri was offside, but Travis knew better. Dmitri's astonishing speed often made him look offside, and besides, the linesman had been right there as he crossed.

The Hurricanes' defence was quick, however, and Dmitri's route to the net was cut off. But for Dmitri it was no problem: he did his reverse curl, heading directly towards the boards, and then cutting back up towards the blueline. The move worked beautifully. As he headed in one direction, everyone else went the other way. He caught Sarah perfectly as she slipped over the blueline. Sarah dished a backhand pass to Travis, cutting in from his wing, and then took out her defender. Travis found he was all alone, one-on-one with the Hanna goaltender. A quick deke to the backhand and Travis lifted the puck high as he could as he flew past the net, the goaltender sprawling. He couldn't see what happened, but the *ping* off the crossbar followed by the whistle told him he had scored – and it was a beauty!

Screech Owls 1, Hurricanes 0.

One shift and they were already ahead. A grateful Mr. Dillinger was all over Travis's line, tossing towels over the necks of Travis, Sarah, and Dmitri as they skated off and took the bench. *Towels* – and they hadn't even broken a sweat! Data wheeled along the cramped space behind the bench and slapped each of them on the back.

Travis turned to high-five Data – and then saw that the Screech Owls had another coach. Kelly Block! He was standing beside Ty, seeming to dwarf the young assistant coach.

"*What's 'Mental Block' doin' here?*" Nish hissed in Travis's ear.

Travis shrugged. "I don't know. I guess he just appointed himself coach."

"If Muck was here he'd toss him out of the rink."

Travis shrugged again. He didn't know. If Muck were here, he doubted Block, for all his nerve, would have the guts to step in beside the Owls' coach. But Muck wasn't here, and Block was trampling over poor Mr. Dillinger right in front of their eyes – or, more accurately, right behind their backs.

Travis felt Kelly Block's hands on his neck, rubbing hard through the towel. He didn't like the feeling at all.

"*Atta boy, Trav! Way to go out there! You just keep open for Sarah to hit you – you got it?*"

*Got it?* Travis wondered. *What's this guy talking about?* Of course he'd try to get open for Sarah. They'd been playing together so long now, neither of them, or Dmitri, for that matter, even had to think about what the play might be. It was as if three players – Travis, Sarah, and Dmitri – shared one mind. But here was this smarmy "sports psychologist" acting as if he'd come up with the play himself.

Soon, Andy had scored a lovely goal on a hard slapshot through traffic. Fahd scored – a bit of a surprise – on a play in which he seemed to walk in, in slow motion, from the blueline and slip the puck under the arm of the falling Hurricanes goaltender. Jesse Highboy scored on a tip-in, and Wilson scored on a weak backhander that went in off a defenceman's skate.

Screech Owls 5, Hurricanes o.

It was clear by the end of the first period that the team from Hanna was badly outclassed by the Owls. Instinctively, the Owls began to hold back a bit, knowing that Muck never, ever wanted them to run up the score on a team. "Never humiliate an opponent," he used to say. "You try to embarrass the team you're playing against, you really just embarrass yourself."

Kelly Block, however, began to take over at the break. While Mr. Dillinger hung his head low and stayed in the background, working on Sarah's skates, Block tried to make a speech that only caused Nish to get the giggles. He talked about how these tournaments are often decided on goals as well as points, and how the Owls had better make every shot count. Kelly Block's eyes, Travis noticed, had taken on a new look. It was as if they were on fire. Travis found he couldn't look him straight in the eye.

By the middle of the second period, Block had taken over completely. He was calling the line changes. He was standing directly behind the players, rocking on the balls of his feet and chewing on ice the way some of the big-league coaches did. He was ignoring Mr. Dillinger and Ty and even Data.

Travis felt the hand on his neck again.

"Trav," Kelly Block's voice growled into his ear, "I'm going to shake up the lines a bit, okay?"

Travis didn't know what to say. *Shake up what lines? And why?* But he knew what he was expected to say, and he said it: "Okay."

"Sarah!" Kelly Block shouted. "Out with Jesse Highboy – and you, Liz!"

Up and down the bench heads bobbed up, helmets turning back and forth as friends and teammates tried to catch each other's eye. *What was going on here?*

Travis noticed that Kelly Block had a list in his pocket that he kept referring to and making changes on with a pen. It was crazy. Sarah had never played with Jesse or Liz in her life. And who did Block want *him* to play with?

"*Nishikawa!*" Block shouted after an offside whistle. "You're centring Travis and Andy!"

Instinctively, Travis turned to see if Nish would look in his direction, and sure enough, his best friend shot him a glance. Nish looked as if they'd just stepped into an insane asylum and some nut had taken charge of the Owls. *Nish at centre?* Not likely.

Sarah's expression said pretty much the same thing: *Who is this guy? What is going on here? Where's Muck?*

Nish didn't even know how to line up for the faceoff. Twice, the linesman had to correct his stance. Then he threw Nish out of the circle. Red-faced and angry, Nish had to let Travis take over the draw.

Travis won the faceoff and sent it back to the defence – but the defence turned out to be Derek Dillinger! Derek, who'd never played defence before, lost the puck in his skates and let it slip away into open ice, where a quick little Hurricanes forward picked it up and flew down on Jeremy, scoring high to the stick side.

When they got back to the bench Kelly Block was furious. He benched Derek for losing the puck and Nish for getting thrown out of the faceoff circle.

"You had nothing to do with it," Travis told his friend, hoping to comfort him.

"He hates my guts," Nish said. "That's all that's going on here. He hates me."

"Maybe he knows what he's doing," Travis said. "He's a sports psychologist after all."

"Yeah, right – and I'm a rocket scientist."

By the third period, Kelly Block was setting lines as if he were drawing names from a hat. The confusion was so enormous, he obviously felt he had to explain himself.

"This is a great opportunity for us to try out some new combinations," he said during a quiet break in the play. "We've got a lot of work to do on team chemistry."

Travis could only shake his head. "Team chemistry" never used to be a problem. Muck hadn't put the Owls together as if he'd dropped a pack of cards and simply picked it up in whatever order he found it. The Owls had been years in the making. Most of them went all the way back to mite together. Travis and Sarah had first played together in novice. And as long as they'd been peewee players, they had played with Dmitri on the first line. The top line.

Now there was no top line. No lines at all, it seemed. Defencemen were playing up, forwards back. Travis wondered if Block would yank Jeremy out of goal in the final few minutes and put him at centre.

The Hurricanes used the confusion to edge their way bit by bit back into the game. They brought the score to 5–3 with two minutes to go, when Sarah, now back on defence, began an end-to-end rush that left a soft rebound lying at the edge of the crease, and Dmitri backhanded it home so high and hard the goaltender's water bottle flew through the air and shot its contents all over the glass in front of the goal judge.

"*Atta girl, Sarah!*" Kelly Block shouted as they returned to the bench. "You're a natural defenceman – sorry, defence-*person*!"

Sarah said nothing. Travis had never seen his friend so unhappy about setting up a goal.

But Sarah's discomfort was nothing compared to Nish's. Nish was sitting at the far end of the bench, pounding his skates into the board to keep the circulation flowing in his feet. Travis could tell, even at that distance, that he was crying. But he wasn't sure why.

*Frozen feet?*

*Or frozen out?*

**5**

n the morning, Kelly Block immediately began to work on building "team chemistry." He had the Screech Owls take turns standing on the chair and falling backwards; they knew that when they fell, someone – a teammate – would be there to catch them. Even Nish managed to shut his eyes and fall back, first into Andy's arms and then Simon's, once he'd seen Sarah and Travis and Lars and Dmitri and Derek and Liz do the same without so much as a nervous tremor.

Travis was beginning to understand what Block was up to. When the sports psychologist talked about a team being like a chain, and "only as strong as its weakest link," Travis could see how that made sense on a hockey team. It was fine to have puck-carriers and goal-scorers, but unless there was a solid defence to back them up, the game would become more like basketball – last shot wins. And it was fine to have forwards who were good in front of the net, but unless there were forwards who were also good in the corners, the puck was never going to get to the front of the net. And as for the goalie, well, that was the most important position of all, wasn't it? Travis didn't think there was a position in all of sports – not baseball pitcher, not even football quarterback – that had as much pressure as goaltender. Pitchers didn't have to play every game, or even every second game. And there was no coach on the sidelines to send in plays to a goaltender the way they did in football.

To reinforce his "link" theory, and to get the Owls depending on each other off the ice as well as on, Block had a few more exercises for them to try. The best involved a nearby creek that emptied into the Red Deer River, a creek that was now swollen with the runoff from the recently snow-covered hills. Block had them build a "bridge" to get across it. He put half the team on one side of the creek, and half the team on the other. They had to assemble a platform on each side using logs and boards, fitting and clamping them together without the aid of plans. Then they had to figure out how to get a cable across from one platform to the other so that one of the Owls could cross the creek. They tried throwing the cable across, but the creek was too wide and the line fell short. On Nish's suggestion, they tried tying one end of the cable to a hammer and then throwing it again. But the hammer was too heavy. It plunged into the water and very nearly snagged the cable permanently on the bottom.

"*Not very bright, Nishikawa!*" Kelly Block called out from the other side of the water.

Data finally came up with the solution. There was a sharp bend in the creek farther up towards the hills. Data suggested that the team with the cable pay enough of it out to span the creek, strap the remaining coils to a board, and carry it up above the bend so that the flow of the water would carry it across the creek as it rounded the corner.

"Now *that*'s using your head!" Kelly Block called over.

"I'd like use this hammer on *his* head!" Nish hissed as he stood by Travis, watching the coils of cable head for the other bank.

Once the cable was across, they were able to mount it like a clothesline, running from one platform to the other. And finally, the Owls on Travis's side figured out how to fit little Simon Milliken into a safety harness and hang him from a sort of "roller skate" device they had fitted onto the cable. His team-mates hoisted him up and launched him over the creek, little Simon sliding easily over the tumbling waters as Screech Owls on both sides cheered him on.

"Now *that*," a proud Kelly Block announced, "is teamwork."

It was, too. Travis felt great about what they had accomplished. They had been given a complicated problem and together they had solved it. Liz and Jesse had seen how to put the platforms together. Data had figured out how to get the cable across. Travis and Nish had worked on how to mount the cable onto the plat-forms. Jesse and Wilson had connected it all. Sarah had known how to work the safety harness. And Simon had flown over the river into the arms of the Owls on the other side – who had then used the same equipment to send Lars back.

"There was another way," Nish grumbled when all the team was once again gathered together.

"And what was that?" asked Kelly Block, suddenly inter-ested.

Nish pointed up the slope, where a concrete bridge spanned the same swollen creek. "We could have driven."

Several of the Owls giggled, but Kelly Block just grimaced. Obviously, he and Nish weren't on the same wavelength when it came to humour – or, for that matter, hockey or anything else. If Block was looking for an example of "bad chemistry," Travis thought, he needed look no further than to Block himself and poor Nish.

Travis knew what was going on. He'd seen it too many times before. Nish was caught in a disaster of his own making. He was digging himself in deeper and deeper, desperately hoping his humour would spring him free when, in fact, it was only making matters worse.

Travis thought that perhaps Nish's luck had turned when Kelly Block announced that he was going to begin one-on-one sessions with the players. They were going to work on self-esteem and concentration and focus, and he was going to teach them some special "envisioning" techniques.

Those Owls who closely followed the NHL knew about "envisioning" and were excited by the prospect of learning how to do it themselves. Paul Kariya, who was idolized by many of the Owls – especially Nish, who still claimed Kariya was a distant "cousin" – was famous for his ability to concentrate fully on the game at hand. Even before a game began, he could "see" the way it would be played, and to the Screech Owls this ability was almost as impressive as his ability to skate so fast and shoot so quickly.

"We're going to do this step by step," Kelly Block announced. "We'll work on those things that distract you and keep you from being the player you can be, and then we're going to work on clearing your mind of everything but the game. We all start *envisioning* the same game; we all start *playing* the same game. And that's where proper team chemistry begins – *up here*." Block tapped his forefinger against his right temple and spun slowly around on his heels so the point was made to every person in the room.

"I've drawn up a list of players in the order I'd like to meet with you," Block said. "You'll find it tacked up at the end of the hall."

The Owls rushed away to see, as if they were racing to slap a teammate who had just scored. Everyone wanted to know when they were going to start learning how to "envision." And everybody wanted to know who was going first.

The most surprised player of all, when they saw the list, was the one whose name was at the very top.

Wayne Nishikawa.

Travis was in his room, changing, when Nish burst in from his session with Kelly Block.

"*This guy is a certifiable class-A nut!*" Nish shouted, flopping backwards onto his unmade bed.

"Whadya mean?"

Nish sat up, his face red and flustered. "Okay," he said, "we go over my 'psychological profile,' right?"

"Right."

"He says I'm an insecure kid who has no sense of himself and doesn't even like himself. That's crap! I LOVE myself!"

Travis couldn't argue with Nish. But he couldn't really argue with Kelly Block, either. The truth, he figured, was somewhere in between.

"He wants me to refocus. He says I play the wrong position for my personality. He says I'm a natural forward and that Muck has messed me up by having me always back on defence."

Travis shook his head in sympathy. "You've always played defence. Muck didn't put you there. He just kept you there."

"I know that. But this lunatic says that I have these *needs* that would make me a great forward. I *need* recognition. I *need* to be the star. I *need* to hear my name coming over the public-address system."

*All true*, Travis thought to himself. But he said nothing. And Nish didn't seem to see any truth in it. He continued, unaware that Travis was stifling a smile.

"So he says he's going to teach me how to 'envision' playing forward. He has me lie down on a couch while he plays this stupid sleepy music like my mother plays, and he tells me to close my eyes while he talks."

"Did you?"

"You have to – wait'll you get in there with him. It's creepy. He's a wacko!"

"Maybe."

"He sits there talking like he's me. You wouldn't believe it! He's sitting there saying, 'I want people to like me. I know my role on the team is to be the funny guy and make people laugh, but I don't really want to do that –'"

"But you do, too!"

"I know that. But he's being me, and he's not doing a very good job, okay. He's saying, 'I want to be Wayne Nishikawa, team leader. I want to be Wayne Nishikawa, good friend. I want to be Wayne Nishikawa, good person' – That's *him* speaking, not *me*. I just want to be Nish, and I'm not too crazy about being a good person!"

"What then?"

"What then? I don't know. I fell asleep."

Travis couldn't help himself. He started to laugh. "*You fell asleep?*"

"Yeah. So what?"

"How could you?"

"It was hot in there. And he had that awful music on. And he was getting pretty boring –"

"*You fell asleep!*" Travis repeated, delighted.

"Big deal. I'm awake now."

"Where was he when you woke up?"

"I don't know. Gone."

"He was *gone*?"

"Yeah. So?"

Travis couldn't believe it. Here was Kelly Block, trying to do what he was being paid to do, trying to do what he was supposed to be an expert in, and the kid he's working on falls fast asleep when he's talking to him.

"He must hate your guts," Travis said.

"Then we're even," Nish said. "Because I hate his."

# 6

ravis and Lars were coming back from breakfast when they looked up the highway and
saw a distant figure, furiously pedalling a
mountain bike towards the camp.

"That's not who I think it is, is it?" said Travis.

"It is," said Lars. "Don't tell me Nish is finally trying to get
in shape."

Nish was now in full view. His red face sweat-covered and
blotched. He skidded in the gravel as he turned hard off the
highway, straightened out and bolted through the gates to Camp
Victory. He sagged on the handlebars as the bike rolled to a stop
near the garage, his chest heaving as he gasped desperately for air.

"He's hyperventilating!" shouted Lars as the two Owls ran
towards their friend.

"No he's not," corrected Travis. "Something's scared him!"

Travis knew his best friend well enough to know when Nish
was badly frightened. Usually Nish was cocky and full of himself,

but every once in a while he got scared into dropping the act and the little boy inside him came out.

"What's wrong?" Travis called as he and Lars raced up. He held the handlebars of the bike as Nish, unsteadily, dismounted and gulped air into his lungs. Travis noticed that Nish's T-shirt and track pants were soaked through with sweat.

"You okay?" asked Lars.

Nish gasped and choked and spat and moaned. He fell to his knees and placed both hands on the ground in front of him, hanging his head as he fought for air and calm.

"*Nish!*" Travis finally demanded. "*Tell us what's wrong!*"

Nish looked up, his face swollen and soaked. Tears? Sweat? Travis couldn't tell.

"You, you . . . won't . . . b–b–believe m–me!" Nish gasped.

"Believe what?" Lars asked. He was gently patting Nish's back, trying to offer him some comfort.

Nish stared hard at them, his eyes pleading for them to take him seriously. Travis had never seen such desperation in his friend's eyes. The look alone scared him – and he didn't even know what it was that had frightened Nish!

"I s–saw . . . some . . . thing," Nish gulped. He seemed about to break into tears.

"What?" Travis asked. "What did you see?" There couldn't be grizzlies around here, could there? And there weren't any buffalo around any more, were there? Except in special parks. Nish couldn't have started a stampede, could he?

But Nish wasn't saying. He seemed to have caught his breath now, but he was strangely silent. This wasn't Nish, Travis thought to himself. Nish was the one who always had to tell everything, first and loudest if possible.

Nish spoke in a very quiet voice. "You won't . . . believe me."

"Try us," suggested Lars. He had a look of utter sincerity on his face. Travis was glad it was Lars who was there with him. Nish could trust Lars the same as he could trust his closest friend, Travis.

"What?" Travis asked.

They helped Nish over to the steps of the nearest cabin. He sat quietly until he had his breath back, then tried to remain calm as he told them what had happened.

The night before, Nish hadn't been able to fall asleep. He had tossed and turned all through the night. He had tried every trick he knew – counting sheep, counting goals, dreaming up gross tricks to play on his teammates – but nothing worked. All he could think about was the look in Kelly Block's eyes as the so-called sports expert told him that he, Wayne Nishikawa, all-star defence at the Quebec City International Peewee Tournament, all-star defence at the Lake Placid International Peewee Hockey Championship, was now supposed to be a forward!

He got up and went to the open window. Everything here was upside down. Defence to forward. Winter to summer.

Nish stared out towards the hills. There was a faint ribbon of red on the high ledge; dawn creeping into the valley. There was no point in sleeping now. No point in even trying.

He had thought of waking Travis up, but Travis was so deep in sleep, Nish was torn between waking him up and doing something funny to him. He thought a dirty trick might perk him up, and headed back to his duffel bag for his special can of shaving cream that had come on every trip Nish had made with the Screech Owls.

He tiptoed back to Travis's bedside and very carefully squeezed out a long unicorn horn of cream on Travis's forehead, teasing and twisting the pile so high that it held just a moment before drooping down over Travis's nose and mouth. Travis, still fast asleep, swatted at the irritation and rolled over, spreading shaving cream all over his pillow.

But Nish couldn't even force a smile. He just wasn't his old self.

He put the shaving cream carefully away – stopping first to fill one of Lars's boots – and sat on the edge of his rumpled bed, trying to decide what to do.

He started to dress, pulling on his Screech Owls sweatpants, a T-shirt, and his Owls windbreaker. If the warm gust from the window was any hint of the day to come, he wouldn't need anything else.

He had no idea what he would do. He didn't want to hang around the camp – Camp Defeat, he was starting to call it – in case Mental Block was also up early and the two of them bumped into each other. Nish wouldn't mind bumping into Block – but only if he, Nish, was driving a train.

He had it in his mind that he had to get away. And the only way to do that was to take one of the mountain bikes and head off for a while into the Badlands. He liked the name – it seemed like a place where he would belong.

Nish slipped out quietly, easing the door shut so that no one would awake. He stepped carefully, avoiding the creaky board on the steps and jumping down from the cabin onto the soft sand that had appeared as the snow ran off towards the river.

There was no lock on the garage that held the mountain bikes. Nish wondered, briefly, how many places there were left in the world like Drumheller and at home in Tamarack, where you didn't need to lock up everything you owned if you ever expected to see it again. He liked this town. He just didn't like Kelly Block and Camp Defeat.

Nish eased out the best bike within reach – a Gary Fisher, with front and rear suspension and a built-in computer that would tell him not only how far he had gone but how long he'd been gone. He was sort of running away, but his stomach was already rumbling with demands for breakfast. He'd just go for a little while, and be back in time to put the bike away and meet the rest of the guys back at the cabin before breakfast.

No, on second thought he'd better just meet them *at* breakfast – Travis and Lars would want to get him back for the shaving cream!

It was beautiful out on the highway. The sky to the east was blue and gold and pink, and the thin light of dawn gave the few houses along the way a blue-black tint, as if they were silhouettes rather than houses. Already there were some people up, and the lights in upstairs rooms gave strange cat's eyes to some of the buildings.

He rode hard until he got to Rosedale and the suspension footbridge. He knew there were good paths on the other side. He tried riding his bike across the bridge, but the swinging motion made his balance uncertain, so he got off and walked, staring down through the steel-grate floor of the bridge at the churning grey-brown water. Any higher, he thought, and he wouldn't have the stomach to make this crossing.

There were no houses on the other side. There had once been an old coal mine, but it was long since abandoned, and though there were signs saying "PRIVATE PROPERTY" bike trails headed off everywhere, disappearing behind the shoulders of the sandhills. There were supposed to be more hoodoos back here – perhaps he'd find some.

Back on his bike, Nish headed into the Badlands. He was breathing hard, pumping determinedly as the bike darted along the trails, the shocks cushioning every small bump and washout. He was alone in the middle of what seemed like nowhere, and he felt completely at ease. It surprised him and pleased him that he felt this way.

He looked around at the barren hills and the strange rock formations. It was no longer the age of TV and video games and McDonald's. It felt as if he had gone back a hundred million years in time. And he was the only human on the face of Earth!

Nish giggled to himself. He was no twelve-year-old kid on the run from Camp Defeat, he was the ferocious Deinonychus they had talked about at the museum. He had the greatest eyesight of all the dinosaurs. He was quickest on his feet, fastest with his hands. No, not hands – long claws, sharp as scalpels. He chomped his teeth together, imagining they were twice the size of a shark's, and ten times as sharp.

The path Nish had taken through the hills rose and fell. He had to keep changing gears and, at times, his rear wheel spun with the extra energy he seemed to have found, small pebbles flying out behind him. He looked back, admiring his own dust. A dust cloud in March, in Canada. Incredible.

Nish was beginning to feel much better. *Why feel sorry for myself,* he wondered, *when the real fool here is Mental Block?* Why worry about anything when he could ride a bike so nice in country like this? The air was warm in his face and fresh with the start of the day. If this was indeed what the world was like at the dawn of history, then he wouldn't mind being there at all.

Nish stood on his pedals to accelerate up a steep incline. The front wheel of the bike rose and twisted in the air. The rear wheel spun hard, jumping the bike hard.

*What was that sound?*

Nish let the bike settle and put one foot on the ground, turning back to see what had made that strange throaty sound behind him.

*Was it the rear wheel catching? Was it a bird? An animal?*

Nish shivered. But it wasn't cold. It was warm, probably heading for hot. He was sweating – but now the sweat felt like little chips of ice running down his back and under his arms.

One hundred million years collapsed in a second. Nish was no longer all alone in the prehistoric world of the dinosaurs; he was all alone in the modern world of the Badlands.

*And he was scared.*

The noise came again. It sounded like it came from a cave. It sounded like it came from some great pit that had no bottom.

The mine? Weren't there still old mine shafts around here?

But what was making the sound? There were all sorts of animals in the West that Nish didn't know anything about. He'd never seen a coyote. He'd never even seen a prairie dog until Andy pointed them out as the bus made its way along the highway from Calgary.

But wouldn't a coyote howl? This was no howl – it was a growl!

Nish got off his bike and stood by it, thinking that in case of an attack he might keep the bike between him and whatever animal it was out there with him.

Nish began to whimper. He began to wish he hadn't made fun of the Little Church. He might need divine help here, and what if there was a Big God and a Big Jesus standing up in the clouds somewhere, remembering that Nish had insulted their church and joked about them being little, and had decided that, as far as they were concerned, Nish was on his own.

"H–help me!" he whined.

Nish realized he had spoken out loud and instantly regretted it. What if someone had heard? What if the sound had come from one of the Owls, getting him back for the shaving cream. Maybe they'd heard him and were standing behind that closest hill, laughing at him right now.

What if it was Kelly Block? What if he'd followed Nish out and now knew what a great big chicken Nish could be when it came down to the crunch?

If someone was indeed watching, Nish couldn't betray his own terror. He had to act brave. His reputation might depend on it. He told himself to remember what Mr. Imoo had taught him in Nagano: to be a Samurai Warrior, to fear nothing. He owed it to his old friend to at least try.

He decided to walk towards the sound.

It had come from behind him, down and to the left, probably from behind that twisted hoodoo that looked like a giant pink-and-brown toadstool.

Nish turned his bike and straddled it, coasting down with his toes clicking the earth and the brakes on, ready to bolt at the slightest sign of a coyote.

"W—who's there?" he called, weakly.

*Again, a throaty roar! Louder this time.*

Nish had never heard such a sound. It sounded like it came from a sewer – or a crypt. Nish had never heard a sound from a crypt. He had never even seen a crypt! But he had seen enough horror movies to know that a sound from a crypt is blood-curdling and filled with all kinds of horrors, from rotting skulls with squashed eyes to hideous snakes and bats and spiders and slugs and maggots and . . .

Nish shook his head sharply. *Idiot*, he said to himself, *you're letting your imagination run away on you! Get a grip! It's one of the team. Or it's nothing. It's probably nothing.*

Nish rolled farther down the hill, coming to a stop in front of the hoodoo. He waited, listening. Nothing. Dead quiet.

*A shadow moved!*

Nish felt his heart in his throat. He felt it choking him. He could hardly keep a grip on the handlebars his arms were shaking so badly.

"W—who's th—there?" he asked in a small, shaking voice.

Nothing.

*The shadow moved again! Large. Huge. And right behind the hoodoo!*

Nish lifted his feet onto the pedals. He flicked the gears down to first, in case he had to jump fast. He pedalled ahead, silently, carefully, easing closer to the other side of the hoodoo.

"T–Travis!" he called. But there was no answer. "M–Mr. B–Block?" He was near tears, biting his lip hard.

THE GROWL ALMOST KNOCKED HIM OVER!

Nish leaped high on his seat and hammered down hard on the pedal, his foot slipping off and the rear wheel digging in sharp and failing to catch on the loose gravel. He lost it, and the bike went down, Nish spilling off the seat, over the handlebars, rolling on the sharp stones.

He lay on his back, wild with panic. He turned his head back towards the growl.

*The shadow moved again!*

And suddenly, from behind the hoodoo, a huge head emerged.

A head as big as the body that followed!

Huge teeth flashing, darting tongue!

Massive scales, rising like little horns along the nose and around the eye!

Green and brown and red and speckled!

Small shrunken hands, with claws like knives!

And a long tail, whipping slowly, menacingly!

The head turned – a small, green, beady eye sizing up its victim!

"I'M SO SORRY, GOD!" Nish screamed.

"Help me!

"Help me!

"HELLLLLLLLLPPPPPP MEEEEEEEEEEEEEEEEEE!"

Nish sighed deeply and looked up at Travis and Lars.

Travis couldn't help himself. A smile quick as a blink flickered on his mouth – and Nish caught it.

"*I knew you wouldn't believe me!*" he wailed. "*No one will believe me!*"

"We didn't say we didn't believe you," argued Travis. "It's just that . . ."

Nish stared back hard, defiant. "Just what? Just that dinosaurs don't exist anymore, is that it?"

"Well . . ."

"Maybe you just saw something like a dinosaur," suggested Lars. "A big shadow, or something."

"I told you. I *did* see a shadow. But then I saw it, face to face."

"What kind?" Travis asked.

"One of those things that looks like the Tyrannosaurus rex – the one from around here."

"Albertosaurus," Lars said.

It wasn't possible. Travis racked his brains trying to think what Nish *might* have seen, might have thought he saw. There were all kinds of phony dinosaurs around Drumheller, on street corners and in parks. The realistic, life-size replicas – including one Albertosaurus in attack mode – outside the main building of the Royal Tyrrell Museum. But Nish was nowhere near there!

"You're sure you went right, not left towards town?"

"I guess I know where I was," Nish said defiantly.

Travis and Lars looked at each other quickly. They had indeed seen him pedalling hard from the east, where the hoodoos were located.

"Nish . . . ," Lars began.

"*What?*" Nish almost shouted. He was angry, impatient. Perhaps he felt he should never have told them.

"This isn't another one of your famous tricks, is it?"

Nish wrenched the bike away from them and threw it to the ground. "Oh, go to hell if you won't believe me," he shouted, his voice choking. "I'm telling you the truth."

Nish walked away, head down, then turned on them, face again swollen and red.

"I SAW A DINOSAUR! A REAL, LIVE DINOSAUR!"

And then he turned and bolted.

# 7

think it was the wind."

Travis couldn't follow Lars's argument. Lars was saying that maybe the chinook had somehow addled Nish's brain. He said there was a similar wind in Europe, the *föhn*, and it was famous for the effect it had on people's minds. Some people, he claimed, even killed themselves when the warm *föhn* began blowing north across the Mediterranean from North Africa in what should have been the dead of winter. Perhaps Nish had just been struck with a similar kind of sudden terror while out on the trail, Lars suggested, and had imagined an Albertosaurus because he'd seen the Royal Tyrrell model just the day before.

"Maybe," Travis said. But he wasn't convinced.

There seemed no rational answer. Nish could act the fool, but he wasn't a fool. Nish loved tricks, but he wouldn't trick about something like this. He knew Nish well enough to know that Nish had been terrified, frightened as badly here in Drumheller as he had been that time in James Bay when they'd been lost in

160

the woods at night and Nish had dreamed he was being attacked by the Trickster and had wet his sleeping bag.

Whatever had really happened, Lars and Travis decided to keep Nish's story to themselves. Nish had been so frustrated he'd gone to his room after breakfast complaining of a headache so severe he couldn't make the exercise class that was about to start. When Kelly Block heard the news, it seemed as if he was somehow satisfied. Maybe he thought Nish was reacting to hearing the sad truth about his personality.

Nish had said nothing more. And neither Travis nor Lars would say anything until they had a better idea of what had happened to their friend on his dawn bicycle ride. Besides, even if they had told the rest of the Screech Owls that Nish had seen a living, breathing dinosaur, it would have paled against the topic that was currently holding the Owls spellbound.

The new team roster.

Kelly Block had posted it while Ty was leading the team through a light workout in the main yard of Camp Victory. It was Sarah who saw it first when they came into the camp kitchen for a short break and some Gatorade.

She wasted no words in her response: "Is this a joke?"

But it was not a joke. Based on his "psychological profiles" and interviews with the players, Kelly Block had designed a roster that he claimed would result in "improved team chemistry."

Sarah Cuthbertson was now playing left defence.

Wayne Nishikawa had become a centre.

Travis Lindsay was on right wing, not left.

Dmitri Yakushev, the quickest skater on the team, was now a penalty killer.

Fahd Noorizadeh, who scored about once every twenty games, was on the power play.

And so it went. Those who were defence were now mostly forwards. Scorers were now checkers. Checkers were now scorers. The only positions that hadn't changed were Jeremy and Jenny in goal, but the way Kelly Block was going about redesigning the Screech Owls, maybe Mr. Dillinger would be in net for the next game.

Travis felt as if his world was spinning out of control. The other players were turning to him, as their captain, in the hope that he might have some answers.

He felt he needed to talk to Muck – but Muck wasn't here. He couldn't even talk to his parents. They weren't here, either. The only Screech Owls parent, apart from Mr. Dillinger, who'd made the trip to Alberta was Mr. Higgins – and Kelly Block was his idea! As for Ty and Mr. Dillinger, both of them seemed overwhelmed by Block's bully tactics and his energetic way of taking charge of everything that happened at Camp Victory.

"I don't mind," said Fahd.

"You're on the power play," said Derek. "Why should you?"

"I'm going to refuse to dress," said Lars, who was now a forward.

"We have to," said Travis. "We're guests here. We can't ruin the tournament just because of Mental Block."

"*No way!* Absolutely no way! I won't. I won't."

"You have to."

Travis was alone with his friend, but getting nowhere. Nish was still in his bed, his pillow pulled down over his face, the covers up to his neck, as if he was expecting snakes to come pouring in under the door. Travis wondered how Nish could stand it. It was boiling hot in the cabin, the chinook still burning down from the hills.

"Look," Travis finally said, "you've got to think about the team, not Mental Block. We're the Screech Owls and we have to show up. We always show up."

"We're not the Screech Owls. He's turned us into a bunch of turkeys."

"It won't work. He'll start out with his new line-up and it won't work, and before you know it you'll be back on defence and Sarah will be back on forward and we'll be the Owls again. You just wait and see."

"You're wrong," Nish said, lowering the pillow just enough to look out with one eye. "You're wrong and I'll prove you're wrong."

"How?"

"I'll go, okay? And I'll play. And you watch. He's too stubborn to change his mind."

Game two was against the Winnipeg Werewolves, a good-but-not-great peewee team from Manitoba that would normally have been hard pressed to stay within three goals of the Screech Owls, let alone beat them.

But this was no longer the Screech Owls. This was confusion.

Kelly Block was now firmly in place as the lead coach of the Owls. Ty was plainly very upset, but, really, Ty was still just a kid himself. He was only a few years older than most of the Owls, and they looked up to him as a fine hockey player and an even better person, but he had no hope of standing up to the force of Kelly Block's personality. Neither did Mr. Dillinger, who was keeping very much to the background, sharpening skates and taping sticks and, for once, not smiling as he went about his job.

Mr. Higgins was no help, either. Poor Andy felt like he had to apologize for his father. "I'm sorry," he said to Travis at one point. "But my dad thinks Kelly Block walks on water."

"I know," said Travis. "Don't worry. We'll soon be back home and all this will have gone away."

But when he thought of Nish, Travis wasn't so sure. Some of the damage done there was going to take more than a flight back to Tamarack to cure. But he couldn't explain that to Andy. No one but Lars and Travis knew about Nish's strange mental state, which Travis thought was probably all due to Kelly Block. And no one but Lars and Travis would be able to help Nish get over it.

The Owls dressed for the game in disturbing silence. It seemed as if they weren't even breathing. Mr. Dillinger was keeping to himself, and Ty was nowhere to be seen.

Kelly Block looked as if he'd been waiting for this moment. He had on a suit, just like a coach in the big leagues, and a tie with so many cartoon characters on it, it looked more like a bad comic book than something anyone would ever wear. He had even been to town to get his hair cut.

"All right, now!" Block had shouted as he stood in the centre of the room. "This is a brand-new start for a brand-new team. We begin today to become the team we were always meant to be."

Travis heard Nish's sigh from the far corner. But no one raised a head.

"We're going to 'envision' this game right now," said Block. "When I stop speaking I want each and every one of you to see the game that's coming up. I want you to breathe the Werewolves. I want victory to be rushing through your blood. I want the Screech Owls to be the only thought that's in your head – the Screech Owls, victorious. Understand?"

He stopped speaking. In the sudden silence Travis was aware of his own breathing. The silence descended in layers, building on them until he wanted to scream.

He wondered if anyone was actually "envisioning" the upcoming game against the Werewolves. *He* couldn't. He didn't think Nish could. He figured his brain and Nish's brain were locked onto the same image – and it had nothing to do with any hockey game.

It was of a monstrous creature that hadn't been seen for a hundred million years.

The game against Winnipeg could not have gone worse. Nish lost every faceoff he took. Sarah got caught out of position on two goals. Fahd had a breakaway on the power play and missed the net. Lars had trouble reading the play. Travis, forgetting that he was now a right-winger, kept criss-crossing at centre ice and bumping into the left-winger, leaving the right side open for every rush the Werewolves cared to start.

If it hadn't been for Jenny and Jeremy, who split the game in net, the score would have been even worse than it was. But in the end the Winnipeg Werewolves had five goals, the Screech Owls only three.

It was the worst team they had ever lost to.

**T**he one-on-one sessions with Kelly Block were over. A few of the Owls, like Fahd, had actually enjoyed them. Fahd said Block had made him feel better about himself and his role on the Screech Owls. Others had hated their time with the sports psychologist – but no one as much as Nish.

Kelly Block was trying to work on the team's "chemistry," Travis reminded himself. Well, he supposed there was good chemistry and bad chemistry. He remembered Mr. Hepburn, the science teacher back home, demonstrating how some things mix and others do not. Mr. Hepburn had sprinkled salt into a beaker of water, and the class had watched as the granules dissolved and were soon, with some stirring, gone altogether – the salty taste the only evidence that anything had been added. Then Mr. Hepburn had taken a small, seemingly harmless piece of material called magnesium and, using forceps to carry it and wearing protective glasses over his eyes, had dropped the tiniest piece into the water – and the explosion had shattered the beaker!

Kelly Block and Nish, Travis supposed, were a bit like water and magnesium.

The morning after the disastrous game against the Werewolves, Kelly Block had summoned six players to his office: Travis, Sarah, Lars, Jesse, Andy, and Jenny. A goaltender and five players – a full unit.

He brought them into a room off his office, a room with bean-bag chairs and soft couches and thick rugs. He suggested they stretch out and relax.

Travis lay on one of the rugs, looking up at the slowly turning ceiling fan and trying to see into the main office. Kelly Block certainly had all the best equipment for running Camp Victory. There were computers and video monitors and book-cases stretching around most of the room. There were model airplanes and model birds hanging from the ceiling, and a miniature basketball net against the door and two small basket-balls carefully set on Kelly Block's big black desk. Everything – paper, books, tapes – was in perfect order.

"You may wonder why you six are here," Block began.

No one said a word.

"That's why we do our psychological testing," he continued. "The questions may not make any sense to you – I know, I giggled too, the first time I saw some of them – but in the end you cannot fool the system. If you answer the way you think I want you to, you end up tricking yourself on the next question, and so on . . ."

Travis's mind had already begun to wander. He wondered if the others were listening. But he could see nothing but the big fan above his head slowly turning.

"I ran your sheets through the computer, did some number crunching, talked to each member of the team, and identified the six of you as team 'generators.' That's not quite the same thing as team 'leaders,' so don't get the wrong idea. You are all leaders, too, but more important, you generate the energy this team draws from. You inspire with your play. You motivate with your emotion. You command respect with your personality . . ."

Travis smiled smugly to himself. This wasn't so bad. He liked being a "generator."

"We have, gathered here, a goaltender, two defence and three forwards. The Russians, as you know, play the game in five-man – sorry, five-*person* – units, not defence pairings and forward lines. Better chemistry. I've identified Jenny as our goaltender of choice and you five as our premier unit."

"*Our?*" Travis wondered. *Since when did Kelly Block belong to the Screech Owls hockey team? And did he talk this way to all teams? What if Muck were here? What would he think? And where was Dmitri? How could Kelly Block dare call something a "Russian unit" and not include the only Russian on the team? And what of Jeremy? If Jenny was the "goaltender of choice," what was Jeremy? The goaltender of second choice?*

It was getting warm in the room. Kelly Block's voice began to take on a purring quality. The fan turned slowly, slowly . . .

Travis tried to stay with Kelly Block this time. He was talking about "generators" and "envisioning" and "imaging" and "focus," and Travis's own focus was beginning to slip again. He wondered how the others were hanging in, but he couldn't see anyone. And he didn't think he should turn his head or sit up to look. There could be no doubt that

Kelly Block was sitting there, staring at the six of them, watching them . . .

⊚

"*Let's head for the hoodoos!*"

Sarah's suggestion had been enthusiastically endorsed by the rest of the "Unit," as the six Screech Owls were now referring to themselves. They had spent nearly two hours with Kelly Block and, Travis was pleased to note, Block had never realized that at least one of the Unit had dozed off in the middle of his presentation. Jesse claimed he, too, had fallen asleep. Jenny said she had just got bored and lost her train of thought.

They weren't much impressed with Kelly Block's inspirational address to the generators, but they did like his suggestion that they head out on the mountain bikes – just the six of them – for some critical "bonding" before the next game.

"If he wants us to bond," Andy said, "why doesn't he just glue us to each other?"

But Travis and Sarah knew what Kelly Block meant. Perhaps he had gone overboard, but there was something to be said for being a true team and having to depend on each other, whether falling backwards from a chair or breaking out of one's own end. A bike ride in the barren hills across the river seemed a perfectly good idea.

Travis and Lars exchanged a quick glance.

*The hoodoos.*

Where Nish had imagined he saw the Albertosaurus.

"Maybe we'll see a Tyrannosaurus rex," Lars whispered.

Travis giggled and kicked his pedal hard, doing a slight wheelie out onto the highway.

The air was warm on Travis's face. He felt happy with his friends – the Unit. He had almost forgotten about poor Nish's run-in with his own panicking imagination.

Poor Nish. Maybe they'd be able to see whatever it was that he had taken for an Albertosaurus.

Maybe they'd be able to show him that it had been nothing but his mind playing tricks on him.

Was it warm enough, Travis wondered, for Nish to have seen a mirage?

# 9

The chinook was holding. The wind was running through the valley like hot air through a heating duct, the river swollen and the ground so quickly dry that small lassos of dust flew up from their tires as they rode off the highway towards the suspension bridge that would take them into the rolling hills and the magnificent, eerie hoodoos.

Travis felt great. The wind was in his face. He had an excellent mountain bike under him. He was taking the runs easily, gearing down for the rises effortlessly. He had a natural eye for reading terrain and moved quicker, more sure, than any of the others. He had forgotten all about Nish and his wild story. He had forgotten all about Kelly Block and his chemistry. He had forgotten about the loss to the Werewolves.

It was so good to be out here with his friends. Sarah was right alongside him, as graceful and sure-footed on a mountain bike as she was on a hockey rink. Lars was letting his back wheel drift around corners, causing Jesse to scream that he was going to lose it, but Lars never did. Andy was strong going up the hills, cautious going down. Jenny was exactly the same on the trails as she was in net: steady.

Deeper and deeper into the Badlands they went. Strange rock formations rose all about them, casting long, bizarrely shaped shadows on each other and along the curling, twisting trails. There was a sense of other-worldliness here. It felt like a different planet, a different time.

Now Travis's thoughts did return to Nish. He could see how someone with a vivid imagination – and Nish had one of the wildest – might think he had seen anything here from giant toadstools to alien statues.

Some of the sandstone structures even had faces – if you looked at a certain angle.

*What was that sound?*

Sarah had moved ahead of Travis on the flat, and dust rose sharply as she braked. Travis braked hard and turned, his rear wheel digging in and sliding to a fast stop. The others braked hard, dust rolling all around them, blocking any clear view.

"Did you hear that?" Sarah asked.

"I heard something," Travis said.

"I heard it, too," said Andy. "What was it?"

"Sounded like a sick lion," suggested Lars.

"There's no lions in Alberta," said Jenny. Travis could detect a little shiver in her voice.

*Again, the same sound – closer!*

Sarah turned sharply, ready to pump. "*What the –?*"

"*My God!*" Andy called out. "L-L-L-OOK!"

Travis turned to follow Andy's line of vision. His eyes moved along the grey-brown trail past a small hoodoo and came to a break between two steeply sloping hills.

What he saw first was the movement – a tail lashing back and forth in the space between the slopes as something moved from shadow to light.

Something with small beady red eyes.

Something with huge horn-like scales about the eye and down the neck.

Something red and rust and dirt yellow and dull green.

Something huge.

*And something impossible!*

*An Albertosaurus!*

"It's a trick!" Travis said, but he didn't even sound convincing to himself.

"*It's coming at us!*" Jenny squealed.

It could not be a model; it moved. It could not be a balloon; the ground rumbled as it stepped. It could not be a trick of their eyes; it roared, and their ears filled with a sound unlike anything any of them had heard before.

It was a sound that seemed to come from the centre of the earth itself.

The monster stepped again towards them and the ground around them trembled!

As a perfect unit, the six Screech Owls turned on their bikes, leapt high above their seats, and pushed down so hard on their pedals that six back wheels spun uselessly in the dirt. A dustcloud rose so high and thick around them that, when Travis looked back, he could barely make out the shadow of the dinosaur.

But it was still there, tail lashing, eyes flashing, tongue flicking. The monster hurled a mighty roar at them, and lowered its head as if preparing to charge.

"GO!" Andy called.

"RUN FOR IT!" Sarah shouted.

"HELLLLLP!" Jesse screamed.

"HELLLLLLP UUUUSSSSSSSS!"

# 10

"I *told* you so."

Travis didn't need to hear this from Nish, but he supposed Nish had to hear himself say it. Nish *had* told them so – and Travis and Lars had dismissed the story as a trick of Nish's overactive imagination.

But now Travis knew that what Nish had seen was real.

There was no keeping secrets this time. The six Owls who had headed out into the Badlands to bond together as a unit had become witnesses to the most extraordinary story to hit the town of Drumheller since 1884, when a young geologist names J.B. Tyrrell climbed one of these strange hills and came face to face with the seventy-million-year-old skull of an Albertosaurus.

It seemed impossible, but now, more than a century later, six kids from a peewee hockey team had found another Albertosaurus – and this one was alive!

Make that seven kids. Nish had already begun to claim his rightful place at centre stage.

"I found it first," he told anyone who would listen.

Unfortunately for the Screech Owls, a great many people wanted to listen. The six Screech Owls who thought they had seen a living dinosaur had come flying back to Camp Victory in such a panic and with so many shouts for help that there was no keeping this a secret. Jenny and Lars had both thrown up they'd been so frightened, and Andy couldn't talk when his father began yelling at him to tell him what had happened. Finally, Sarah and Travis managed to force the story out, in the midst of gasps and sobs from their teammates.

Someone must have made a call, for within half an hour a reporter from the local newspaper, the *Drumheller Mail*, was at the camp gate. An hour later the *Calgary Herald* was there demanding interviews with the kids who claimed they'd seen a living dinosaur. And not much later people from the wire services and television stations had flooded the town.

And then came the Royal Canadian Mounted Police.

Mr. Higgins and Kelly Block met the police car at the front gate and let them in. On Block's insistence, the television cameras had not been allowed through, but they were set up anyway all along the edge of the highway, filming anything that moved and calling questions over the fence to any Screech Owl who happened to walk between cabins.

"DID YOU SEE THE DINOSAUR?"

"CAN YOU TALK TO US?"

"WHERE ARE THE KIDS WHO SAY THEY SAW THE MONSTER?"

On Mr. Higgins's advice, the Owls didn't try to answer the reporters' questions. The police were there, he said, and the police would take charge of matters.

After an hour or so, it struck Travis as odd that the most natural thing to do had not been done – or even suggested.

"Why aren't they going into the hills to look for it?" he said to Sarah.

"They don't believe us," she said.

"They think we made it up," said Lars.

"I know what I saw," said Nish, growing prouder by the moment. "I know what I saw, and I know what it was."

Nish wanted to go out to the fence and talk to the camera crews, but the other Owls wouldn't let him. They milled around the kitchen area, waiting to see what the Mounties and other adults would decide to do. For the first time since he had met him, Travis began to feel sorry for Kelly Block. All this attention couldn't be doing his camp much good.

There were now many more people here than just the police. Some looked like scientists. They had gathered with Kelly Block in a meeting room to discuss the situation. Sarah went over and sat close to the door, trying to hear what was being said inside.

She soon reported back, unimpressed.

"They think it has something to do with the chinook," she said. "There's a guy with them who I think might be a psychiatrist. He's talking about 'mass hysteria' and things like that. He says we suffered some kind of 'gang delusion.'"

"What language are you talking?" demanded Nish.

Fahd, who knew something about everything, explained. "He thinks you all dreamed the same thing at the same time."

"That's impossible!" said Andy.

"No," said Fahd. "It can happen. Lots of experts think that's what UFOs are. Somebody thinks they see a flying saucer, and suddenly everybody in town thinks they see them."

"We don't *think* we saw anything," said Nish a bit testily. "We did see a dinosaur. And *I* saw it first!"

# 11

**B**y morning, the story was out of control. The claim of the six kids – "*Seven*," Nish kept correcting – who said they had seen a living, breathing dinosaur had travelled around the world. American stations were sending in television crews. CNN was on the scene, broadcasting live. The Screech Owls were headline news, but it was hardly the kind of publicity they might once have dreamed of as they headed into a hockey tournament:

"CANADIAN CHILDREN TELL MONSTER FIB!"

"TINY HOCKEY PLAYERS ATTEMPT PREHISTORIC HOAX"

"CHINOOK BLAMED FOR YOUNGSTERS' WILD CLAIM"

"FAIRIES AND FLYING SAUCERS – NOW LIVING, BREATHING DINOSAURS!"

"TERROR IN THE BADLANDS!"

Their parents had all phoned. Some of them were beside themselves with worry. Sarah's mother had been in tears. Travis's father had told him to remain calm, to say only what he knew to be a fact, and not to be afraid of the truth. Nish asked his mom to clip out all the newspaper stories.

The angle that most of the media had taken concerned children making up stories to draw attention to themselves. One story cited dozens of examples of stories where youngsters had fabricated huge lies and fooled their families and everyone else, at least for a while, and sometimes for years. Many of the news reports compared the "Drumheller Dinosaur Sighting" to an event that took place in England back in 1920. Two little girls who lived in a village in Yorkshire claimed to have played with real fairies since they were tiny, and had been able to take two photographs of the tiny flying creatures with a camera. The story had been such a sensation, and so many people had believed the two girls and their photographic evidence, that even the famous writer Arthur Conan Doyle, creator of the Sherlock Holmes mysteries, was called upon to give his opinion. The great man gave his backing to the little girls' amazing story. The hoax was not revealed for decades, when one of the little girls, now a very old woman, decided she could not go to her grave carrying such a fib.

There were no photographs of the Alberta dinosaur, all the stories gleefully pointed out.

"No one believes us," Sarah said despondently.

The police briefly interviewed the seven Screech Owls, and one of the Mounties, who seemed very cross with them, warned that they could be charged with public mischief if they didn't own up to the truth.

"This is a very serious charge, young ladies and gentlemen," he said. "It would be a most serious blemish on your record and your families' good names."

"But it's the *truth*!" said an exasperated Lars. "We saw a real, live dinosaur."

"*I* saw it first," added Nish.

If the reporters and the Mounties didn't believe the Screech Owls, there were soon lots of others who did. Within a day Drumheller was flooded with the curious. Before long there wasn't a vacant hotel room to be found between Drumheller and Calgary. They arrived first from all over Canada and the United States, and in the days after from England and France and Germany and Japan . . .

Several of the supermarket tabloid papers then hit the stands with stories – including photographs! – that seemed to back the seven kids' version of what had happened. One of these papers even had a front-page headline that claimed, "CANADIAN AUTHORITIES DESPERATE TO SUPPRESS KIDS' DISCOVERY OF THE MILLENNIUM!"

The Owls were able to hear some of the debate on the local radio talk shows. Most of the discussion involved dinosaur jokes at the expense of the Screech Owls, but several callers seemed to think that this extraordinary chinook had somehow, in some unknown way, released a slumbering, frozen giant from pre-history. Fahd was quick to point out that this explanation didn't make sense – but then, what part of the story did make sense? All they knew for sure was that it had somehow captured the imagination of a good part of the world.

Traffic out to the Badlands became so frantic that the RCMP put up roadblocks and declared the barren hills beyond the suspension bridge off-limits – which only served to convince many that there really was something out there.

It seemed insanity had come to Dinosaur Valley. European television crews rented helicopters and were even flying about at night with huge searchlights bouncing over the hills. Hikers were walking in from the opposite direction, ignoring the roadblocks.

And hour by hour, the Mounties were getting angrier with the seven hockey players who refused to back down on their story. There was even a rumour that the seven youngsters were about to be formally charged with public mischief.

Mr. Higgins, looking very worried, gathered the seven Owls in the camp meeting room. He had Kelly Block with him and another man, Mr. Banning, who was a Calgary lawyer.

"The police are getting very concerned that this has gone too far," the lawyer said. "I happen to know they are right now preparing charges against you."

"They should be out looking for the Albertosaurus," said Sarah, "not worrying about us."

"Well, miss," said the lawyer. Travis glanced at Sarah and saw her grimace; Sarah hated to be called "miss." The lawyer didn't even notice. "Well, miss, they are indeed worried about you," he continued. "I have been asked by them if perhaps you would all, or even a couple of you, be willing to undergo lie-detector tests."

The Owls looked at each other.

"That proves they don't believe us!" said Nish.

Sarah shook her head. "But it also gives us a chance to prove we're telling the truth."

"Let's do it," said Lars.

"I don't know, son," cautioned Mr. Higgins. He seemed distinctly uncomfortable with the idea.

"Come on, Dad," said Andy. "Or don't you believe us, either?"

Mr. Higgins stumbled and mumbled. It was clear that he did not.

"I'll do it," said Travis.

"So will I," said Nish.

All around the circle, the Owls nodded their agreement.

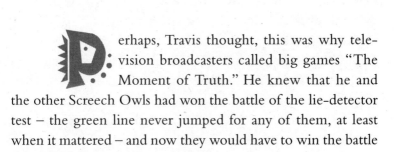

erhaps, Travis thought, this was why television broadcasters called big games "The Moment of Truth." He knew that he and the other Screech Owls had won the battle of the lie-detector test – the green line never jumped for any of them, at least when it mattered – and now they would have to win the battle of game three of the Drumheller Invitational.

The tournament wasn't about to stop just because the town had filled up with news reporters and the curious. There was still a schedule to be played out and a trophy to be won. The Screech Owls, however, seemed hardly in the running any more. Lose this game, and they would be headed home, with nothing to show for their trip but a bunch of newspaper clippings about an imaginary dinosaur.

The opposition was, appropriately, called the Predators. The Prince Albert Predators from northern Saskatchewan. They were, by all accounts, a good team, strong up centre and solid in goal. In any other circumstance, the Screech Owls versus the Predators would have been a great match.

But these were hardly normal circumstances. The little Drumheller arena was packed, not by hockey fans, but by those who wanted a look at the seven players who claimed they'd seen the monster. There was a television crew from Japan filming the game, and another one from Mexico. There were reporters and tourists and even a crazy man with a rainbow fright wig holding up a sign saying that "The End of the World Has Come," complete with a crude drawing of a dinosaur – not even an Albertosaurus – to back up his claim.

Nish, apparently, had even signed some autographs. But if Nish liked all the attention, Travis hated it. He was captain of the Screech Owls, and the Screech Owls were in tatters. Their lineup was as confused as a game of pick-up-sticks. They didn't seem to have a coach. They had played the worst game of their lives against the Werewolves. And considering they had come out to Alberta to work on their "focus," they were so out of focus as they headed onto the ice to face the Predators that some of the Owls had even forgotten what position Kelly Block had decided they now played.

"I think I'm a goalie," Jeremy joked. "The pads have my name on them, anyway."

Jeremy wasn't even set to start this critical game. Block wanted to go with his Unit: Jenny in net, Sarah and Jesse on defence, and Lars, Andy, and Travis up front. All of them at positions they had never before played.

"Let this experience bring us together," Kelly Block had told them in the dressing room. "Let us use the crowd for energy. Let us show the world that the Screech Owls stand for the truth, not lies!"

"What the heck did that mean?" Nish hissed to Travis as the Owls made their way down the corridor towards the ice surface.

"I haven't got a clue," said Travis. "Maybe he saw the Albertosaurus, too."

"Mental Block seems awfully upbeat for a guy who's about to embarrass himself in front of a full rink."

"Yeah, I know. He's weird, that's for sure."

Up ahead, Sarah turned around abruptly.

"You guys see Data?"

Travis said nothing. He knew Data hadn't been on the bus. He knew Data was staying deliberately back at the camp, pretending to be "tired." In fact, Data had told Travis he wanted to check around when no one else was there. For what, Travis didn't know. Probably Data didn't know, either. But Travis was still all for Data looking.

"Data's got too many brains to associate himself with this disaster," said Nish.

"You're probably right," said Travis.

There was no more talking to be done. They were at the rink boards now, the noise of the crowd so loud they couldn't hear each other. The crowd was not, however, cheering for hockey. They were cheering for celebrity. The Screech Owls were now world-famous. They had made CNN. They were on the supermarket tabloids.

They were the kids who had seen the dinosaur!

Just to be sure, Data had checked everywhere. He had rolled himself up the ramp into the kitchen and looked for signs of life – even a repairman or a cleaner. But there was no one. The cook must have gone to town for groceries. The Camp Victory parking lot was empty of vehicles. The Owls' bus was at the rink. Kelly Block's fancy 4x4 truck was missing. There was just Data – all alone.

He had told Mr. Dillinger he didn't feel well, but he'd known immediately that Mr. Dillinger wasn't buying it. Mr. Dillinger didn't argue with him, though. Data could tell by the look in Mr. Dillinger's eyes that he was as upset as any of the players. This had turned into a hideous, awful experience. If Mr. Dillinger could have, he would have stayed back at the camp with Data and let Kelly Block have exactly what he wanted: total control of the team, the spotlight his alone.

Data had grown deeply suspicious of Kelly Block. Block had ignored him and treated him like some sort of hanger-on, rather than as a real assistant coach, as Muck always treated him. Data seemed to be just a nuisance to Block, always in the way, so now he was out of the way. But he had no intention of lying in his room sulking.

Because he had been largely ignored by Block, Data had found he could pretty much come and go as he wished. He had puzzled over the "psychological profiles" that Kelly Block had been so keen on. He had wondered about the "focus" sessions and the "envisioning" and "imaging" and whatever else was supposedly going on in the minds of his teammates as they struggled to remain the team that Muck Munro had so carefully built over the years.

When Block had met with the six key players, the Unit, Data had tried to listen in by pulling his wheelchair right up to the door and putting his ear to the keyhole. But the drone of Kelly Block's voice had been so low, Data couldn't hear anything clearly and was no wiser about what Block was up to.

He was almost certain, however, that none of the six players in that room had said a word back – and that just didn't seem right.

From the kitchen area, Data made his way around to the office. He tried the door to Kelly Block's inner office and found it locked. He pulled and rattled, but it would not give.

Data had no idea whether it would work, but he had seen a hundred television shows where an actor had sneaked into a locked room by sliding a credit card past the bolt of a locked door and turning the handle. He didn't have a credit card, but he did have his student card, and it was wrapped in plastic hard enough that it felt like a credit card. If the lock was a deadbolt, though, he wouldn't have a chance.

Carefully, Data slipped the card in between the door frame and the lock. He worked it down, then up, then down again, and felt it rest against something hard.

He pushed, pushed again, and felt something give way. He pushed again, harder, and turned the handle at the same time.

*He was in!*

"We've got to do *something*!"

Travis heard the anxiety in Sarah's voice, but could not even look up to see her expression. He was beat, exhausted. His heart was pounding wildly and his breathing felt as if someone had stuffed his lungs with cotton balls, leaving no room for oxygen.

He kept his head down, the sweat dripping off his forehead and into his eyes. He flipped up the mask, plucked the towel from around his neck – thank heavens Mr. Dillinger was still here! – and wiped his face.

When he finally looked up, Sarah was still staring at him, challenging. "Travis!" she said. "*It's up to us!*"

Travis nodded. He knew. The Predators had moved immediately in front when Fahd, on for the power play, had tried to get a little too fancy in his own end and attempted to beat the forecheck. He'd lost the puck – "It stuck in a wet spot!" Fahd claimed, near tears – and the checker had been left alone with Jenny in goal, who got a piece of his sharp shot but had the puck dribble down her back and in when she flopped back in desperation.

The Owls were going nowhere. They couldn't mount a breakout, they couldn't hang on to the puck in the Predators' end, they couldn't send the quick skaters, like Dmitri, off on fast breaks, because, of course, skaters like Dmitri and Sarah were now playing defence.

All they could do was try to hold the Predators at bay. So long as they played one-on-one checking hockey – sticking close to their opposite numbers on the Prince Albert team – they could just manage to stay in the game. Sarah, of course, was probably the finest checking centre Travis had ever seen at peewee level. Now, on defence, she seemed uncertain where she should be, but she never left her check.

Early in the second period, the Predators went ahead by a second goal when Nish, playing centre, tried to hit Wilson breaking up left wing but had his pass knocked out of the air by a pinching Predator defender. The Predator threw a cross-ice pass to a teammate just circling behind Jenny, and the teammate tipped the puck in the far side.

Predators 2, Owls 0.

"*Chemistry!*" Kelly Block kept yelling. "*Chemistry!*"

"Biology!" Nish mumbled back. "History! Math! Recess!"

Travis was giggling on the bench when Block suddenly leaned low over his shoulder and, for once, said something that made sense.

"I'm going to try moving Sarah up front," he said. "I want you to switch over to left, and I'll try Dmitri on right."

*What a phony!* Travis thought. Here's this guy pretending he's just come up with his own new line combination. *But all he was doing was putting back the original first line – Muck's line!*

"*Let's do it!*" Sarah shouted as she leapt over the boards with new energy.

"*Yes!*" shouted Dmitri, who hardly ever shouted anything.

For Travis, it was like putting on his old sneakers after a painful Sunday morning in church shoes. From the moment they lined up for the faceoff, he felt as if he had found his game again. Sarah waiting for the puck to drop, her skates stuttering back and forth. Dmitri with his stick blade flat on the ice, poised to break. And back on defence, Nish, the former centre.

Sarah took the puck before it could even strike the ice. The linesman jumped back and Sarah used him as a shield while she circled quickly, throwing off the Predators' centre. She fired the puck hard off the left boards.

Travis knew his play. He was back in his own world now. As soon as he saw Sarah look at the boards, he took off, bolting around the Predators' defender at the blueline and picking the puck up as it bounced off the boards on the other side of the flailing player.

He had it on his stick now – puck, stick, hands, arms, body, legs, skates, all in familiar territory for the first time in two games. He didn't even need to look to know what Dmitri would be doing.

Flipping the puck high, Travis lobbed it past the outstretched glove hand of the remaining defence. The Predators' player was wisely trying to stay between Travis and Dmitri to block the shot, but when Travis flipped the puck the defender fell for the bait and tried to knock it out of the air. To do so required stopping, and stopping ended his backward progress. Dmitri was already past him, the puck slapping onto the ice and into the embrace of his stick blade.

Dmitri was in alone, and Travis already knew exactly what would happen. The shoulder fake, the move to the backhand, the goalie going down to protect the post, the puck flying high and hard over the goaltender's shoulder, the water bottle flying.

Predators 2, Owls 1.

Data stared at the bookcase, his mind racing.

Kelly Block must have had a thousand books in his office. Most were on psychology and sports psychology and motivation, but here was an entire bookcase devoted to a single, unexpected topic.

Hypnosis!

Data scanned the titles. *Stage Hypnotism: Mass Illusion. Hypnosis and the Control of Fantasy. You Can Control the Minds of Others. Triggering Minds: The Art of Suggestive Hypnotism. . . .*

And on the bottom shelf there were at least a dozen videos, all devoted to the art of hypnotism. There was hypnotism for psychologists, hypnotism for therapists, even hypnotism for circus performers.

Data moved to the filing cabinet. He knew what he was doing was wrong, but he was starting to believe that whatever Kelly Block had been doing was even more wrong. He didn't like snooping – but he liked even less what had been happening to his friends. And if the only way to correct a terrible wrong was to do something just slightly wrong, and which hurt no one, then Data felt, on balance, he would be right.

The filing cabinet was locked. He tried the desk drawers. Nothing. He tried the pen drawer. Nothing. He picked a small wooden box off the desk and rattled it. There were keys inside.

Data had difficulty manoeuvring. His right arm was almost as good as new but he still couldn't do much with the other one. It took him more than ten minutes, but he finally found the right key and got the drawer open. He had to reach up and grab files at random, lifting them high enough to read what they were.

"CORRESPONDENCE"

"GUARANTEES."

"REPAIR WORK, COMPLETED."

"REPAIR WORK, SCHEDULED."

He was getting nowhere fast. He selected a lower drawer.

He could see these files. His eyes moved quickly, trying to take everything in at once.

"RESERVATIONS."

He pulled the file out and glanced quickly at the record. The Owls were the only team to come to Camp Victory so far this year. That explained the musty smell they had detected when they first arrived. It was only March, however.

But there were hardly any bookings for the months to come. A couple in June, three in July, then more blank spaces.

Data looked at the previous year's bookings. More blank spaces.

He put the file back and searched for another that had caught his eye. "FINANCIAL STATEMENT."

He pulled out the file and opened it. Why hadn't he paid more attention in business class? The statement, stamped by a local accounting firm, made very little sense, but Data knew just enough to come to a quick conclusion.

Camp Victory was losing money – big time.

He selected another file. "BANKS."

The letters enclosed were far more easy to interpret. Some were registered letters. Some read like legal documents. Camp Victory was on the verge of being declared bankrupt. Kelly Block had been given huge loans – hundreds of thousands of dollars – and the banks wanted their money back.

Data was about to close the drawer when a file he hadn't noticed caught his attention.

"CAMP DINOSAUR BUSINESS PLAN."

He plucked the file out, placed it on his lap, and opened it.

"This is a business plan for a new Alberta tourist enterprise to be known as Camp Dinosaur," the opening paragraph began. "It is based on an anticipated surge in international tourism, attracted to the most renowned dinosaur grounds in the world: the Drumheller Badlands. Camp Dinosaur, with an initial start-up investment of $5 million, will capitalize on increased interest in the Badlands and the Royal Tyrrell Museum, and will feature expeditions into the dinosaur grounds in search of fossils and prehistoric evidence. The Jurassic Park theory of the possibility of restoring dinosaur life will be a central theme to this ambitious and easily realized project. An initial share offering of . . ."

Data had seen enough.

Now he knew.


In the third period, Kelly Block began throwing Travis's line out on every second shift, his "chemistry" theories forgotten, as most of the team were back in their original positions. They were almost the Screech Owls again. All they needed now was Muck Munro behind the bench and Kelly Block out of their lives and, just as importantly, out of their minds.

Fahd, of all people, scored the equalizer when he picked up a loose puck in the opposition's end after Derek had squeezed a Predator out of the play. Fahd had meant to pass over to Wilson, pinching in off the far defence, but the puck had glanced the wrong way off Fahd's stick, catching everyone, especially the Predators' goaltender, off guard. With the goalie committed, all she could do was look back helplessly as she slid out towards Wilson, and the puck drifted in over the line.

"We're going to have to do it," Sarah said as the seconds ticked down.

Travis nodded. He knew their line would be on in the final moments.

They changed on the fly, Kelly Block worried now that he'd never get the whistle he was hoping for in the Predators' end. Sarah hit the ice first, racing back into her own end as Nish circled behind the Screech Owls' net with the puck. Nish saw Sarah coming, and dropped the puck for her. He then "pic-ed" the first incoming checker to give Sarah free space up the side.

Travis leapt for the ice as Simon lunged to get off. He hit the ice in full motion, and flew cross-ice, Sarah hitting him with a perfect pass just onside, and Travis cut for the Predators' blueline.

He used the boards to get clear of the first check, but the defence had him lined up perfectly, so he stopped hard and circled. Sarah was flying over centre, with Dmitri now on the ice and charging down his off wing. Travis faked the pass, losing one of the defenders.

Nish was coming late. Travis just dropped the puck so it was on side, barely inside the Predators' blueline, and skated hard for the remaining defender, forcing him to shift sideways in the hopes of beating Nish to the puck. But Nish was already there.

Nish picked up the drop pass in full flight. He had a clear route to the net, the Predators' goaltender skittering out to cut off the angle.

Nish raised his stick for the hard slapper.

The goalie went down on his pads, glove ready.

Nish dropped his stick, and danced sideways, skirting the helpless goaltender and lofting the puck easily into the wide-open net.

Screech Owls 3, Predators 2.

Data was sweating. He knew he would need the files as evidence, particularly the business plan that revealed that Camp Victory was about to be transformed into a dinosaur adventure camp where tourists would scour the Badlands in search of fossils – perhaps even hoping to find proof that dinosaurs hadn't all died out a hundred million years ago. He had the business-plan file, and the bank file, and the reservations file. He would need them all.

He was worried sick he'd be caught. This was break and enter. This was stealing.

But what about Kelly Block? Data still wasn't sure what he had been up to, but he knew, in his heart, that Block had done something to his friends. Something wrong. And he knew that Block was behind this whole mad rush to Drumheller to see if there really was a live dinosaur hiding out among the Badlands.

He wheeled outside and carefully shut the door, listening to the lock click back in place.

He turned, the files on his lap, and began steering his chair out towards the front door.

He would go to his cabin, he figured, and there he would hide the files.

Just as Data was about to reach the door he heard a sound outside.

He stopped so hard the files spilled to the floor. He scrambled to pick them up, leaning far out of his wheelchair to reach the papers that had slid across the polished hardwood.

It was a car door slamming!

Data's heart was pounding. He had the last of the files gathered up, but nowhere to hide them or, for that matter, himself. He would have to bluff his way past whoever had just pulled into the parking area.

He opened the door, cringing. Better to be seen leaving the office than to be caught inside, he figured. The sun cut into his eyes. He squinted in the light, unable to see anything but the blinding red and yellow through his eyelids.

"Data?" a voice called.

He recognized that voice. But it couldn't be . . .

Data closed his eyes hard, then slowly opened them.

A man was paying off a cab driver. The cabby was pulling away. And then the man was standing in the centre of the parking lot, smiling, an old suitcase in one hand, his other hand raised in greeting.

"MUCK!" Data called. His voice broke. He had never been so glad to see anyone in his life.

Travis was passing along the handshake line, Nish behind him, Sarah in front. He was tapping shin pads and punching gloves, and trying to say the right thing – "Nice game . . . Thanks for the game. . . . Good game" – but he knew it should never have been this close. The Owls had been lucky to get the win in the end, but they should have beaten the Predators easily. And they should never have lost to the Werewolves.

Without even looking at the standings posted in the lobby, the Owls all knew where this left them. The win had given them one more game in the tournament, but not for the championship. They had made it to the "B" side, and would play for the consolation title. It wasn't the same as making the big game.

In a way, though, it hardly mattered. For the first time ever, the Owls would probably have preferred just to go home and not play at all any more. The excitement had all been off the ice instead of on. Drumheller was a wonderful town, but Kelly Block had made their stay an experience they would rather forget. And as long as he was around, none of them felt much like playing. He wasn't their coach – and they weren't the old Screech Owls.

Sarah waited until Travis had passed the last Predator in the line, then together they turned towards the exit.

"Do you see what I see?" she asked.

"What?"

"What?" repeated Nish from behind.

"By the Zamboni entrance."

The doors were open, the big machine ready to come out and flood the ice after the handshakes were over. But to one side was Data, pumping his fist in the air.

And behind Data, holding on to the handles of his wheelchair, was Muck!

# 13

"We owe you young people an apology."

The deep and confident voice belonged to the senior officer in the Drumheller detachment of the Royal Canadian Mounted Police. He was standing in the centre of the camp kitchen, the only room large enough to hold all those who had been called together for this moment.

Travis sat at a table with the other six who had seen the dinosaur. Nish was beaming, as if he were about to be knighted by the inspector. Sarah was there, smiling. And Lars, Andy, Jesse, Jenny. All of them. And all of their teammates. And, of course, Muck.

"Mr. Block has been arraigned this morning in a Calgary court. He is in custody, pending Monday's bail hearing. We cannot comment on the charges or the case, of course, but we can tell you that it seems you were right and we were wrong to doubt you."

"ALLLLL RIIIIGHT!" Nish shouted. Everyone in the room, Mounties and players, looked at him as if he had just dropped in from another planet.

"We knew, naturally, that there never was any dinosaur," said the inspector. "That was impossible. But we knew nothing about the powers of hypnotism and suggestion. I'm told, however, that while under hypnosis, you can't be made to do anything you don't *wish* to do, but you can be made to imagine things, even as a group, if conditions are right and the hypnotist knows what he is doing."

It was all becoming clear to Travis. Nish, after all, had said he'd fallen asleep while undergoing that one-on-one session with Block, and they'd thought it a great joke, but it now seemed clear that Nish was *intended* to fall asleep. All the other talk, about "chemistry" and "focus," was just blarney while Block used the hot room and his purring voice to get people to fall under his hypnotic spell. And the fan that Travis had watched before he dozed off – it was the same thing. All part of the scheme.

"You will be interested to know that my men did indeed find something in exactly the place you identified out in the hills," the inspector continued.

Travis could sense the room go very quiet.

The inspector laughed. "No, I'm afraid *not* an Albertosaurus, though I think some of my officers wondered at times if they might come face to face with a monster."

Everyone chuckled politely. Travis and Nish strained to see what it was that two of the Mounties were carrying into the room.

"This," the inspector continued, "is a remote-control sound system. It's not very big, you'll notice. But it certainly sounds big."

One of the officers flipped a switch. The machine hissed, then growled deeply, the fierce sound filling the room and threatening to burst the walls.

*The roar of the Albertosaurus!*

"Turn it down, Mac!" the inspector shouted. The machine clicked off. "We believe this device was hidden out there by someone, probably our Mr. Block. It was set off by a remote sensor. Body movement, say a bike passing by, would set it off. Anything that happened after that probably took place in your imaginations."

In some ways it was really quite simple, thought Travis. Block had probably found it quite easy to insert the idea of a living Albertosaurus in their heads. They'd all seen the life-size models at the Royal Tyrrell Museum and were all excited about dinosaurs. All they had to do was hear that sound, and their minds would do the rest of the work for Block. He'd probably experimented first with Nish, who obviously had the wildest imagination on the team, and then tried it out on the six he'd selected.

They weren't a Russian unit at all. And their selection had nothing whatsoever to do with playing hockey.

It had everything to do with a very public hoax, and millions of dollars.

"I think Mr. Munro has something to say to you all," the inspector said.

He nodded to Muck, who fidgeted awkwardly, then stepped forward. Nish began a small smattering of applause that caught on, and grew. Muck grimaced and shut them down by raising his right hand.

"We have a game to play," Muck announced. "We're still here for a hockey tournament."

## 14

he Drumheller rink was filled to capacity for the second straight day – but the crowd was hardly the same this time. This time the merely curious had stayed at home. The people of Drumheller had come out to see hockey, not the little kids who had played a part in what the papers were now calling the "hoax of the century."

The crowd had gathered early. The big championship game was still two hours off, but they had come to cheer for the Screech Owls, and also to show them that in Drumheller they were not all like Kelly Block. They cheered the warmup and they clapped for the players coming onto the ice and they even cheered when Travis Lindsay, the little captain, succeeded in firing a puck off the crossbar and over the glass into the crowd.

The Owls were up against the Lethbridge Lasers, a fine team that had missed the championship round by a single goal. Since the Owls had struggled so badly, even against weak teams, the crowd expected the Lasers would have little trouble taking the consolation title.

Muck's entire speech before the game, Travis figured, could be written down on a tiny scrap of paper and stuffed inside a fortune cookie.

"Same lines as always," he said. "Jeremy and Jenny split the goaltending. Play your best."

Nothing about "chemistry," no fancy words out of a psychology textbook, no crazy theories – and certainly no hypnotism.

Sarah and Travis and Dmitri started.

They dominated the first shift, up and down the ice, with pinpoint passing and deft drop plays that sent Dmitri in for a superb chance, only to be turned back by a fine stacked-pads save by the Lasers' goalie.

Halfway through the first period, Nish saw little Simon Milliken breaking for centre and threw a high pass that went over Simon's shoulder like a football and dropped just ahead of him a second before he crossed centre ice. Simon was onside and had a clear break. He went backhand-forehand and then slipped the puck in on the short side as the goalie butterflied too late.

Screech Owls 1, Lasers 0.

It was clear there was not going to be much scoring. First Jenny and then Jeremy, who came in at the halfway point, played magnificently. The Lasers' goaltender, staying in for the whole game, seemed unbeatable except for Simon's lucky break.

Into the third period the Lasers finally struck when they turned a two-on-one into an open chance. Wilson, back-pedalling fast, guessed it would be a pass and dropped to block it, but the Laser centre held fast to the puck and slipped it quickly across in front of Jeremy, and the winger fired it fast into the open side.

Owls 1, Lasers 1.

What a game it had become. The crowd was screaming with every rush. If this was a consolation match, Travis thought, what would the championship game be like?

Travis watched happily as Muck walked along behind the players the way he had a thousand times before. Mr. Dillinger was back, patting backs, rapping helmets, dropping towels around necks, slapping pants as players rose and leapt over the boards and into the play. Ty was once again Ty, whispering strategy to Muck and talking to the players about other things they might try, and complimenting them on the things they were doing right.

*If I could spend the rest of my life on this team*, Travis thought, *I would*. And then he realized what that meant.

*Chemistry.*

The Screech Owls had had it all along. It took Kelly Block to ruin it.

The consolation match ended in a tie, 1–1, and they announced an immediate ten-minute, sudden-death overtime. First goal wins.

Muck was at Travis's back, leaning down.

"Don't be afraid to carry," Muck said. "They're keying on Sarah and Nish, expecting them to have the puck."

Travis nodded. He felt Muck's big, rough hand on his neck. It was like a comforter.

Next shift, Wilson pounded the puck around the boards to

Nish, who stopped, seeming almost to tread water as he stared down the ice, challenging the Lasers to forecheck.

Travis turned back sharply, rapping his stick on the blueline as he cut into his own end. Nish hit him perfectly.

A winger was chasing him, closing in on him fast. Without thinking, Travis did something he had only dreamed about before. Still skating towards his own net with the puck, he suddenly dropped it back so it passed through the checker's skates. At the same time, Travis turned abruptly, picking up his own back pass as he headed straight up ice towards the Laser end.

He could hear the roar of the crowd. What sound would they have made, he wondered, if it hadn't worked?

*The roar of the Albertosaurus?*

Travis moved over the red line, with Sarah ahead of him, slowing so she wouldn't go offside. The Lasers were double-teaming her. Travis bent as if to fire a pass in her direction, then brought the heel of his stick down hard on the puck – sending it backwards through his own skates!

Travis cringed, praying that Dmitri would be there.

*He was!*

Dmitri had read the play perfectly. He took up the sliding puck and flew across the line, Sarah and Travis barely staying onside, each with one leg straddling the Lasers' blueline.

Dmitri broke for the corner, spinning away.

Travis read the signal. Dmitri was going to drop the puck and take out his checker. They were cycling the puck – Russian style.

Travis headed for the corner, and the puck came instantly back to him. Dmitri had the checker under control – he'd have to be careful he didn't get called for interference – and Travis looked back towards the blueline, certain of what he would see there.

A locomotive coming full bore: Wayne Nishikawa.

Nish was already poised to shoot, his stick sweeping back for the one-timer.

Travis held to the last microsecond, then sent the puck out fast. Nish had to time it perfectly. He brought his stick down hard.

The puck shot forward, then Travis lost it, then the crowd roared as one.

Travis spun, looking at the net. It was bulging with the puck. The Lasers' goalie was fully extended, legs out, arms out, stick swinging wildly – but the puck was already by him.

*We did it!* Travis shouted.

The Owls poured onto the ice. Travis heard Sarah screaming in his ear.

"*Trav! We won! WE WON!*"

It looked as if the Screech Owls had won the Stanley Cup, not the consolation round of a small-town tournament. The entire arena seemed to explode, as if all that had happened to the Owls was now forgotten, as if everything in the world was now right once more and would never go wrong again.

Ty was running into the crowd of Screech Owls that had smothered Nish into a corner.

Even Muck was out on the ice, moving as fast as his bad leg would take him. He was holding both arms in the air, fists up high, a big grin from ear to ear. Behind Muck, Mr. Dillinger was pushing Data out onto the ice, Data's fist pumping the air.

Travis and Sarah pushed into the crowd. Dmitri leaned over and smacked Travis's helmet. It rattled his brain but felt like a caress. Travis threw his arm around Sarah's shoulder and hugged. Jenny leaped onto their backs from behind.

They threw their gloves and sticks and helmets off, and pushed and shoved and cheered and screamed until, finally, they broke through to reach the Screech Owl who had scored the winning goal in overtime.

Nish was beet-red and covered in sweat, but there was no smile on his face, no life in his eyes. "What's going on?" he asked Travis. "What's everybody yelling about?"

"You, you stupid idiot – great goal! WONDERFUL GOAL!"

"*What goal?*"

"We won, you jerk. Don't you realize what you've done."

Nish shook his head, not comprehending. "I can't remember a thing," he said.

"*What?*" Travis yelled, unbelieving.

"I must have been hypnotized."

And then Nish winked.

**THE END**

# The Ghost of the Stanley Cup

# 1

*ish was dead!*

One moment he was screaming "*I'M GONNA HURL!*" from the seat behind Travis Lindsay – who was desperately hanging on to the bucking, slamming, sliding monster beneath them – the next he was airborne, a chubby twelve-year-old in a red crash helmet, a black rubber wetsuit, and a yellow life jacket, spinning high over the rest of the Screech Owls and smack into the churning whirlpool at the bottom of the most dangerous chute of the long rapids.

Nish entered his watery grave without a sound, the splash instantly erased by the rushing, tea-coloured water of the mighty Ottawa River as it choked itself through the narrow canyon of wet, dripping rock and roared triumphantly out the other end. Screaming and spinning one second, he was gone the next – his teammates so terrified they could do nothing but tighten their iron-locked grips on their paddles and the rope of the river raft.

*Nish was dead!*

Travis closed his eyes to the slap of cold water as it cuffed off the dripping rock walls and spilled in over his face. *Would any of them get out alive? Would it be up to him, as team captain and best friend, to tell Nish's mother?*

"Did my little Wayne have any last words?" poor sweet Mrs. Nishikawa would ask.

"Yes," Travis would have to answer.

"What were they?" Mrs. Nishikawa would say, a Kleenex held to her trusting eyes.

And Travis would have to tell her: "*'I'm gonna hurl.'*"

The Screech Owls had come to Ottawa for a special edition of the Little Stanley Cup. Instead of in January or February, it was being held over the Canada Day long weekend and was going to honour the one hundredth anniversary of the Ottawa Silver Seven – hockey's very first Stanley Cup dynasty. It was to be a peewee hockey tournament the likes of which had never been seen before. The Hockey Hall of Fame in Toronto was bringing up the original Stanley Cup that Governor General Lord Stanley had given to the people of Canada in 1893, there was going to be a special display of hockey memorabilia from the early 1900s, and the Governor General herself was going to present the cup to the winning team. The Sports Network was going to televise the final, and special rings – "*Stanley Cup rings!*" Nish had shouted when he heard – would be awarded to the champions.

But it was unlike other tournaments for more reasons than that. Muck Munro, who always said he had little use for summer hockey, wasn't there to coach. Muck had told them he couldn't get off work, but the Owls figured he hadn't tried all that hard. If Muck took a summer holiday, he preferred to head into the bush for a week of trout fishing. Muck's two assistants, Barry and Ty, hadn't been able to get away either. The team was essentially under the control of good old Mr. Dillinger, who was wonderful at sharpening skates but didn't know much about breakout patterns, and Larry Ulmar – Data – who was great at cheering but not much for strategy. Right now, Data was waiting for the Owls at the end of the ride, deeply disappointed that the river guides hadn't been able to figure out a way to strap his wheelchair into the big, bucking rafts.

Nor were the Screech Owls staying with local families for this tournament. Instead, they were camping, along with most of the other teams, at a church camp farther down the river, within sight of the highrises of Ottawa. It was an ideal location, and the tournament games were deliberately spaced out to allow for day trips. The teams were booked to go river rafting, mountain biking in the Gatineau Hills, and even off to world-famous Algonquin Park, where they hoped to see moose and bear. The tournament final itself was to be played in the Corel Centre, where the Ottawa Senators had played only the winter before. Nish had said it was only proper that he win his first Stanley Cup ring on a rink where NHL stars had skated.

But now Nish was lost overboard, bouncing, spinning, bumping along the bottom of the Ottawa River, snapping turtles pulling at his desperately clutching fingers, leeches already sucking out his blood.

It had been the guide's suggestion that one of them join him at the back of the raft and help steer. Nish, of course, had jumped up first with both hands raised and shouted out that the seat was his. The new player, Samantha Bennett, had also raised her hand to volunteer, and Travis was quick to notice a small flash of anger in Sam's green eyes when the guide gave in and picked Nish. Sam, who'd only moved to Tamarack two months earlier, was Data's replacement on defence. Big and strong, she was as competitive off the ice as on, and almost as loud and just possibly as funny as Nish himself. Andy Higgins had even started calling her "Nish-*ette*," though never to her face. Nish, to her, was a rival as top Screech Owls' defender, not an example for her to copy.

The waters had been calm when Nish went back to sit with the guide. Once, Travis thought he had seen Nish unbuckle his safety harness while the real guide – "Call me Hughie" – pointed out the sights along the river. Travis hadn't worried about Nish's harness until, around the next bend in the river, his ears were filled with a frightening roar, and the water, now rushing, loomed white and foaming ahead of them.

It hadn't seemed possible to Travis that a rubber raft could chance such a run. What if it was punctured on the rocks? But the guide had sent them straight into the highest boils of the current, and the huge raft had folded and sprung and tossed several of them out of their seats as it slid and jumped and smashed through the water. They turned abruptly at the bottom and rammed head-on into a rooster tail of rolling water, the rush now flinging them backwards as if shot from a catapult.

Nish had held on fine through all that – despite his undone safety harness.

Down the river they went, the water roaring and thundering between tight rocks as the runs grew more and more intense. But always the big raft came through, the Screech Owls screaming happily and catching their breath each time they made it down a fast run and shot out the other side into calmer, deeper waters.

But this last time had been too much. The big raft slid into the channel, snaking over the rises, and up ahead Nish saw Lars Johanssen, Wilson Kelly, and Sarah Cuthbertson being bounced right out of their seats. But they had their hands looped carefully around the rope, as instructed, and fortunately they came right back down.

Travis had also left his seat, the quick feeling of weightlessness both exhilarating and alarming. He held tight and bounced back down, hard, and was instantly into the next rise.

That was when he heard his great friend's famous last words – "*I'M GONNA HURL!*" – and the next moment he was watching, helpless, as Nish slipped into that horrifying watery grave.

Nish, lost overboard.

Drowned.

His body never to be recovered.

# 2

"*KA-WA-BUN-GA!*"

Travis spun so fast in his seat he almost turned right around. But then he realized the raft was also turning. They'd reached the bottom of the run. The water was slowing, circling back in small eddies and swirls. Hughie, laughing and digging in hard with his steering paddles to follow the flow, was pointing back up the water.

"*KA-WA-BUN-GA!*"

*It was Nish!* He was lying flat on his back as if the chute were a La–Z–Boy and he was casually watching television, not magically returning from the dead. His chubby hands were folded behind his head for a pillow, and the life jacket had him riding high as a cork as he came down, feet first, and spun into the small whirlpool at the bottom before bumping gently into the raft filled with astonished, delighted Screech Owls.

"*Can we do that again?*" he shouted to the guide.

Hughie laughed so hard Travis thought he might fall in too.

"*Get in here!*" Hughie said, and with some difficulty hauled Nish up over the side.

"CHUCK HIM BACK IN!" a loud voice shouted from the front of the raft. "WHALES ARE OUT OF SEASON!"

It was Sam. The Screech Owls – with one exception – roared with laughter. Nish rolled on his side and spat a mouthful of river water in Sam's direction. Travis caught sight of his friend's face. It was burning so bright it almost turned the water on his cheeks to steam.

Hughie, still laughing, helped Nish back into his seat and, this time, tied him to the raft. They continued downriver, flowing with the current and shooting fast through the narrows. Several times riders flew into the air and bounced on the thick sides of the raft, but they all held tight to the ropes and, when necessary, to each other. Despite Nish's recommendation, no one wanted to shoot a rapids without the raft under them.

It was a wonderful way to spend a day. The river seemed designed for rafting, with long, luxurious drifts between the white-water chutes and, around noon, a rocky river island suddenly looming before them with a calm, sheltered landing area downriver and a large, flat, rocky surface for lunch by the shore.

Hughie broke out two large coolers that had been secured by Velcro straps at the centre of the raft. Several Owls helped him haul them over to a flat rock where several wooden blocks were scattered around a black and damp-looking fire pit. The thick cedar blocks made perfect stools, and several of the Owls shed their helmets and life jackets and sat down to watch the guide work.

Inside one cooler was paper and dry wood, pots and pans and cooking oil, and tin cups and paper plates and towels. Inside the other was food: hot dogs and buns, boxes of Kraft Dinner, Kool-Aid, tins of cookies, and several thick bundles wrapped in tinfoil which, when carefully folded back by the guide, revealed the pink flesh of lake trout. "Caught 'em myself," Hughie bragged.

He began to set the fire, carefully crumpling up the paper, then building a thatch of thinly sliced kindling on top before striking a match. The fire caught quickly and he began feeding it, first with the dry dead branches of a nearby spruce, then with split birch that had been piled there earlier, presumably by the rafting company.

"Go explore the island while I get things ready," Hughie suggested. "Just make sure you have your life jackets on."

The Screech Owls began walking about the small island. It was hot in the sun with the wetsuits and bulky jackets on, and Travis could feel his skin prickling with sweat. If he felt uncomfortable, he thought, how must Nish feel?

But if Nish was bothered by the heat, he didn't show it. He was up ahead and in full voice, surrounded by his friends on the team – Wilson, Andy, Lars, Fahd Noorizadeh, Derek Dillinger, Gordie Griffith, Jeremy Weathers, and Jesse Highboy. Slightly ahead of them, Sarah was walking with Sam, Liz Moscovitz, and Jenny Staples. Travis could see Sam whispering and the other girls giggling.

"I coulda died back there," Nish was saying just a bit too loudly.

"I thought you *were* dead," said Fahd.

"Just lucky for them it was me who flew off," Nish boasted. "Good thing for them I'm such a strong swimmer."

Sarah couldn't resist. She turned, her face questioning: "You looked like you were 'floating,' not swimming."

Nish dismissed her with a wave of his hand. "I had to get clear of the bottom first. You wouldn't believe what it's like down there. Just look at how hard that water's going" – he pointed to the wildest section of the river as it pounded and churned and roared through the narrow stretch between island and shore – "Nobody'd survive that if they weren't a strong swimmer like me."

"I wouldn't," agreed Fahd.

Travis wasn't so sure. It seemed to him that the wetsuit and life jacket may have done all the work, that Nish was merely along for the ride from the moment he splashed in. But he supposed if Nish wanted to make himself out to be a hero, he'd let him. After all, it had happened a million times before.

"HEY – HUGHIE!"

It was Sam's big voice again, calling over the roar of the river. The guide stepped back from his blazing campfire and looked over to where Sam and most of the other Owls were standing.

They were right below the high bluff that formed the upstream end of the island. It was like a miniature mountain, with a small pine tree hanging on valiantly to the side.

"OKAY IF WE CLIMB UP?"

"*I'll have to come up with you!*" he called. He threw more wood on the fire. It would be a while before there were coals enough for cooking.

Sam was already scrambling up. There seemed to be a series of hand- and foot-holds all the way to the top, and her hands and feet moved deftly from grip to grip. She was halfway up by the time the guide made it over to them.

"*Slow down up there!*" Hughie called after her. But he didn't seem angry. He took a run and leaped to the first grip himself, moving up surely and quickly, as if he knew the face of the bluff by heart. Dmitri Yakushev, Sarah, Simon Milliken, and Jesse were right behind him.

"Let's go!" Travis said to Nish.

"Ah, who wants to do something stupid like that?" Nish said.

But Travis wasn't listening. He was hurrying to join the scramble up to the top. The view from up there would be fantastic. With the thick mist rising off the river as it roared by on both sides of the island, the top was barely visible. Once up there, it would probably feel as if they were floating on a cloud.

Travis joined in with Andy and Jenny and Willie Granger, who were about to start climbing.

Andy looked at Travis, puzzled. "Isn't Nish coming?"

"Sure," Travis said as he turned – only to realize Nish hadn't come with him.

*Of course – Nish was terrified of heights!*

"What's wrong with him?" demanded Andy.

Andy hadn't been with them at Lake Placid, when Nish had freaked out on the drive up White Mountain. He'd panicked again at the CN Tower in Toronto, but Andy was new to the team then and probably hadn't noticed. The truth was that Nish – big brave Nish – had one remarkable weak spot: he could not bear heights.

"C'mon, Nish!" Travis shouted encouragingly. "It's not so high."

Too many of the Owls were watching for Nish to ignore the challenge. He swaggered over, but Travis noticed that Nish's high colour from his fall overboard had vanished. He was growing whiter by the moment – almost as if the blood were draining straight out the bottom of his wetsuit.

"Get going, then," Nish ordered. "I'm right behind you."

The others scrambled up with Travis at the rear. It was hard work, but relatively easy climbing. The route had been well established. Travis reached the first ledge and paused to catch his breath. He looked back. Nish, barely two metres off the ground, was staring up helplessly, his face pale and frightened. He looked on the verge of tears and was breathing heavily.

Travis gave his friend an easy way out. "You're probably beat from the spill," he said.

Nish nodded gratefully. "Yeah, I think you're right. I'll maybe just hang back a minute and catch my breath."

"See you up there," Travis said, knowing he wouldn't.

Travis hurried to catch up. He soon settled into a rhythm, finding a handgrip whenever needed, a foot-hold at just the right distance, roots and rock edges and branches perfectly placed for reaching out to and pulling yourself up. It was fun, and he moved quickly.

When Travis looked over the top of the rock face, he saw the Owls already there, gathered around Hughie. He was pointing out the far Gatineau Hills.

It was a beautiful place to stand. The rocks were stark and wet with the mist that rose like steam all about them. It seemed they were in a dream world, walking among the clouds, able to fly if they wished.

"Anybody ever fall off?" Sam was asking, her green eyes flashing with excitement. Now that they were in the sun, her red hair sparkled wildly with the mist settling on it from below.

"You'd die," pronounced Fahd with his usual air of disaster.

"Nah," laughed Hughie. "The water's forty feet deep on this side. You couldn't touch bottom if you tried; you'd be swept away downstream before you'd gone three metres deep."

"Anybody ever jump?" Sam asked.

"You nuts?" Fahd said.

"Sometimes," said Hughie. "There's a few guides who'll do it. We once had a television crew here filming it for *Extreme Sports*."

"Did you jump?" asked Jesse.

"I'm not that crazy," laughed Hughie.

"Well," said Sam, "*I* am!"

And with that she turned and raced for the edge, springing once on both feet high out over the gorge then tucking her legs into her body in a full somersault.

"*Hey!*" shouted the guide.

They all raced towards the empty space where a half-second earlier Sam had stood. Travis reached the edge just in time to see her disappear down through the mist and into the churning, boiling river.

"SHE'LL DROWN!" screeched Jenny.

"She can't," said Hughie, gathering himself. "She's fully outfitted. She'll be all right."

The Screech Owls stood leaning over the edge, all of them

staring into the hump of rolling water where Sam had disappeared.

"She won't come up there," said the guide. "Watch for her downstream."

The Screech Owls stared down towards the calmer water where they'd drawn the raft up onto the rocks.

They saw Nish first. He was standing alone down by the raft, looking completely lost, trying to stay out of sight of the others.

And now they were all staring at him.

"What's Nish doing there?" Fahd asked, although it was all too obvious.

"*There she comes!*" called Hughie, pointing.

They followed his finger. Travis noticed the red crash helmet first, then the bright yellow life jacket. Then the fist, pumping the air as if she'd just scored the winning goal in the Little Stanley Cup.

"*KA-WA-BUN-GA!*"

Nish's call, but clearly not his voice.

It was Sam, pumping her fist and hollering at Nish.

"*KA-WA-BUN-GA! CHICKEN BOY!*"

Sam was swimming, strong and easily, towards the shallows where the raft was docked. She kept pumping her fist.

"*KA-WA-BUN-GA!*"

Travis could see Nish look up at them, his face filled with the painful knowledge that he had just been humiliated. Now they all knew he had chickened out of the climb. And now they all knew there had been nothing particularly brave or talented about his overboard ride down the river.

Nish had just been out-Nished by Sam.

He was a long way away, and there was heavy mist in the air, but Travis didn't need to see Nish's face clearly to be able to read it.

Total fury.

# 3

'll get her back – don't you worry."

Nish might have been talking to himself. He was flat on his back, wearing only his boxer shorts, his sleeping bag kicked off to the side and his pillow covered with candy wrappers: Tootsie Roll, Mars Bar, Mr. Big, Milky Way. In Nish's opinion, a four-course meal.

The boys had woken early. There was so much going on during the Little Stanley Cup, it seemed there was no time left for sleeping. They'd been up until midnight watching the Canada Day fireworks on Parliament Hill – the greatest display of brilliant colour and raw *noise* that Travis had ever experienced – and this morning they had been roused at 7:30 to get ready for their first practice. It was, for the Screech Owls, even better than a game, for they were going to skate on the Corel Centre ice and use the same dressing room as the Ottawa Senators.

Travis lay in the big, army-style tent, half-listening to Nish ramble on about getting his revenge on Sam, and half-watching the sunlight play over the tent. The light seemed to pour through a thousand pinpricks in the canvas – yet it had rained during the night and they'd remained warm and dry.

"But how?" Andy finally asked Nish.

Travis winced. The worst mistake you could make with Nish was to lead him on. The others in the tent – Fahd, Jesse, Lars, and Dmitri – knew it too, but Andy had been unable to resist.

"I'm not sure yet," Nish answered, then giggled softly to himself. "But it'll be good, *real* good, I promise you that."

Travis closed his eyes, not even daring to imagine what schemes were racing through his best friend's twisted little brain.

The sun was now so strong on the tent, it seemed Travis's eyelids had been spray-painted red from the inside.

It was already getting too hot – he could hardly wait to hit the ice.

Travis could never quite understand what Muck had against summer hockey. Muck always said summer was for other sports – baseball to improve your eye-hand co-ordination, soccer to help your footwork and passing, biking for conditioning – and claimed that the reason so many kids dropped out of hockey in their teenage years was that they were sick and tired of playing the game twelve months of the year. Perhaps Travis would one day agree with his coach, but not now.

He loved the way everything about summer hockey was backwards. In winter you came in to the warmth and shed bulky outdoor clothes; in summer you came in to the cool and put on bulky equipment. Travis liked the dressing up instead of dressing down. He liked that first step onto a fresh ice surface when he could kick once and just glide freely. He often thought that the first turn around the rink in summer must be as close as a kid can come to feeling like an astronaut stepping outside the spaceship: so heavily insulated, head helmeted, gravity and friction defied, his body drifting and soaring with the slightest effort.

Even better, the Owls were in a rink where NHL players had performed. Here, on this very ice surface, was where Alexei Yashin and Daniel Alfredsson and Marian Hossa had starred for the Senators. Here was where Jaromir Jagr had scored, where Patrick Roy and Dominik Hasek had kicked out the shots. And here, he suddenly remembered, was where Wayne Gretzky had played his final game ever in Canada. Because of that, it was a rink that belonged to Canadian history.

Mr. Dillinger was doing the best he could. He set out pylons and dumped a bucket of pucks, and he tried to talk like Muck and outline plays like Ty, but it wasn't the same. Poor Mr. Dillinger, sweat beading on his bald head, could barely skate. He needed his stick on the ice for support, and when he tried to fire a puck into a corner so the power play could work on their cycling, he fell over onto one knee.

"*Need some help out there?*" a voice called from behind the bench.

Mr. Dillinger stood up, knocked the snow off his leg and stared over, not sure whether he was being laughed at or not.

A handsome young man was standing beside Data, who had pulled his chair up to the bench and was following the practice with a playboard on his lap. The man had short dark hair and was smiling – a nice smile, an inviting smile. He was holding up his skates, tied together at the laces, as if to suggest he be asked out on the ice.

Mr. Dillinger skated over, stopping so awkwardly he threw his big hip into the boards and sprung open the bench gate. He almost fell, catching himself at the last moment.

"What makes you think we need help?" Mr. Dillinger said, with as much dignity as he could muster.

The young man smiled again – his teeth flashing under the strong lights of the Corel Centre – and Mr. Dillinger was instantly smiling back, then laughing at himself.

"I'm Joe Hall," the young man said, holding out his hand.

# 4

"**G**lad to meet you, Joe Hall," Mr. Dillinger said, taking off his hockey glove and reaching for the young man's hand. Mr. Dillinger's hand seemed to disappear into Joe Hall's like a gopher into a large hole.

"I live down by the campsite – heard some of the other coaches saying your coach couldn't make the trip. True?"

Mr. Dillinger was nodding, catching his breath. "I'm just the manager and skate sharpener. Data here's more of a coach than I am."

Joe Hall turned his beaming smile on Data. "I can see that," he said. "You've got some drills worked out on that board, I see."

Data seemed shocked, instantly shy. "Oh, I was just fooling around."

"Nah, they're good," protested Joe Hall. He turned his gaze back on Mr. Dillinger. "I'd be honoured to help you run the practice. Just say the word."

Mr. Dillinger nodded gratefully. He looped off Muck's whistle and tossed it to Joe Hall, who slipped it around his thick neck and sat down on the bench to put his skates on. A stick and gloves lay behind him. He'd come prepared.

"Just what we need," Nish whispered into the back of Travis's helmet. "Another *expert*."

Travis turned, irritated. "We need *somebody* who knows what he's doing."

"I think he's kind of cute," said Sam.

"So do I," agreed Sarah.

"Better than anything else we've seen around here, that's for sure," added Sam.

"*Get a life!*" Nish practically spat in her direction.

Sam rolled her eyes. Sarah giggled. Usually it was Sarah who took the shots at Nish and kept him in line. She seemed happy to be sharing her duties.

Joe Hall was ready in less than a minute. He stepped out onto the ice surface and flexed, stretching carefully before looping around the rink a couple of times. It seemed to Travis that Joe Hall hadn't been on skates for some time, but he could see that, even on rusty legs, he had a marvellous, powerful stride.

"Okay, Owls," Joe Hall said when the team had gathered around. "Let's have us a practice."

Twenty minutes later, Travis was bent over double, sucking for wind. Nish, splayed out flat in the corner, was groaning and gasping for air. Andy was hanging over the boards, gulping his breaths. Everywhere it was the same, with one – no, two –

exceptions. Sarah, who seemed to find skating easier than breathing, was still flying about the ice in her lovely, effortless stride. And right behind her, a little less elegant but more powerful, was Sam. They were laughing.

Joe Hall was a taskmaster. He skated them until most of the Owls had either dropped or were about to drop. He ran complicated breakout drills that sent the puck flying out to centre ice so quickly that Sarah, waiting for the pass, barely had to flick it on her backhand to send the swift Dmitri in on clear breakaways. He had them working the corners, practising penalty-killing and switching, on a rap of his stick, from zone to man-on-man coverage. It was exhausting, but it was a superb, hard practice. Muck would have approved.

Joe Hall blew hard on the whistle, calling the players down into a far corner. He had them drop to one knee when they arrived. Nish arrived on both knees, spinning wildly, and knocked into Andy and Fahd and Lars so hard he sent them tumbling like bowling pins.

Joe Hall waited until everything was absolutely silent, then he stared at Nish and spoke in a low, steady voice. "You can go and sit on the bench, mister. We've still got some business to do here."

Nish looked stunned. He turned, mouth open, and Travis could see the pink spreading across his cheeks. But no one was offering any sympathy.

"Get going," Joe Hall said. "You're wasting our ice time."

Nish rose to his skates. Slowly he skated away, the rasp of his skates uncannily loud in the empty rink. Not a single Screech Owl even dared to breathe.

But Joe Hall was smiling again. He had forgotten already about Wayne Nishikawa, troublemaker. "Anyone here know about the Silver Seven?" he asked.

"Data would," Sarah said.

"They were hockey's first dynasty," offered Fahd.

"That's correct," said Joe Hall, nodding. "They were the original Ottawa Senators. Four Stanley Cups in a row at the start of this last century. Not even Gretzky's Edmonton Oilers managed that. Guys like Harry 'Rat' Westwick, 'Bones' Allen, 'Peerless' Percy LeSueur, and 'One-Eyed' Frank McGee."

The players giggled at the names.

"You don't hear nicknames like that these days, do you?" Joe Hall said. "The kid I just sent off, what's his name?"

"Wayne Nishikawa," Fahd offered.

"And his nickname?"

"Nish."

Joe Hall shrugged. "Figures. There's no imagination in hockey any more. All you kids should have nicknames – they're as important in this game as numbers. What *should* be Nish's nickname?"

"'Chicken'?" suggested a voice from the back. It was Sam.

The other players giggled. Joe Hall looked from face to face, waiting for an explanation, but no one was volunteering.

"Did you have one?" Fahd asked.

"Me? Yeah, I did."

"What was it?"

Joe Hall shook his head: "You'll have to figure that one out for yourself."

"No fair!" protested Fahd. But Joe Hall was already changing topic.

"Let me tell you something about 'One-Eyed' Frank and Harry the 'Rat,'" he said. "They're both in the Hockey Hall of Fame, you know."

"We were there!" said Jenny.

"Then you should know *why* they're in the Hall of Fame. The 'Rat' was one of the best skaters who ever played the game. If you really had to have a goal, you counted on him. Frank McGee once scored fourteen goals in a single Stanley Cup game – a record no one's ever going to break. How do you think they scored those goals?"

Fahd raised his hand like he was in class. Joe Hall nodded at him.

"Breakaways," he suggested.

Joe Hall shook his head. "How do you get a breakaway?" he asked Fahd.

"You fire the puck up to someone who's breaking."

Joe Hall smiled and pointed. "Exactly! But what if you couldn't do that?"

"You mean offside?" asked Andy.

"No," said Joe Hall. "I mean what if the rules didn't allow you – or anyone for that matter – to pass a puck *up* to a teammate?"

"What kind of a rule is that?" asked Lars.

"It was the rule they played under. It wasn't until 1929 that hockey brought in the forward pass. Did anyone know that?"

"No," Fahd answered for them all.

"For more than thirty years they played the game by using only drop passes and back passes – and still 'One-Eyed' Frank McGee was able to score fourteen goals in one game. It worked for the Silver Seven, don't you think?"

"I guess," said Fahd.

"I guess so too," said Joe Hall. "And so we're going to bring that pass back to this tournament. We're going to move ahead by going backwards."

For more than thirty minutes, Joe Hall had the Owls work on drop passes and back passes. He had them scrimmage with one new rule added – no forward passes. At first it confused the players terribly, but after a while they started to get the hang of it and began moving up the ice in waves, with each successive wave rushing quicker just as pucks were dropped back to them.

"We look like Russians!" shouted Dmitri proudly.

"We look like idiots!" corrected Nish, who had been allowed back into the play.

But Travis didn't think so. There was method to Joe Hall's madness, and the Owls were starting to look for the play developing behind them. They were using themselves as decoys, drawing off checks while leaving pucks for teammates rushing up behind. It might not have looked quite right, but it was working.

Sarah looped behind her own net and, with a burst of speed, slipped straight up centre, sending the opposing defence – Nish paired with Lars this time – backpedalling wildly. She dropped the puck neatly to Sam, charging up from her defensive position.

Travis could see the play. Sarah had used her body to "accidentally" brush Lars back and take him out of the play. It was just Sam on Nish, with Travis coming up fast.

If Sam could drop to Travis, he would have a clear shot on Jeremy, who was already shimmying backwards into his net, glove ready.

Sam saw the play, too. She dropped the puck deftly between her skates and turned to see if Travis was in his expected position.

And that's exactly when Nish "smoked" her.

The sound was astonishing. It was more like a collision in the parking lot than a hit just inside the blueline. There was the sound of air bursting from lungs, pads giving, plastic cracking, sticks and skates and bodies colliding.

Sam went down hard, sprawling toward the corner.

Nish, who barely kept upright, staggered once, then dropped his stick and gloves.

He tucked his hands under his armpits, dropped into a crouch, and began skating in a wide circle past the fallen Sam.

"CLUCK! CLUCK–CLUCK–CLUCK!" Nish cackled as he looped around the ice in an exaggerated chicken dance. "CLUCK! CLUCK–CLUCK–CLUCK–CLUCK–CLUCK!"

Joe Hall's whistle sounded like the scream that had never come from Sam. Travis had often wondered how Muck could put so much emotion into his whistle – shrill for anger, slow and rolling for contentment – but this was a new sound, a frightening one.

Nish stopped his stupid show. Joe Hall came skating back, pointing, his hand shaking.

"*You're outta here, Mister! The dressing room — and make it fast!*"

Nish didn't argue. He left his stick and gloves on the ice and never even broke stride as he leapt through the gate leading to the dressing room.

Travis turned his attention back to Sam. She was on her knees, fighting for wind. Sarah was already there, an arm over Sam's shoulders.

Sam gathered her breath, put her skate down, and stood, a bit unsteadily.

*She was laughing!*

# 5

The Screech Owls played their first game against the Rideau Rebels at the Kanata Recreation Centre, a double ice-surface rink within sight of the peach-coloured walls of the Corel Centre. It was almost as good, Mr. Dillinger said, because this was where the Senators practised when the Corel Centre was unavailable. There was even an elevator for Data to use to get down to the dressing-room level.

Data had struck up a fast friendship with Sam. She seemed to know almost as much about *Star Trek* as he did, and on the bus the two of them argued endlessly about which was superior, *Star Trek* (Data's choice) or *Star Wars* (Sam's choice). The day after practice, when Sam stood outside the bus, heavy equipment bag slung over her shoulder, and shouted up to Mr. Dillinger "*HIjol!*" – Klingon for "Beam me up!" – she won Data's heart forever.

Nish seemed unwilling to take any competition from Sam for the spotlight. On the night the Owls had a team dinner at the camp with the tournament organizers, it looked as if he was going to behave himself, until the visiting church minister suggested that, instead of a prayer before the meal, they go around the tables and tell the gathering one special thing in their lives for which they were particularly grateful.

"My grandparents," said Travis.

"My country," said Lars, who was fiercely proud of being from Sweden.

"My new friend and teammate, Data," said Sam.

"Mail-order catalogues," said Nish.

The minister, already moving his finger on to the next Owl, jumped back, his attention returning to Nish, a puzzled expression on his face.

"Why, son?"

Nish grinned. "I'm grateful for the lingerie ads."

The girls on the team all groaned. Lars and Andy started giggling and couldn't stop, finally ducking down and hiding underneath the tablecloth until Mr. Dillinger, his own face flushed red, went over and shooed them out. Travis looked over at Sarah, who rolled her eyes and spun a finger beside her right temple. Travis just nodded back. Good thing for Nish that Joe Hall hadn't been able to make the dinner.

Travis thought he understood Nish's bizarre behaviour, but Joe Hall was a puzzle. He seemed to be around, much of the time – then suddenly gone. They asked him where he lived, and he pointed up the river and said he had the first cottage on the shore around the point. But some of the Owls had gone hiking that way, and they had seen nothing. They asked him what level

he'd played at – he had clearly been a superior hockey player –
and all he'd said was "high."

"Why'd you quit?" Fahd wanted to know. "Injury?"

That's what Travis had figured. That's what had happened to
Muck, who still limped from the bad break that had ended his
junior career and ended, forever, his dreams of making the NHL.
Joe Hall didn't limp, but it could have been something else. An
eye? Concussion?

"No," he said. "No injury."

"Well, what then?" Fahd persisted.

Joe Hall stared at them a moment, as if unsure whether to tell
them.

"I . . . ," he began. "I . . . just got sick, okay?"

Nothing more had been said. But it didn't stop the team
from talking about Joe Hall among themselves. Lars was fascinated by Joe Hall's way of playing the game. "European," Lars
called it. "Russian," Dmitri argued. But it was neither, Travis
figured. It was *old* – like Joe Hall himself had said – the way
"Rat" Westwick and "One-Eyed" Frank McGee used to play
the game in this very city.

"Did you notice his stick?" Sarah had asked Travis after that
first practice.

"No. What kind does he use?" Travis asked, thinking that's
what Sarah meant: Sherwood, maybe, or Easton, or Titan, or
Nike.

"The blade's completely straight," she said. "I couldn't tell
whether it was right or left when I picked it up."

"*Straight?*"

"As a ruler."

Travis shrugged. Made sense, he figured, if you were going to use a lot of drop passes and back passes. He'd noticed himself how often the puck rolled off the backside curve of his blade. He just couldn't be as accurate with back passes as he was with forward.

"What make is it?" he asked.

"That's what's really strange," said Sarah. "It looks home-made – almost like somebody carved it out of a tree branch."

6

There was a good crowd to watch the Rideau Rebels play the Screech Owls. The Rebels were the media favourite in the tournament. Not only was the team made up of local kids, it was the namesake of one of the first teams ever to play in the Ottawa area. The modern Rebels even wore replica jerseys.

According to the *Citizen* newspaper, if there hadn't once been a team called the Rebels, there would never have been a Stanley Cup. Two of the players on the team had been the sons of Lord Stanley, the Governor General of the day. Lord Stanley, who had come over from England, never tried to play himself, but he enjoyed watching, and at the end of his appointment in Canada he decided to leave behind a "challenge cup" for hockey teams to play for. Lord Stanley spent $48.67 of his own money on the trophy, but never once saw it played for. He could not have imagined that, a century after he'd returned home to England, the Stanley Cup would be the most easily recognized trophy in professional sport.

Two of the Rebels' players, Kenzie MacNeil and James Grove, were the *Citizen*'s choice as most likely candidates for the Most Valuable Player award, which was to be presented on the final day by the modern Governor General. If the award were to go to one of the two Rebels, said the *Citizen*, it would be "poetic justice."

"What the heck's *that* mean?" Nish demanded when Travis showed him the article.

"That it should happen. That it's the right thing."

"Yeah, *right!*" Nish said with great sarcasm.

Nish didn't miss a beat. Just before the puck dropped on the opening faceoff, he skated past Kenzie MacNeil, lining up to face off against Sarah, and quickly whispered his own version of "poetic justice":

> *"Roses are red, violets are blue.*
> *I'll be MVP – not you."*

MacNeil just looked at him and shook his head, baffled.

Halfway through the shift Travis could see why Kenzie MacNeil might be the early favourite as the tournament's top player. Joe Hall had switched the lineups around a bit, perhaps sensing that Nish and Sam would hardly be able to play together. Nish was out with Lars, and Lars made the mistake of trying to jump into the play right after the faceoff. Sarah tied up MacNeil, but just as Lars tried to slip in and away with the puck, MacNeil used his skate to drag the puck through the circle and up onto his stick. Sarah stuck with him, but he was able, one-handed, to flick a backhand pass to his left winger, James Grove, who suddenly had open ice with Lars out of the picture.

Nish cut fast across the blueline to cover for Lars, but to do so he had to leave the far wing open. The Rebel left winger was able to fire a rink-wide pass, blind, knowing that the Rebels' other winger would be open.

Travis was the Owls' only hope. He chased his check and caught him just inside the Owls' blueline. Travis began leaning on the player to force him off towards the boards, but he should have tried to play the puck. The winger flipped an easy drop pass that looped over Travis's stick and fell, like a spinning plate, on the safe side of the line.

Kenzie MacNeil, moving up fast, was all alone. He came in on Jeremy – who was coming out to cut the angle – and instead of cutting, or faking a shot, MacNeil simply hauled back and slammed a vicious slapshot that tore right through Jeremy's pads and popped out the other side into the Screech Owls net.

As the starting lineup skated off, their heads hung low, Sarah said to Nish,

> "Roses are red, violets are blue,
> When that guy scored, where were you?"

"Ahhh, drop it!" Nish said angrily, slamming his stick down.

Travis felt bad for his friend. He'd seen that Nish had simply tried to cover for Lars, who made the initial mistake, and that in doing so he'd left his side open and gave the Rebels the opening they needed. Sarah was also at fault, Travis said to himself, for she was supposed to have stayed with MacNeil. He'd learned long ago, however, that there was no point in arguing over what had happened out there. The only thing that mattered was what would happen *next* – and the Screech Owls had to get back into this game.

"Everyone noticed how they scored that goal, I hope," said Joe Hall. "Drop pass."

Joe Hall decided to counter the Rebels' big scoring line by putting Sam out every time MacNeil was on the ice. Sam's only job was to stay back and make sure the big Rebel centre didn't get free. As the game continued, she stuck to him, in Nish's words, "like gum to the bottom of a school chair," and it was clear that the star player was growing frustrated.

So, too, was Nish, who was not seeing his usual amount of ice time. On a Rebels power play he let little James Grove slip in behind him, and the talented Rebel got away a hard shot that Jeremy in goal took on the shoulder, sending the puck flipping high over the boards. The whistle put an end to play, but Nish continued right on through the little forward, running him over like a Zamboni and picking up a second penalty for the Owls.

Joe Hall was not amused. He waited until Nish returned to the bench from the penalty box, then very calmly he told him he had all but cost them the game with that stupid after-the-whistle hit.

"If you can't control your temper," Joe Hall said in a steady voice that must have sounded like a scream in Nish's burning ears, "you'll never control the play."

Nish didn't play another shift. Joe Hall began double-shifting Sam, pairing her first with Lars and then Wilson – and the more she played the more she shone.

In the second period, Gordie Griffith picked up a bouncing

puck at centre and broke up alone, dishing off to Dmitri, who was just coming over the boards on the fly. Dmitri raced in and beat the Rebels' goaltender with his trademark backhand high into the net.

MacNeil might have scored a second when he got in alone, but a sprawling, stick-swinging desperation move by Sam knocked the puck off his stick and into the corner as she fell to the ice. MacNeil came to a sharp stop, his skates deliberately throwing snow into Sam's face.

She got up, laughing.

If it had been Nish, he would have come up swinging.

In the third, the two teams exchanged goals: one by Fahd on a weak, looping shot from the point that bounced in off the butt of one of the Rebels' defenders – "*Exactly the way I planned it!*" Fahd claimed at the bench – and one by the Rebels when little James Grove came down one-on-one and slipped the puck through Wilson's skates. The little Rebel then pulled out Jeremy just as deftly, sliding the puck in so slowly it looked like he was in a curling match.

Travis had one good chance. He broke up ice with Sarah charging behind him through centre, but when he tried to cut to the defence and drop the puck for Sarah – a no-no, according to Muck – he blew the opportunity, leaving the puck for the second defenceman instead. The defenceman simply chipped the puck off the boards and the Rebels had a three-on-two that, once again, Sam foiled with a poke check.

"You have to get the puck to your centre," Joe Hall said when Travis skated off. "It's not a package you leave at the front desk for her to pick up when she's got time."

Travis nodded, knowing he'd blown it. Next time, if there was a next time, he'd make sure the puck was on Sarah's stick before taking himself out of the play.

But there was no second chance for Travis. The horn blew – a 2–2 tie – and the teams lined up to shake hands. Travis was right behind Sam. Big Kenzie MacNeil was coming through the line, barely touching hands rather than shaking them. When he came to Sam, he scowled.

"Keep off my case," he hissed, "or I'll take you out."

Sam yanked off her helmet and shook out her bright red hair. She blinked several times, faking delight.

"My, my, Kenzie," she said, smiling, "are you asking me out on a *date?*"

It was MacNeil's turn to blink – but in genuine surprise. Had he not realized Sam was a girl?

"*Go to hell!*" he snarled.

He refused to shake Sam's hand, slamming his fist into Travis's glove instead and turning abruptly to leave the line.

Sam was laughing loudly.

It was a good thing, Travis thought, that Joe Hall had already ordered Nish to the dressing room.

Sam had scored another bull's eye, and Nish would not have been pleased.

# 7

**W**HERE ARE MY GAUCHIES?"

The players had just come back from an early-morning dip in the Ottawa River and were supposed to change quickly for the long bus ride to Algonquin Park. Nish had been first in the water, first out of the water, first dried off, and first back to the tent. Travis was only stepping off the beach when he heard the yells from inside their tent.

"*WHO TOOK MY GAUCHIES?*"

Travis hurried up, pulled back the flaps, and there was Nish, buck naked in the centre of the tent, kicking everyone's sleeping bags and clothes as fast as his feet could move. He seemed near panic.

"*My boxers are gone!*" he shouted at Travis, as if Travis would know what had become of them. "*All of them. What the hell's going on here?*"

"Calm down," Travis said. "You've just misplaced them like you do with everything."

"Somebody's stolen them."

"Who'd want to touch *your* boxer shorts?" Fahd asked as he ducked inside.

"That's what *I* want to know," cried Nish, missing Fahd's point.

Travis, who was the most organized, led them on a careful check of all their clothes. This wasn't the first time they'd been on a hunt like this: Travis still chuckled when he remembered how Nish's boxers had once ended up in the freezer. The boys carefully made piles of Lars's stuff, and Fahd's, and Andy's, Jesse's, Dmitri's, Travis's, Nish's – but nowhere could they find any of Nish's distinctive yellow-and-green boxer shorts.

"Call the police," Nish said.

"And what?" Travis asked. "Ask them to put out an all-points-bulletin on missing underwear? You'll just have to borrow some."

"Not mine!" said Fahd with alarm.

"Not mine!"

"Not mine, either!"

"Nor mine!"

"Forget it," Nish said angrily. "They're all too small anyway."

They poked around in the clothes some more, but it was futile. Finally Nish sighed heavily, a sign that he was giving up.

"What'll you do?" asked Fahd.

"Go naked, pal – that okay with you? Will you mind my big white butt sitting on your lap?"

"Oh, God!" said Fahd. "Can't you find something?"

"You can wear your bathing suit," Travis suggested. "We'll probably be swimming again anyway."

"It's wet."

"So what? Put it on."

Nish made a face and stepped back into his bathing suit, then pulled his wide khaki shorts over top. The wet bathing suit immediately soaked through to the front of his shorts.

"Jeez," said Nish. "Now I look like I wet myself."

"Better that than naked," said Fahd. "C'mon, let's go – we're already five minutes late."

They finished dressing, grabbed their towels, and ran to catch the team bus, which Mr. Dillinger had already pulled up to the front gate of the camp. The rest of the Owls were already aboard, and a great cheer went up when the stragglers came into sight.

Nish, worried about the wet spots on his shorts, wrapped his swimming towel around himself as he ran. He was last to the bus, and had to wait while the others filed by Mr. Dillinger.

Joe Hall was already there. He shook a finger at each late boy, but didn't really seem all that angry. His eyes went wide when he saw Nish wrapped in a damp towel.

"You got anything on under there, big boy?" shouted Sam from well back in the bus.

Nish looked up, his face reddening. "Somebody stole my boxers. *You* wouldn't know anything about that, would you?"

The whole bus broke into laughter. They'd been waiting for this moment.

"Check the flagpole!" Jenny shouted.

Nish looked from face to face, but saw no allies, no explanation. Finally, he bent down and leaned towards the window, staring up as far as he could see.

There, at the top of the camp flagpole, Nish's boxer shorts flapped in a gentle breeze.

"Who did that?" Nish asked, unnecessarily.

"*We did!*" the girls on the team all said at once.

"We're all just so grateful for *men's* lingerie," Sam said, her voice almost exactly the same as Nish's at the camp supper.

The bus broke up. Red-faced and furious, Nish bolted past Fahd for a seat by the window. He swept the towel from around his waist and threw it over his head to escape his tormentors.

Mr. Dillinger helped poor Nish out. He slammed a Sum 41 CD into the bus player and cranked it up loud.

The bus jumped as it pulled out, wheels spinning and screeching slightly as the dirt changed to pavement. Everyone in the bus broke into a cheer.

They were headed for Algonquin Park.

They were off to visit a ghost.

@

The "ghosts" had been Mr. Dillinger's idea. He'd spent all of June planning this trip. He'd been delighted when the organizers of the Little Stanley Cup had insisted that the tournament be as much about seeing new things as playing new teams, and he'd enthusiastically signed the Owls up for the river rafting and mountain biking and watching the magnificent fireworks on Parliament Hill.

But the ghost idea had been his alone. He'd read an article about all the ghosts the area could lay claim to, and he asked the Owls if they had any interest in trying to see one. It was a crazy idea – just the sort of brilliant, offbeat activity Mr. Dillinger was so good at coming up with – and they'd cheered the suggestion loudly.

He took them down to Sparks Street and had a local historian point out the precise spot where Thomas D'Arcy McGee, one of the Fathers of Confederation, had been shot in the back by James Patrick Whelan as McGee fiddled with his latch key. The historian was wonderful, even dressing up in period costume to tell the story of the assassin, the last person publicly hanged in Canada. "It happened on February 11, 1869," the historian told them. "The people came by the hundreds, from all over, to watch Whelan hang from the gallows just down the street from here. To this day, there are people who claim the ghost of James Patrick Whelan still walks the streets of Ottawa on dark, misty nights. And there are those who say Thomas D'Arcy McGee sometimes rises to speak in the House of Commons on nights when Parliament isn't in session."

They'd toured Laurier House, where Prime Minister Sir Wilfrid Laurier had once lived. The staff who looked after the house told them of the strange happenings that had occurred there: furniture that had been moved in the night, lights on in the morning that had been turned off when the house was closed the previous day. They went to the William Lyon Mackenzie King estate in the Gatineau Hills and toured the strange grounds where King, who seemed a madman to the Owls, had brought relics of old churches and buildings from as far away as London, England, and erected them in the woods. A tour guide told them how King, even when he was prime minister, held seances to consult his dead dog and mother on how to run the country.

And now, Mr. Dillinger had said, they were off to visit "the greatest Canadian ghost of them all: Tom Thomson."

It was a long bus ride to Algonquin Park. Some of the Owls slept. Fahd played with his Game Boy. Sarah read. Wilson and Sam listened to hip-hop on their portable CD players. But Travis just turned to the window and stared out at the glittering lakes and endless bush.

They were well inside the park when Travis felt the bus suddenly slow and pull off to the side of the road.

"Shhhhhh," Mr. Dillinger said from the front of the bus. "Everyone out, but keep it quiet."

Travis wasn't sure at first what they were getting out for, but when he stepped down into the bright wincing light of the day he realized the bus was not alone. Several vehicles, some wearing canoes on their roofs like caps, had also stopped. And up ahead, a crowd of visitors had gathered, many of them with cameras raised.

"A moose cow and her calf," whispered Mr. Dillinger. "Go gently."

Travis and Nish pushed through to the front of the crowd. They faced a bog, which farther out gave way to water, and here the moose and her calf were standing, shoulder deep, calmly biting down into the water and then slowly chewing as they gazed about like moose tourists who had suddenly come upon a herd of humans.

"Who chews their water?" Nish asked.

"They're *eating*," said Travis. "There are weeds growing just under the water."

"Gross!" Nish said.

But Travis was fascinated by the big animals and, in particular, by their lack of fear. Surely they had noticed the people standing about, the cars and trucks pulling off to the side of the road and stopping in a cloud of dust. But they seemed, if anything, amused by all the attention.

Travis took a few photographs on his disposable camera and then, almost in an instant, the moose were gone, dark shadows slipping into the darker shadows of the deep bush.

"Wow!" said a voice beside Travis.

It was Sam. She was shaking with excitement. "Did you ever see anything so beautiful?"

Travis didn't know if he had. But it was more than the moose. It was the park itself, so green, so wild, the hills so sudden and the rock cuts so deep, the lakes so blue and clean and inviting. They stopped at the Lake of Two Rivers picnic grounds and had lunch and swam – Nish first in because he was already in his bathing suit – and then continued to Canoe Lake, where the ghost of Tom Thomson was supposedly waiting for them.

"This ghost business is a load of garbage," Nish was saying in a seat far behind Travis. Nish's voice was back to normal: a touch too loud, a bit too confident, a little too much bluster. "It's like UFOs," he said. "You got all these people claiming to see one, but how come nobody's ever got a picture of one?"

"There's lots of pictures of UFOs," said Data, who counted himself an expert on anything to do with space.

"They're all fakes," Nish said.

"How do you know the authorities don't just say that so people don't panic?" said Data. "Just imagine for a second if the government came out and announced that aliens from outer space were really flying over New York or Vancouver – or Algonquin Park, for that matter."

"I'll believe it when I see it for myself," said Nish, as if that was an end to the argument.

They pulled off at Canoe Lake. Mr. Dillinger had arranged everything. There was a barge boat waiting for them at the Portage Store, big enough to hold everyone, as well as a couple of park rangers, one to run the outboard and one, an older man who smoked a pipe, to point out the sights.

On the long run up the lake, the older ranger told the Owls the essentials of the Tom Thomson story. Now Canada's most famous painter, he was unknown when he first came to the park just before the First World War. Some of the rangers at the time thought he should be arrested as a madman for setting up a three-legged stand, resting a board on it, and then slapping paint all over the board. "They'd never ever *heard* of an 'artist'!"

Over the next few summers, however, Thomson had become as much a part of the park as the rangers themselves. They taught him how to paddle a canoe, how to fish for lake trout, how to set up a camp, and how to find his way around the intricate highway of park lakes.

"People came in then by train," said the ranger. "Train's long gone, so's the lodge he stayed at when he wasn't camping. The woman he was engaged to marry died a lonely old woman years ago, convinced to the end that Tom's body still lay in a shallow grave at the top of that hill there with the birch trees."

He pointed to the shore, to a splash of white birch on a small hill overlooking the lake. Travis felt a chill run down his back.

As an island came near, the ranger steering the boat killed the outboard. The silence was shocking. The older ranger waited, knowing he had his audience in the palm of his hand.

"Right here," he said, pointing down into the calm black waters off the island, "is where Tom Thomson's body rose to the surface in July of 1917."

"What happened?" asked Fahd, his eyes wide open.

The ranger shrugged and smiled. "No one knows. Eight days earlier he'd set off from that far point over there on a short fishing trip and never returned. They found his canoe, but never his paddle – and paddles float. So do bodies after a few days in warm water, but they didn't find him for more than a week, and when they did they also found a length of wire wrapped round and round his ankle – almost as if he'd been tied down to something – and a small, bleeding hole in his temple."

"Murder!" Fahd practically shouted.

"Maybe. There'd been a fight the night before, people say, and the lodge owner, Shannon Fraser, had supposedly struck Tom a blow, and Tom fell down and cracked his head on the fire grate. Some say Fraser and his wife dumped Tom overboard that night with something heavy tied to his ankle, and then cast his canoe adrift, hoping people would presume he'd drowned and wasn't ever coming up. Tom had also argued with an American cottager down the way" – he pointed to the opposite shore – "about the war (Canada was in it, the United States not yet) and the story goes that the hole in Tom's temple came from a .22 fired by the cottager as Tom paddled by. There's also those who say he struck his head when he fell in his canoe while standing up to take a leak –"

"*What?*" Nish screeched.

"That's one theory," the ranger said, smiling. "But none of us here put much stock in it. It only takes a few paddle-strokes to reach shore around here – so why would anybody be so stupid?"

"What do *you* think happened?" asked Sarah.

The ranger nodded. "I think he was murdered. I think that's why people say they keep seeing him come back. He's trying to tell us something."

**8**

hey tied the boat up to a small island – Little Wapomeo, the old ranger called it – and explored before taking another swim. The Screech Owls were getting hungry again, and the rangers were already making a fire as the players dried off and strung their towels over a rope the younger ranger had strung between two spruce trees. There were hot dogs and marshmallows to toast, and cold canned pop. Mr. Dillinger had certainly planned well. And long after they'd eaten their fill they continued to sit around the fire, talking easily with the rangers about their fascinating jobs.

Travis noticed that it was quickly getting dark. The smoke from the fire was gathering about the island. There was also a mist rising from the water, swirling and shifting mysteriously as if something unseen were controlling the air currents.

He watched the older ranger and Joe Hall for a while, the two of them standing down by the water and talking quietly. Travis couldn't hear what they were saying.

When the ranger came back he had his pipe out and was poking at it with his jackknife. He loaded it up again and made a great show of lighting the pipe from a flaming stick he plucked from the fire. He sat down on a large block of wood, leaned forward, and began what everyone had been waiting for – the tale of Tom Thomson's ghost.

Travis couldn't stop shivering. It was partly that the day was cooling down, partly the way the smoke from the fire and the mist from the lake moved about the edge of the island like dancing clouds, and partly the tone of the older ranger's voice as he told the story.

Tom Thomson's body had surfaced, "all swollen and coming apart, white skin waving in the water," and his fiancée, Miss Trainor from the cottage across the way (he pointed with his pipe), had demanded to see the body. No one wanted her to see it, but she insisted. She would believe to her dying day that this had been no accident.

"They buried him right away. Had to. Not to put too fine a point on it, he was rotting. They took him by cart up that hill I showed you, wrapped him in a cloth, and buried him. Next day this undertaker shows up, claims he's been sent by the Thomson family, and refuses any offers of help to dig up the body so he can take it back to where the family lived.

"The undertaker went up there with a big black coffin and a lantern and worked through the dark night. In the morning, when the men went up by horse and cart to get him, he was sitting there happy as a clam, the coffin all sealed up and ready to go.

"Some of the men – and I knew some of them, too – claimed he hadn't done a thing. Couldn't have done anything; nobody could dig up and move that body all by himself. One of the rangers who helped load the coffin on the train said he could hear sand sliding inside. The sand all slid to one side when they set it down. Shouldn't have done that if a body was inside, should it?"

"No," answered Fahd unnecessarily.

"There was a lot never explained about this. If they took his body, how come his fiancée, Miss Trainor, kept cleaning up his grave there on that hill? She did it for more'n forty years – right up until she died.

"A few years back a bunch of men on the lake decided to check and dug up where Tom'd been buried. Found a skeleton there with a hole in the skull. Government and police came in and investigated and claimed it wasn't Tom at all but some Indian. Said he'd probably been buried there long, long ago. Makes no sense to me. No Indians around here that I ever knew of – but they always said Tom Thomson looked like he was Indian with those high cheekbones of his.

"One of the old-timers on the lake even said there was a third grave, that they'd gone up and stolen Tom's body away after the first burial up on the hill to make sure he stayed here at Canoe Lake – and that was why the undertaker had nothing but sand in his coffin. He wouldn't admit he couldn't find anything, see?"

"Yeah," said Fahd.

"This old guy said he was going to show people once and for all what had happened. Told his story one late winter's day to a newspaper reporter, and then came back here to that old house up the narrows where he and his brother lived. Was walking across the iced-over lake with their groceries when he fell through – right there, believe it, right at the spot where they found Tom."

No one said a word this time. A loon called far out on the lake, sending shivers up more than a dozen spines. The fire cracked, causing several of the Owls to jump.

"There was a woman, lived here for years, and she swore that on a night with a mist just like this she got lost in her canoe. This man in a canoe slips out of the mist, smiles, and guides her back to shore. She swore it was Tom – but he'd been dead nearly twenty years.

"Another time two guides were travelling behind a party of American fishermen when a man suddenly appeared out of the mist and called towards them that there'd been a drowning at the rapids up ahead. Sure enough, when they got there one of the American fishermen's canoes had gone over and a man was lost. Both guides swore it had been Tom who called to them.

"There's some say you can hear him paddling by on a night like this . . ."

The ranger cocked his ear. The silence was astonishing, and all strained to listen. The loon called again. The fire sparked. Travis could hear the light lick of water – Tom paddling? – but realized after a while it was just the lake playing on the rocks along the shore.

They sat a moment, the smoke and mist swirling about them.

"*I think I hear him now!*" the ranger said in an urgent whisper.

They strained to hear.

"*What a crock!*" Nish whispered in Travis's ear.

"*Look to the point!*" the ranger hissed.

Travis looked, but could see nothing. He strained and thought he could sense the mist moving, and a distant object growing. It had to be his imagination.

But it wasn't. The object, whatever it was, grew closer, and slowly the sound of a canoe in the water fell over the camp and drowned out all other sound, their ears filling with the light kiss of a well-stroked paddle on water. It was almost as if a wind had come up – suddenly the mist parted and a dark canoe slid out of the night, the water licking on the sides, the bow sizzling lightly as it broke the water.

"OH MY GOD!" screamed Sam, bringing everyone to their feet.

"*Fake!*" whispered Nish. "*What a wuss she is!*"

The canoe came closer. The older ranger moved back, as if caught by surprise, and as he moved, everyone moved.

"*Who goes there?*" he called. There was real urgency in his voice.

Sam screamed. Nish giggled.

But Sam wasn't the only one frightened. Travis could hear Fahd whimper. There was a quick shuffling movement on the shore now, almost as if all the Owls were trying to gather so tight together they would become one.

The canoe came closer, closer.

At that moment a white light appeared on the water. Cast up from inside the canoe, it revealed a man paddling. His face, streaked with dark shadow, was ferocious.

*Sam screamed!*

*Jenny screamed!*

*Lars screamed!*

*Jesse screamed!*

*Sam screamed again!*

Travis remembered his disposable camera. It was in his pocket. He pulled it out.

The flash exploded like sunlight over the scene. For an instant, they could see everything: the grey-green canoe, the dark-haired paddler, his paddle raised for the next stroke . . .

Then the flash was gone. And at the same instant the light casting shadows on the paddler's face was gone, and, in another instant, the canoe itself was gone, with not even the sound of a paddle touching water.

"*What the devil was that?*" the ranger asked.

"T–Tom T–Thomson," Fahd suggested.

"*Wow!*" whispered Nish with great sarcasm. "*How'd he ever figure that out?*"

"I don't . . . know," the ranger said. "I've never seen anything like that before in my life." He sounded shaken.

"*He probably sees it every week at exactly the same time,*" hissed Nish.

Travis didn't know what to think. If it had been a trick, it was a spectacularly successful one. He was shaking like a leaf, and so, too, he suspected, were the others. Probably even Nish.

But it couldn't have been a real ghost. It couldn't have been Tom Thomson – could it? No. Not possible.

"Check around," whispered Nish. "Where's Joe Hall?"

Travis looked about the campsite. He could account for everyone – the two rangers, Mr. Dillinger, the Screech Owls – but not Joe Hall. Nish might have guessed correctly. Had Joe

Hall sneaked off and slipped a canoe into the water on the other side of the island?

But there was Joe Hall now! He was moving near the trees with Sarah and Sam, an arm around each of them. Sam seemed terrified. She was sobbing as she held on to Joe Hall's powerful arm.

"*Look at her!*" hissed Nish. "*She's bawling like a baby. What a wuss!*"

The rangers were already packing up quickly to go. They drowned the fire and loaded the barge and told everyone to get on. Joe Hall held a flashlight so no one would fall climbing on.

A large flashlight? *Perhaps he had also held it between his knees and shone it up onto his face!*

Travis borrowed one of the rangers' flashes on the pretence of helping others pick their way along the shore, and he used it to sweep over Joe Hall and examine him. His knees were soaking wet – *as if he'd been kneeling in a canoe!*

"It was him," announced Nish, delighted with their detective work.

Maybe that was what Joe Hall had been whispering about with the ranger, thought Travis: a plan to trick the Owls into thinking the ghost of Tom Thomson had appeared.

"We'll find out for sure tomorrow," said Travis.

"How's that? You expect him to confess?"

Travis smiled and held out his camera. "I took his picture, remember?"

"I can hardly wait to show her."

"*Her?*" Travis asked.

"*Sam! Who else?*"

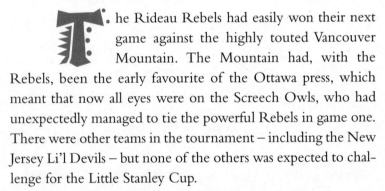

he Rideau Rebels had easily won their next game against the highly touted Vancouver Mountain. The Mountain had, with the Rebels, been the early favourite of the Ottawa press, which meant that now all eyes were on the Screech Owls, who had unexpectedly managed to tie the powerful Rebels in game one. There were other teams in the tournament – including the New Jersey Li'l Devils – but none of the others was expected to challenge for the Little Stanley Cup.

Nish was in a wonderful mood. He'd come back to the camp to find his boxers down from the flagpole and returned to the tent. Even better, he figured he was about to go one-up on Sam, once Travis turned his camera in to the little shop down the road and got his photos back. He'd be delighted to show her what had terrified her at Canoe Lake: the very person she'd run to for comfort.

They arrived at the Kanata Recreation Centre early, and Joe Hall asked Travis if he could see him a moment out in the corridor. *Had he noticed the camera?* Travis wondered. *Was he going to try to get it from him so the identity of "Tom Thomson" would remain a mystery?*

But Joe Hall had no intention of talking about photographs. He had his stick with him – the strange stick that Sarah had noticed was as straight as a ruler and seemed somehow homemade. He told Travis to bring his stick along as well.

With Joe Hall leading the way, the two walked through to the smaller of the two rinks, which was not being used. It was cold and empty, with fog gathering in one corner of the ice surface on such a hot day. It made Travis think momentarily of the canoe in the mist, but Joe Hall didn't want to talk about ghosts either, real or otherwise.

"I like what I see in you, Travis," Joe Hall said.

"Thanks," said Travis.

Joe Hall dropped a puck he had been carrying in his pocket. It sounded like a rifle shot in the empty rink. He stickhandled back and forth a few times, the straight blade as comfortable on one side of the puck as the other.

"You had a chance to win that opener for us, you know," Joe Hall said.

"I guess," admitted Travis. He knew what the coach was getting at. The drop pass to Sarah that didn't work.

"I want you to stand on the blueline," said Joe Hall. "And just watch something – okay?"

"Okay," said Travis.

Travis hurried to the blueline, sliding easily in his sneakers. He wished he was in his skates. He'd feel taller, more himself.

Joe Hall began moving away from Travis towards the net, stickhandling easily. He moved almost as if daydreaming, the puck clicking regularly from one side to the other as he moved in and stared, as if a goalie were there, waiting.

Suddenly there was a louder click – and the puck was shooting straight back at Travis! It was right on Travis's blade, but it had happened so fast it caught him completely off guard. Travis fumbled the pass, letting the puck jump outside the blueline.

"How'd you do that?" Travis asked.

"Fire it back," said Joe Hall. "And this time be ready for it."

Travis passed the puck back. Joe Hall again stickhandled back and forth, the steady click of puck on wood almost soothing. Then the louder click – and the puck was shooting back at Travis! He was ready this time, and could have fired a shot instantly.

"I still don't know how you're doing that!" Travis called.

"Come and see," Joe Hall called back.

Travis skidded on his sneakers to where Joe Hall was waiting. Travis gave him the puck and he stickhandled a bit, then he brought the heel of his stick down hard and fast on the front edge of the puck, sending it like a bullet between his legs and against the corner boards.

Joe Hall looked up and flashed his amazing smile. "'Rat' Westwick came up with it," he said. "He called it the 'heel pass.' He and 'One-Eyed' Frank McGee used to bamboozle other teams with it. They never knew when it was coming. Watch."

Joe Hall retrieved the puck and stickhandled again, effortlessly, and then suddenly the heel came down hard on the puck instead of passing over it again, and the puck shot, true and accurately, right between Joe Hall's legs and into the corner.

"Let me try," said Travis.

He took the puck, stickhandled, and chopped down, but the puck stayed where it was.

"You have to hit the front edge," said Joe Hall.

Travis tried again. This time the puck flew, but into his own feet. It wasn't clean and straight like it was when Joe Hall did it.

"It's your stick," said Joe Hall. "Try mine."

Travis handed over his new stick – Easton, special curve, narrow shaft, ultralight – and took Joe Hall's from him.

It felt heavy. It felt wrong. He set the blade on the ice, and it looked to the left-handed Travis like a right-hand stick. As if the curve was going the wrong way. But it wasn't a right stick either; it was perfectly straight. There was no name on it, only "J. Hall" pencilled near the top of the handle.

"Where'd you buy this thing?" Travis said.

"You can't buy them," said Joe Hall. He didn't offer where it had come from.

Travis worked the puck back and forth. He lost it several times, being used to the cup of a curve that was no longer there.

"Try the heel pass," Joe Hall said.

Travis did. The stick came down perfectly on the puck, and it shot straight and true between his legs. Joe Hall was waiting and timed a shot perfectly with Travis's stick. The puck stuck high in the far corner of the net.

"Wow!" said Travis. "That worked perfectly."

"You like to try the stick in a game?" Joe Hall asked.

Travis felt the stick again. It still didn't feel right to him. "Maybe," he said, looking up to make sure he wasn't hurting Joe Hall's feelings. "But I'm so used to mine."

Joe Hall took his stick back and handed Travis his. "Suit yourself," he said. "But you'll never master the heel pass with that curved blade."

Game two was against the Sudbury Minors, a gritty little team with tremendous heart but limited talent. The Owls jumped to a quick three-goal lead on a clean breakaway by Dmitri, a hard blast by Andy, and an exquisite end-to-end rush by Sarah in which she split the Sudbury defence and roofed a backhand as she fell into the corner.

Travis noticed almost immediately when Nish began to wander. Had Muck been here, he would have called Nish on it immediately, but Joe Hall was new to the team, and Mr. Dillinger and Data had other duties apart from trying to figure out when Nish was about to go off the deep end.

The first hint was on a play when icing was waved off and Nish picked up the puck in his own corner and failed to hit Sarah with the usual breakout pass. Instead, Nish started his old river-hockey routine, trying to stickhandle through the entire team so he could be the hero and score the goal. He made it all the way down the ice, moving superbly, but he cranked his shot off the crossbar. Which only made matters worse from then on. Now Nish was absolutely determined to score.

Travis could see Joe Hall's frustration mounting. He told Nish to stay back, but Nish ignored him. The Owls were up 6−0 when Nish tried a stupid play. Turning his stick backwards, he tried to skate up the ice with the puck held by the knob of the handle.

Muck hated hot-dogging. Perhaps it was because Muck wasn't here that Nish was getting so out of control, but he picked the wrong team to try to humiliate. The Sudbury team might have been a bit low on talent, but they lacked nothing in courage. Nish was barely over centre when the captain of the Minors hit him so hard he flew in a complete somersault. He landed on his skates, wobbling a bit before he crashed into the boards.

The referee was signalling charging. Nish should have been happy – it would have given the Owls the advantage – but he wanted revenge. He jumped to his feet and charged the Sudbury captain back. The crowd roared as Nish put his shoulder into his opponent. The big Minors captain never moved. Nish shook off his gloves, deliberately tossing them so they struck the other player. The linesmen moved in quickly before anything could happen. Nish was lucky the referee called him only for roughing – one blow would have meant an automatic game ejection.

Nish knew his shifts were over when he finally got out of the penalty box. He skated casually across the ice to the Screech Owls' bench and yanked open the gate.

"Wrong door," said Joe Hall, his lips tight.

"What do you mean?" asked Nish.

"The Zamboni doors for you, buddy. You're through this game, *and the next*. We don't need that."

Nish's mouth went so round it could have held a puck.

"W–w–what?" he stammered.

"You heard me. Get off the ice."

Nish looked desperately around for support, but he found none, and then began to make his way to the far end of the rink. He stared at his teammates as he passed by, but none would look back. None except Sam.

She laughed.

Nish paused, about to say something stupid, but then thought better of it. He didn't need any more trouble from Joe Hall.

The game seemed to die after that. Sudbury had clearly given up, and thanks to lessons taught them by Muck Munro, the Owls weren't inclined to run up the score any further.

They played the clock out cleanly and quickly, working more on their passing than their shots, careful at all times to remain in position.

Travis had one glorious moment near the end of the game when Dmitri flipped a pass high from his own blueline and Travis gloved it down right at the red line. He had the puck, and he had space to work. He looked up: one defence back, Sarah coming up clear from her own end.

Travis began moving with the puck, happy with the way it felt on his stick, glad he'd stuck to the Easton instead of taking up Joe Hall's offer of the straight blade.

He cut towards centre, the defence keeping an eye on him but refusing to commit. Travis worked the puck across the blueline, then cut across again so that he drew the defender with him while Sarah moved across the blueline and into position.

He laid the puck out in front, exactly where he wanted it. He stickhandled once, twice, then came down hard on the puck with the heel of the stick.

The puck shot to the side and into the corner!

The play had failed, but it had still fooled the defence, who turned to chase the lost puck. Sarah was there ahead of him, and she quickly fired the puck back to Travis, who snapped it into the open side.

Screech Owls 7, Sudbury Minors 0.

He had scored, and his teammates were cheering, but Travis knew he had failed. He looked up at Joe Hall as he came off the ice, teammates slapping his pants and shoulders.

"Wrong stick," said Joe Hall.

"I know," said Travis.

"It's there any time you want it."

Travis smiled, not yet ready. "Thanks," he said. "Maybe next game."

# 10

"I've figured it out," Nish said.

Travis didn't dare ask what. *How to behave during a hockey game? How to be a real team player? How Joe Hall pulled off that Tom Thomson stunt?* It could have been anything.

They were lying in the tent, a light rain drumming on the canvas. They'd practised earlier and had eaten and were resting.

"Figured what out?" Fahd finally asked. He couldn't resist.

"How I'm going to get her."

"Get who?"

"Oh, just the one who tried to make a fool of me on the river, just the one who put my gauchies up the flagpole, just the biggest pain in the butt this team has ever known, that's all."

Travis couldn't resist. "Who's that?" he asked.

"Very funny," said Nish. He was sucking loudly on a Tootsie Roll, offering none around as usual, and thinking out loud, also as usual. "It's got to be embarrassing, right? Really embarrassing."

"Why?" Fahd asked.

"Because she embarrassed me. All that 'Ka-wa-bun-ga' crap and stealing my boxers. It's got to be just as good from my side."

"Let it go," said Travis. "She's a good sport. The team likes her."

"This isn't about the team," countered Nish. "This is about her and me."

"You're too competitive," said Lars.

"Not at all," said Nish. "I'm just getting even. Like in a tie game. What's competitive about that? I don't have to win, just get even."

*Yeah, right*, Travis thought to himself. *Who's he kidding?* But he said nothing.

Nish went on. "You know where the women's washroom is?"

"You mean the outhouse," Fahd corrected.

"Whatever – you know where I mean."

"You'd better be careful there," warned Travis.

"Nah. She has to go sometime, doesn't she? I mean, girls do go to the bathroom, don't they?"

Lars couldn't believe it. "You want us to sing, '*We-know-where-you're-go-ing!*'? That's a bit childish even for *you*, isn't it?"

"Nah, no singing. I got a much more sophisticated plan than that. Say she goes in and shuts the door, and a few seconds later there's this enormous explosion that everybody in the camp hears. You think she wouldn't find that a bit embarrassing?"

"You can't bomb an outhouse!" protested Fahd.

"Not a bomb, stupid – a harmless cannon cracker. Like the ones they set off on Canada Day."

"Where are you going to get a cannon cracker?"

"They sell fireworks at that little shop," he said.

"Not to kids they don't," said Travis.

"They'll sell to me," said Nish. "Just you watch."

"How would that work?" Fahd asked. "How would you set it off, even if you got some fireworks?"

"Very simple. The boys' outhouse is right next to it. I run a fuse from one to the other and you signal me."

"*Who?*" they all asked at once.

"*You!*" Nish said loudly. "*My friends, that's who?*"

"Those pictures should be ready," Travis said later that afternoon. "You want to come pick them up with me?"

"I'll be right there," Nish said. First, however, he dashed into the tent. Travis thought he was writing something down. It wasn't like Nish to keep a diary.

"What was that all about?" Travis asked when Nish returned. "Writing home?"

"You'll see," Nish answered. "Let's get going."

It was a brief walk down the highway to the store. It had everything – food, milk, videos to rent, live bait, a film drop-off and, of course, fireworks. It was run by an elderly couple. The woman was French – Sarah had talked with her for quite a while – and her husband was hard of hearing. Apart from Sarah, no one was able to have much of a conversation with either of them.

"I'm here to pick up my pictures," Travis said as they entered the store.

"Eh?" the old man called back, cupping a hand behind his ear.

"My photos," Travis said, louder. "They're supposed to be ready today." He waved his pick-up slip. The old man recognized it and grabbed it out of Travis's hand. He led him to the rear of the store, where the film was kept.

Nish wandered over to the old woman. He smiled his best Nish smile, the smile that meant something unexpected was coming.

Travis couldn't see what was going on. The old man was rummaging through the photos waiting to be picked up, checking Travis's slip against a dozen numbers. Nish and the old woman were bent over a sheet of paper, the old woman asking questions.

Finally the old man came up with the processed film. He handed it over to Travis. "That'll be $12.81, young man."

Travis fumbled with his wallet. Just like Nish, he thought, to make himself scarce when the bills were being paid. He knew Nish would be first to scoop up the picture that showed Joe Hall in the Tom Thomson canoe.

Travis paid up and left. Nish was standing at the front door, counting out his own change. He had a large bag under his arm.

"What's in there?" Travis asked.

"I'll tell you outside. You get the pictures?"

"Yeah, let's go."

Once out and back on the highway, Nish looked around like a man about to hold up a bank. Then he pulled open the bag so Travis could look in.

Inside were dozens of firecrackers: some large, some small and attached to lengths of string, even a few rockets and Roman candles.

"How did you get all that?"

"I bought 'em. She even threw in a few extra for free."

"You can't buy fireworks. You're not old enough."

Nish grinned. "Apparently I am – when I have a note from the church camp that this is for a special ceremony."

"*You lied?*" Travis asked, exasperated with his friend.

Nish shrugged innocently, looking deeply offended.

"Lie? Me? Where's the lie? The note was written on church camp stationery. And it is going to be a special ceremony – a *very* special ceremony."

"But you wrote the note yourself!"

"We never discussed that," Nish said triumphantly. "She didn't ask, so I didn't say."

"And you can't call your stupid plan a 'special ceremony.'"

"It will be when you see it, pal. It will be, I promise you. Now let's have a look at those pictures."

Reluctantly, Travis peeled open the flap of the envelope. He pulled the photos out and began thumbing through them. The moose. The picnic grounds. The barge. . . . He could see the edge of the next photo, showing mist and water.

Travis held his breath. Now they would know. He pulled the photograph free of the others.

It was Canoe Lake all right, the mist swirling on the water. *But nothing else!*

"*You blew it!*" Nish said angrily.

"But I couldn't have. I caught him perfectly."

"You blew it, obviously. There's nothing there. You either snapped too soon or too late. You blew it – and now I got nothing to shove under Sam's nose."

Nish yanked the photo away and spun it into the ditch. He patted his haul of fireworks. "Thank heaven I got this. Good thing *somebody's* reliable," he said, and began walking back to the camp.

Travis made his way down into the ditch and retrieved the photograph from where it had lodged in a milkweed plant. He started walking, well behind Nish, who was hurrying ahead, happily swinging his bag full of treasure. He carefully studied the photo again.

Nothing.

Nish was right. He'd failed to catch the canoe or the person paddling in it. Too soon or too late.

But it made no sense. How could it show nothing? Travis wondered.

He'd seen the canoe light up when the flash went off – how else would they have known that the canoe had been grey-green, the same colour as Tom Thomson's canoe? And yet this photograph showed nothing but mist and water.

No canoe.

No paddler.

Could it really have been Tom Thomson's ghost? No, Travis decided. Impossible.

But if it was Joe Hall pulling a trick – he remembered the flashlight and the wet knees – then where was Joe Hall? Why was *he* not in the picture?

# 11

"This game is a must win for us," said Joe Hall. He was standing at the front of the dressing room, leaning on his straight-as-a-ruler stick. He seemed worried.

More than worried, thought Travis. He looked ill. His face was pasty, and he was sweating. And it seemed, at times, as if he was leaning on the stick for support.

Nish remained in the corner, arms folded. He was the only Screech Owl not dressed. He sat by his locker, staring defiantly. *If this game is so darned important*, he seemed to be saying, *how come I'm not playing?*

"I know what you're thinking," said Joe Hall, almost as if Nish had been talking out loud. He walked over to Nish and prodded him gently with his stick. He smiled, but the smile had lost its former brilliance.

"Joe doesn't look very good," Sarah whispered beside Travis. She had noticed as well.

"You might make a difference in the game," Joe Hall said to Nish. "You might make *the* difference."

Nish seemed happy to hear this. Travis could tell his best friend was fighting off a big smile.

"I'm not a fool," Joe Hall continued. "I can tell when a player has talent or not – and you, sir, have big talent. You might well make the difference in the game . . ." He paused, seeming to have to gather his energy. "But this game can make a difference in your life . . . and I think that's more important."

Nish looked up. He didn't have a clue what Joe Hall was getting at.

"You've got a temper, haven't you?" he said to Nish.

Nish shrugged.

Joe Hall turned to the team. "He's got a temper, doesn't he?"

"The worst," said Sarah.

Nish sneered at her.

"I had a temper," Joe Hall said. "It was the worst part of my game. It almost cost me my career. I had to learn to control it, or else. Who was it asked me what my nickname was the other day?"

"I did," said Fahd, raising his hand like he had to go to the bathroom.

"Well, I didn't tell you what it was, did I?"

"No," said Fahd, his hand still up.

"They called me 'Bad' Joe Hall – and I hated it."

No one spoke. They could hear the sound of Mr. Dillinger's skate-sharpening machine hard at work in the corridor. Joe Hall stumbled slightly, caught himself on Nish's locker. Nish looked up, frightened, but whether he thought Joe Hall was going to fall on him or strike him, Travis couldn't tell.

"You're too good a kid to get hit with a tag like that," said Joe Hall. "Besides, 'Bad' Wayne Nishikawa sounds pretty stupid, doesn't it?" He smiled, and for an instant the old brilliance was back.

Nish was flushing red. "I don't know," he mumbled. Travis knew what Nish was thinking: he'd *love* a nickname like that!

"You play *with* a label, you *become* that label," said Joe Hall. "People came to see 'Bad' Joe Hall, so I gave them 'Bad' Joe Hall – and by the time I realized how stupid I was being . . . it was too late."

Travis knew that Joe Hall was talking about Nish, and about how Nish had to grow up if he ever wanted to be a real player. But there was something more he was trying to say, something about Joe Hall himself. And Travis didn't know what.

"So you're going to watch this game," said Joe Hall. "And I want you to watch a particular player out there all game long – and learn from her. Understand?"

Nish looked up, eyes batting in confusion. "*Her?*" he asked.

"Sam."

"*Sam?*" Nish asked, incredulous.

"Yes, Sam. She's so good at letting nothing get under her skin, she ends up under *their* skin. You saw it the other games."

Joe Hall was right. Sam laughed when she was dumped. She laughed when Kenzie MacNeil sprayed snow in her face. She just laughed, then she kept on doing whatever would drive them crazy.

"I have to watch her?" Nish asked, not believing.

"Every single shift," said Joe Hall. "Now let's get out there!"

The Screech Owls rose to cheers and backslapping. Travis, as team captain, waited to go out last, and he alone saw the exchange of glances between Nish and Sam as she left the dressing room.

Sam's eyes filled with triumph.

Nish's eyes squeezed tight with revenge.

Sam was certainly well worth watching against the Vancouver Mountain. The Owls were in tough, with the Mountain also having a real chance of reaching the final if only they could beat the Screech Owls. The Rideau Rebels had easily won their third game against the team from New Jersey, and were sitting atop the standings, waiting only to discover who they would meet in the final: the Owls or the Mountain.

The Mountain were looking to win. They were quick, smart, and strong. By the end of the first, with Jenny struggling in the Screech Owls' net, the Mountain were ahead 3−0. If they could hang on to their lead, they were on their way to the final.

Travis had several chances, but couldn't seem to get a good shot. As soon as he took possession of the puck in the Mountain end, they closed in on him and took away any space for him to work with. He tried setting up Sarah and Dmitri, but the Mountain were keying on Sarah's playmaking and Dmitri's speed and neither of them ever seemed free.

Sam began the turnaround midway through the second. She had already played extremely well, and had yet to be scored on when on the ice, but it was her offensive move that caught the attention of the large crowd. She blocked a shot just inside her own blueline and, still down, used her wide sweep to chip the puck up along the boards by centre. Derek Dillinger beat the Mountain defence to it, sending a cross-ice pass to little Simon Milliken, and Simon crossed the blueline and fired the puck hard around the boards.

Derek made the blueline just in time to keep the puck from sailing out. He kicked it up to his stick, deked towards the boards, then sent a sharp backwards pass to the high slot, where Sam was charging under full steam.

Travis had seen this play before – only it was always Nish charging up centre to join the play late.

Sam faked a slapshot, stepped around the single defence between her and the goal, fired a hard shot the Mountain goalie stopped by stacking his pads, and then clipped her own rebound over him and in under the crossbar.

The tide had turned for the Owls. Inspired by Sam's goal, they kept coming against the strong Mountain team, and soon it seemed only a matter of time until the Owls scored again.

It was Fahd, of all people, who gave them their next goal. He scored his second goal of the tournament on a hard, low shot that screamed right along the ice, through a crowd in front of the net, and caught the goalie by surprise as it ripped just under his stick.

Ten minutes into the third, Sarah took a beautiful pass from Sam and flew up the ice with Dmitri and one defence back. Travis had seen this play a hundred times. Across to Dmitri, back to Sarah, back to Dmitri, the water bottle flying against the glass.

Screech Owls 3, Vancouver Mountain 3.

At the end of regulation they were tied.

The first game had been left with the score even, but now they needed a tie-breaker to decide which team would advance to the final. The tournament rules called for immediate sudden-death overtime, with four-a-side for the first two minutes, then three-a-side, then two-a-side.

After four minutes with no score, the referee signalled for two-a-side. Travis was halfway over the boards when he felt his sweater being pulled back.

It was Joe Hall. Travis wasn't going.

"Sarah and Sam!" Joe Hall called out.

Travis slunk back onto the bench. He'd been caught by surprise. He'd assumed it would be him and Sarah out – captain and top player – but now it was Sarah and Sam. Two girls. He could see the Rideau Rebels up in the stands, laughing and pointing. The big centre, MacNeil, was on his feet, shouting something, but Travis couldn't make out what it was. He guessed it wasn't complimentary.

He turned and looked at Nish, standing behind the bench in his street clothes. Nish had a smirk on his face and was shaking his head in disbelief.

Things soon changed, however, as Sam chased down a loose puck and used her powerful body to ride off the Mountain player who got there first. She turned as soon as the puck came free and lifted the puck so high it very nearly hit the clock, the rolling puck falling with a slap just across centre.

Sarah had read the play perfectly. She picked up the puck in full flight, completely free of the defence.

Across the ice, the Mountain coach almost came over the boards screaming. "*Offside! Offside!*" But the linesman had waved it off.

The crowd was on its feet.

Sarah came in gracefully, stickhandling carefully, and moved to her backhand – or so it seemed! She made the motion, but just as it appeared she was shifting to go to the short side, she moved the puck back to her forehand and fired a hard wrist shot.

The Mountain goalie, who had a great glove hand, got a small piece of the shot – but not enough.

The red light came on!

The Mountain coach was screaming again!

The Owls poured over the boards, heading to pile onto Sam and Sarah.

They were going to the final!

Travis threw down his stick and gloves and hurled himself into the writhing mess in the corner. Buried somewhere underneath was the player who had set up the winner and the player who had scored it. He could see neither of them.

But he could see Nish. Still standing on the bench. On his face, a look of shock.

# 12

*"PERFECT! ABSOLUTELY PERFECT!"*

Nish sat in the centre of the tent rubbing his hands together and chuckling. Travis had rarely, if ever, seen his friend so pleased with himself.

"I've really outdone myself on this one, I think."

"You've come undone," corrected Travis. "You're nuts."

"It's going to work. I promise you."

Nish had been working away like a mad scientist any chance he got. He'd taken apart several of the larger fireworks, saved all the powder inside, and used the fuses to build one very long one. He'd sneaked into the women's outhouse and wired several cannon crackers deep below the seat. Then he'd run his long fuse out through a crack in the outhouse wall and over to the men's' outhouse a short distance away, where he'd hidden it carefully from sight.

"How did you stand it?" Fahd wanted to know when he heard.

"I held my breath, stupid – and worked in shifts."

"I'd have gagged," said Fahd.

"How are you going to catch her going?" Lars asked.

"She'll have to go sometime," Nish said, lightly clapping his hands together, "and when she does, I'll be there with my trusty lighter."

He pulled out a lighter and flicked it on, holding the flame out for all to see.

"Where'd you get that?" Travis asked.

"My good friends up the road," Nish said.

Travis shook his head. "I don't want to know."

Travis left the mad scientist and his admiring throng and set out to walk around the camp. It was a beautiful afternoon, the day before the final game, and the sun was gold and dancing on the river. There was a pair of Canada geese near the shore with a family of puffy little ones, and Travis watched awhile and tried to take his mind off everything. Nish's mad scheme. The mysterious photograph. Joe Hall.

He was worried about Joe Hall. Sarah had noticed the coach's ill health as well, but he'd seemed to rally for the game against the Vancouver Mountain, and by game's end they'd forgotten all about it.

Travis decided to track down Joe Hall and see for himself how he was doing. He headed up the nature trail that led out past the point. His cottage had to be somewhere up that direction.

"Hey! Where're ya goin'?"

It was Sarah. He turned and waved back.

"Just going for a walk."

Sarah smiled. "Like some company?"

"Sure."

Sarah hurried to join him on the trail. "You're looking for Joe Hall, aren't you?" she said in a quiet voice.

"I guess," Travis answered. He really wasn't sure what he was trying to do.

They walked out past the point, then took to the shoreline and made their way upstream. The bush was tangled and the rocks sharp, but by working half through knee-deep water and half through the underbrush, they steadily made their way.

There was no sign of a cottage.

"*Hey!*" a voice called. "*What're you kids up to?*"

Travis and Sarah stopped dead in their tracks. They tried to make out who it was through the thick brush, but could only see a figure moving and a flash of something yellow. Yellow fur.

It was a dog – the setter that belonged to the farmer who cut the grass at the camp. Travis felt his heart begin to beat again.

"Hi!" Sarah called when the farmer came into sight. The setter raced at them, leaping high in an attempt to lick Sarah. She caught the dog by the fur of its collar, settling it and patting it gently.

The farmer seemed to recognize them now. "Youse two are from the camp, eh?"

"Yeah. I'm Travis Lindsay. This is Sarah Cuthbertson."

"You both swim?"

"Yes."

"Well, you got to be careful walking along there, you know. Not much of a current here, but enough to drown more than a few that slipped in."

"We'll be careful," said Travis. "We're looking for Joe Hall's cottage."

"Who?"

"Joe Hall – our coach for the tournament. He's staying in a cottage up here."

The farmer shook his head. He took off his cap, sweat heavy on his brow, and rubbed it off with his shirt sleeve.

"No Hall along here," he said. "No cottage for that matter. Next property north is a park."

"There's no cottage here at all?"

"None's that anyone can use," the man said. "Abandoned place up around the next point – but nobody's been there for years. People owned it must have died, I think."

"You're sure there's been nobody there?"

"I'm sure. They'd have to cross my land to get to it, and I ain't seen nobody around here all week but you two kids. And what I can't see my dog smells – and she ain't said nothing about any stranger being around here."

"Can we walk further up?" Sarah asked.

"Long as you're careful," the farmer said. "Don't go near the cottage, though – it's a trap. Floor wouldn't hold you."

"We'll be careful," Travis said again.

The farmer nodded and moved back towards his field. They could see a large green tractor in the distance. He must have been taking off hay.

The dog stayed with them, dancing around them and splashing out into the water after imagined sticks. Travis was glad of the company.

Before long they rounded the next point.

"There it is!" Sarah said.

At first Travis couldn't see it, then gradually it came into focus: a black and grey, sun-bleached shack so old it seemed to blend in with the landscape. He could see broken windows, and a large tree branch that had fallen and caved in a portion of the roof.

"Let's get a closer look!" Sarah said.

"Okay," Travis said. He could hear the lack of confidence in his own voice, but Sarah was already splashing ahead, taking a shortcut through the shallows. Travis followed and expected the setter to splash ahead and catch up to Sarah, but there was no dog.

He turned. The setter was sitting there, whimpering, her tail wagging fast, her eyes filled with worry.

"What's wrong, girl?" Travis called.

Sarah stopped. "What's up?"

"The dog won't move."

Sarah shrugged. "Maybe she's trained to stay on her own property. Don't worry about her – she'll find her way back."

Travis stepped out into the water to join Sarah. It was cold against his bare legs and it tickled. The rocks were slimy. He slipped and nearly fell several times, but soon Travis and Sarah were almost to the broken-down dock that had once belonged to the cottage.

The dog was moaning. She was still sitting on the other side of the shallow bay, whining and wagging her tail hopefully.

"She's chicken!" said Travis.

"No way! Setters *love* water," Sarah said. "She's just trained not to wander, that's all."

"I guess," Travis said, but he wasn't so sure. Something was making him feel uneasy, too.

There was another moan, louder this time.

"Stupid dog," Travis said.

Sarah had stopped abruptly. "That wasn't the dog!" she whispered.

Travis felt a sharp chill run down his spine. He listened, and heard a low sorrowful groan from the cottage.

"I'm getting outta here!" he said.

"What if it's Joe Hall?" Sarah hissed.

"It can't be. The farmer never saw him. The dog would have known if someone was here."

Sarah pointed back to the setter, still watching, still fretting. "Maybe the dog *does* know," she said.

Travis felt his heart pound hard against his chest. He tried to speak, but his voice broke and creaked. "We're . . . not supposed to go in," he reminded Sarah.

"What if he needs help?"

"It's not even him," said Travis. "It's some animal. Maybe a skunk. Maybe even a *bear*."

"I'm going in," she said.

Sarah stepped up on shore. The dog on the far side of the water howled and barked. She began running back and forth frantically along the shore, but was afraid to come to them.

Sarah stepped cautiously along the dry, broken planks of the dock. Several were rotten and had turned to dust around the rusted nails. But she picked her way carefully, and Travis followed.

They could see where once there had been a path to the cottage. It was overgrown now and barely identifiable. Sarah pushed through, lowering her head against the flicking branches.

Travis was right behind her.

When she reached the cottage Sarah held up her hand for him to stop. The only sound was the frantic whining and barking of the setter in the distance.

"You hear anything?" Sarah asked.

"No," Travis said. He wanted to bolt. He wanted to run all the way back to his sleeping bag and jump into it and pretend that he'd never even heard of a cottage upstream from the camp.

Sarah stepped up onto the broken-down porch. A chipmunk scurried under, chattering wildly and frightening them both. But Sarah kept going. She came to the door and turned the latch. It swung open, surprisingly easily. Almost as if it had been recently oiled.

They stepped inside, Travis brushing aside cobwebs that clung to his hands like cotton candy. He almost gagged from the smell of must and rot.

Sarah stopped. She was shivering, uncertain where to head.

Travis didn't dare move.

*Then he felt a large, cold, clammy hand settle on the back of his neck!*

# 13

"What are you two doing here?"

The voice was familiar, though weak. Travis turned and stared up into the drawn, pale face of Joe Hall. He didn't look like "Bad" Joe Hall at all. He looked like "Sick" Joe Hall.

"We, we were looking for you," Travis admitted.

"Are you all right?" Sarah asked.

There was a long silence, then Joe Hall sighed. He seemed very tired.

"I'm fine," he said, unconvincingly. "You may as well go ahead in — but step carefully."

They edged past old furniture and even raspberry shoots that had pushed up inside the abandoned cottage. They passed through into a sitting room, where the light was falling in shafts through torn curtains.

There was a cot in the room. Joe Hall must have been lying there.

The light was better here, and the two Screech Owls took the opportunity to look more carefully at their new friend. Joe Hall looked terrible. His eyes seemed sunken and every few moments he shook from the inside out with a deep, quiet cough.

"You're sick!" Sarah said.

"It's just the flu," Joe Hall said. "I'll be fine for the game."

Sarah pushed aside the tattered curtains. The sun poured in through the broken and cobwebbed window, causing Joe Hall to blink and Sarah's and Travis's eyes to widen. He looked terrible. He'd lost weight.

"You need a doctor," said Sarah.

"I'll be fine," Joe Hall argued. "The worst is over."

"What're you doing here?" Travis asked.

"I come here sometimes," Joe Hall said. "No one knows about it. Place used to belong to the Westwick family. You remember I told you about Harry, the 'Rat'? I'm a bit of a student of 'Rat' Westwick, you might say." He smiled at Travis. "He's the one taught us that heel pass, remember?"

Travis nodded. He couldn't believe anyone would want to come here on their own. Especially if they were ill.

"If I'm the same after the big game," Joe Hall said, "I'll see a doctor. I promise you that, okay?"

He flashed his old smile and immediately looked much better. Sarah and Travis couldn't help themselves. They nodded, though they still felt he needed help now, not tomorrow. But Joe Hall wasn't going to listen to a couple of kids.

"You better head back to camp now," he said. "They'll be sending out a search party."

"I guess you're right," said Sarah. "You're sure you're going to be all right here, though?"

"I'm fine," Joe Hall said. He smiled again, but it wasn't so convincing this time. "I'll see you two at the rink, okay?"

They nodded in agreement.

Joe Hall walked them down to the dock, and when the setter caught sight of them it began to howl and moan. The dog seemed frantic, racing back and forth in the water, snapping and growling and barking.

"She's still waiting for us," Sarah said. "She wouldn't come across the water with us."

Joe Hall nodded, swallowed hard. "There's been a skunk around," he said. "I guess the dog smells it."

"I guess," Travis said.

The dog obviously had a better nose than he had. All Travis could smell was the musty old cottage and the river.

*H NO!"*

Travis had been first to break through the thick bush and find the path leading down into the camp. But when he did he saw that Nish's mad plan was already under way.

Fahd was waving frantically from near the flagpole. He was trying to catch Nish's attention. Nish was standing behind the boys' tent with Andy and Lars. Lars caught the signal and punched Nish's shoulder.

They peeked around the side of the tent just in time to see Sam leave the dining hall and head for the women's outhouse.

Nish broke across the camp at full speed, jumping from tree to bush to tree, as if no one would notice.

Sam went inside the outhouse and closed the door.

"What's going on?" Sarah asked from behind Travis.

"It's Nish's revenge," Travis said. "He's wired the outhouse for when Sam goes."

"*'Wired the outhouse'?*"

"He set some fireworks. He's going to fire them off when she's in there."

"That's *dangerous!*"

"Nish claims it's only a couple of big firecrackers, and they're well below the seat in a wire cage."

"How'd he get down in there?"

"He won't say."

"He's insane."

"I know, I know."

Nish was now racing as fast as he could to the men's outhouse. Fahd already had the door open. Nish was in in a flash. Fahd shut the door and ran for the tent.

"What's happening?" Sarah asked.

"He's got this long fuse and he's going to light it from where he is."

"He knows what he's doing?"

"Nooo – but when has that ever stopped him?"

They waited. Sarah seemed apprehensive, worried about her friend. Travis was nervous as well, but worried also about his friend, Nish. He couldn't afford to get in any more trouble here.

There was a long pause. They could hear giggling coming from the direction of the boys' tent. Andy was making farting noises under his arm.

"How mature!" Sarah said.

They waited, but nothing happened. After a while the door to the women's outhouse opened and Sam came out. She walked right past Nish's hideout and washed her hands in the outside basin.

Still there was no explosion.

The boys had left the safety of their hideout behind the tent and were moving closer to the scene of the misfire.

"Nish?" Fahd called tentatively.

The door to the men's outhouse slipped open and a furious-looking Nish stepped out. He found the fuse on the ground and began tracing it along to the women's outhouse. He opened the door and slipped inside.

"What's that?" Sarah asked.

"Nish's fuse," Travis said. "It didn't work."

"No — what's *that*?" Sarah repeated.

She was pointing back to the men's outhouse. From the grass just outside came a small puff of smoke, followed by a little burst of light that sizzled and sparked and raced along the fuse right behind Nish.

Travis couldn't help himself: "*Nnniiiiiisshhhhh!*"

KAAAAA-BOOOOOOMMMMMMM!!!

KAAA-POWWWWWWWW!

Travis had never seen anything like it. The women's outhouse seemed to jump about three feet in the air before crashing back down and wobbling from side to side. Smoke billowed from the air vent.

The door opened.

Out walked Nish, his arms straight down and his blinking eyes forming pink holes in the dark sludge that coated him from the top of this head to his sandals.

Nish was covered — completely, absolutely, and disgustingly — from head to foot *in human waste!*

@

"Very funny! *Very, very* funny!"

But it *was* very funny. No matter what Nish said. Sam laughed so loud and long she eventually pitched over onto her side and kicked her legs like she was riding an imaginary bike. Sarah laughed so hard she fell down on her knees. Fahd was crying he was laughing so hard. And Travis was laughing so hard he couldn't speak.

"*Stay still, you idiot!*" Mr. Dillinger shouted.

But even Mr. Dillinger was laughing. He was trying to be tough, but it wasn't working. Mr. Dillinger had a garden hose out and was standing a safe ten feet away from Nish and spraying him with the nozzle on full. Nish was turning, round and round and round, as the hose cut through the sludge and, slowly, a pink and highly embarrassed Wayne Nishikawa began to emerge.

When Mr. Dillinger had sprayed the worst parts with water, he shut off the hose and threw a bar of soap at Nish. "In the river, Mr. Manure," he said, fighting back a giggle. "You've got a good day of scrubbing ahead of you before anyone will even go near you."

Nish fumbled the soap, bent to pick it up, and slipped and fell, which only caused more laughter. He cradled the soap and began walking down towards the beach. When he reached the water he just kept on walking, almost as if he expected to walk across to the other side of the wide Ottawa River, but eventually he bobbed to the surface and began singing as he scrubbed.

He had obviously decided there was no use in fighting it. He may as well join in on the laughs.

"I do think he's insane, you know," Sarah said as she and Travis watched from the shore.

"He's different, that's for sure," said Travis.

"I think he's *neat!*"

Both Travis and Sarah turned at once.

It was Sam, flushing beneath her flaming red hair.

# 15

"Hey, Data – how ya doing?"

Data swivelled around in his chair. "Oh, hi, Travis. Nish all cleaned off yet?"

"It'll take him all summer – and even then he'll still smell like Nish."

Data laughed. He'd missed the explosion but had made it out in time to see Mr. Dillinger go to work with the hose. Data had been looking up *Star Wars* and *Star Trek* stuff on the Internet. The camp management had let him spend as much time on the camp computer as he wanted.

"What's up?" Data asked.

"I want you to find out something for me," Travis said.

"Shoot."

"I want to know more about Joe Hall."

"Get a grip, Travis – there's going to be about a million Joe Halls on the Web."

"But there's something different about this one. He used to play hockey. There's hundreds of hockey Web pages."

"And probably hundreds of Joe Halls who play or played hockey."

Travis was disappointed. The World Wide Web wasn't suddenly going to reveal all about Joe Hall. "I guess so," said Travis. "Thanks anyway."

Travis turned to go, but Data called him back.

"Don't give up so easily, Trav. What else do you know about him?"

"Nothing – that's the point. I wanted to see if there was *anything* I could find out."

"What do you suspect?"

"I don't know. Nothing, I guess."

"There must be something."

"I don't know, honestly. It's just that there's something not quite right about Joe Hall."

Data took a piece of paper and began scribbling. "'Joe Hall,'" he said. "Anything else?"

"I think he played at a high level, but I don't know when."

"What about a nickname?" Data asked.

"Yeah! 'Bad' Joe Hall. He told us."

"'Bad Joe Hall, hockey player,'" Data said. "I'll let you know."

"Thanks," Travis said. "Thanks for trying."

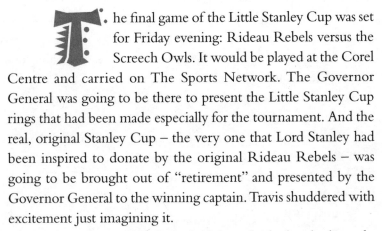

he final game of the Little Stanley Cup was set
for Friday evening: Rideau Rebels versus the
Screech Owls. It would be played at the Corel
Centre and carried on The Sports Network. The Governor
General was going to be there to present the Little Stanley Cup
rings that had been made especially for the tournament. And the
real, original Stanley Cup – the very one that Lord Stanley had
been inspired to donate by the original Rideau Rebels – was
going to be brought out of "retirement" and presented by the
Governor General to the winning captain. Travis shuddered with
excitement just imagining it.

But there was more. The original trophy had to be brought
up from the Hockey Hall of Fame in Toronto, and the Hall was
also going to put on a display at the Corel Centre featuring all
the greats who had ever played for the original Cup, including
Harry "Rat" Westwick and "One-Eyed" Frank McGee.

The excitement was getting to the whole team. Mr. Dillinger
had sharpened everyone's skates so many times some of the Owls

were deliberately "dulling" them by running the blades along the edge of an old hockey stick. Even Joe Hall seemed miraculously recovered. He was smiling again, that wonderful shining smile. And he looked freshly showered and shaved and was walking with a bounce.

"He's faking it," said Sarah. "Listen to him breathe."

When Joe Hall came up to Travis just before the warm-up, Travis immediately noticed that Sarah was right: his breathing was shallow, quick, and the quiet cough was still there.

"How about it today, Travis?" Joe Hall asked. "Try the stick?"

He seemed so hopeful, Travis had to think fast to come up with a way to please Joe Hall and, at the same time, get out of this predicament.

"I'll try it in the warm-up," he said.

"Go ahead," said Joe Hall. "It's all yours."

He got the stick for Travis. He seemed pleased. Travis put the stick to the side of his stall, not wanting anyone else to notice.

They entered the rink to pounding rock music and dazzling lights, brighter than they had ever seen. Of course, they were special lights for television, Travis realized. He instantly felt their heat.

But he was warm also from excitement. The crowd was enormous. There might be ten thousand people here, he thought. And there, in the special box to the right, was the Governor General! She was waving to the crowd, and the people were applauding.

Everything felt wonderful to Travis – except the stick. It felt like a foreign object in his hands, something he had never held before.

He stickhandled a bit with it, then tried a shot. It rang off the crossbar – his good luck omen! Travis smiled to himself.

"*Where'd you get the goofy stick, jerk?*" a voice snarled in his ear.

It was Kenzie MacNeil, the big Rideau Rebels centre. He was laughing and pointing Travis out to his teammates.

"Is that some kind of joke?" James Grove asked.

"We'll see who's laughing at the end," Travis said. He sounded cocky, but he dumped the stick at the first opportunity and pulled out his Easton instead. He hoped Joe Hall wouldn't notice.

But he hoped in vain. Lining up for the opening faceoff, Travis glanced back at the bench. Joe Hall was staring right at him. He looked heartbroken.

It's not my fault, Travis thought. I never asked to use that stupid stick.

But there was no time to worry about it. The puck had dropped, the crowd exploded with noise, and the Rebels had possession.

Big MacNeil was turning in his own end. He seemed even larger this game, more assured of himself. He came up slowly, and Travis made his move to poke check.

Like a snake, MacNeil's stick moved back, tucking the puck away and then flipping it ahead, well out of Travis's reach. He was beaten. MacNeil moved down ice and ripped a hard slapper that Jeremy took on his pads.

Nish picked up the puck and cracked it off the boards back out to Travis. He cradled the puck, then began moving up ice. He faked a pass to Dmitri and instead fired the puck on his backhand off the near boards, neatly stepping around the player coming to check him. He was in three-on-one, with Sarah coming up fast.

Travis held the puck until the last moment, then tried to drop a pass to Sarah, but it rolled off the back of his curve and was lost.

He headed for the bench, anxious for a change. Joe Hall said nothing, but he didn't need to. Travis already blamed himself.

The game kept sailing end to end, but without a goal. Jeremy was fantastic, stealing goals from MacNeil twice with his glove, and once getting lucky with a shot that bounced away off the post. The Rebels' goalie was also hot. Twice he foiled Dmitri, and once he made a great blocker save on a hard drive by Nish from the point.

Nish was playing great. This was the Nish of championship games. He was all business, no nonsense. Perhaps Joe Hall had got through to him about his temper. Twice Joe Hall even paired him with Sam, and Nish kept his feelings, whatever they were, to himself. Perhaps he was still too embarrassed about the exploding outhouse to dare say anything to anyone.

The Rebels scored on a tip-in during a power play, and the Owls tied it up on a slick move by Simon Milliken when he was able to slip the puck over to a charging Andy for a hard back-hand that beat the Rebels' goaltender. After one period it was 1–1, still 1–1 after two.

Late in the third period, with the score still tied, Travis chased MacNeil into the Rebels' corner. MacNeil stopped abruptly and turned so fast he ran over Travis, snapping Travis's stick as it fell between MacNeil's powerful legs.

Travis tossed his broken Easton away and made fast for the bench. Derek Dillinger saw him coming and leaped over the boards to replace him.

Data was already making his way to the rack to get Travis his second stick when, suddenly, Joe Hall grabbed Travis by the shoulder. Even through his shoulder pads and jersey he could feel the shake in Joe Hall's hand. He was very ill.

He looked up at his coach. Joe Hall's eyes were sunken again, but they held so much light they seemed to glow on their own. It had to be the television lights, Travis figured.

"Try mine," Joe Hall said.

Travis nodded. What choice did he have?

Joe Hall reached behind the bench and came up with his stick. Travis took it, reluctantly. It felt heavy, all wrong.

Travis looked up at the clock. Less than five minutes to go. At least he wouldn't have to use it for long.

*But what if he had a chance and blew it? Would it be his fault – or Joe Hall's?*

The Rebels almost scored with less than two minutes left when MacNeil broke in with his wingers and faked a shot that sent Sam to her knees and out of the play. He selfishly wound up for a hard slapshot and Nish threw himself in front of the shot, the hard drive glancing off his mask, then off the crossbar, before flying harmlessly over the glass.

Nish had saved the day.

He lay on the ice, not moving. Sam was already back on her feet and racing to him. She knelt down. Nish was blinking up, still stunned by the shot.

"That was sure no chicken play," she said, and smiled.

Nish got up slowly, feeling his helmet as if it might have been shattered. Sam gave him a grateful tap on the shinpads. The crowd applauded warmly. They knew they'd just seen a great defensive play.

"Great play, Nish!" Travis called as Nish came off the ice. "You saved a certain goal!"

Nish only nodded and sat to catch his breath. Travis didn't need to see his friend's face to know what colour it would be.

Travis took his first shift with Joe Hall's stick right after Nish's moment of glory. MacNeil was still out, and the Rebels' star pointed at Travis's old-style straight-as-a-ruler stick.

"The secret weapon?" MacNeil asked. His linemates laughed.

Travis rapped Joe Hall's stick hard on the ice. He wouldn't let them get to him.

The linesman held up his arm. The Owls were making one last change.

It was Nish – on with Sam – still shaking his head, but back to play.

Sarah won the faceoff. She pushed the puck to her left and bumped MacNeil out of the way.

Travis picked up the puck and immediately wished he had his Easton. The puck felt like lead. He stickhandled back and forth but worried he'd lose the puck.

He fired it back to Nish, who looped back into his own end. Slowly Nish went around the net, checking the time left – barely a minute – then doubled back again, unsure what to do.

Finally Nish fired the puck hard off the backboards to Sam, who reversed direction and circled behind the net herself. She saw Travis free at the blueline and hit him with a perfect pass.

This time Travis didn't even try to stickhandle. He began, instead, to push the puck ahead of him and race down the side.

Travis's good speed gave him a jump on the Rebels' defence, and he made it to the blueline before his man turned on him.

Travis shot the puck across the ice to Dmitri. The lack of curve threw his aim off, and it flew ahead of Dmitri, who dashed into the corner to pick up the puck.

Dmitri made a beautiful move on his checker, passing to himself by backhanding the puck off the boards as the checker tried to take him out. He sidestepped the check, and the puck was instantly his again.

Dmitri hit Sarah coming in hard. She beat the one defence and backhanded the puck across to Travis.

Travis was afraid to shoot. He couldn't be sure he'd even hit the net. And the other defender was already on him, wrapping long arms around him.

The puck was loose in front of the two struggling players. Travis stared helplessly at it a second, then, without even thinking, hammered the back of the blade down hard on the edge of the puck.

The puck shot back between his legs – right back onto the stick of Sam, who was charging towards the net.

Travis clamped his arms down on the defender's arms. If he was going to be held, he'd hold, too. The defender couldn't move on Sam.

Sarah had the other defender out of position and pic-ed him so he couldn't get back in the play.

Sam faked once to her backhand, then blew right around the

Rebels' goaltender and smacked the water bottle off the back of the net.

Owls 2, Rebels 1.

Fourteen seconds to play.

The players on the ice were all over Sam and Travis, but their teammates on the bench didn't dare jump over. With time still remaining, it would mean a penalty. But they were on their feet, stomping and yelling and high-fiving each other.

They lined up for the faceoff. MacNeil scowled at Travis, who held the stick blade up to his mask and pretended to kiss it. He felt like Nish doing it.

Sarah took the puck off MacNeil and shot it back to Sam, who dumped it back to Nish. The Rebels charged in desperation. Nish waited until the last moment before lobbing it out over everyone's head. Dmitri cuffed it at centre and the puck rolled into the Rebels' end, no offside, and big MacNeil, skating hard, barely got to it as the buzzer sounded.

The Screech Owls had won the Little Stanley Cup.

With "Bad" Joe Hall's heel pass.

# 17

he celebration seemed to go on forever. The teams shook hands – "Great stick!" big MacNeil acknowledged with a good-hearted smile. The Governor General made her way down onto the ice for the presentation, and the ice filled with television cameras and radio and newspaper reporters asking for interviews, and photographers snapping shots of the Screech Owls as if they'd just won the Stanley Cup.

Which, of course, they had.

The first presentation, however, was to the Most Valuable Player. The public address system roared out the name – "SAMMM-ANTHA BENNNNN-ETTTTT!" – and Sam, standing down the line by Jenny Staples, threw off her helmet and shook her head as if she hadn't heard right.

But if Sam was surprised, no one else was. The crowd roared its approval and the Governor General handed her a beautiful little Inuit carving. Sam hugged the Governor General. Travis, hitting his stick on the ice, could only wonder if you were allowed to do that.

But the Governor General didn't seem to mind. She hugged Sam back. Then a large figure on skates stepped out of the Owls line and skated down to tap Sam's shinpads.

It was Nish, glowing like a goal light.

A moment later, a man wearing a dark blue suit and the whitest gloves Travis had ever seen came out from the Zamboni chute carrying the original Stanley Cup. It was so much smaller than the one Travis was familiar with from TV, but he knew that this one, the small one, was the *real* one. The same one that Lord Stanley had paid $48.67 for more than a century ago. Today, it was priceless.

The Owls and Rebels lined up and the Governor General presented the Rebels with silver medals, which she placed around their necks. The Owls raised their sticks in salute and cheered the home-town team.

Travis turned to Sarah. "Find Joe," he said. "And fast."

Sarah skated away.

The Governor General then picked up the original Stanley Cup. She looked around for the team captain.

"Go, Trav!" Nish called, hammering his stick.

"Yeah, Travis!" Sam shouted.

Travis noticed Sam and Nish were now standing side by side. Something seemed to have changed between them.

But he wasn't looking for Sam or Nish. He had to find Joe Hall.

The Governor General was walking towards Travis with the

Stanley Cup in her hands. The Rebels were pounding their sticks on the ice in salute. The entire Corel Centre was on its feet, cheering.

Travis looked around, nearly frantic.

*There was Sarah!* And she had Joe Hall with her.

Joe Hall, white as the ice, was leaning heavily on Sarah. He looked terrible.

Travis turned first to Joe Hall. He handed him back his stick. The sparkle was missing, but Joe Hall managed a thin, quick smile.

"You won the Stanley Cup for me," he said.

Then the Governor General presented the Stanley Cup to Travis. With trembling arms he took the trophy, thanked her, and raised it over his head to thunderous cheers.

Travis knew that everyone expected him to hand the Cup next to his assistant captain, Sarah. But Sarah stepped aside, and Travis, smiling, did what both of them knew needed to be done. He handed the original Stanley Cup to Joe Hall.

Joe Hall reached for it. He was crying. Sobbing openly, huge tears welled up in his eyes and rolled down his cheeks, splashing into the Stanley Cup.

"Thanks, Joe," Travis said. "And congratulations."

Sarah reached up and kissed Joe Hall. Still sobbing, he handed the trophy to Sarah. Sarah lifted it, then handed it off to Derek, then Nish.

Nish pushed past several of the Owls to make sure Sam got it next. She raised the cup and did a little dance, much to the delight of the crowd.

# 18

"Where did Joe Hall go?" asked Travis.

Sarah looked around. "I hope he's gone to see a doctor."

Travis had no time to go look for him. There were photographers and reporters and more cheers and a Little Stanley Cup ring to try on. Soon an hour or more had passed, and they still hadn't seen Joe Hall.

Finally, with the cheering over and the ice already being cleaned, the triumphant Owls made their way back to the dressing room. Mr. Dillinger was there, packing up the equipment for the long bus ride home.

But still no Joe Hall.

Travis undressed, showered, and changed. He was just doing up his shirt when Data wheeled up and handed him a folded piece of paper. "You might want to look at this, Travis."

It was, as Travis expected, the results of Data's computer search for Joe Hall. Sure enough, it turned out there were hundreds of Joe Halls, even several Joe Halls in hockey. But only one "Bad" Joe Hall.

Travis read frantically.

*Hall, Joe: "Bad" Joe Hall was born in England but was raised in Canada. He played professional hockey at the beginning of the 20th Century, mostly for the Montreal Canadiens. He was famous for his bad temper — he was once taken off the ice in a police paddy wagon! — but later came to regret the playing time his temper had cost him. Hall's Canadiens met the Seattle Metropolitans to decide the 1919 Stanley Cup, but the Spanish flu struck the Montreal team badly. Five players were too sick to play, and when Joe Hall died, the championship was cancelled that year — the only time in history there has been no Stanley Cup awarded.*

Travis read it twice. He could make no sense of it. *It was impossible.*

Sarah popped her head into the dressing room.

Travis looked up, hopeful. "Did you find him?"

Sarah shook her head, then she stopped and smiled. "I don't know — maybe I did."

Travis was more puzzled than ever. Either she had found Joe Hall or she hadn't.

"Come on out here a minute," Sarah said.

She took him up the back stairs to the front foyer of the Corel Centre, where the original Stanley Cup was back on display and the fans were lining up by the hundreds to have their pictures taken with it and the other trophies from the Hockey Hall of Fame.

But it wasn't the trophies that Sarah wanted to show him. "Over here," she said. "The display cases."

They moved over to several large glass cases containing memorabilia from the Silver Seven and the early Ottawa Senators. There were even photographs of the Rideau Rebels, and a great picture of "One-Eyed" Frank McGee and Harry "Rat" Westwick.

But she wanted to show him something else. "Look in this case," Sarah said.

Travis peered in. Old skates, equipment, sweaters, a hockey stick. He saw nothing to tell him where Joe Hall had gone.

"What?" he said.

"Recognize the stick?" she asked.

Travis looked again. It was in the far corner of the case. An old, perfectly straight hockey stick.

And at the top, near the handle, was pencilled a single name.

"J. Hall."

### THE END

# The West Coast Murders

**1**

t was Sarah who spotted the first body.

She was standing high on the bridge of the Zodiac, staring out over the rolling sea off the San Juan Islands.

Travis had seen her get to her feet and point, but with the wind roaring in his ears he couldn't hear what she had shouted to the guide on the tour boat. Whatever it was, it caused the guide to stand, draw her binoculars up, and stare in the direction Sarah was pointing for some time before suddenly turning the Zodiac and revving the engines.

The big open tour boat headed towards the area where Sarah was still pointing. The swells were high along the Strait of Juan de Fuca this early in the year, and at times the islands dropped out of sight for a moment before the Zodiac roared up the next wide, rolling wave.

Travis didn't mind the rolling. The same, unfortunately, could not be said for Nish, who lay flat on the floor of the Whale

Watch tour boat and had turned the oddest colour of green Travis had ever seen in a human face.

This was not the Nish they had started out with from Victoria Harbour. Before the Zodiac had rounded the breakwater and headed out into open sea, Nish had bounced about the big rubber-sided boat like a tropical storm – "Hurricane Nish," Sarah had tagged him – and soon had everyone on the tour, Muck and Mr. Dillinger, all the Screech Owls, even the guide, howling with laughter as he kept interrupting the guide's talk about where they'd be going and what they'd be seeing.

They would be watching for dolphins and porpoises, the guide told them, and with luck they might even see a massive grey whale. She explained how to tell the porpoises from the dolphins. She told them there were more than thirty different kinds of dolphins in the world, and how it was important to protect them.

"Not long ago we were losing twenty thousand of them a year in gill nets," the guide said. "Tuna fishermen were letting them get tangled in the nets they were using to catch tuna, and the dolphins were drowning. Like us, they need to breathe air. We've saved a lot of them, but it still happens. That's why all the dolphins we find off the coast of British Columbia are protected by law; we don't want anybody, or anything, hurting them.

"Everyone knows they're mammals, of course, not fish. They're as intelligent as chimpanzees and have memories like elephants. They're better with numbers and better at following complicated instructions than most of us are – so treat them with respect. They may be smarter than us."

"Certainly smarter than *some* of us," Sarah added, with a withering look at Nish.

Nish crossed his eyes and rolled his tongue before sticking it out at Sarah and violently shaking his head.

The guide said any dolphins they saw today would likely be Pacific white-sided dolphins, which were common along this coast. Killer whales, she added, were also dolphins and could be found off the coast of British Columbia as well, though they are rarely seen. They might get lucky, but more likely they'd see a big grey, which was just as good, in her opinion.

"Greys are beautiful animals," she said. "Some of them are longer than a city bus, and once they get here they spend most of their time eating tiny little sea creatures they find in these waters. An adult grey will eat about twelve hundred kilograms of food a day – that's the equivalent of ten thousand Big Macs."

"*That's what I usually order!*" Nish had shouted.

The dolphins, the guide said, prefer salmon, but also love a good feed of anchovies.

"*They order pizza out here, with anchovies?*" Nish had screeched. "*I think I'm gonna hurl!*"

And less than ten minutes later, with the sea rolling and sliding and slipping under him, he had indeed "hurled," a small figure in a rain suit and life jacket hanging over the back of the Zodiac and barfing into the open sea as seagulls screeched overhead and the rest of the Owls mercilessly applauded and cheered his every retch.

Now Nish was flat out, green and groaning – but at least he was quiet. This was no time for wisecracks. Whatever Sarah had sighted, it seemed to have the guide deeply concerned.

Twice they turned and circled back, the guide continually rising from her pilot's chair to lift the binoculars and scan the rolling sea for whatever it was that Sarah had seen.

"*There!*" Sarah called, pointing. This time Travis heard her.

The guide turned the Zodiac sharply, easing it up one long, rolling swell and down the other side, where, almost magically, the boat drew up alongside the object of their search mission.

Travis, sitting on an outside seat beside Sam, Nish's new partner on defence, leaned over the round rubbery wall of the Zodiac and stared hard.

It was a dolphin – rolling lifelessly in the sea, shreds of pale, white flesh stringing out in the water from its underside.

And something else – fading to pink in the water, but dark red closer to the rolling, unreal looking dolphin.

*Blood*.

"I think *I'm* gonna hurl," said Sam in her deepest voice.

"What happened?" Travis asked.

"Maybe it got struck by a ship?" suggested Data, who was strapped into a seat just the other side of Sam.

The guide was out of her pilot's seat and down close to the side of the Zodiac. She had out a long pole with a hook on the end and reached with it into the water. But the boat was rolling too much. Muck, the Screech Owls' coach, stood to help. "You take the controls," he said to her. "I'll pull it in."

The guide nodded, and a moment later she had put the outboard engines into reverse and pulled the boat around so that it and the dolphin were at least drifting in the same direction.

Muck, his lips tight and jaw set, reached for the dolphin with the pole and caught it along a front flipper, the hook pulling the creature so it rolled over completely as it came towards the Zodiac.

There was a black, gaping hole on the dolphin's other side, fresh blood still streaming from the wound.

The guide came down from her seat for a closer look. "What the —?" she said.

"A swordfish?" Data suggested. "Ran it right through?"

Muck was shaking his head. "I don't think so," he said. "It's been shot."

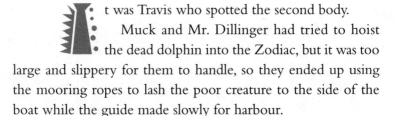

t was Travis who spotted the second body.

Muck and Mr. Dillinger had tried to hoist the dead dolphin into the Zodiac, but it was too large and slippery for them to handle, so they ended up using the mooring ropes to lash the poor creature to the side of the boat while the guide made slowly for harbour.

All of the Screech Owls were upset. They'd come out to see grey whales swimming and playing in the sea, and they'd found, instead, a dead dolphin. "Shot," Muck had said, but it made no sense to Travis. Shot for what reason? he wondered. And who would do such a thing?

Jenny Staples, the Owls' goalie, was sobbing. A few of the others, Fahd included, were brushing away tears and trying to pretend that it was just the splash from the sea. Travis's throat felt tight and he avoided having to talk. He sat, staring at the rolling horizon, and tried to think of anything but the death of this beautiful creature that now lay strapped to the side of the boat, blood stringing out pink behind the small wake that rippled from its tail fin.

Muck and Mr. Dillinger talked in low voices as they leaned over the side making sure their ties held. The coach said it must have something to do with tuna fishermen and gill nets, but Mr. Dillinger didn't think there was any tuna fishing done off these waters. Mr. Dillinger said it must have been some idiot with a rifle out for nothing more than a kick, but Muck shook his head in disgust. Muck looked angry, as if somehow this attack on an innocent sea creature had been an attack on himself and his team of peewee players.

On the slow journey back to shore, a huge, mottled grey whale breached off to one side. The next time the gigantic dark creature rose out of the water, several of the Owls raised their disposable cameras and clicked off a few shots before it disappeared again in a thundering crash of spray, but they did so without much enthusiasm. Hardly anyone said a word, except to point out where the whale was coming up again.

Soon, however, it had moved off and there was only the slow drone of the engines on low speed, the trickling sound of water as it played between the trussed dolphin and the side of the boat, and the hypnotic rise and fall, rise and fall of the wide, rolling sea.

Some of the Owls were dozing off. Fahd was slumped over. Sarah was leaning on Sam, both of them nodding sharply from time to time as they bobbed in and out of sleep. Andy lay against Wilson in the seats up ahead. Dmitri and Lars and Simon were asleep too, their hooded heads down low as if in prayer.

Travis kept watching the sea. He could not stop wondering how this had happened. If Muck was right and the dolphin had been shot, could it really have been for *sport*? For a *kick*? Maybe it was a fisherman who'd accidentally caught the dolphin in his nets, and when he couldn't untangle the poor creature he had put it out of its misery.

But that didn't seem possible. There was no torn netting on the dolphin, just the gaping black hole in one side where dark blood was still seeping out and thinning to pink, eventually fading to nothing as it washed away in the sea.

Perhaps the dolphin hadn't been shot. Maybe Muck was wrong. Maybe it was a shark attack! A swordfish, like Fahd said. A bite from some fierce sea creature. Maybe it was the mark of a suction cup from the arm of a giant squid or octopus.

But Travis knew nothing about the ocean and decided he shouldn't pretend to. He'd have to wait, like everyone else, to find out what had happened. He just hoped it wasn't a gun that had done this.

Would it be murder? he wondered. Can you *murder* a dolphin? Or does it have to be a human before it counts for that much. But then the guide had said they're smart as us, they breathe like us, they can learn, they speak to each other.

It would be murder in Travis Lindsay's opinion, anyway.

He tried to doze off, but couldn't. He watched, instead, the slowly approaching land and the islands merging into the horizon behind. It was difficult adjusting to the size of the ocean after all those summers at his grandparents' little lake up near Algonquin Park, where he and Nish last summer had managed to swim from shore to shore while Travis's dad stayed alongside in the rowboat and kept a sharp eye out for waterskiers and wakeboarders. At the lake he was never out of sight of the shore. Here, if he looked to his left – what had the guide called it, port? – he could see nothing. For all he knew, there *was* nothing in that direction all the way to Japan.

He was staring out, thinking of Japan and Nagano and the Big Hat arena, when suddenly he thought he saw something. He half stood, but then crouched back down. He didn't want to shout out if it was nothing. Maybe it was just his imagination playing tricks on him.

He waited for the next long roll of the sea. Then he saw it again – a flash of something white.

*Another dolphin?*

He waited until he had seen it twice more before he said anything. By now he was sure. He stepped over to the pilot's seat, where the guide was nursing the controls and staring ahead towards her destination.

When Travis finally caught her eye, she looked down, wary. It occurred to Travis that she, too, might have been crying.

He pointed to the west. His voice caught slightly. "I-I see something over that way."

The guide said nothing. She stood up, raised her binoculars, and stared for a long time. One long swell, then a second, then a third, the guide still staring, seemingly as uncertain as Travis had been.

She put the glasses down, and Travis saw a look of extreme anger flash across her face. She said nothing to him, but turned back towards the two men on the far side still holding the dolphin tight to the Zodiac.

"We have another sighting on the port side!" she called.

Muck and Mr. Dillinger looked up, Mr. Dillinger's eyes blinking behind water-spotted glasses. "Of what?" he called.

"I don't know," said the guide. "I'm not sure."

Muck got to his feet, lifted his hand to shield his eyes, and stared. "We'd better check it out."

The guide said nothing. She turned the boat at once towards the object Travis had seen. The movement jolted the dozing Screech Owls and several stirred. Sam and Sarah stood up together, staring out to see where they were going.

"W-wh-what's goin' on?" said a voice below Travis. He stared down into a face that was not nearly as green as it had been a half-hour earlier. Still, Nish did not look at all well.

"We're turning," Travis said. "There's something in the water."

"*Fish?*" Nish said sarcastically.

Nish was trying to smile. He was coming back, recovering from his bout of seasickness.

"You want to sit up?" Travis asked.

"Give me a hand."

Travis helped his pal onto the seat beside him. Nish shook his head and rubbed his face.

Slowly, at times almost seeming to go backwards, the Zodiac crawled over the rolling swells towards whatever was floating in the distance.

Most of the Owls were awake by now and knew they were headed for something in the water. Sarah and Sam were trying to stand in order to see better, but with the rolling waves and slippery floor of the Zodiac, it wasn't easy. They plunked down and waited like everyone else.

Travis could feel the tension rise around him. The white thing he had first seen in the distance was drawing closer, visible now with each swell rather than just every so often. From time to time the guide lifted her binoculars to check. Her concern seemed to be growing.

She pulled the Zodiac around to starboard, then hard left again to port. The Zodiac rose up and over a wave, and then slipped down into the same trough of sea that held the mystery object.

Travis and Nish both moved to the side of the boat, staring hard.

It was a white shirt, drifting slowly in the water.

And from inside the shirt came a familiar dark stain, fading to pink, just as it had around the dolphin.

The object rolled easily in the waves, tumbling to reveal a gaping black hole in the white cloth almost exactly the same as the wound on the dolphin.

*Only this was a man!*

Travis turned in shock to Nish.

Nish had gone green. He looked like he was about to be sick all over again. But he was pointing, his finger shaking.

"What?" Travis asked impatiently.

"*W-we . . . know . . . him!*"

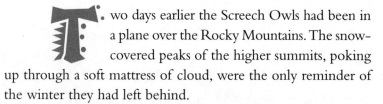

**3**

wo days earlier the Screech Owls had been in a plane over the Rocky Mountains. The snow-covered peaks of the higher summits, poking up through a soft mattress of cloud, were the only reminder of the winter they had left behind.

In Vancouver, their destination, it was more like early summer. On the long ride in from the airport, they were thrilled to see pink cherry trees, red and yellow tulips, gardens like living rainbows with everything in full bloom.

Rarely had the Screech Owls looked forward to a trip so much. It was not just that this was beautiful British Columbia, with everything from the mountains to the ocean; they'd also be playing in a totally new kind of hockey tournament. Vancouver was hosting the first-ever "3-on-3" International Peewee Competition. Several of the matches were to be played in nearby Bellingham, Washington, just across the Canada–U.S. border, which would give the tournament a genuine *international* flavour. Teams from all over North America had been invited – from

Quebec City to Anaheim, from Winnipeg to New York City –
but they were not going to compete as teams. Instead, each team
would be split into groups of three skaters – usually two forwards
and a defence – which would compete in different divisions for
separate championship trophies.

It was an idea that Wayne Gretzky and other hockey leaders
came up with when they met to talk about what was right and
what was wrong in minor hockey. A great many of the top
National Hockey League stars these days came from Europe,
even though far more people played hockey in Canada and the
United States. So what was their secret?

Wayne Gretzky and the others came up with a number of
suggestions. First – and much to the disgust of Nish – Canadian
and American minor hockey teams needed to practise more and
play fewer games and tournaments. "*Gimme a break!*" Nish had
howled. "*That's like choosing school over summer vacation!*"

But another idea sounded more attractive. What about bringing shinny back into the organized game? Gretzky said he'd
learned his skills in his backyard, not through organized practices where he couldn't work on the tricks that would make him
the greatest player of all time.

Perhaps "3-on-3" hockey should become part of the organized game. In Europe, where they play on a larger ice surface,
they had been playing 3-on-3 for decades, using the width of
the ice rather than the length. They could, by dividing the rink
at the bluelines, run three games of 3-on-3 at the same time.

In Canada, a group of former NHLers was now building
smaller 3-on-3 rinks around the country, and the game was
catching on with everyone from little kids to old men. The first

rinks had been built around Vancouver, and so this was where
the idea for the first international 3-on-3 shinny tournament
had taken root.

To the Screech Owls' great surprise, Muck Munro had been
enthusiastic about the tournament. He believed in tradition,
and didn't much care for newfangled ideas. But for Muck,
shinny was not a new idea. And when the Owls remembered
the joy in Muck's face when Tamarack froze over and he'd
come out to play on the frozen fields, they understood why he
was all for this "new" idea of bringing fun and creativity back
into the game.

Each group would, of course, also have a goaltender, but
Jeremy Weathers and Jenny Staples would split those duties. The
hard part was figuring out who would play with whom, and
some of Muck's combinations were surprising.

One Monday evening after practice, he pinned a notice to
the bulletin board in the Owls' dressing room:

## Screech Owls 3-on-3 Teams

### Elite Division
**Team 1:** Sarah Cuthbertson – Travis Lindsay – Wayne
Nishikawa
**Team 2:** Dmitri Yakushev – Andy Higgins – Lars Johansson

### Canucks Division
**Team 3:** Fahd Noorizadeh – Gordie Griffith – Samantha
Bennett

### Rockies Division

**Team 4:** Liz Moscovitz – Derek Dillinger – Willie Granger

### Pacific Division

**Team 5:** Simon Milliken – Jesse Highboy – Wilson Kelly

"*Not Sarah!*" Nish shouted as he leaned over Travis's shoulder, reading Muck's list. "*Why is she on my team? Why me? Why me?*"

Travis just shook his head. He knew Muck's decision was a good one. Nish and Sarah actually played wonderfully together, even if sometimes it seemed they were more interested in taking shots at each other than at the opposing goaltender. Travis was delighted to be included on the first team with them.

Muck had done a splendid job. He'd entered two 3-on-3 groups in the toughest division, and had spread the Owls' talent evenly through the other divisions. Travis could sense how disappointed Sam was not to be included on one of the top two lines, but with only one defender in each group, what else could Muck do? Nish was, well, Nish, and he always came through. And Lars had grown up playing 3-on-3 in Sweden and was probably the best shinny player of them all.

From Christmas on, the excitement built. The Owls still played in their league, but sometimes they could think of little but the upcoming tournament. They practised hard, spending the last twenty minutes of every session on 3-on-3 shinny, just getting used to each other and trying tricks they wouldn't dare attempt in a real league game.

The tournament was scheduled for the Easter long weekend, and an extra day was being added at each end, giving them nearly a week in Vancouver for the tournament and plenty of time for sightseeing.

"*Wreck Beach!*" Nish announced. "That's the only thing I want to see."

"What's Wreck Beach?" Fahd asked.

Nish looked at Fahd as if he had just crawled out of an old hockey bag and had never before seen the real world.

"*Are you serious?*" Nish asked. "It's the *nude* beach. I'm going as soon as we get there."

"You'll freeze," said Sarah.

"Come and see for yourself," Nish challenged.

"We will," said Sarah.

"And we'll be bringing cameras," laughed Sam. "*With telephoto lenses!*"

"Very funny," Nish sneered. "*Very, very funny.*"

So far, however, they hadn't come within a mile of Wreck Beach, wherever that was (How does Nish find out about these things? wondered Travis), but they had all walked across the famous Capilano rope bridge, which hangs, and swings, high above a gorge. All, that is, but Nish, who stayed in the van claiming he had food poisoning when, in fact, he was just terrified of heights. They saw the steam-powered clock in Gastown, the harbour, they walked around Stanley Park, and had a wonderful time at the Vancouver Aquarium.

Sarah and Sam were particularly keen on the Aquarium. They had wanted to see the killer whales – a baby had just been born – and all the Owls were fascinated by the special tour the staff put on for them.

They were allowed to feed the sea lions. Sarah and Sam were kissed by a killer whale. They saw the penguins, and when Fahd said how much one chubby, preening penguin in the corner looked like Nish even the staff laughed at the red-faced exhibitionist. They heard a lecture on dolphins and porpoises and grey whales, and one of the attendants, Brad, even took them into the research area and showed them how the dolphins could talk to each other and how, in a matter of a few minutes, he could teach them a new trick.

It had been, until now, the most riveting moment of the trip.

*"W-we . . . know . . . him!"*

The urgency in Nish's voice was real. He wasn't kidding. He was dead serious, and terrified.

Travis turned back from his friend and stared into the water just in time to see the head roll around again, eyes open and blank and very, very dead, the mouth twisted in pain that could no longer be felt.

"IT'S BRAD!"

The scream came from Sam, pushing hard against Travis's shoulder.

"OH MY GOD!"

That was Sarah. She was already bursting into sobs.

Travis forced himself to look again when the body rolled over once more. It *was* Brad, the marine biologist from the Vancouver Aquarium.

Brad, who had taken them to see the dolphins.

Brad, who had so charmed Sarah and Sam.

Brad, with a gaping black wound in his chest that matched the wound on the dolphin now strapped to the side of the Zodiac.

**4**

ravis was grateful that Muck and Mr. Dillinger had come out whale watching with the team. The two men had taken care of the dolphin, and now they quickly took charge again. Muck ordered the Screech Owls to look in the other direction, which they did; not even intense curiosity could cause Travis to turn around. Nor did Nish turn, proof that the one thing more frightening than anything he could imagine was at that moment being lifted up out of the sea by Muck and Mr. Dillinger and hauled into the Zodiac.

When Travis finally did look, the body had been covered by a plastic tarpaulin and Mr. Dillinger was tying down the ends, making sure the wind blew nothing free. Muck went back to hold tight to the strapped dolphin, and the guide turned the boat, once again, towards shore.

No one said a word the whole way in to Victoria Harbour. The guide had obviously radioed ahead, because there were police cars with lights flashing and an ambulance and first-aid workers waiting for their arrival. They must have known it was a dead body coming in – two, if they counted the dolphin – so Travis figured the first-aid people could be there for only one reason: the Screech Owls.

But the Owls all seemed to handle it well. There were some sobs, of course. And Travis could see Fahd shaking and pretending it was because of the cold. But Mr. Dillinger and Muck's quick thinking meant the shock was not as bad as it might have been. The first-aid workers talked to them all and checked them over, and Nish was given a Gravol for his still-churning stomach. Everyone else was fine – at least physically.

A windowless van from the Aquarium took away the carcass of the dolphin, and a special police vehicle showed up to cart the body of the marine biologist away to the morgue.

The police interviewed the guide and Muck and Mr. Dillinger, and after they'd all signed statements and given their addresses and telephone numbers while staying in Vancouver, the police told the Screech Owls they were free to go.

"Why wouldn't they interview me?" Nish whined as the last of the police cars pulled out. "I'm the one who identified the body."

"Perhaps you could tell them how he was killed, too," said Sam with more than a touch of sarcasm. Her eyes were red from crying.

"Obviously," protested Nish, "he was shot."

"By *who?*" Sarah asked. "And *why?*"

"You expect me to know *everything?*"

"You always act like you do."

But not this time, Travis thought. No one knew.

Why had there been a dolphin out there floating dead, a gaping black hole in its side?

And why a short distance away a man – a man who knew everything there was to know about dolphins – obviously murdered?

Mr. Dillinger was wonderful on the way back to Vancouver. He cranked up the rock music on the old bus the organizers had made available to the various teams, and once they were on the ferry he got change for a hundred-dollar bill and walked around handing out money so the Owls could lose themselves and their thoughts in chips and gravy and video games.

Nish, now fully recovered from his seasickness, was intent on winning a wristwatch from a machine that required him to work a crane with a metal grab over the desired object, drop it down, snatch the prize and then drop it into a chute. So far he'd won three "prizes": a key chain, a pair of ruby-red plastic lips, and a badly stitched, stuffed doll. He hadn't even come close to the watch.

Travis left his pal pumping in quarters and cursing the fates, and went out on the deck for a walk around the big ferry. The wind felt fresh on his face. The sun was out, a spring sun burning like summer, and he thought he'd walk back towards the stern of the boat – "The *poop* deck!" Nish had happily shouted when one of the deckhands asked the Owls if they knew any of the names for the parts of a ship – and watch the gulls swirl above the wake.

Travis hoped Nish left his brain to science when he died. It was worth taking a closer look at the mind of a twelve-year-old whose great ambition in life was to find a nude beach. Of course, they'd have to scrub it down before touching it.

The ferry was just crossing a narrows between two large islands. It was such a beautiful sight, the leaves already out, the trees and bushes in bloom, the hills in the distance and rocky shoreline so near. He could see a farmhouse on one side, and wondered what it was like to live there and be able to look out one window and see horses grazing and out the other and see a huge ferry filled with people and cars and trucks churning by, everyone on deck trying to stare in at you and see what you look like.

There were others out on the deck. An old couple, just standing at the rail and staring, their arms linked. A student sitting up beside one of the vents, an open book on her lap with the pages flipping in the wind. And down towards the stern, Nish's "poop deck," he could make out a couple of Screech Owls windbreakers.

Their backs were turned to Travis, but he knew who it was. The flying, waving light brown hair was obviously Sarah. And the carrot top bouncing wildly in the wind was Sam.

The noise was extraordinary. He could hear the big engines churning and pounding. He could hear the bubbling roar that came up from the big propellers.

"*Hey!*" he called out over the noise.

Travis wasn't sure exactly what he saw next. A quick motion by Sam. Sarah hunching her shoulders as if she was trying to hide herself in her windbreaker. Something spinning out into the wake. Perhaps it was only a gull twisting down.

Sarah turned, sheepishly. "Hey, Trav – how's it going?"

"Okay – what's up?"

"Nothin'," Sarah said. He couldn't help but notice the high colour in her cheeks. It couldn't be from the sun; the clouds had parted only half an hour before.

Sam was breathing out, hard, her lips so tightly pursed it looked like she was whistling. Only instead of a shrill whistle coming out, there was a steady, thin flow of steam. Like winter breath in Tamarack – only here it wasn't cold.

*It wasn't steam, it was smoke!*

Travis tried to think of something to say but found he couldn't.

"You guys see Lars?" he asked instead. He hadn't even been thinking of Lars up to this moment.

Sarah seemed relieved. She smiled, flushing even deeper. "I saw him earlier. I think he's on the upper deck."

Sam said nothing. She was looking warily at Travis, as if trying to figure out how much he'd seen.

"Okay," Travis found himself saying. "Thanks. See you later."

He was gone before they said anything, gone in one quick turn, and was soon bounding up the stairs in search of time to think, not looking for Lars at all.

*What was happening here?*

Bodies in the water?

Murder?

Sarah Cuthbertson smoking?

This latest development was almost as upsetting.

*Sarah Cuthbertson smoking?*

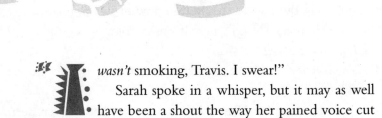

# 5

*wasn't* smoking, Travis. I swear!"

Sarah spoke in a whisper, but it may as well have been a shout the way her pained voice cut through the small dressing room. She was hurt, and it showed in her eyes and sounded in her voice.

Sarah hadn't denied that Sam was smoking. She said Sam had bummed the smoke off another passenger, an older teenager. This older girl had even offered Sarah one and just shrugged when Sarah refused. Sam had taken the second one and had smoked them both.

"Sam was upset about what we'd seen," Sarah said. "That was all."

"Muck would suspend her if he knew," Travis said. "Besides, she shouldn't smoke."

It rattled Travis to think that a teammate – someone exactly the same age as he was – would be smoking. And not one cigarette as an experiment, but a second, almost as if she *needed* it.

"He'd have kicked you off the team, too," Travis thought to add.

Sarah looked on the verge of tears. "I was just *standing* with her," she protested.

"You didn't stop her."

Sarah was frustrated. "I'm not her mother!"

"You're her teammate," Travis said. "You both have a responsibility to the Owls."

Inside, Travis winced. It was he who sounded like someone's mother. But he was captain, wasn't he? He was supposed to set an example. And if he saw something that wasn't right, he had to say so. Either that or go to Muck.

Any further discussion on the matter was over when a large rear end came through the door. It was Nish, in full gear except for skates, pushing the door open with his butt while he made sure his freshly sharpened blades didn't nick up against the door frame.

Right behind Nish – well, technically, right in *front* of Nish, since Nish was walking backwards – was Lars Johansson. Lars, Dmitri, and Andy, and Jenny in net, had already won their first game with an 11–3 victory over a weak threesome from Seattle.

Nish backed in, sweeping his arm low in a deep bow as Lars followed, laughing.

"The Master of 3-on-3 will now address us!" Nish announced.

Lars blushed slightly and plunked himself down on a bench. "Muck asked me to talk to you," he said. "This is going to be different from anything you guys have ever done before. A couple of practices don't prepare you for how quick it's going to be and how confusing it can get."

"Your team had no trouble," said Sarah.

"We were up against three big kids who couldn't skate with us," Lars said. "Muck says your opponent is going to be one of the top teams."

Nish looked up, confused, moving his head quickly from side to side.

"Who *are* we up against?" he asked.

"The Portland Panthers," Sarah said. "Ring a bell, big boy?"

"No!" Nish shouted up from tying his skates. "Should it?"

"Lake Placid?" Sarah said.

"Billings and Yantha?" Travis said.

Nish looked up, blinking, and Travis could see it was all coming back to him: Billings, the shifty little defenceman on the team that had almost beaten the Owls at the Lake Placid tournament; Yantha, the big centre with the booming shot.

"Wedgies . . . ," Sarah said, encouraging Nish to remember. "The time you rewired the hotel television . . ."

Nish was already blushing. "Okay, okay, okay – I remember. Big deal. We beat them then, we'll beat them now."

"Not the same thing at all," Lars said.

"What makes *you* the big expert?" Nish challenged.

"He's played it more than any of us," Sarah said, defending Lars. But Lars's feelings weren't hurt. He was well used to Nish's big mouth.

"It's easy," Lars said. "For 3-on-3 you just have to remember three things."

"*Skate! Shoot! Score!*" Nish shouted.

No one paid him any attention. Lars counted off the three points on his fingers: "One, pass to open spaces. Two, use your body to create holes for your teammates. Three, don't be afraid to slow things down."

"*And four!*" Nish shouted. "*Fire the stupid puck in the stupid net!*"

Travis had never felt so big. He could see his reflection in the glass as he swept the length of the little rink in three hard, extended strides. If the Olympic-sized ice surfaces in Lake Placid and Sweden had seemed as big as a frozen lake, this was like a puddle.

He loved it. He and Sarah and Nish were swirling so fast during the warmup it felt dizzying. A shot on Jeremy, the next player in dropping the rebound for the next shot. Shot, rebound, drop, shot . . . He rang his third one off the crossbar: it was going to be a great game.

First, though, there was a small ceremony. The organizers came out onto the ice and a man said what Travis supposed were a few words of welcome into a microphone – the echo in the arena was so loud, Travis couldn't make out a word the man was saying – and then a man and woman came out pulling large boxes alongside them on the ice and handed out gifts to the players on both teams.

"T-shirts, I hope," said Nish.

"Looks like something much more than that," said Sarah.

She was right. It was far more, in fact, than Travis had ever heard of for a peewee tournament. He'd been given T-shirts before – they were Nish's favourite souvenir – and mugs and little trophies and even a set of kids' books about a hockey team that travels to tournaments all over and gets in all kinds of trouble. But he'd never been given anything like this.

First, each player was given a brand-new equipment bag, with the tournament logo and the player's number on either end.

"*Awesome!*" said Nish as he examined his treasured number, 44. "Just like the pros!"

And as if that weren't enough, there was also a second gift, in a black-and-gold presentation box.

Nish, of course, was into it like a small child at Christmas. He pulled out a round plastic ball that had water inside.

"Am I expected to drink this?" he shouted, exasperated.

Sarah, shaking her head, ripped it out of his hands, turned it over once, and handed it back. Instantly the globe was filled with a swirling flurry of snow, the white flakes tumbling about in the liquid until they settled around a beautiful miniature scene of a ski hill.

"It's a souvenir of Grouse Mountain, dummy," she said. "Where they snowboard."

"*Ohhh,*" said Nish, as if he'd never heard of such a thing. He turned the globe over, shook it hard, and watched the snow swirl and settle again. "*Outstanding!*" he said.

"Here," Mr. Dillinger said, holding out his hands. "Give me those bags. I'll be transferring the other kids' gear over to theirs, so I'll set yours up by your lockers so you can put all your stuff in after the game."

"What about our snow globes," asked Nish.

"Don't worry – I'll put them in the bags, too. For safe keeping."

Nish reluctantly handed over his equipment bag and new toy. Mr. Dillinger reboxed the globe and, with Lars's help, gathered up the other, unopened boxes and equipment bags from Jeremy and Sarah and Travis. The rest of the team could put their own away.

These four had a game to play.

# 6

ravis placed his stick across the top of his shin pads and coasted, looking down into the ice and off to the far end – which wasn't very far away – to check out the Panthers. He recognized Yantha immediately: big and dark and smooth. It looked as if he'd grown since Lake Placid. He looked at Billings, the quick little blond defenceman who was such a wonderful skater. Billings looked back, winked, and raised his stick in salute. He, too, had recognized his opponents. Travis remembered they'd exchanged autographs at the end of the Lake Placid tournament. He still had Billings's autograph. He wondered if Billings had kept his.

It felt funny. It felt weird. It felt neat. He was happy for the first time since they'd gone out whale watching and come upon the floating bodies. The two officials came out, and the little ice surface seemed magically filled with skaters. They lined up for the faceoff, Sarah to take it, Travis to the side, and Nish well back by Jeremy. It was, Travis thought, just like playing shinny in the basement.

But as soon as the referee dropped the puck, the novelty turned to challenge. With only three on the ice, the players were free to go anywhere, yet in such a small area, there were few hiding places, and no place to coast and suck up your wind. There were, as well, no changes, meaning they had to take a whole new approach to the game. You couldn't go flat out all the time. You had to pick your spots. You had to gather energy and not waste it. Never had Muck's warnings about "skating around in circles like chickens with their heads cut off" made more sense.

Muck was still coach, but it wasn't the same. With no changes, he could talk strategy only at the break. He could have yelled over the noise of the thin crowd, but Muck, of course, never yelled. Travis could hear Data screaming, and thought he heard Sam's big voice a couple of times, and once he heard Lars yelling for them to *slow it down!*

Lars's instructions were making more sense than they had in the dressing room. With the Owls swirling and the Panthers sticking with them, there was little point in direct passing. Better to drop it in an open space when you could see that Nish or Sarah was headed that way. Travis also found he was most effective in leaving passes and using his body to brush away his checker. But as for the advice to slow things down – how was that possible?

The games were two periods, twenty minutes of straight running time each, and at the break all six players and the two goaltenders simply collapsed onto their backs in exhaustion. They'd been going full out for most of the period, pausing only for the faceoffs and after goals. The two teams were almost perfectly balanced, with five goals for the Panthers, including a spectacular backhand roofer by Billings, and five for the Owls, including three pretty dekes by Sarah.

Travis's lungs were burning, but he felt wonderful. The game had been spectacular – fun and clean, quick and well-played, like both a championship game and a Sunday afternoon on the frozen creek at home. He felt the pressure to win, but it came from himself and his teammates, not from the stands. And there was none of that terror of making a mistake that so often turned regular hockey games into dull demonstrations of how to dump a puck in and how to chip it back out.

Muck said something during the break that Travis never expected to hear coming out of his coach's mouth: "You're too predictable."

Travis blinked, the salt of his sweat biting into his eyes. He was surprised at how much he was sweating.

"Try something they're not expecting," Muck said.

A hundred games of being coached by Muck flashed before Travis Lindsay's eyes. He remembered the back pass that Muck had so hated. He remembered Muck's frown when he tried that silly little dance of the puck off his skate blades. But now here was Muck telling Travis to cut loose. Use a little driveway ingenuity. Try some of those basement tricks.

The Panthers went ahead in the second, and final, period on two quick goals by Yantha, one of which almost ripped Jeremy's arm off before bouncing through and over the line. Nish scored on a pass that accidentally clipped off Billings's skate, and Sarah hit the goal post on a backhand after she'd cleanly beaten the Panthers' goaltender.

Travis tried everything. He lost the puck in his own skates trying to click it up onto his blade, and Billings picked it off and scored. He tried a back pass, but Yantha read it perfectly and used Nish for a screen, firing a puck between Nish's legs that found the far corner of the net.

The Panthers had a three-goal lead and Travis could hear the crowd getting louder. He could hear Data's anxious, high-pitched voice calling for them to get going. But no sound came from Muck. Even if the Owls were down by ten goals, Muck would never shout.

Sarah picked up a rebound that Jeremy fed to the corner, then flipped the puck back into the far corner for Nish. Without even looking, Nish dumped the puck cross ice and bounced it off the boards for Sarah in full flight. She flew down the wing and blew a slapshot past the Panthers' goaltender to reduce the lead to two.

With five minutes left and the tension rising, the Owls took their game up a level. Nish stickhandled end to end before slipping a drop pass back between his own legs to Travis, and Travis threw a quick pass across the crease to Sarah, who scored again.

A minute left, and Nish scored on a fabulous rush that forced Yantha to trip him as he flew past the Panthers' big centre. Nish managed to take the shot by sweeping his stick blindly across the ice, but a second later crashed heavily into the boards.

Travis hated that sound. No, it wasn't the sound at all; it was the *silence* he hated at the end of a bad fall. It was as if all the noises of the arena – the skating, the yelling, the crowd, the whistles, the puck on blades, the crash of the sliding body into the boards, the echoes – all suddenly came to a stop, with every breath in the building held for fear of losing all breath entirely.

Both Sarah and Travis raced for their fallen teammate. Muck was already over the boards and making his way across the ice, Mr. Dillinger, with the first-aid kit, slipping and sliding along behind him.

"Anyone in the crowd holding a video camera?" Nish asked as Travis and Sarah leaned over.

"*What?*" said Travis. He wondered how badly Nish had smashed his head into the boards.

"I wanna know if anyone caught my goal," Nish said.

Sarah shook her head. "You're *pathetic.*"

Nish grinned up, sweat covering his face. "I know," he said with enormous pride.

Mr. Dillinger checked him over. The referee checked him over. They decided that nothing was broken and helped Nish to his feet. Sarah picked up his stick, Travis his gloves. The crowd began cheering, and the Panthers, led by Yantha, pounded their sticks on the ice in tribute.

Travis felt proud of his friend – right up until Nish began blowing kisses to the crowd like he was some famous actor taking a curtain call.

"Next time, I might hit him myself," Sarah said, shaking her head.

Nish skated about for nearly a minute, then lifted his stick towards the referee to signal he had his wind back and was ready to finish the game.

The puck dropped and Sarah clipped it right out of the air back to Nish, who turned and raced back towards his own end.

"*You're goin' the wrong way, idiot!*" Sam's big voice bellowed through the rink. Travis could hear them laughing in the stands.

But Nish knew exactly what he was doing. With Yantha giving chase and the Panthers' other forward trying to cut off his passing lane to Sarah, Nish used the net to shake free of Yantha and, reversing suddenly, headed to the far side, with Yantha now trying to cut back across ice to head him off.

It was a brilliant tactic. The other forward, thinking Yantha was out of position, moved to cut off Nish. Nish waited, teasing with the puck on the end of his stick, and just as both Panthers came down on him, he flipped a backhand saucer pass that hit Sarah perfectly as she moved through centre.

Sarah snapped a quick pass to Travis, who moved over the blueline with it, Billings trying to stay level between the two rushing Owls.

Travis faked a pass to Sarah, but Billings was too smart to bite. He wasn't playing the puck; he was playing the zone, trying to stay between the two so Travis couldn't slip a pass across the crease to Sarah and would have to take a shot from well out.

Travis pulled the puck back tight to his skates and cut for centre. Sarah, reading him perfectly, cut from the opposite direction, hoping the criss-cross might confuse Billings.

But again, Billings was too smart. He kept to his position, and just as the two Owls began to cross, he began to go down, hoping to use his falling body to block the drop pass he believed Travis was planning.

Travis held. He held, and everything seemed to slow. He held, and Sarah blew past him, and Billings, already committed, went down onto his side, spinning perfectly to cut off the pass that never came.

Travis held, and drifted. As he slowed, everything else sped up, and instantly he understood what Lars had meant. Going slow, as long as it surprises, can open up space just as surely as speed can.

He was all alone now. Sarah had cut across, her skates now rasping on a hard turn. Billings was lost, his stick teasing help-lessly like the sword of a defeated warrior.

The goaltender's pads stuttered. Travis held still, and waited. He seemed to be drifting like an astronaut, defying gravity, and the goalie, rattled by this neverending pause, gambled by flop-ping to his side and stacking his pads.

In a normal game, with two defencemen pressing him in the slot, Travis would have panicked and shot, praying the puck would somehow trickle through.

But this was not a normal game. This was 3-on-3 hockey, with everyone else out of the play, just Travis and the Panthers' goaltender alone with a slow-moving puck and a waiting net.

He held, seemingly forever, and continued to drift: past the goaltender's stick, past the stacked pads, past the skate blades until, finally, there was a small unblocked channel into the net.

Travis fired a backhand, low along the ice.

He heard so many sounds at once it was almost impossible to separate one from another: the horn, a whistle, cheering, cursing, Sarah screaming as she cut behind the net from the other side.

"TRAAAAVISSSS!"

Travis spun, his back slamming hard into the boards, but he felt nothing. He could see the referee, his hand pointing to the back of the net. He could see Yantha roaring back up ice, slamming his stick angrily. He could see the dejected look of the Panthers' goaltender, beaten.

The Screech Owls number-one team had won its first game.

They shook hands as the Zamboni came out to clean the ice. Yantha just slapped at Travis's glove, but Billings took his hand warmly.

"Nice goal, Travis," he said.

"Thanks," Travis said. He couldn't believe the little Portland defenceman still knew his name. Perhaps he had kept the card with its autograph – but he hadn't the nerve to ask.

The other Owls came onto the ice in their street clothes: Muck, Mr. Dillinger, Sam pushing through like she owned the place, then Lars.

Travis and Lars high-fived at centre ice.

"Slow enough for you?" Travis asked.

"It worked, didn't it?" Lars laughed.

"Perfectly."

**N**ever had Travis seen a tournament so wonderfully run. The organizers even took each team's equipment after the players switched over to the new tournament bags, and special locked "cages" had been provided in a rear storage area so teams could, if they wished, keep their equipment at the main tournament rink. Sarah and Sam, for example, wanted to take their equipment back to the motel and wash things out in the laundry room. Nish, red-faced, said he wanted to do the same and yanked his new pride and joy – "Official Competitor, First International 3-on-3 Hockey Tournament, Vancouver, B.C., No. 44" – off the nearest trolley, threw it over his shoulder, and headed out to catch the bus back to the motel.

"Nish has never washed his stuff in his life," noted Data as several of the Owls watched, astounded.

"He always says his stink is his good luck," said a mystified Jesse.

"He just wants to play with his new toy," said Travis. He made shaking motions with his hands and pretended to turn over a snow globe, his eyes widening in mock amazement.

"Didn't he have a childhood?" Wilson asked.

"He's still having it," said Sarah. "It's his missing adulthood that worries me."

The motel was simple, but nice, with a good view of English Bay and, on the far side, the green edge of Stanley Park. Sarah and Sam headed down to the laundry facilities to wash their hockey gear, Data and a few of the players started up a Nintendo round-robin, and Lars and Travis, who were rooming with Nish and Andy, lay down for a quick nap before dinner.

Travis was just dozing off when the quiet was broken by a cursing, angry Nish.

"*Damn it, damn it, damn it!*" Nish wailed. He sounded truly upset.

"*What?*" Travis shouted.

"My snow globe's broken!"

Travis sat up. At the foot of his bed was Nish, crouching over his new equipment bag. The box his snow globe had come in was torn at his feet and the beautiful gift in his hands.

"What's wrong?" Travis asked.

"Look!" Nish said, holding it up.

Travis stared at the snow globe. Only the snow inside wasn't swirling. It wasn't tumbling or falling.

It was doing nothing. More a solid snowball than a snowfall.

"What happened?" asked Travis.

"I dunno," said Nish. "I just pulled it out and it was busted."

Lars was already on his feet. He took the globe from Nish and rolled it over slowly in his hands. Nothing moved. "You must have shaken it awfully hard," he said.

"I didn't shake it at all," Nish protested.

"Maybe it got shaken on the bus," suggested Travis. "Or when they threw it on that trolley."

"That's probably it," said Lars, nodding. "It got so badly shaken it crystallized."

"*What?*" Nish asked, his face twisting into a puzzled prune.

"Crystallized," repeated Lars. "Sometimes things that are in liquid can crystallize and turn solid. Kind of like ice – only it doesn't need the cold."

Nish looked baffled. But he seemed to accept Lars's explanation. "I guess," he said. "But I don't want a broken one. I want a good one."

Lars smiled. "You can have mine. I don't care about it. I just like the equipment bag."

Nish looked relieved. "You're sure?"

"Sure. I'll give you mine next time we're back at the rink. It's in my new bag. That's where the rest of us put them."

Nish took back the broken snow globe and stared at it. "What'll we do with this one?"

"Put it in the drawer," Lars said. "Maybe I'll show it to someone and try to get a replacement."

Nish nodded. Perhaps he didn't understand crystallization, but he understood what he needed to know: that he would have a good, working snow globe to take home to his mother. Travis grinned slightly to himself. He knew Nish too well. If only the others knew what a big softie Nish was when it came to his mom. It was good of Lars to make such a generous offer – but then, that was typical of Lars, too. Always helping out. Always doing the right thing.

There was a loud rap on the door.

"You in there, Travis?" a voice called.

It was Sarah.

"Yeah, whadya want?"

"Muck wants to see us all down in the lobby – right away."

T he rest of the Owls were already hanging around the lobby. A few parents were there as well – only a handful had made the long trip – and Mr. Dillinger was organizing coffee. Muck was deep in conversation with a heavy-set, grey-haired man in a dark blue suit. Waiting to one side, both with Styrofoam cups of coffee steaming in their hands, were two other, powerful-looking men, also in dark suits.

Muck moved to the centre of the floor and cleared his throat. Everyone fell silent at once; they all wanted to know what was up.

"This here," said Muck, again clearing his throat as he turned to the grey-haired man, "is Inspector Bronson of the Royal Canadian Mounted Police. He's going to fill you in on what's been happening regarding the . . . incident."

Inspector Bronson, ruddy-faced and smiling, rubbed his hands nervously as he took his place beside Muck. He introduced the two men who had come with him, also with the RCMP.

"This has been a complicated investigation," said the inspector. "We've tried to co-ordinate matters, but it's also involved the Coast Guard, City of Victoria Police, and the Department of Oceans and Fisheries. We've also been helped out by the good people at the Aquarium.

"I also want to thank you all for your valuable contribution. If you hadn't sighted that body –"

"Two bodies," a voice interrupted.

Travis turned sharply. It was Sam, her green eyes flashing with something very near anger.

The inspector's red face turned even redder.

"Yes, well, of course," he sputtered, the air before him raining with spittle. "But we're conducting a murder investigation, miss. For the purposes of that, we are speaking of one deceased . . . Mr. Bradley Cummings."

"The dolphin was murdered, too," protested Sarah.

"Yes, well," the inspector began. A fleck of white foam danced ridiculously on his bottom lip as he fumbled for his words. The girls had clearly thrown him off. "The dolphin was killed, we have now ascertained, by fishermen's nets. The animal pathologists at the Aquarium found rope burns on it. We believe that Mr. Cummings was engaged in some sort of effort to rescue the fish from the netting –"

"A dolphin's not a fish!" Sam insisted.

"Whatever, miss," the inspector smiled lamely. "Mr. Cummings was vitally involved in dolphin projects at the Aquarium and was known to go out often on his own in search of them.

"He was a card-carrying member of Greenpeace," the inspector added, with a hint of a sneer as he mentioned the well-known environmental protection group, "and had been involved in disputes with drift-net fishermen in the past. He was a key leader in the fight to have them banned."

"What happened?" asked Fahd.

"We don't know exactly what happened, son, but what we *believe* happened is that Mr. Cummings came upon a fishing boat illegally using drift nets. Perhaps he tried to challenge them in some way. Some of these Greenpeace guys can be quite aggressive, you know."

It was clear that the inspector had no use for Greenpeace. He spoke as if everyone in the room shared his opinion, though Travis doubted any did – with the possible exception of the two policemen standing by the doorway.

"We imagine there was a confrontation. We think it was settled with a gun."

"But why shoot the dolphin, too?" asked Sam.

The inspector turned, blinking with surprise. He shrugged. "Perhaps to put him out of his misery. We don't know exactly, of course. All we do know, and all we are investigating, miss, is that someone shot Mr. Cummings and killed him. Through the Coast Guard, we are now conducting a thorough search of the waters around the area in question. All fishing vessels will be searched."

"You expect to find the weapon?" Muck asked.

"If we do, we'll find the killer," the inspector said smugly.

"Wouldn't the gun be at the bottom of the ocean by now?" said Fahd.

"Not necessarily, son," the inspector said, glad to have sensible questions from a sensible young man like Fahd. "Some fishermen believe in the law of the high seas. They might feel perfectly entitled to defend their property with firearms."

"It's hardly like Brad was out to torpedo them!" Sam shot back.

The inspector turned, staring hard, his colour rising again. He clearly did not like to be interrupted, especially with sarcasm.

"Where is his boat?" Sarah asked.

"Whose boat?" the inspector snapped.

"Brad's."

"We have found no vessel," he said.

"Isn't that a bit odd?" Sarah asked.

There was spittle again on the inspector's lips, dancing as he blew out impatiently.

"It's a very big ocean, my dear," he said, as if speaking to a little child. "Things can get lost at sea. They can even sink. Perhaps they sank his boat after they shot him."

"But *why* shoot the dolphin!" Sam demanded, all but stomping her feet.

# 9

**T**ravis blinked several times, unable to believe his eyes. Maybe he'd lost his mind and was seeing things. Perhaps he was having a nightmare.

"What's wrong with *you*?" a familiar voice whined.

But there was nothing wrong with Travis. It was the *thing* standing in front of him that had a problem.

Whatever it was, it was standing in the harsh light of the motel room's bathroom door. It was wearing a floppy bucket cap with the Vancouver Canucks logo in the middle. It had mirror sunglasses on, sending Travis a reflection of himself, his mouth and eyes wide open in shock. It was wearing a thick smear of white sunscreen right down its nose and onto one cheek. It was carrying a small gym bag – again, Vancouver Canucks colours, Vancouver Canucks logo – and out of the top of the gym bag stuck a huge bottle of blue Gatorade, an opened plastic bag of long red licorice sticks, and the earphones to a portable CD player.

Over its shoulder it wore a gaudy orange-and-yellow towel – *and apart from that nothing else!*

Not a stitch.

"*What're you looking at?*" the familiar voice whined from behind the sunscreen and mirror sunglasses.

Travis wasn't exactly sure. The big mirror on the bathroom door played off the wall of mirrors over the sink, so that Travis was staring at not just one shocking, incredible sight, but at more than two dozen. *More than two dozen buck-naked Wayne Nishikawas!*

Nish smiled. "You coming with me?"

"Coming *with* you?" Travis said incredulously. "*Where?*"

"Wreck Beach, stupid."

"*Where?*"

"The nude beach. I checked at the front desk. It's just past the university – about a dozen blocks from here."

"You're not going like *that?*"

"What's wrong with this?" Nish asked, twirling like a fashion model. "I'm dressed perfectly for Wreck Beach. Sun's shining – perfect beach weather."

"How you gonna get there?"

Nish turned and looked at himself in the mirror – hat, sunglasses, towel, sandals, *nothing* else . . .

"You plan to *walk?*" Travis asked, laughing. He could just picture Nish waddling down the street, bare cheeks wobbling behind him, cars honking and swerving, police sirens screaming.

Nish shook his head with pity for Travis. "I'm not that dumb, you know. This is how I'll look when I get there. What do you think?"

"I think you're crazy. They'll never let you on – you're a kid!"

"And kids can't be nudists? Is that what you're saying?"

"Nobody's going to be there. It's still spring, for heaven's sake!"

"It's warm out. Nobody's going to freeze their pinkies off."

Travis rolled his eyes. "It's not your pinkie I'm thinking of."

Nish wasn't even listening. He was looping a big unbuttoned shirt over his shoulders and kicking around his dumped luggage for his bathing suit. He was getting dressed to go out – getting dressed to go out and get undressed.

"Are you coming?" he asked as he lifted the bathing suit on one sandalled toe.

"Not a chance, pal."

Nish stepped into the suit, shrugging. "Suit yourself – but it's the chance of a lifetime."

"To see *you* naked? I've already seen enough of that to last a lifetime!"

Travis had no idea what would become of Nish. Nor did he much care. Some of the other Owls were gathering in the lobby, getting ready to strike out for the nearest McDonald's and talking excitedly about the 3-on-3 tournament.

There was a buzz to this competition that Travis had never before experienced. At every other tournament, the Owls had talked about their own team, and other teams, and how they were doing, and who they might meet if they made it to the finals. But now that they were split into teams within teams, all the talk was about themselves. Gordie, Fahd, and Sam had two easy wins in the Canucks Division, and Derek, Liz, and Willie had won one and then been beaten badly in the Rockies Division.

Dmitri, Andy, and Lars were soon to play their third match in the Elite Division, after losing their second. This one would be against the Portland Panthers, who had already been beaten by Travis, Sarah, and Nish. Travis's team was now 2–0, as was Jesse's team, with Simon and Wilson.

The Owls' excited chatter was brought to an abrupt end by a loud rumble of thunder. Travis looked out and saw that dark clouds were moving in fast. It amazed him how quickly the weather could change in Vancouver. A few minutes ago there had been bright sunshine – "beach weather," Nish had called it – and now it looked like it was going to storm. What was it the motel manager had said to them the other day? "You don't like our weather? Wait five minutes and it'll change – I guarantee it."

They decided they'd better head for McDonald's before the rain hit, and were just on their way out when Sarah and Sam burst in, their arms filled with newspapers. They seemed very excited. Sarah was holding out the front page of the *Vancouver Sun*, tapping her finger hard against the headline.

"AQUARIUM SCIENTIST HAILED AS HERO."

"*They're saying Brad gave his life for the dolphin!*" she shouted.

Sam handed out copies with the front-page stories and photographs of Brad Cummings. There were quotes from his fellow workers, who all said Brad went out on the water every chance he got, searching for dolphins and warning fishing trawlers to stay away from spots where he'd seen them swimming.

There was talk of naming a park after Brad, talk of a special scholarship fund being set up at the university to encourage the study of endangered species. Travis read all the reports, and while he still felt terrible about what had happened to Brad – could barely stand to think of him rolling about in those waves with that hideous black hole in his chest – he felt proud of what Brad had been doing and happy that there were people who had appreciated his efforts. He was, indeed, a hero.

Sam was in tears reading one of the papers. It was a story about Brad's mother and how Brad had always cared for her and how, ever since he was a little boy, he had cared more for wild creatures than for anything else. There was even a picture of a young Brad, aged thirteen or fourteen, feeding one of the killer whales at the Aquarium, and Sam clutched the newspaper picture to her heart as if she were about to faint.

"Listen to this!" shouted Data, who had wheeled over and picked up a copy of the *Vancouver Province.*

Just then there was a tremendous clap of thunder and a roar as the rain burst outside. Travis was glad Sarah and Sam had come along with the papers. They'd saved them from a soaking.

"'COAST GUARD FOLLOWING LEAD IN CUMMINGS MURDER,'" Data read, almost having to shout over the rain drumming on the motel windows. "'The Canadian Coast Guard has stopped and searched more than twenty fishing boats and trawlers in the past two days in an effort to find more details on the death of Bradley Cummings, twenty-seven, the marine biologist who was found floating off Victoria Harbour Monday with a bullet hole in his chest.

"'The RCMP Forensic Division in Vancouver has tentatively identified the murder weapon as an old-fashioned .303 Lee Enfield rifle, a war weapon once popular with deer hunters.

"'According to sources, the Coast Guard has interviewed at least two witnesses who reported hearing a shot, or several shots, fired in the vicinity Monday morning. Numerous fishing vessels – Canadian, American, Japanese, and Russian – were reportedly fishing in adjacent waters at the time.

"'Officials hope to find the weapon involved. A rifle, however, is easily lost to deep waters, and the Coast Guard is aiming its investigation more at interviews and possible eye-witnesses.'"

"Let's hope they find the murderer," said Wilson.

"I still can't understand why they'd shoot the dolphin, too," said Sam.

"You care more about a fish than a person?" asked Simon.

"It's not a fish. It's a dolphin. And of course I care about Brad – I just don't understand why they'd do that to a dolphin."

"It was caught in their nets," suggested Data, "and that's how they get rid of them. It was going to die anyway. Brad must have heard the shot and come after them. Or maybe he saw them do it. And then they shot him."

"I hope they catch them," said Liz.

"So do I," said Sarah.

"*What the hell is that?*" howled Derek, staring in the direction of the glass front door.

The Screech Owls all turned at once. The door opened, wind and rain bursting in as if someone had turned a fire hose on the motel entrance.

And with the wind and rain came a strange wet creature. It put its back to the door, pushing hard to close it. The latch caught, shutting the storm outside, and the room filled with silence. Silence but for the huffing and puffing of the creature who had burst in.

It wore a soaked bucket hat that hung so limp over the creature's face they couldn't see its eyes. There was something white smeared down its nose and cheeks. There was an unbuttoned shirt, wet through and clinging like paint to the heaving chest of whatever was beneath it. There was a bathing suit, halfway down the creature's hips, heavy with water and threatening to drop. There was a dripping sports bag, a half-finished bottle of blue Gatorade sticking out past the dangling earphones of a portable CD player.

"*Nish?*" Sam ventured.

Travis said nothing. He didn't need the creature to speak to know what it was.

The creature was shaking and shivering right in front of them. Its teeth were clicking together. It was moaning.

"*Where were you?*" Sarah asked.

The soaking wet bucket cap came off, revealing a very wet Wayne Nishikawa. He wiped the back of his arm across his face, smearing the white sunscreen from ear to ear.

"Nowhere," he mumbled through chattering teeth.

"*You weren't looking for that nude beach, were you, Nish?*" Sam demanded loudly.

Everyone started laughing.

"*None of your business!*" Nish practically spat.

"Whadya see, Nish," Andy teased, "barenaked . . . *ducks?*"

Nish scowled in Andy's direction. He shook himself like a big dog and started to walk towards the corridor leading to his room. His sandals squished as he stepped, large, wet footprints mapping his progress.

Nish paused at the doorway, peeled off his drenched shirt and shook it, spraying water in the Owls' direction without so much as turning around.

His wet bathing suit had slipped down even further, his cheeks bulging above the elastic. He stuck his bum out, half-mooning the Owls.

"I'M GONNA HURL!" howled Sam.

# 10

ravis's team was scheduled to play its third game in the Elite Division, this time against a spunky little side from Boston that had already beaten one of the better Canadian teams in the tournament. Muck and Data had "scouted" the Boston threesome in its previous game, and Muck asked the Owls' top team, plus Jeremy, to show up early to go over a few points with him.

Nish and Sarah carried their new equipment bags over their shoulders. Sarah had washed her jersey and socks and aired her equipment, and Travis could smell Fleecy fabric conditioner wafting up from her bag. Travis couldn't think of many peewee players who actually washed their gear. He might "air out" his stuff once or twice, but most of the players here, he figured, wouldn't even think to check their equipment from the day they arrived to the day they left. Still, it was such a pleasant change from Nish's equipment, which usually smelled like a giant's armpit whenever he unzipped it in the change room and dumped the damp, unwashed contents out in a huge pile. Nish, of course, had done nothing to his equipment, despite his threats. He'd only wanted to get his hands on the snow globe, which had also proved to be a huge disappointment.

They took over a small dressing room at the far end of the corridor. Mr. Dillinger helped Travis collect his new equipment bag – with the number 7 sharp on both ends – from the locked storage section that had been assigned to the Owls, and when he came back to the room Nish was staring down at his freshly dumped equipment in total shock.

No smell whatsoever.

No stink, no crumpled, caked socks, no damp, sticking sweater, no rolls of shin-pad tape, no half-empty bottles of Gatorade, no candy-bar wrappers – nothing to identify this as the pride and joy of Wayne Nishikawa, number 44, Screech Owls.

"What the hell's going on here?" Nish demanded.

"I can't believe it," said Jeremy. "Your equipment bag's open and I'm not gagging."

"*It's not my equipment!*" Nish whined.

"You're number 44," Travis said, gently kicking the end of the bag where Nish's number was clearly stitched.

"But look at the stuff!" Nish protested. "It's all brand new!"

Nish was right. New shin pads, new shoulder pads, new pants, new skates, new socks, new helmet, new gloves, new rolls of tape, garters, jock, everything.

"It's never been used," said Jeremy.

"That's crazy!" said Nish. "That makes no sense."

"Wait a minute!" Travis interrupted. He had just thought of something. "Where'd you get the bag from?"

"They *gave* them to us, remember?"

"No, no, no – I mean, where'd you get it from when you picked it up to go back to the motel?"

Nish looked puzzled. "Off the cart. Mr. Dillinger was just about to put them away, remember?"

"Yeah, I do. But the Panthers were putting theirs away at the same time. You're positive you got yours off the right cart?"

"Yeah – I guess," Nish said, but he didn't sound very sure.

"Mr. Dillinger's still out there," Jeremy said. "He's setting up his skate sharpener."

"He'll know," suggested Travis. "Let's go check with him."

They went into the corridor and down to the storage area, where Mr. Dillinger was already at work on a skate, a long spray of red-orange sparks shooting out from the blade as he expertly drew it along the spinning stone. Data was with him, lining up the skates as Mr. Dillinger finished sharpening them.

Mr. Dillinger shut the sharpening machine off when he saw them and lifted his safety glasses, smiling.

"We think Nish got the wrong bag," Travis said.

Mr. Dillinger chuckled. "Pretty hard to mistake Nish's equipment for anyone else's, isn't it?"

"Very funny," Nish said. "I took it off the cart – but this is what I ended up with."

He tossed the equipment bag down in front of Mr. Dillinger, the brand-new shin pads sticking up through the opened zipper. Mr. Dillinger leaned over and drew a deep, contented breath, like a man taking the first smell of spring.

"It isn't Nish's stuff – that I assure you," Mr. Dillinger said.

"Where'd my stuff go?" Nish asked.

"Maybe it's still on our cart," suggested Jeremy.

"That's where I got *this* one," Nish argued.

"Maybe you took it from the Panthers' cart. Don't forget — they got new bags at the same time."

Mr. Dillinger considered a moment. "It's possible," he said. "Why don't I just check our stuff to make sure."

He laid down the skate he'd been holding and fumbled in his pockets for a key chain. He picked out a shiny new key and headed back down to the storage locker. The others, including Data, followed.

He worked the key quickly into the lock, opened up the gate, and entered. The three players followed him in. Mr. Dillinger pushed and pulled at various bags. He reached deep in the pile and tugged hard at one buried near the bottom. With a grunt he pulled it free.

"There she be," said Mr. Dillinger, moving aside so they could see a large white number 44 on one end.

"Let me check," said Nish, pushing his way through.

He reached over and unzipped the bag. He breathed deep, imitating Mr. Dillinger, the smell like fresh-baked bread to him. "I'm home!" Nish announced.

"Zip it up!" Mr. Dillinger said. "You're peeling the paint off the walls!"

Nish snorted and zipped his bag up. He threw it over his shoulder and bounced the weight happily. He had his equipment back.

"Leave the other one with me," said Mr. Dillinger. "I'll be seeing the Panthers' manager — they play right after you. I just hope they didn't need it before this."

"It's just extra equipment," said Nish. "Brand new stuff just in case, I guess. They wouldn't have needed it."

"Lucky for you, young man," said Mr. Dillinger. "Lucky for you."

Nish was happily getting into his wretched equipment when Muck and Data arrived with Sarah. They all pushed into the little dressing room and Muck went over some last-minute reminders for the three players and their goalie.

"They've got one great shooter," said Muck, "and they won their first match by setting him up in the slot. There's a young woman on the team who's quick but doesn't see the ice nearly as well as you, Sarah. And their third is the most incredible pest you're every going to see on the ice. He never stops working, and he's going to get to you, Mr. Nishikawa, unless you promise to put a lid on that temper of yours."

Nish blinked and smiled like a choirboy. "You can't be talking about me, coach, surely . . ."

Muck shook his head. "Their goalie's good, but I think he's weak on low shots."

"I *know* he's weak on low shots," said Data. He was consulting a detailed scouting report spread across his knees. If hockey could be reduced to a mathematical equation, thought Travis, Data would be the one to calculate it. Unfortunately, there were two elements of the game that could never be figured out entirely, never reduced to simple equations: surprise and luck. Though without those two unknowns, figured Travis, hockey wouldn't be near the delight it is, both to those who play and to those who are just fans.

"He had eight scored on him last game," said Data. "Of the twelve shots on goal, seven were low – five right along the ice. He has the best glove hand I've ever seen – sorry, Jeremy."

"That's okay," Jeremy said, flapping his catching glove like a lobster claw.

Muck was ready to sum up: "Keep the big guy out of the slot. Watch the playmaker and try to surprise her. Don't let the checker pester you. And keep the shots low. Okay?"

"*Okay!*" they all said at once.

"Then let's go."

Muck and Data had done their job. From the moment the puck dropped it was clear that the Boston team was like a one-song band: let the shooter find the slot, feed him the puck, and let him shoot. Not very imaginative, Lars would have said, but it had worked before and, despite Muck's and Data's warnings, was working again against the Owls' top threesome.

Boston was up 3–0 before the Owls even managed a good shot on goal. In part it was Jeremy's fault – maybe Data had put him off by saying how good the other goalie was – but it was also Travis's fault for letting the playmaker get away from him, Sarah's fault for letting the slot stay open, and Nish's fault for letting the chippy little checker get to him. Nish had already swung his stick hard at the little checker's heels.

"You connect with one of those swings and you could be kicked out of the game," said Muck. "You might want to consider that, young man."

Nish never lost it again. He began to play as only Nish could play, when he wanted to. He was cool, methodical, careful, smart.

He blocked shot after shot from the shooter. He fooled the play-maker by letting her think she had room to pass, only to dive and frustrate her best efforts. He ignored the chippy checker, who soon seemed much closer to losing his temper than Nish was.

Sarah scored on a high backhander. Travis scored on a shot that never left the ice, causing a loud "*Whoop!*" from Data. And Nish scored on an end-to-end rush where he pulled the goalie out and gently tucked the puck in behind him as if he were placing an egg back in the refrigerator.

"Now we've got a game," Muck said. He was almost smiling.

It was a game indeed. Travis kept tight to the playmaker, making sure she had little ice to work with, and tried to force her to dump the puck to empty space. Sarah, with her great speed, was able to beat the others to loose pucks, which she then got to Nish, letting him work as a kind of quarterback as they moved up the ice.

Travis tried to keep in mind what Lars had told them. He used location passes. He used his body well. And he used slow-ness as a tactic, which worked beautifully.

It was on Travis's second goal that he realized the goaltender was guessing where the shot would go. The goalie had got it right almost every time, until Travis discovered the slightest pause could cause him to drop down, stack his pads, and even drift right out of the net.

"*Keep it! Keep it! Keep it!*" Travis whispered to Nish and Sarah as they lined up for the faceoff. Both understood. Both began keeping more.

The Owls went ahead 5–3. Boston tied it up. The Owls went ahead on a lovely little deke from Travis. The Owls went two up on a rocket from Sarah that never left the ice. And the Owls went ahead to stay on a blistering slapshot from Nish that bounced off the checker *and* Travis before tumbling up over the fallen goalie and into the net.

Final score: Owls 9, Boston 6.

Sarah, Travis, and Nish – and Jeremy – were undefeated.

"Good work," Muck said when he and Data came into the dressing room. He was carrying cold cans of Coke, and handed them out. For Muck to do something like this, Travis figured, was roughly the equivalent of buying them all new cars and handing out Stanley Cup rings. He must have been delighted. He even opened Nish's drink for him, Nish pretending to be unconscious as he lay flat on his back with his feet up on the bench.

"I-have-got-to-let-the-blood-flow-back-to-my-head," he groaned.

"We'll let you know if it ever gets there," said Sarah.

Nish stuck his tongue out at her and guzzled from his Coke, the dark liquid running down his cheeks and onto the floor. He then burped, loud as a car backfiring – a sure sign he was happy with his game.

Mr. Dillinger came in and congratulated them all.

"Did you get the bag back?" asked Travis.

Mr. Dillinger scratched his head. "I tried," Mr. Dillinger said. "But it wasn't the Panthers' – they don't even have a number 44 on their team."

"Whose was it, then?" Nish asked from the floor.

"I don't know," said Mr. Dillinger. "And they don't know. I guess it was just an extra."

"That doesn't make any sense," said Data.

"I know it doesn't, son," said Mr. Dillinger. "But you explain it, then."

Data shrugged. He said nothing.

But Travis could tell from the look in Data's face that he wasn't going to be satisfied with no answer at all — not when there had to be an explanation for such a simple mistake.

# 11

ravis decided this time to take his equipment back to the motel. He was sure he had been sweating much more playing 3-on-3 hockey than he normally did. Not only was it a lot more fun and relaxed than regular games, it was harder work. There were no changes, no long breaks, fewer faceoffs – and only two other players on the ice to pick up the slack if you missed your check or dogged it backchecking. At the end of each game, Travis felt drained, and by the weight and smell of his equipment, he knew exactly where he had drained to: it was time to air out the equipment.

He obviously wasn't the only player with this in mind. A couple of the Boston players had their equipment slung over their backs. And Sarah was again taking hers with her. Not Nish, though. His recovered equipment was zipped up and festering at the back of the Owls' storage area.

"Hang on there a minute, son!"

Travis turned, not recognizing the voice.

A man was walking towards him fast. He had on a dark bulky windbreaker and tinted glasses, the kind that seem to darken as the wearer moves from shadow to light, from inside to outside. He had a buzz-cut, his hair clipped so close his scalp seemed to shine in the arena lights. He had one large earring in his left ear.

Nish was pushing through the door already and turned back as the man reached them.

The man was smiling. They could see a crest on the windbreaker now, a tournament crest. He was one of the organizers.

He held his hands out helplessly, almost signalling an apology. "Look, you'll have to excuse me," he said, "but I've been asked to do a quick check of every bag leaving the building. Would you mind, son, if I took just the quickest peek?"

"What's the problem?" Nish asked.

The man shrugged, smiling. "There's been a thief at work here the last few days. Couple of wallets. Some skates. Look, I'm not even suggesting it might be either of you guys – in fact, we think it's just someone creating mischief. You know, putting stuff in other guys' bags to get them in trouble. I can guarantee you no trouble – just a quick glance to be sure, okay?"

"Sure," said Travis. "Go ahead."

Travis slipped the bag off his shoulder and dropped it onto the smooth concrete floor of the entranceway.

"Thanks," the man said. He unzipped the bag, ran a hand quickly down both sides, checked the end pocket.

He pointed to Travis's tournament present, the boxed snow globe.

"That what they gave you?"

"Yeah," Travis answered.

"What're they like?" the man asked.

"Neat," said Travis. "It's a snow globe."

The man was already opening the box. He peered down at the snow globe, gave it a little shake, and laughed.

"I love these things," the man said.

Travis grinned. For an "official," this guy wasn't doing much of a job of checking things over. He seemed too easily distracted. He put the snow globe back in its box, carefully closed it, and returned it to Travis's bag.

"Thanks a lot," the man said. "Sorry to be such a hassle."

"No problem," Travis said.

He hoisted his bag up over his shoulder again, and Nish pushed open the doors and held them for Travis. It had been raining when they arrived, but now the sun was shining.

Nish was already babbling about getting back to Wreck Beach. He said he knew he'd never talk Travis into going with him, but perhaps Lars would go. Lars, after all, came from Sweden and was used to saunas and didn't think there was anything particularly odd or funny about walking around naked and . . .

But Travis wasn't even listening. Nish went on and on, and Travis tried to concentrate the way he would on a difficult math problem. This tournament was wonderful – in a way, he'd never enjoyed the game of hockey more – but there were also some very strange things going on around them.

The Owls had stumbled across a murder. Two murders, if you counted the dolphin. They knew the victim, even if only slightly. That was the first mystery, and now there was this second, completely different one.

Hockey bags.

Nish had walked off with a bag that didn't belong to him – and, as far as they could tell, didn't belong to *anyone*. And now this tough-looking man had asked to search through Travis's hockey bag with some weird story about stolen equipment. It hadn't rung true when he said it, and it didn't ring true now that Travis thought it over.

No, this was much worse than any math problem. In this case, nothing at all added up.

Lars met them in the motel lobby, holding out a snow globe with a perfect little blizzard inside. Nish grabbed it and kissed it. Now he had a present for his mother, and this one worked.

"Did you exchange it?" Nish asked.

"Nah – I'll ask about it later. You can have mine. I picked it up at the rink for you."

"They didn't accuse you of stealing it, did they?" asked Travis.

"No. Why do you say that?"

"They checked my bag on the way out."

"Mine, too," added Sarah.

"There was a guy at the door asked if he could see it," said Lars. "But he never said a word about stealing."

"Did he check it?" asked Travis.

"Yeah," Lars said, his voice trailing with wonder. "He said he just wanted to see how it worked."

"Same with me," said Sarah.

"Maybe there've been complaints about other globes that don't work," suggested Nish.

"Maybe," said Travis, but he didn't think so. Surely the man with the earring would have said something about faulty snow globes when he was looking at his. But instead, he'd acted as if he'd never seen one before, even though Travis was sure Sarah had left before Travis and Nish.

"This guy shaved practically bald, with a big earring?" Travis asked Sarah.

"Yeah," said Sarah. "Why?"

"I don't know – just wondering."

# 12

Nish was still gazing at his perfect new snow globe when the doors to the motel burst open and Sam roared in, brandishing the morning newspaper.

"*There's something weird going on here!*" she announced. She seemed both angry and determined at the same time.

"What is it?" Sarah asked.

"Just look at this!" Sam said. She spread the newspaper out on the lobby coffee table and her teammates clustered around, peering down at the place on the front page where she was tapping her finger.

"TIME OF DEATH A PUZZLE," said the headline.

Sam read out loud:

"Medical experts have concluded that Brad Cummings, the twenty-seven-year-old marine biologist found murdered off Victoria Bay last weekend, died as much as three hours before the dolphin found shot in the same waters. Early investigation had been based on the assumption that the dolphin had been killed first.

"It had previously been presumed Mr. Cummings got into an argument over the fate of the dolphin, which led to a confrontation between the marine biologist, a known environmental activist, and fishermen who may have snagged the dolphin in illegal nets.

"The dolphin, Vancouver Aquarium scientists confirmed today, showed faint signs of abrasion on one side, consistent with injuries found among fish and animals that have struggled in fishing nets.

"Both victims, RCMP sources say, were killed with the same weapon, a Lee Enfield .303-calibre rifle once popular with local hunters.

"No weapon has been found, nor have any witnesses stepped forward in the case."

Sam finished reading and stood nodding with great satisfaction. "I knew there was something fishy about this whole thing," she said.

"Of course there was," Nish shot back. "They murdered a fish, remember?"

"You're too stupid to bother with," Sam said, dismissing him.

"I don't understand," said Fahd.

"Why would they kill Brad first?" Sam said. "It makes sense if he'd come along right *after* they'd shot the dolphin. Maybe he was even filming it. But why kill him and then, hours later, kill the dolphin?"

Everyone thought about it a while. No one had any idea why.

"Maybe they thought the dolphin knew something?" suggested Andy.

"Or *had* something?" offered Lars.

Sam looked up from the paper. "What do you mean?"

"I don't know," said Lars. "It just seems they must have had to chase the dolphin. Maybe it had run off with the nets?"

"I doubt that," said Andy.

"Well, something," said Lars.

"What?" Nish demanded.

"I don't know," said Lars. "Something."

It doesn't add up, Travis kept saying to himself. It just doesn't add up.

# 13

"Let's get naked!"

Nish was at the open window, ducking low to stare up into a soft blue sky. The sun had been out all morning, and the air pouring in was warm and filled with the promise of summer.

Nish was in his boxer shorts, visible to anyone in the parking lot who happened to pass by.

"Let's just get to the rink," Travis said. "You do what you want later – by yourself!"

"I think you should go see a psychiatrist," said Lars, flossing his teeth as he walked out of the bathroom.

"You can talk!" Nish barked back. "Only a nut would floss when there's no one to make him. I don't even brush my teeth when I'm on the road!"

"*Or shower!*" shouted Andy, who was just coming in from the hallway.

"*Or use deodorant!*" called out Wilson, right behind Andy.

Nish drew himself up and puffed out his chest. "That's because I believe in the cleansing power of nature. You see, *I* am a nudist!"

"You're a nudist *and* a nut," said Travis, surprising himself by saying so. "Now let's get dressed and get out of here. We want to see Gordie's group up against that team from California, don't we?"

"I'd rather see Wreck Beach!" protested Nish.

"You're pathetic!" said Andy.

The Owls had almost reached the little 3-on-3 rink when Travis, slightly ahead of the rest and helping push Data along, saw the quick flash of a Screech Owls sweater as someone ducked around the far corner of the arena, where the Zamboni came out to dump the snow.

"They're out back," Travis announced, turning and walking backwards as he informed the others.

With Travis and Data leading the way, the group headed down the side of the arena and around the corner to the rear of the building. Travis expected to find all four of the Owls who would playing that afternoon – Fahd, Andy, Sam, and, in goal, Jenny – but when he turned the corner he realized there was only the one.

Sam . . . smoking.

She turned when she heard them and coughed out a lungful of cigarette smoke. Travis could see she was trying to hide the burning cigarette behind her back, but then, realizing it was only the boys, she slyly drew her hand forward and attempted to look natural.

But it didn't look natural at all. It looked ridiculous. Especially with her dressed for a game of hockey.

"You'll stunt your growth," Data said.

"Mind your own business," said Sam.

Travis winced. He hadn't expected such a sharp response to Data's comment. He watched her face as she dragged deep on the cigarette. Her eyes were red; she looked like she might be on the verge of tears.

Was it the smoke? Or the murders? None of the Screech Owls had seemed as caught up in and upset about the murders as Sam had. Each morning she was up at dawn to grab the early papers. She listened to the newscasts. She had even phoned the Aquarium to see if there was any more information on the death of the dolphin. Twice she had exploded at teammates for talking about the "murder," as if the word could only apply to people. She referred to the "murders," and she grieved as much for the poor dolphin as she did for Brad Cummings.

Sam flicked the still-burning cigarette away. She coughed once but then held the smoke for some time before expelling it in a long, elegant plume that rose over her head and vanished into the air.

"Muck catches you, you're dead meat," said Nish.

"Muck catches me, I'll know who told," she said, and stomped in through the Zamboni doors towards the dressing room.

"What's with her?" Nish asked.

"She's upset," said Andy. "She's been like that ever since the whale watching."

"What can we do about it?" said Wilson. "The police are working on it."

"They're not getting anywhere," said Andy. "I think that's what's wrong with Sam. No one seems to care about the dolphin, and no one seems to be getting anywhere on the murder."

"Murders," corrected Data.

"Murders," agreed Andy.

"We better get inside," said Travis. He started to turn Data's chair around, but Data held up his hand for Travis to stop.

"Just leave me here," Data said. "I can get in the Zamboni entrance easier than the front."

"You're sure?" asked Travis.

"I'm sure. I want to check out something anyway."

Travis shrugged. He knew better than to hound Data about what he was up to. If Data wanted him to know, he would have said.

"Suit yourself," Travis said. "You know where we'll be."

ata was happy to be left alone, to move at his own pace on Nish's great puzzle, which Data found both confusing and fascinating. Too many voices tended to cloud the issue, too many ideas sent his own mind in wild circles – but always, always returning to the one point that made no sense to him: the hockey bag that had no owner.

He kept his brain locked on that one troublesome fact. He wouldn't let his thoughts drift off to puzzling over why, or how, the man in the water might have died before the dolphin. He refused to think about the snow globes and why the organizers would have a man checking the players as they left the rink. These were significant factors – they might even turn out to be critical clues – but Data had a gut feeling he couldn't shake about the mysterious hockey bag.

Everything else might have an explanation. The man and dolphin might have been murdered by different people. The autopsy reports might even be wrong. And there might have been a problem with kids stealing from the tournament, even if Data had trouble believing they would do such a thing.

But there could be no easy explanation for the hockey bag. It wasn't Nish's, even though it was exactly the same as the one he'd been given and had his number on it. A mix-up would have been understandable, and at first that's what it had appeared to be. But once it turned out that the Panthers had no number 44, and the only trolley Nish could have gotten mixed up over was the Panthers' – all the other teams' equipment being locked up – it seemed to Data to make absolutely no sense at all.

But he had a notepad and he had a hunch. He rolled his wheelchair down past the dripping Zamboni, over a hose line, and down a corridor towards the large storage area at the back of the rink.

He could hear the high, dry song of a skate-sharpening machine. It didn't sound like Mr. Dillinger's, and he hoped it wasn't. He was looking for another equipment manager, from another team altogether.

He rolled as fast as he could towards the sound.

Travis, Nish, and the rest sat in the stands, cheering on their teammates – Fahd, Gordie, and Sam – against a tough, quick team from California, the Arrowhead Rangers.

"Fahd may finally have found his game," said Lars.

Travis nodded in agreement. It was somewhat surprising to see, but Lars was correct: in 3-on-3, Fahd was two or three times the player he was in regular hockey. Fahd had always moved so slowly and deliberately on the ice, but here, with more space to work in, his slowness worked at times to his advantage. It was just as Lars had said. And Fahd seemed able to keep track of his opponents far better when there were just three of them instead of five. He suddenly seemed smarter, niftier, slicker, and if he still lacked speed it was hardly a disaster, because, unlike in other games, he was always moving the puck just before an opposition player caught him.

Gordie and Sam were playing as expected. Gordie's long reach was a great advantage on the smaller rink, and he was able to read his teammates well. And Sam, by sheer desire, was able to drive directly for the net from almost anywhere, panicking the Rangers so much they put two checkers on her, which only opened up either Fahd or Gordie for an easy pass and shot. And if the puck found Gordie, with his hard, quick wrist shot, it seemed to end up in the net every time.

The Owls' threesome, with Jenny in net, was up 5−2 at the break. Mr. Dillinger had come around and was sitting with the others, and he started up a great cheer for the skaters before the puck dropped again.

"Muck's betting they make the finals," said Mr. Dillinger when he sat back down beside Travis.

Travis looked to make sure Mr. Dillinger wasn't joking. He wasn't. He wasn't even looking to see Travis's reaction − if he had, he would have seen Travis's jaw drop.

*The finals?* Travis thought he had a pretty good fix on which threesomes were moving ahead, and he'd already figured on his own group, with Sarah and Nish; the Panthers' top threesome; the Owls' other elite team, Dmitri, Andy, and Lars; and perhaps a team from Winnipeg battling it out to see which two met in the "A" championship. He'd never for a moment considered one of the teams from the Canucks Division jumping up, even though they'd been told from the start that crossovers were possible. He'd figured the Elite Division had been given its name for a reason.

And yet he had to admit, they were playing extremely well. It was as if he was seeing skinny little Fahd for the first time. Fahd combined with Gordie's shot and Sam's strength made a formidable team, and the way Jenny was playing goal for them was equally astounding. Perhaps Muck was on to something.

Travis began watching his fellow Owls more closely. He was *scouting* them, even though he knew the four players on the ice almost as well as he knew himself.

There was something different about Sam. He began to focus on her, watching her even when she wasn't directly involved in the play, and it took him several minutes to realize what had changed.

Sam was running out of gas. She was gasping when the play left her. And she was coasting when she should have been skating.

It was as if she had no breath left.


Data found who he was looking for. The equipment manager was in charge of the California team, the Arrowhead Rangers. His name was Mr. Williamson – sort of a skinny Mr. Dillinger, with a full head of grey hair – and he was both very friendly and helpful.

"Funny you should bring that up," the Arrowhead equipment manager said when Data got around to asking his one important question. "We had the same thing happen here. I do my morning check – I like to sharpen all the kids' skates right away – and I pull out the bags and then restack them when I'm done. Same darned thing happened to us."

"What do you mean?" Data asked.

Mr. Williamson studied his nails as he thought about it. "We had one too many bags. I figured one of the equipment guys from one of the other teams simply got mixed up and put it with our stuff. All those new tournament bags look exactly the same. So I just handed it back in."

"To who?"

"The organizers. They seemed pretty darned glad to get it, too."

"What number was it?"

"Huh?"

"The number – do you remember the number on the side?"

Mr. Williamson ran a hand through his thick hair. "Oh, that number. Yes, as a matter of fact I do, son."

"And it was?"

"Number 17. And you know what? We don't even have a 17 on the Rangers."

Data nodded and scribbled down the number on his notepad.

A number the Rangers didn't have. Just like the Panthers never had a number 44.

What did it all mean?


Travis could tell Fahd was starting to understand his new abili-ties in 3-on-3. With time running out on the Rangers, Fahd picked up the puck behind his own net, began coming out the left side, then twisted back to the right. The Rangers' quickest player swept around the net, chasing.

Fahd seemed so cool it was almost as if he was moving in slow motion. He tapped the puck back against the boards and turned again, just as the checker flew by and slashed his stick. It didn't even matter; the puck wasn't on Fahd's stick anyway.

He picked off his own pass and began to move up ice at such a leisurely pace it looked like he was on a public skating rink instead of in a high-pressure hockey tournament.

Andy slammed his stick hard, calling for a pass on the other side. A second Rangers checker tried to take the pass away, and went down on one knee as Fahd casually faked the pass to Andy. The checker lost his balance and twirled off into the boards.

Fahd kept the puck and moved directly to the net. He motioned as if to make a drop pass – the pass that was working so well for the Owls – and again a Rangers player went for it, lunging behind Fahd in the hopes of plucking the puck away from Sam, who was waiting to pick it up.

But again no pass. Fahd still had the puck, each of the Rangers now out of his zone and only the goaltender left. Fahd held on, waiting, moving slowly past the net until the Rangers' goalie flopped and kicked high with his pads in desperation.

Just as Travis had done against the Panthers, Fahd kept the puck and slowed even more, waiting while the goaltender drifted helplessly out of his own net, and then backhanded the puck high under the crossbar.

The stands exploded in appreciation. Travis could feel Mr. Dillinger's big hand pounding into his back. He could hear a wicked, high-pitched giggle as Nish pumped a fist for Fahd. He could see Sarah dancing with delight.

He felt good for Fahd. He felt, for a moment, as if he no longer knew Fahd. *Fahd, the star of the game?* Never before – but he sure was now.

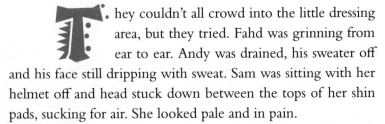

# 15

hey couldn't all crowd into the little dressing area, but they tried. Fahd was grinning from ear to ear. Andy was drained, his sweater off and his face still dripping with sweat. Sam was sitting with her helmet off and head stuck down between the tops of her shin pads, sucking for air. She looked pale and in pain.

Travis felt a finger poke in his back. He turned around quickly. It was Lars. "Data wants to see you," he said.

Travis backed out of the dressing room, the door muffling the sound of the happy players and their fans as it closed.

Data was sitting a little way down the corridor. He had his notepad on his knee, and looked extremely worried.

"What's up?" Travis asked.

"The snow globe that came out of that bag Nish carried back to the motel," Data said. "What became of it?"

Travis thought about it for a moment. "We put it in one of the drawers," he said. "Lars was going to exchange it, I think."

"Did he?"

Travis shook his head. "I don't think so," he said. "I think it's still there."

The worry lines on Data's face deepened. "I think we'd better go back to the motel as quickly as possible," he said.

Data explained on the way back. He had discovered that the confusion over Nish's bag wasn't an isolated incident. The Arrowhead Rangers' equipment man, Mr. Williamson, had also found a bag that didn't belong with his team's equipment. An extra bag, and a number on it that didn't connect to any of the Arrowhead players. A bag number 17, but no 17 on the team.

It seemed too much of a coincidence. Nish had picked up a bag intended for the Portland Panthers, and they had turned out not to have a number 44 in their lineup.

Data had borrowed a master team roster from Mr. Dillinger. It listed all the teams, all the players, and all the numbers. He couldn't find any other equipment managers, but he had been able to do a visual check of several of the other teams, counting their bags stacked up inside the locked storage areas. He was convinced several of the teams had one more bag than players on their roster. He hadn't been able to check if in each case there was a number that didn't fit on the team, but he had seen enough to become suspicious.

"Maybe they just threw in an extra bag for each team," suggested Nish. "A bag for the coach, or equipment manager – and extra equipment, in case somebody forgot something."

Data wasn't convinced. "Don't you think if that was the case they would have told the equipment managers?"

"What then?" Sarah asked.

"I don't know," Data said. "But I want to check out that snow globe Nish gave Lars."

"It's no good," Nish said, shaking his head. "We should have taken it back."

"That's just what I'm worried about," said Data.

They had almost reached the motel when Sam, who'd been hanging back with yet another of her cigarettes, caught up to the rest of the Owls and walked quickly, breathing hard, right through the centre of the gang.

Travis thought it was rude, and quite unlike Sam.

As she pushed through, her head held straight ahead, she whispered quickly out of the corner of her mouth: *"Don't anybody turn! There are three men following us!"*

"Impossible," said Nish, threatening to turn.

*"Don't look!"* Sam hissed again, her whisper almost becoming a shout. *"One's the guy Travis said was checking bags. The buzz-cut guy with the earring."*

Travis had to fight not to turn. He kept facing straight ahead, and the Owls, as a group, picked up the pace.

As they rounded a corner Travis allowed himself the quickest, tiniest peak back. He saw the man in the tinted glasses. His windbreaker was gone now – it was warm, the sun still out – and he was wearing a dark golf shirt. And two other men, both bulky, both in black T-shirts that showed off their beefy arms, were moving with him.

"What do we do?" asked Fahd.

"We get to the motel and find Muck," said Data. He had his wheelchair going full speed. Nish was pushing from behind, almost running.

"What do they want?" Sarah asked him.

"I think I know."

They made it to the motel, and once inside looked out through the glass door. The men had vanished.

"They weren't after us at all," Nish sighed in relief.

"Think again," advised Andy. "Look at the back of the parking lot."

The men were walking casually across the parking area, pretending to be moving towards their vehicle, but in fact they were turning to watch the kids and slipping in among the cars for cover.

"Get me to your room as fast as you can," Data ordered Nish.

"Somebody track down Muck or Mr. Dillinger," Travis called back. He was already fishing out his key to the room he shared with Nish and Lars.

Fahd and Andy split off to find the coach and the equipment manager. The motel seemed empty. It was such a fine day, everybody was probably out exploring. Travis had a sudden wish it was still raining, and that everyone was still in the motel. It was warm, but he shivered suddenly, worried that Muck and Mr. Dillinger wouldn't be around to help if the three men came after them.

But why? he wondered. Why would they come after a bunch of kids? What did they think they had?

Once Nish had pushed him into the room, Data began taking charge.

"The snow globe," he said. "Where is it?"

"It's in the bottom drawer," said Lars.

"It's no good," protested Nish. "It's broken, remember?"

"I'm not so sure," said Data.

Lars removed the box and opened it for the second time. The globe was still there. It hadn't been touched. The "snow" was still crystallized, meaning it was still broken. Travis couldn't see what the point was.

Data had Lars bring the globe to him. He set it in his lap and, with his good hand, began rolling it back and forth.

"See?" said Nish. "It's busted."

"I don't think so," said Data.

"What is it then?" Nish asked sarcastically. "*Fixed?*"

Data looked up at them all, his eyes filled with the same worry Travis had noted before. "It's cocaine."

"*Cocaine?*" Sarah and Sam said at once.

"*Drugs?*" Travis said.

"I think so," said Data. "We're going to have to call the police to be certain."

"I'm not so sure we've time," said Sam. She was looking out the window. "Those three guys are coming in the back way."

Travis looked out just in time to catch the third of the big-muscled men dip in the back entrance.

"What if they're coming after this?" Travis asked.

"If they get it," said Data, "there goes the evidence. It would just be our word against theirs."

"Like they're going to believe us!" said Nish.

Andy burst into the room, scaring them all. He seemed out of breath, frightened himself.

"Muck and Mr. Dillinger are out," he said. "There's nobody here."

"We better call the police," said Sarah.

"We better hide this," said Lars, picking up the snow globe.

"*Where?*" asked Nish. His voice cracked with fear.

"I don't know," said Lars. "Let's get it out of here. The window, maybe – those three thugs are inside the building."

Travis hurried into action. He was captain, after all. He was supposed to lead in moments of crisis. "I'll take it," he volunteered.

"I'm comin' with you!" Nish said at once.

"I'll come, too," said Sam.

Travis was already half out the window. Nish followed, then Sam.

Lars leaned out with the snow globe and passed it into Travis's outstretched hands.

He took it carefully, afraid of dropping it and breaking it. He cradled it like a baby against his chest.

"*Someone better be calling the police!*" Sam called up.

"*Sarah's already on the phone!*" Lars shouted down. "*Just get it out of here until they get here!*"

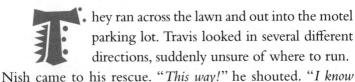

hey ran across the lawn and out into the motel parking lot. Travis looked in several different directions, suddenly unsure of where to run.

Nish came to his rescue. "*This way!*" he shouted. "*I know where it goes!*"

With Nish leading, the three Screech Owls began running as fast as they could. Nish moved quickly, puffing loudly but running well. He was already sweating. Sam covered the ground as fast as she moved on the ice, seeming to eat up the distance. Travis brought up the rear, finding it difficult to run as quickly as the others without his arms free. But he was holding the evidence, and had no intention of dropping it or leaving it or, worst of all, giving it up.

He heard Nish's voice, but at first he wasn't sure it was Nish. It sounded like a trapped animal, a squeal more than a voice, and filled with sudden terror.

"*They're coming!*"

Out of the corner of his eye Travis could see two burly

figures moving out of the side door of the motel and into the parking lot. One pointed – *at him!* – and they began running in the Owls' direction.

"M–M–MOOOOOVE IT!" Travis found himself screaming.

The men were giving chase, the buzz-cut guy and one of the two muscle men. The third must have still been back in the motel, checking the rooms.

Nish was in full flight now, tearing down the streets past the university buildings, headed towards a dark, green park at the far end. Travis didn't know what to think. Perhaps they could lose the men more easily in a park. But then, if they did get caught, who would be there to help them?

There was no time for debate. They made for the park.

Travis could feel his chest burning. His breath seemed on fire as it jumped from his lungs. He was sweating, his heart pounding. Nish's face was beet red, his mouth wide open, and sweat danced in drops off his cheeks and forehead. Sam was breathing terribly, but still seemed strong.

Sam looked back at Travis. "*Here!*" she puffed, reaching out with both hands. "*I'll take it a bit!*"

Travis handed the snow globe to her gratefully. He felt instant energy, new speed as he gave it up, but the relief didn't last. Another dozen strides and his lungs were again on fire, his legs turning to rubber.

But he was doing better than Sam. She was suddenly falling back, crimson in the face, and gasping horribly for air. She stumbled once and nearly fell with the snow globe. Travis reached over and she handed it back. She seemed angry – but whether at him or herself, Travis couldn't tell.

Into the thick of the park the three Owls ran, their pounding running shoes snapping twigs and sending dirt flying. Branches stung their faces as they pushed through, hoping that around the next tree they would find an adult, a policeman – anyone who could help.

Sam was still slipping back. Her breathing seemed loud enough for all of them, deep rattling gasps that cut sharply through the silence of the bush they were invading.

Travis could hear the men crashing through the trees. They were cursing the branches and snapping them off as they elbowed deeper and deeper into the wooded park. Fortunately, the big men were slowing down in the thick bush. Had the branches not blocked them, they might already have reached Sam, who was steadily falling behind the two boys.

Did Nish really know where he was going? Travis wondered. He was acting like he knew, but Travis had known Nish to fake it a million times before. This was no time for bluffing.

Nish was up ahead, picking the path they would take. His head was spinning from side to side, a sure sign he was getting confused. Travis suddenly felt angry with Nish for bringing them there – but still, where else could they have gone? At least the men weren't gaining on them any more.

Sam suddenly stopped, gagging alarmingly as she tried to breathe. She leaned over and held one arm out, begging them to wait. She was beat, exhausted. It seemed she couldn't go on.

Up ahead, Nish stopped and spun on his heels, terror in his eyes.

"*We're trapped!*" he shouted back.

They had come to the ocean. They could go no further.

Travis could hear the men thrashing through the bush towards them.

"There's . . . b–beach . . . that . . . w–way!" Sam gasped, pointing.

They looked to their left. The woods gave way to open ground; beyond that was sand.

There were bodies in the distance.

*Naked bodies!*

Nish smiled. "I'm home!"

"You're dead!" Travis shouted angrily at him. This was no time to fool around.

*Nish had led them to Wreck Beach, the nudist beach!*

"*I can't run any more!*" Sam cried, her eyes filling with tears. She was puffing terribly, gasping for air.

"What'll we do?" Travis asked.

Nish had already decided – his shirt over his head, his shorts dropping over his sandals, his boxers down past his knees.

"*They'll never chase me there!*" he shouted.

He turned, buck naked, and yanked the snow globe out of the Travis's hands. Before they could say a word, he bolted out of the cover of the woods and onto the beach.

"GO FOR IT, NISH!" Sam called.

Travis couldn't believe it. He couldn't even speak. He could only stare at the back of the best friend he had in the world, Nish's barenaked cheeks churning as he hurtled, sand flying all about him, directly into the throng of early-season nude sunbathers.

Nish was wearing nothing but a snow globe, clutched so tight to his chest he looked like a football player heading for a touchdown.

"HEY!" a nasty, deep voice shouted. "STOP!"

A little distance away the two men had also broken clear of the woods. They couldn't see Travis and Sam in the cover of the branches, but they could plainly see Nish charging across the sand with the prize they were after.

They never even looked for Sam and Travis. They set off across the soft sand, sinking and stumbling with each step, two fully clothed men in dress shoes running and yelling into a crowd of peaceful nudists, most of whom were scattering with their towels and umbrellas to make way for the miniature nudist who was barrelling straight down the beach with what appeared to be a crystal ball in his arms. The stumbling men pushed on in pursuit, oblivious to the sudden rise of a police siren ahead at the far side of the beach.

Two police cars with flashing lights and sirens pulled off the hard ground and fishtailed onto the beach, throwing sand in every direction.

Nish never looked back. He kept on going towards the police cruiser, his legs a blur, his pink round body hunched protectively over the snow globe. And as the first policeman jumped out of the car, the naked young runaway blew right past him into the safety of the front seat.

The two men tried to turn back, but it was too late. They stumbled on the soft sand and went down, stumbled over each other again as they tried to get back on their feet. They fell back, cursing, as the police moved in on them with service revolvers drawn.

The two men threw up their hands in surrender.

Beaten by a naked twelve-year-old.

# 17

**N**ish and Fahd came into the motel lobby, their arms filled with copies of the *Vancouver Sun* and the *Province*. Nish's photograph was the entire front page of one paper – "PEEWEE NUDIST FOILS DRUG CARTEL," blared the huge red headline – and his face beamed out in a smaller photo in the other paper, with a large map beside him showing the various places the RCMP had raided following the arrest of the thugs on Wreck Beach.

"The pictures are inaccurate," Nish announced as he handed out the newspapers to his teammates. "I shouldn't have any clothes on – but the stories are pretty good!"

The stories were astonishing. Travis and Sarah leaned over a copy of the *Sun* spread out on the floor, and raced each other to see who could come up with the most amazing detail.

"'PEEWEE TOURNAMENT PART OF INTERNATIONAL DRUG SCHEME,'" Travis read from one headline.

"'AQUARIUM COLLEAGUES STUNNED TO LEARN BIOLOGIST

PART OF SMUGGLING RING,'" Sarah read, her voice sad rather than excited.

The story *was* sad. Exciting, obviously. Dangerous, obviously. But sad, too, for none of the Owls could take any pleasure in learning that Brad Cummings – the marine biologist who had been so kind to them during their visit to the Aquarium, the body they had found floating in the rolling seas off Victoria Harbour, the sweet, gentle man they all thought had been murdered because he tried to rescue a dolphin – had, in fact, been up to his neck in a very dangerous and criminal business.

"This is too much," Sarah said. And it was, for all of them. She was teary-eyed as she examined the newspapers. And Sam could only read a little bit before crunching up her newspaper and throwing it hard against the wall. She had then stomped out into the light rain, where she could now be seen, walking around the parking lot with her hands wrapped around her bare arms.

Travis read on, switching from one paper to the other, then back, trying to put it all together in a way that made sense.

But it was almost beyond sense. It seemed like they'd all been watching some fantastic, outrageous television show. But there was no remote you could push to turn it off, no happy ending, no feeling it was make-believe.

The mystery had been solved, but Brad and the dolphin were still dead.

Two other things were also certain. The mystery would never have begun to unravel if it hadn't been for Data's curiosity about the hockey bags. And the bad guys would never have been caught if Nish hadn't made that daring, naked dash across Wreck Beach with the broken snow globe in his arms. In fact, the snow globe wasn't broken, had never been broken. It had been exactly as Data had suspected, an ingenious way to smuggle cocaine.

If Travis had to take all these newspaper stories and reduce them to one simple explanation, the way they sometimes had to do in school, he would have written it down this way:

Smugglers had been using dolphins to get illegal drugs into the North American market. Cocaine was shipped up from South America, where it was manufactured. The fishing vessels carrying the drugs really were fishing along the Pacific Coast of the United States, but once they reached British Columbia the "fishermen" quickly became drug smugglers.

Canada is considered much easier to smuggle drugs into than the United States, so the smugglers chose the waters off Vancouver Island as the place to get the cocaine ashore. This is where the dolphins and Brad Cummings, a marine scientist with the Vancouver Aquarium, came in.

The story of Brad Cummings is unfortunate. He was, as friends and admirers believed, absolutely devoted to the welfare of dolphins. He was a leading expert in the training of dolphins and the study of their behaviour, and after many years of research he had developed a complex "language" of whistles that he used to communicate with them. To help finance an international campaign to outlaw the use of gill nets that have killed so many dolphins, Cummings had let himself become involved in helping the smugglers. He helped them land the drugs in return for tens of thousands of dollars, all of which he apparently turned over to various agencies devoted to animal welfare.

One dolphin, raised from infancy by Cummings, had been trained to carry waterproofed packages of drugs from the fishing vessels to a smaller boat closer to the shore, thereby avoiding detection by the Coast Guard and RCMP drug patrols.

According to an informant connected to the drug operations, shortly before his death Cummings came to believe he had been tricked by a smuggler and was owed ten thousand dollars. He instructed the dolphin to head out into open water with the drug payload instead of taking it directly to the drop-off point, and he refused to call it back until he'd received the money. The ransom trick failed. Cummings was murdered by the smugglers, who then used his special series of whistles to track down the dolphin, which was shot and the payload of drugs removed from its body.

This explains why the autopsies had discovered the man was killed some time before the dolphin. It also explains the markings on the dolphin, which had previously been mistaken for gill-net markings.

Once the drugs were taken to Vancouver, an elaborate scheme was devised to get the drugs across the border into the U.S. Shipment was to be arranged through the use of "mules" – innocent drug carriers – which in this case turned out to be peewee hockey players.

Teams from all over the United States and Canada were coming into Vancouver for a special 3-on-3 hockey tournament, and the smugglers arranged to have snow globes and new bags given out to each player participating. The smugglers then arranged to add an "extra" bag to each team, which would contain a snow globe with roughly $300,000 worth of high-grade cocaine in it.

Each team would play a single game just across the Canada–U.S. border at Bellingham, Washington, and the organizers would transport the teams' equipment in a truck separate from the buses carrying the players. Once at the Bellingham rink, the "extra" bag containing the cocaine would be removed from the rest of the bags. The likelihood of border guards checking through the sweaty equipment bags of several dozen peewee hockey teams was remote indeed.

Had it not been for the work of Larry Ulmar, known to his teammates as "Data," the trick would never have been discovered. And had Wayne Nishikawa, better known as "Nish," not used his ingenuity to draw two of the smugglers to Wreck Beach, where they were immediately apprehended by police, the smugglers might have gotten away with their drugs *and* the murder of Brad Cummings.

Travis, on second thought, would change "murder" to "murders." He could not forget the poor innocent dolphin whose only crime was to obey instructions.

# 18

"We better find Sam," Sarah whispered to Travis. She looked worried. Travis nodded and folded up the newspaper he'd been reading. The stories were all beginning to repeat themselves anyway.

"She's in the parking lot," Travis said, but when they got outside they could see nothing. The parking lot was empty but for some swirling candy wrappers.

"I know where she'll be," said Sarah.

She led Travis out back where the garbage dumpster was, and there, as expected, was Sam, sitting on the curb, her legs folded in front of her. Her head was down. She was staring, almost as if hypnotized, at a dried leaf she was holding in one hand. Beneath it, in her other hand, she held a cigarette lighter, the flame licking upward towards the bottom of the leaf. The leaf began folding in on itself, almost as if panic had somehow struck it, as first smoke and then orange flame licked up through the centre.

Neither Sarah nor Travis said a word. They waited. And for a while it seemed Sam had no idea they were there.

Sam shook the leaf until it was nothing more than a stem and some black, curled char. She clicked off the flame, dropped the burned leaf onto the pavement, and getting up she tossed the lighter into the dumpster. She turned and looked at the other two. Her eyes were red. Possibly from the smoke of the leaf, but probably, thought Travis, from something else.

Sam looked a bit sheepish.

"The cigarettes are already in there," she said, nodding at the dumpster. "I've had my last smoke – I almost got us caught . . ."

Sarah looked perplexed, but Travis understood. Sam was looking straight into his eyes, as if searching for a signal – but what kind? Forgiveness? Blame? Travis could not blame her. Sam had helped as best she could. She had run for it with Travis and Nish when the easy thing to do would have been to stay in the motel and wait for the police. She had carried the snow globe when Travis had faltered. She had simply run out of gas, just like in the hockey game.

Travis smiled a smile that made words unnecessary. And from the look in Sam's eyes and her shaky smile in return, it was much appreciated. Sarah, ever wise, asking for no explanation, also smiled at Sam.

Sam caught Travis off guard with a huge hug. For a moment it was he who had trouble breathing. Then Sam broke it off and hugged Sarah, who hugged her back.

"I wasn't a very good smoker anyway," Sam said, half laughing, half crying, "was I?"

"No, you weren't," agreed Sarah, also laughing.

All three turned at a sudden voice, calling out from the front corner of the motel. It was Fahd. He'd come looking for them.

*"Muck wants to talk to us all together!"*

"The tournament goes ahead," said Muck.

He was standing in the centre of the little motel lobby, turning as he spoke to the Screech Owls and the handful of parents who had come out to Vancouver with the team.

"I just got off the phone, and it's still a go," he continued. "The city has taken over and wants to ensure that the original intent comes off. Every team has agreed to a new format that will shorten things up.

"We're not playing any games in Bellingham. We're going directly to the finals. They did some kind of calculation to work out where each team stood, and for us it means some good news, some bad."

Muck pulled a sheet of motel stationery out of his pocket. He unfolded it, turned it around, and stared hard, trying to make out the scribbles he'd made in pencil.

"Dmitri?" he said slowly, looking up in search of the Owls' quickest skater. Dmitri raised his hand from the chair he was sitting in. "Your team's out, I'm afraid. Means nothing, okay? Just the way they juggled things around so they could wind this thing up fast."

Dmitri looked over at his teammates, Andy and Lars. Out because of a single loss. All they could do was shrug. It didn't seem fair — but who knew how they'd calculated which teams would continue? Some of the teams had played only two rounds of the 3-on-3, others had played as many as four.

"Liz, Derek, Willie?" Muck read out.

The three raised their hands.

"You're in the Rockies finals, okay? Game's in an hour, so you better go get your stuff together."

The lucky team whooped and high-fived their way out of the lobby.

Muck kept turning the paper one way, then the other, squinting hard as he tried to read his own terrible handwriting.

"Simon?" he said.

Simon Milliken raised his hand. Simon's teammates, Jesse and Wilson, moved closer.

Muck looked up. "Sorry, boys. Don't take it personally, though. Two wins and a tie, you should expect to go on. They must have just flipped a coin on some of these final match-ups."

The three looked stunned. They hadn't lost a single game. They'd played as well as they possibly could. Jesse slammed his fist into an open hand, Wilson dropped into an open chair, sighing.

Muck kept fiddling with his paper. He looked up a couple of times, peering about the room as if in search of someone who could help.

But there were only the two teams left. Sarah's team, with Travis and Nish, playing in the Elite Division, and Sam's team, with Fahd and Gordie, playing in the Canucks Division.

Travis's heart sank. Muck was just stalling. He hadn't the nerve to tell them they were out of the tournament, that the most fun Travis Lindsay had ever had in a pair of skates was about to come to an unexpected end.

"Sarah, Travis, Nishikawa?" Muck read.

"Yes," Travis said, speaking as captain.

But Muck didn't even acknowledge him. He read on: "Sam, Fahd, Gordie?"

"Here," said Sam. "Just put us out of our misery."

A slight grin flicked at the corners of Muck's mouth. He folded the paper and tucked it back into his pocket. "You two teams are meeting for the overall championship," he said.

The players looked at each other in shock.

"But we're not even in the same division," said Sarah.

"Don't ask me," Muck said, grinning. "All they told me was to have both teams there for seven o'clock. Travis, you're wearing home sweaters. Fahd, your team's in away, okay?"

Fahd looked at Travis; Travis at Fahd.

"Okay," said Fahd.

"O-KAY!"

# 19

"*This is embarrassing!*"

Nish was almost completely dressed – pants, shin pads, socks, even skates complete with tape around the tops – everything but his shoulder and elbow pads and sweater. He was sitting, but leaning forward over his knees, his face red from the strain. Or perhaps it was anguish, given the way he sounded.

"What's *your* problem?" Sarah demanded as she pulled her sweater over her head.

"We're the *Elite* Division," Nish moaned. "We're not supposed to be playing against *Fahhhhdddd.*"

The way Nish said the name, it sounded as if Fahd had never held a hockey stick, never worn skates, never touched a puck. It sounded as if he had no feet, no hands, no brain.

"Fahd's excellent at 3-on-3," said Jeremy, who had played more games than any of the others, since he and Jenny were in goal for five "teams."

"It's *em-bar-rass-ing*," Nish howled, as if the mere thought were painful.

Sarah shook her head. "You're the last person on earth to decide what's '*em-bar-rass-ing*,' Mr. Wreck Beach."

Nish straightened up, looking hurt. "Hey, c'mon, *I'm* the one who solved the murder, aren't I?"

Travis was about to argue the point when the door opened and Muck came in, smiling. He'd been in a great mood since Liz and Derek and Willie won the Rockies Division championship in a close 5–4 game against the team from Boston. But it wasn't his usual smile. It was almost as if Muck was enjoying some little private joke.

"Ready to go?" Muck asked, and they shouted that they were.

Travis pulled his number 7 sweater over his head, quickly kissing the collar as it passed his lips. Now, if he could only hit the crossbar during warm-up, he might have a good game.

"It wouldn't be fair of me to give you any scouting report on the other team," Muck chuckled. "All I can say is they're Screech Owls. That's usually enough to make any team play their best, and that's the least I expect of you. Now go out there and have fun."

"Who's coaching us?" Nish asked.

Muck winked at Sarah and Travis. "Not me, thankfully. I got the team that listens to its coach."

"What's that supposed to mean?" Nish said, trying to look innocent.

"It means, Nishikawa, that your coach is Data. Why don't you surprise him by doing as you're told, for once."

And with that, Muck turned and left. Only Travis was in a

position to see that Muck was laughing to himself, enjoying the moment.

Data didn't have much to tell them. With Mr. Dillinger's help, Data had settled his chair behind the bench, where he was able to talk to the Owls as they leaned over the boards, but in fact there was little for a coach to do in 3-on-3 hockey. No lines to change. No big breaks or time-outs or ways of mapping out plays. Nothing but a few early instructions and then a lot of loud encouragement.

"Keep your eye on Fahd," Data said. "He's pretty good at this."

"'Keep your eye on *Fahhhhddd*,'" Nish mimicked. "C'mon, Data, get with it. This is a hockey game, not a spelling bee."

Nish turned and skated away, laughing at his own stupid joke. Fahd was, in fact, a pretty good speller at school, but he was also a pretty dependable little hockey player and, in 3-on-3, a crafty playmaker.

Sarah and Travis touched gloves for luck and skated back towards the faceoff circle. It felt odd to be out on the ice with Screech Owls sweaters skating around on the other side. Fahd and Sam and Gordie and Jenny were opponents, not teammates, and even though Travis knew each of them so well, even though he counted them among his best friends, they were a bit like strangers now, their personalities and talents unknown.

But still, he felt good. He'd kissed his sweater. He'd touched gloves with Sarah. He'd hit Jeremy's pads in exactly the right order – right pad, left pad, left pad, right pad, blocker. He'd even hit the crossbar. He was ready to play.

He couldn't, however, say the same for Nish, who seemed to be taking this game far too lightly. Perhaps all the publicity had gone to his head.

The puck dropped and there was no more time to think. From now on, for Travis, it would all be action and reaction.

Sarah won the drop easily from Gordie. She fired the puck back to Nish, who turned and began skating casually back towards Jeremy. Nish rounded the net, came out the other side, and lofted a high pass that slapped and bounced past centre. Travis raced for it, but Fahd beat him to the puck.

Travis turned sharply, almost jumping back in the opposite direction. Normally he would have had a check, but Fahd, moving so slowly, so surely with the puck, wasn't doing what Travis expected. Instead of driving towards Travis's net, Fahd turned and skated cross-ice to the far boards, and Travis flew by.

Fahd held the puck and deked past Sarah, then flipped a quick backhand to Gordie, who fired a hard slapper as soon as the puck came within range. The puck slammed hard into Jeremy's pads and bounced straight out into the slot. Sam, driving from the point, hammered the puck home.

Owls 1, Owls 0.

No – Fahd 1, Nish 0.

Ten minutes into the game, Fahd's side was up 4–2 and dominating play. Sarah was skating well, and Travis felt he was playing fine, but Nish seemed oddly out of it, as if he wasn't taking anything seriously.

"Let's get it going!" Travis said as he brushed past Nish just before a faceoff.

"Don't worry," Nish said. "I've got it completely under control."

Sarah scored a beauty on an end-to-end rush in which she pulled Jenny out and roofed a backhander Dmitri-style. Fahd scored on another slowed-down play. Nish scored on a deflection. Fahd scored on yet another slow-down. Nobody seemed able to read him.

The rink was loud. It was packed with Owls and parents, and their cheering and yelling bounced off the ceiling and walls to combine into one great roar. Travis was sure he could pick out Lars's shouts at one point, and he thought he heard his own name being called, as well.

Lars would be shouting instructions. *Pass to open space. Use your body to open up holes for the others. Don't be afraid to slow things down.* Travis was trying them all, but it wasn't working.

Sam picked up the puck behind her own net and used the angle to beat Sarah's forecheck. She roared up over centre. Travis left her to Nish and concentrated on Gordie, trying to make sure Gordie wouldn't have space to get a good shot away.

Sam came straight at Nish. He was backing up, his hips working fast, and he was staring right at her. Perfect: just the way Muck taught. One-on-one, ignore the puck, play the man – or in this case, the woman.

Sam shifted the puck out on her stick, teasing.

Nish went for it, trying to poke it away, but Sam tucked the puck back in, and slipped it between his skates and out the other side.

Using her momentum she beat him on the inside, and looped around into the clear, scooping up the puck she'd just slipped through.

Nish turned the other way, sweeping his stick across the ice as he fell.

But it was too late. Sam was clear. She moved to her backhand, delayed, waited with the patience of Fahd, and then drilled a backhand high and so hard that it blew the water bottle off the top of the net.

The rink erupted in cheers. It had been a sweet enough play on its own, but it was the move on Nish that had electrified the crowd.

"Kind of undressed you there, didn't I, big boy," Sam said as she skated back past Nish. "Too bad this is a hockey rink and not Wreck Beach."

Nish never said a word, but Travis could tell he was steaming. And he could hear Sam's breathing, shallow and hard. She'd just skated the length of the ice, and they were all tired, but her breathing was louder and quicker than the others.

As Sam's game began to slip, Nish suddenly took his play up another notch. He hadn't said a word in answer to Sam after her magnificent goal, but Travis knew his friend well enough to know that his beet-red face was a sign Nish was ready to get serious.

Travis caught Muck's expression just before the faceoff. Muck was coaching from the other side, but he, too, had seen the change come over Nish. Usually Muck tried to provoke this in Nish to get him into a game, but now Sam had done it for him. Travis decided that Muck would probably be pleased. He wanted all the

Owls to play well, even if it was against him. And getting Wayne Nishikawa to play the best hockey he could was something Muck counted among his greatest, if most difficult, achievements.

In the second half, Nish was like a whole new player. He was suddenly faster, smarter, slicker. He checked better. He passed better. He shot better.

Nish scored first on an end-to-end rush when he deked past Sam in a play almost identical to the one she had scored on. Nish scored on a terrific blast from the point after Sarah set him up and used her body to block Sam from getting to him. Nish scored on a two-on-one where Travis kept the puck for a long delay then slid a back pass to him for a hard, high one-timer.

They played, back and forth, for the full two periods of straight time, and when the horn finally blew the score was Owls 9, Owls 9.

It didn't matter which side was Fahd's, which side Nish's. The two teams were tied.

# 20

"What happens now?" Nish asked Data as they gathered at the bench to catch their breath and take in some water.

"Shoot-out," said Data.

"Who shoots?" Nish asked, expecting it would be him.

"Everyone," Data said. "Three shots – and if it's still tied, then it's one after another until one team goes ahead."

Nish scored. Travis scored. Sarah hit the post. Fahd scored. Sam scored. Jeremy caught Gordie's hard wrist shot.

Owls 11, Owls 11.

"What *now*?" Sarah asked when they returned to the bench. Nish was spraying water directly into his face.

"We pick a single shooter," said Data.

"Who?" Travis asked.

Data seemed reluctant to say.

"I've got to go with Nish," he said finally.

Nish shook his head. "Like there was ever any other choice."

Sarah turned to Travis, her eyebrows raised. "Is it ever okay to cheer for the other side?" she asked.

Travis just laughed. There was no answer for that. There was no explaining Nish.

The other side chose Sam. It caught Travis by surprise, because Fahd had played such a great tournament, but Sam was the better regular hockey player and had the good shot.

Sam was first. She went in fast, braked suddenly and slipped the puck through Jeremy's five hole.

Nish went second. He flew up and blasted a slapshot that went in under Jenny's arm.

Owls 12, Owls 12.

Sam went again, and scored again, this time on a pretty play where she deked left and scored from the right side, one-handed.

"It's all up to you," Data said to Nish.

"I know."

Nish picked up the puck at centre, moved slowly, then began cutting for the net. He faked and held, and Jenny moved with him, ready to stack her pads. He held still, waiting for the net to open, but Jenny held her position, drifting with him.

She'd obviously been studying Fahd's play. She was just as patient, just as determined.

Nish ran out of space. He had to shoot. He tried to lift it over her pads, but it was too late and the puck rang off the outside of the goal post and bounced harmlessly away.

Fahd's Owls had won the 3-on-3 tournament!

The rink erupted, as much in relief as in excitement. It had been an odd feeling, with everyone cheering for the Screech

Owls and determined to be happy no matter what the score.

It had been a wonderful game. It had been a difficult tournament. It had been a terrible experience at times. But now, with the murders solved, with the tournament completed, and with the Screech Owls both champions *and* runners-up, life was returning to normal.

Finally.

The organizers came onto the ice for the presentation. There were gold medals for the winners and silver for the runners-up.

Then they announced the tournament MVP, and to no one's surprise, it went to Sam.

A woman came out carrying a square, silver-covered box and began to open it.

"*Hey*," called Nish. "*Maybe it's a snow globe!*"

"Get a life!" snapped Sarah, standing beside him.

But it was not a snow globe. Slowly the woman drew the trophy from the box.

It was a beautiful West Coast native wood carving.

Of a dolphin.

Sam burst into tears as she accepted it. She held it tight with one arm and threw the other around the woman, hugging hard.

The smiling organizers took it for tears of joy.

Everyone else in the rink knew that was only part of the story.

**THE END**

Ron Devries

Roy MacGregor has been involved in hockey all his life. Growing up in Huntsville, Ontario, he competed for several years against a kid named Bobby Orr, who was playing in nearby Parry Sound. He later returned to the game when he and his family settled in Ottawa, where he worked for the *Ottawa Citizen* and became the Southam National Sports Columnist. He still plays old-timers hockey and was a minor-hockey coach for more than a decade.

Roy MacGregor is the author of several classics in the literature of hockey. *Home Game* (written with Ken Dryden) and *The Home Team* (nominated for the Governor General's Award for Nonfiction) were both No. 1 national bestsellers. He has also written the game's best-known novel, *The Last Season*. His most recent nonfiction hockey book is *A Loonie for Luck*, the true story of the famous good-luck charm that inspired Canada's men and women to win hockey gold at the Salt Lake City Winter Olympics. His other books include *Road Games*, *The Seven A.M. Practice*, *A Life in the Bush*, and *Escape*.

Roy MacGregor is currently a columnist for the *Globe and Mail*. He lives in Kanata, Ontario, with his wife, Ellen. They have four children, Kerry, Christine, Jocelyn, and Gordon.

You can talk to Roy MacGregor at **www.screechowls.com**.